"You mean you kissed me to find out if I'd been telling the truth about slipping liquor into your mother's tea?"

At least she had the good grace to blush. In fact, she looked as if she was on fire. "You *can't* think that I would have kissed you for any other reason!"

He was shocked. She had kissed him—for *investigative purposes?* Little Miss Innocent had braved the fevered lips of a bad man just to ensure her home remained whiskey free?

But hadn't he had an ulterior motive, too? He had been trying to play scare-the-virgin. And then the virgin had turned the tables on him.

But in the end, anger won out over guilt. "Lady, that takes the cake! You are, bar none, the most irritating, suspicious female I've come across—and believe me, I've come across some doozies."

* * *

Blissful, Texas
Harlequin Historical #661—June 2003

Praise for Liz Ireland's latest titles

Trouble in Paradise

"Liz Ireland's latest Harlequin Historical
is an adorably funny romance guaranteed to bring
a smile to your face...."
—*theromancereader.com*

"An excellent multi-layered story with deep secrets
and several abiding love stories. Come visit Paradise."
—*Rendezvous*

The Outlaw's Bride

"Ms. Ireland has written a fast-paced,
adventurous tale about two lonely people
who find love amid the Texas plains."
—*Romantic Times*

BLISSFUL, TEXAS

LIZ IRELAND

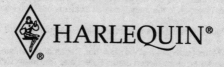

HARLEQUIN®

TORONTO • NEW YORK • LONDON
AMSTERDAM • PARIS • SYDNEY • HAMBURG
STOCKHOLM • ATHENS • TOKYO • MILAN • MADRID
PRAGUE • WARSAW • BUDAPEST • AUCKLAND

ISBN 0-373-29261-9

BLISSFUL, TEXAS

Visit us at www.eHarlequin.com

Printed in U.S.A.

Please address questions and book requests to:
Harlequin Reader Service
U.S.: 3010 Walden Ave., P.O. Box 1325, Buffalo, NY 14269
Canadian: P.O. Box 609, Fort Erie, Ont. L2A 5X3

Chapter One

Texas, 1882

The stage to Blissful jolted along the dusty, deeply rutted road west from San Antonio, flinging its six passengers against the windows one moment then hurling them against one another the next.

After two hours of this treatment Lacy Calhoun felt utterly exhausted. The temperature inside the coach was stifling; the opened windows let in more dust than air. Much longer inside that hot box and she feared she would simply wither. In fact, she would have loved to give up the fight altogether like the man next to her, whose corpulent body periodically flopped against her shoulder, his mouth gaping in slumber. Even while she winced at the spittle coming out the side of his tobacco-stained lips, she envied him his remarkable technique of relaxation under duress.

But of course her neighbor wasn't stuffed like a sausage into a brand new corset that pinched. His legs weren't encased into thick, sensible stockings. And naturally he was immune to the pungent smell of sweat emanating from their fellow passengers, since a large part of the odor seemed to originate with him. The pains Lacy took trying not to breathe through her nose almost equaled the efforts she expended to keep herself sitting in her rightful place every time the stage wheels hit a nasty hole. Otherwise, she would have landed in the lap of the passenger across from her. Which, taking into account the raw masculinity of the man, was somewhere a young lady who'd just spent the past fourteen years in a convent shouldn't want to be.

Bluntly speaking, he was the most attractive, virile man Lacy had ever laid eyes on. Granted, after her time at Our Lady of Perpetual Mercy, she didn't have a wide sampling to draw comparisons from. But she was still fairly certain she was looking at—or rather, pointedly trying *not* to look at—a specimen most women would call a handsome devil.

Emphasis on devil. The man's deep brown eyes were so piercing they sent a little shiver through her every time she caught him staring at her, which he had been doing all the way from San Antonio. The rich, dark depths of those eyes made her understand, all at once, what Sister Mary Katherine had meant when she warned Lacy against *earthly thoughts.* Something in his countenance made her feel warm all over, from her scratchy straw bonnet right down to the cramped, pointed toes of her new boots. Maybe it had to do with the knowing grin he directed at her—even the curve of his thick mustache seemed to be turned up in a seductive smile. Whatever the cause, Lacy was sure that the dizzying, irregular beat of her heart was what happened to women when they fell under a man's spell…and thereafter became fallen women.

The trouble was, if she looked away from the man's handsome face, it was impossible not to be mesmerized by the rest of him. He was built like Greek statuary, in epic proportions. Broad shoulders emphasized the smart cut of his dark coat, and the legs that jutted out to a point just a hair's breadth from her own knees were massive trunks. Even his hands, so large and browned, seemed imposing. She could imagine those hands touching her, as indeed they had as he'd handed her up into the coach back in San Antonio.

At the memory of his warm flesh against her left elbow, she blushed. What a silly reaction to have about such an innocent little gesture. It wasn't as if the man had actually touched her in an intimate manner....

She hazarded a glance at the man, caught his eye, and felt her heart thump dangerously—like a primitive native drumbeat in her breast.

For pity's sake, she upbraided herself, *two hours away from the sisters and you're already contemplating sinning!* And to think, she'd actually considered taking the veil herself. The sisters at Our Lady of Perpetual Mercy had obviously wanted her to stay—had practically begged her not to go home—and Lacy did believe she would make an excellent novice. But her duty lay elsewhere. And as Sister Mary Katherine had told her, a good heart could always find good works to do.

The driver hit another bump, and Lacy tensed every muscle in her body to keep herself rooted to the hard bench seat. One gloved hand was splayed against the edge of the opened window in an effort to hold herself in place, while the other, in a bow to ladylike behavior, rested in her lap with her embroidered reticule.

Lacy had outfitted herself to make a good impression. At Christmas when her mother had visited her at the convent, she'd told Lacy that she was tired of seeing her in drab shapeless clothing. So Lacy had been preparing for this day ever since, sewing herself a new lavender dress in the latest style—well, the latest she could gather from her limited view of the world at the convent. She'd found a magazine, two years old, featuring a picture of a dress with a fitted bodice and tight sleeves, with sweet accents of lace at the collar and the cuffs. The fitted skirt was rather immodest by her standards, so she had taken a creative liberty by making it a little fuller than the picture had indicated.

She wanted her mother to see how well she could do needlework. For fourteen years, her mother, a widow, had worked her fingers to the bone running a large boardinghouse and taking in sewing and mending to provide for Lacy's education. Now Lacy wanted to provide for her mother for a change.

"Where are you headed, miss?"

The devil's dark eyes peered straight at her. The other people in the cramped stage, another man and an elderly woman, were also eyeing her curiously. The question had even roused the fat man next to her.

She cleared her throat of the layer of dust and grit lodged there. "Blissful."

"You don't say." Another wide, dazzling smile spread across the devil's face, revealing a row of even white teeth. "What takes you there?"

The question seemed a little impertinent to her, since they hadn't even been introduced.

"My mother lives there," she revealed cautiously. To rebuke him for his forward manner, she turned, directing the rest of her explanation exclusively to the others. "Mama sent me to be raised by the sisters at Our Lady of Perpetual Mercy in San Antonio, but she's getting older now and no doubt could use my help." She sighed, feeling pleasantly martyrlike. "So I've decided to surprise her and return at last to the bosom of my childhood home."

She immediately regretted the figure of speech. She could swear she felt the stranger's dark eyes ogling her chest.

Only the elderly lady next to the opposite window seemed duly impressed by her daughterly devotion. "Very kind of you, dear."

Encouraged, Lacy was about to engage the woman in further conversation when the devil poked his large paw toward her. "The name's Lucas Burns."

She kept her own free hand fisted around her reticule and nodded at him curtly. "How do you do."

At her cool response, he withdrew his hand and used it to tip his black hat back on his head. He chuckled. "I see. The high-tone type. Well, young lady, you might be interested to know that we're going to be neighbors."

Lacy's mouth dropped open in surprise. "*You're* from Blissful?"

Her mother always described Blissful as such a sweet little community—and her memories from childhood made it seem that way, too. She just had vague recollections, of course. Of the house, full of music and gaiety. Her sociable mother was never at a loss for laughter, and they were always surrounded by company. In those early years, it seemed her mother had an endless stream of friends who enjoyed playing with Lacy and bringing her treats. At the boardinghouse, Lacy had been treated like a little princess. That was another reason her mother always gave her for sending away for her education to the convent. She told Lacy she didn't want her to be spoiled.

No chance of that at Our Lady of Perpetual Mercy. Not only had she received instruction along with other girls, but she had lived and toiled alongside the sisters in exchange for a portion of her board.

But now...was she really going to be *this* man's neighbor? Of course, on the surface there was nothing terribly wrong with him. His clothes seemed fine and certainly the others in the carriage weren't ostracizing him, but to Lacy something about the man smacked of the disreputable.

"I've spent a decade in Blissful, but I never saw *you* around before," he went on, staring at her closely. "You say your mother lives there?"

"Yes." She pointedly focussed her gaze out the window, away from him, and was rewarded with a faceful of dust.

He laughed. "Well, aren't you going to give me any hints?"

Lacy coughed, then lifted her chin and forced herself to look him in the eye. "You *might* know her." She hoped not, but from letters and holiday conversations it seemed her mother knew everyone in Blissful. "Mama runs a boardinghouse."

His face screwed up in puzzlement. "A boardinghouse in Blissful?"

"Mama also sews. She says she does quite a good little business." She remembered, however, to whom she was speaking. "Of course, a man probably wouldn't know about these things. What call would you have to buy women's clothes?"

Lucas shot a sidewise grin to the other passengers. "No call whatsoever, I assure you…except for an occasional gift to a special lady friend.''

The way he said *lady friend* implied something carnal. Something…

She looked into his dark eyes.

Something…very appealing.

''What did you say your name was?'' Lucas asked.

She shook her head and dragged her gaze away from his lips, giving herself another upbraiding for her wayward thoughts. All the hot air in the coach was obviously affecting her reason. ''I didn't.''

He sat back, arms crossed, sizing her up. ''Well, Miss…whatever your name is, I imagine we'll be bumping into each other quite often. See, I run the Rooster Tail.''

Her brows knitted in confusion. ''I beg your pardon?''

''The Rooster is Blissful's saloon.''

It was all Lacy could do not to let out an indignant huff. She might have guessed the man would make his money in a scandalous way—since he could encourage scandalous thoughts in her with just one look. She lifted her head loftily. ''Well we certainly won't be bumping into each other *there*, I assure you.''

He drew a long face—one she suspected was meant to be mocking. ''I take it you don't approve.''

''I most emphatically do not. I think it's disgraceful for a person to profit off the weakness of men.''

His eyes flashed and for a moment she regretted speaking so candidly. Yet why shouldn't she speak her mind? Especially since she was so right.

''I'm sorry you feel that way, Miss…''

''Calhoun,'' she said proudly, finally supplying the man with the information he had been angling for. ''My name is Lacy Calhoun.''

The man's mouth popped open in recognition. ''You mean your mama is *Flossie* Calhoun?''

''*Florence* Calhoun.'' What was so astonishing about that fact?

Lucas barked out a laugh, and the man next to her sniggered as well.

Irritation flashed through her. "I don't see what's so funny."

Lucas took a moment to tamp down his chortling. "I think you've got things a little confused, Miss Calhoun. If there's one business in Blissful men know about, it's the Satin Slipper."

"The what?"

He cleared his throat. "Your mama's…boardinghouse."

He and the other man, the one who had laughed, exchanged a glance that caused apprehension to tingle in Lacy's spine. To hear Lucas Burns tell it, her mother was involved in something shady. But that was nonsense!

Of course, her mother did sometimes wear clothes that seemed more revealing than was proper. Lacy had often spied the disapproval in Sister Mary Katherine's eyes during Flossie's visits to the convent. But just because her mother had daring taste in clothes, or perhaps *sold* clothes that were risqué…

Unfortunately, there was no time to refute the man's innuendo, because in the next minute the stage sped into a barely-there town consisting of one long main street lined sporadically with buildings in a mix of adobe and clapboard facades.

"Blissful!" the driver bellowed as he yanked the team of horses to a stop that sent the passengers careening about the little coach one last time. In a heartbeat, Lacy was flung into the arms of Lucas Burns. She butted up against the rock solid wall of his chest with a gasp.

Lucas didn't seem in a hurry to let her go, even once the stage was at a full stop.

He grinned that wolfish smile at her as he pinned her in his lap. "You say you've come here to work for your mother?"

For a moment Lacy's mouth felt so dry she couldn't speak. "Yes!" she finally croaked. The man had as much give in him as a granite boulder, and she wriggled against him in a futile panic until she realized she was making a spectacle of herself.

His smile broadened. "I'll look forward to that, Miss Calhoun. I'm mighty interested in sampling your talents myself."

Lacy hardly knew how to respond. She'd never been on the receiving end of such brazen suggestiveness. And to think this was just her first day out of the convent!

Blushing furiously, she wrenched herself free and then allowed herself to be yanked out of the stage by the driver, who was already impatient to be moving along again. Lacy landed unsteadily on her feet, wobbly after the bone-rattling ride, weak-kneed from her fleeting moments in Lucas's lap, then jumped aside as her bag was hurled down from the top of the wagon. A few inches and her own luggage would have brained her. The bag was heavy; she couldn't say how she was going to get it to her mother's house. Wherever that was.

Bewildered, she spun in a circle, taking in what little there was to see of the town she hadn't laid eyes on since she was five years old. This was the moment she had awaited for fourteen years. The one she'd dreamed about nights in her bed at the convent.

But the handful of buildings did not spark any fond recollections, nor did they inspire enthusiasm in her breast. The dry, withered look of the place wasn't helped by the glaring noonday sun beating mercilessly down. The only sound was of the snorting horses of the stage, anxious to get away, accompanied by the buzzing of several varieties of bugs, a few of which homed in on the new arrival. Lacy flapped her hand to shoo them away.

"Like me to carry your bag for you?" Lucas's question felt more like pestering than a sincere offer, especially when she looked up and saw those humor-filled eyes boring into her.

She was tempted to hop back into the stage and go round-trip back to San Antonio, but of course there could be no returning there. She had bidden the sisters goodbye. She was nineteen, a grown woman, and she owed it to her mother to help out now, bugs and Lucas Burns notwithstanding. She couldn't allow herself to be put off by the insinuations of one man—a scoundrel who made money plying liquor into innocent souls. The whole world wasn't like this one pushy rascal.

And hopefully, the entire male population of Blissful wouldn't make her pulse pound so erratically.

"No thank you. I can handle my own luggage."

"Really? You seem kind of puny to be toting big things like that around."

She eyed her bag doubtfully. Heat and exhaustion were making her mind sluggish. "I'm sure it's not far."

"Oh, that's right." He smirked. "You don't even know where you're going."

To her dismay, the man grabbed hold of her shoulders and wheeled her around, pointing her toward a large house at the far end of town. The edifice was impressive. In fact, it was the tallest, most prominent building in the whole town. There was certainly no missing it. The house was two stories high, with gables and a cupola sprouting out irregularly. Peacock-blue painted clapboards with scarlet scalloped woodwork blared brightly in the sunshine, and an elaborately lettered sign hung off the front porch.

As Lacy stared at the house that was to be her home, her apprehension bumped up a notch. It certainly seemed very colorful for a boardinghouse…but of course her colorful mother lived there. With some of her friends. Lacy sifted through her memory for their names. Sal. Bernice. Squirrel-Tooth Shirley.

She gulped anxiously. Perhaps she should have warned her mother she was coming.

Perhaps she should just go back and become a nun after all.

"Sure you don't want me to accompany you?" Lucas asked.

When Lacy saw his big grin, her spine stiffened with resolve. What a little idiot she was being! He was just teasing her because she'd insulted his saloon.

"No thank you. You just run along back to the Chicken Coop, or whatever you call it."

''The Rooster Tail.''

With one last haughty lift of her chin, she said to the odious man, hopefully in parting, ''Please don't waste any more time on me, Mr. Burns. I'm sure there are men lined up at your door waiting for cheap gratification.''

If she had hoped the man would recoil from her stinging insult, she was doomed to disappointment. Lucas tossed back his head and howled with laughter. ''Unfortunately not as many as there are lined up at your mother's, Miss Calhoun.'' He tipped his hat and turned away.

She watched him stride down the street, his shoulders still shaking with laughter, and with small clouds of dust billowing at his boot heels. His infuriatingly ominous words were still ringing in her ears. Why, from what he'd said you'd almost think…

Well, not even almost. Absolutely. But that was impossible!

She peered at the garish house. It *was* impossible, wasn't it?

With more strength than she would have guessed she had, she lifted the handle of her valise and dragged it along behind her through the dusty street.

She tried to shake off the man's terrible innuendo. What a fiend Lucas Burns was—slandering her mother like that in front of a coachful of people! Now Lacy wished she had put the man in his place. Yes, and stood up for her mother as vociferously as her mother would have for her. Flossie wasn't a bad person. If she were, would she have sent her one and only daughter to be raised in a convent? Would she have made extra donations to Our Lady of Perpetual Mercy every Christmas and Easter?

As she came closer to the house, the doubts Lucas had planted in her mind began to scatter as her eagerness to see Flossie again bloomed. She loved her mother—and part of what she loved about her was that they were so different. Her mother was flamboyant, and had always loved loud music and good food and fun. So what? Perhaps her mother even engaged in a little gambling, too. Sinful—but hardly the end of the world.

As Lacy picked up her pace, she hit upon an idea that surprised her. Maybe her mother felt stifled in Blissful! After all, there was nothing really here to speak of. A general store…the Rooster Tail…a jail. A few lean-tos connected together that proclaimed itself a blacksmith shop and livery. The houses scattered about were little more than shacks. It was barely civilized, this town, with no sidewalks, no school, and certainly no church that she could see. What kind of society could exist here for a vibrant woman like Flossie Calhoun?

What kind of place was this?

Lacy reproached herself for not having come sooner. Of course, Sister Mary Katherine had been loath to let her go, and her mother naturally hadn't wanted to be selfish and insist she leave a place where she'd been so happy. But looking around the town, Lacy realized how much her mother needed her. Now she and her mother would be able to laugh together and keep each other company during the long evenings. Lacy had learned how to cook and do fine needlework from the nuns—perhaps she could share these skills with her mother and her friends. Also, for her departure, the nuns had given her several books. She could read her mother *The Confessions of St. Augustine* and *Lives of the Saints* and—Oh, all her favorites!

Just that moment, the door of the big blue house blew open and a shirtless, unshaven cowboy flew off the porch backward, shoved by a stout, striking blond woman with ample breasts her thin wrap took few pains to conceal. Meaty arms tossed the cowboy's hat, belt, and boots after him. The blizzard of garments settled on the ground around their stunned owner, who hurriedly collected his clothing. Meanwhile the woman, whose hair and painted face gave her the artificial look of a china doll, planted her fists on her hips and let loose a barrage of insults.

"Don't you come 'round here tomorrow night, Boot Withers, expectin' to drink and be entertained all night for nothin'!

If I'd a known you was broke, I'd a kicked your skinny fanny off this porch seven o'clock last night!''

The young cowboy sent her a supplicating look as he hurriedly buttoned his shirt. ''Aw c'mon, Sal. Other men keep tabs!''

Several shuttered windows on the top floor opened, and suddenly, Boot and Sal had an audience of laughing women. Even from a distance Lacy could tell they were all in various states of undress. The sight made her blush...as did the memory of Lucas Burns throwing back his head in laughter and taunting her.

If there's one business in Blissful men know about...

A sinking foreboding took hold of her. *Oh, lord...* But of course, Lucas could still be wrong, Lacy told herself, using up her last scrap of optimism. This *could* be a boardinghouse....

''Other men who ain't longtime freeloaders!'' Sal yelled at the man.

''I told you I could pay at the end of the month.''

''What do you think Flossie's running here, a boardinghouse?''

Lacy's heart sank.

''Fat chance of that!'' The man had his boots on and his shirt half buttoned and was obviously feeling a bit more confident. He jutted his chin cockily. ''Not if this is your idea of hospitality!''

The girls in the upper windows cackled with delight.

''Sounds like you've got an unsatisfied customer, Sal!'' one of them chided.

At the taunt, Sal whirled in indignation. ''And what would you know about satisfying any man, you skinny little piece of nothin'! The Slipper'd go broke if all we had to peddle was your bucktooth charms!''

Just then, the front door banged opened and another woman stomped out on the porch. A strangled gasp of recognition caught in Lacy's throat. *Mama?* Flossie Calhoun's startling red hair was tousled from sleep, and her clothing could only be described as…inadequate. A scarlet nightgown and a robe so sheer as to be practically no cover at all for her curvaceous frame. Flossie, older by more than a decade, made Sal seem almost dainty.

Seeing her mother this way, Lacy felt as if she had swallowed a stone. A fine film of sweat broke out on her brow. She was dumbstruck.

When Flossie spoke, her voice was a trumpet blast of authority. "What's all the yellin' about?" She looked with barely veiled impatience at the cowboy. "Boot, you mean to tell me you're stiffin' the house again?"

"I get paid Saturday, Flossie," Boot argued. "A man can't always match up his desires with his bankroll, you know."

Flossie tossed her pile of red curls and laughed. "That's just the kind of half-cocked thinking that always gets you into trouble, Boot. Sal here's not one to take credit. In fact she might just march right over to Sheriff Turner and report you for theft."

The cowboy looked outraged—and nervous. "Theft?"

"I believe that's what you call takin' goods without payin'."

"Aw, Floss, you *know* you can't do that. That judge in San Antone said that if I get in one more scrape with the law, that'll be the end of me."

"Then next time you should put off comin' round here till the Widow Wallace has paid you for whatever it is you do around her place." Flossie chuckled. "I still haven't figured out what that could be."

Boot cut off the discussion before he had to endure more insults. "All right, all right. I'll bring the money on Saturday."

Sal yelled at him. "And don't expect to stay over again!"

Boot spun on his heel, prepared to make his getaway, but was stopped when he spied Lacy. Startled, both of them jumped a foot backward. On second look, Boot's eyes bugged then gave her a long once-over. Lacy's face felt fiery with embarrassment. "Say, Flossie—is this a new one?"

Lacy looked pleadingly toward her mother, denials sputtering incoherently on her lips.

Flossie's mouth scrunched unhappily as she turned her attention to the visitor. "Lord I hope not! Business is pokey enough already."

Tears stung Lacy's eyes. This homecoming wasn't working out at all the way she had planned. In fact, it was a disaster. All these years, her mother had been sending money to the convent for her upkeep. All these years, her mother had been…well, she couldn't even form the words in her mind.

She wasn't even sure if she *knew* the correct words.

No wonder Sister Mary Katherine had begged her to stay in San Antonio! She must have known about Flossie all along. The thought that everyone at the convent had known the truth while Lacy had been blissfully unaware made her feel ill. Oh, why hadn't Sister Mary Katherine told her what awaited her in Blissful? A two-hour stagecoach ride had led her from her life as a near-novice to *this*. She felt as if she were a soiled dove herself.

She dropped her bag, which hit the dirt and sent up an explosion of dust. Her whole body felt leaden with disbelief and disappointment, and she collapsed on top of her luggage. Her head hurt from the sun beating down on her bonnet. *Don't cry,* she admonished herself. If she cried, she would make a fool of herself and embarrass her mother. Her poor mother…tarnished and besmattered with shame.

She hiccupped and bit back hysterical tears.

There was a gasp, and footsteps clattered down the porch stairs. "Lord-a-mercy! It's *Lacy!*"

Lacy looked up to see her mother fluttering toward her in her indecent clothing in the broad daylight. It was all she could do not to shrink back in horror. She was trembling now in her effort to keep moderately composed.

"Baby, what are you doin' here?"

Flossie didn't seem the least bit discomfited by the fact that her daughter had arrived and discovered her disgraceful, well-kept secret. Well kept from Lacy, that is. Flossie was apparently too distracted by the sight of her upset daughter standing in front of her to remember that she was supposed to be running a boardinghouse, not a...

Brothel.

The very word made Lacy feel woozy, but for her mother's sake, she tried to put on a brave face. All these years at the convent, she had defended her mother's loudness in manner and dress as being part of her blowsy charm. Lacy wouldn't hear a word spoken against Flossie Calhoun. And why should she? The woman had given birth to her, supported her, educated her. She owed Flossie everything. *Everything.*

"Honey, you got tears in your eyes! What's the matter?" Her mother put her arms around her and pulled her into a fierce protective hug, burying Lacy's face in sheer red ruffles and giving her a choking lungful of tart, flowery perfume. "Did something happen at school? You should've told me you was comin'!"

As she crumpled into her mother's embrace, it was tempting to say that *nothing* was wrong. Anything her mother did was right—or at least was surely done for the right reasons.

And yet, Lacy thought, drawing strength as she hugged her mother back, didn't she owe more than simple acceptance to Flossie, who after all had educated her and made her a better person? Wouldn't the right thing be to return the favor? To show her the error of her ways?

Surely that's what Sister Mary Katherine would have admonished her to do. A good heart can always do good works, she had said.

Flossie gazed down at her with a worried brow. "Land's sake, Lacy—say something! You could have knocked me over with a sneeze, you're arrivin' here so sudden. Did you have a fight with the nuns?"

Lacy choked back tears. "N-no!"

"Well then, what is it? What are you doing here?"

"Oh, Mama!" she exclaimed, finally finding her voice. "The question that concerns me is, what are *you* doing here?"

And then, despite all her efforts to be brave, she exploded into sobs.

Chapter Two

"Things'll never be the same in Blissful again!" wailed Boot.

"You can say that again!" George Oatley, the blacksmith, agreed. And it wasn't often that the two men agreed on anything.

But on this day, all the men sitting around the Rooster were of one mind.

Lucas listened to his customers bemoan the exodus of fancy women from the town and got bristled up all over again. That very morning, a stream of gals had poured out of the Satin Slipper—ousted by Lacy Calhoun, a woman who, heretofore, most of the town had only heard about when Flossie had a few too many and got sentimental. Almost no one could remember when the little girl lived with Flossie. For years the newer arrivals had even doubted that this sainted daughter in San Antonio really existed.

This fateful day had made believers out of all of them. Though nobody could understand how the arrival of one nineteen-year-old girl could suddenly turn their world upside down.

Only Lucas wasn't surprised. Oh, no. He knew well how women could wreak havoc on one man—why not a community? Plus he'd had hours in that cramped stage yesterday to study their new adversary's icy blue eyes and determined, pointy chin. Not to mention those little dewy lips that seemed pursed in disapproval at *everything*. If there was one woman in the world who could spell trouble for Blissful, Lacy Calhoun was that woman. Sure, she looked all pretty and rosebud sweet. For a short while he had even enjoyed flirting with her and teasing her.

The more fool him. He should have known right then that she meant trouble.

Lucas's son, Jacob, a gangly eleven-year-old who was already sure that his life was getting away from him, sighed wearily as he dried a glass. "I don't know what ya'll are complaining about," he said. "I never even got to step foot in the Slipper!"

Lucas glowered at him. "You didn't miss much." The last thing he needed right now was for his kid to start moping about women. Jacob's not having a female influence in his life was a raw point with Lucas.

Boot looked aghast. "Not miss much?" His voice cracked with emotion. "Why, between the Slipper on one end of town and the Rooster on the other, Blissful was the most hurrah town in all of Texas. Outside of San Antone, we're practically the South Texas tenderloin."

"Besides, it wasn't just the women that were the big draw, Lucas," Harry Bean pointed out. "There was always real good music at the Slipper, too."

The other men gaped at the storekeeper as if he'd lost hold of his reins.

"Maybe old Myrtle will believe you're there listening to piano music, but not us!" Boot said, zinging him.

Harry's entire balding head turned beet colored on him. Harry's cantankerous wife was involved in a silent war with Harry's spinster sister, Birdie, who lived with them. Birdie was quiet and shy, but also immovable. The three were locked in domestic disharmony in the small rooms above the store…except when Harry could sneak away to the Slipper for a little peace.

Harper Cooley, who was prone to giving windy treatises on

the state of the world, cleared his throat. If anyone should have been upset about the Slipper's closing, it was Harper. Since the old drifter arrived in town three months before, Flossie had been paying him to be doorman at the Slipper. For a brothel heavy, Harper was about twenty years too old and physically not very imposing. But pickin's in Blissful were slim, and Flossie liked arguing with him, and it turned out Harper didn't need brawn. He could wear a man down just by talking. Now he was out of a job.

He wasn't out of breath, however. "I guess what Harry is trying to say was that there was a cultural aspect to the Slipper, if you've a mind to look at it that way. Nobody can deny the Slipper sort of gave Blissful its identity."

"Hear that?" Boot moaned. "We've lost our girls *and* our identity!"

George frowned. "What are you going to do now, Harper? Move on?"

The saloon's batwing doors swung open and Flossie came swooning in, making her way to the bar as quickly as possible. The men parted for her and gathered around for news.

But Lucas saw at once that Flossie was in a bad way. She was wearing one of her oldest dresses—a mustard colored muslin that couldn't be said to flatter her. The drab rag wouldn't have flattered anybody. Her face, devoid of its usual paint, was washed out, and there were dark circles under her eyes. A little of her sparkle was gone.

"What's going on, Flossie?" Boot asked eagerly.

Flossie broke the bad news as gently as she could, but everyone still took it hard.

"Closin' down!" George repeated mournfully. Though of course all morning they'd known that Flossie was closing down the Satin Slipper. She couldn't run the place without her girls. But now that they had heard it from the horse's mouth it was official.

"You *can't* close down, Flossie," Harper said. "It's a matter of principle. What will Blissful be without the Slipper?"

Flossie shook her head and poured herself a shot of whiskey. "Beats me, old man."

Lucas looked at her, concerned. "Don't you think you ought to go easy there, Floss?"

After all, it was still early and she seemed beat. Granted, Flossie had been dealt a blow by Lacy's surprise arrival in town. He didn't blame her one bit for being upset. That haughty priss of a daughter had already caused this town more trouble than it had seen since the last Comanche raid. But he didn't want to see Flossie take it out on herself.

Flossie sighed. "I got to take it when I can get it now, Lucas. Lord only knows when I'm gonna escape Lacy's watchful eye again."

Boot snorted in disgust. "Don't tell me she's banned liquor from your house, too!"

"Poured out practically every drop," she said. "I managed to salvage some by stashing it behind the parlor curtains, but I've got to save that for emergencies."

The men in the bar protested Flossie's being treated so cruelly in her own home.

Yet Flossie still appeared resigned to going straight. She exhaled a long sigh. "I'm sorry, boys, but I raised a respectable gal, and now I got to go respectable myself."

"Respectable!" Boot practically spat the word. "You're respectable now, ain't you? You run the biggest money-making enterprise in Blissful."

"Yeah!" Harry Bean chimed in. "I'll bet your outfit made more money than my store, even. More than the Rooster, even. Didn't you tell your daughter that?"

Flossie looked depressed. "I did."

"Well?"

"She got hysterical on me." She shook her head and winced a little at the memory. "I tell you, boys, I can take her lecturing. But the *weeping*. I thought it would never end. That girl's got more saltwater in her than the Gulf of Mexico." Flossie's expression turned unspeakably sad. "She said she'd rather we'd both starved to death or became beggars than keep the Slipper open.''

Boot's face collapsed in stupefaction. ''She said that to *you?* After all you done for her?''

Flossie shook her head. ''You can't blame Lacy for the way she thinks. I was the one who packed her off to that convent, on account of I didn't want her to be raised around the same rough element I was. The Slipper wasn't a place for a little girl. At least, not *my* little girl. I wanted my daughter to grow up to be an educated, upstanding lady, and now she is one.''

''That's just fine and dandy,'' George broke in. ''*Let* the girl be a lady. Why the heck should you have to be one too?''

''I'm her ma. I gotta set an example.''

A sea of blank stares met this pronouncement.

''Okay…'' Harry said, restarting the conversation. ''But why should the rest of us suffer? Heck, half my business probably came from your girls, Flossie. Now when cowboys get days off they'll take their trade someplace else.''

''Before you know it, the stage probably won't even stop here,'' George chimed in.

Harper shook his grizzled head sagely. ''See, friends, once civilization gets its claws on you, pretty soon it'll have you in a stranglehold. In the history of the world—''

Boot sighed in irritation. ''Aw, heck, Harper! We don't none of us care about history. We just want the girls back!''

''I was just trying to put the closing of the Slipper into a larger context,'' Harper explained.

George chortled. ''Girls are the only context Boot's interested in.''

Boot, who had a hair-trigger temper and didn't appreciate teasing, especially from George, snapped back at him, ''That ain't true! I got other interests.''

''Oh, sure,'' George said, guffawing. ''You probably developed quite a few of them in jail when you were the infamous outlaw, Boot the Kid.''

''Shut up!'' Boot had already hopped off his barstool and

was ready to start swinging before Lucas reached across the bar and stopped him.

"Simmer down! Can't you tell when you're being teased?"

Boot bounced on his heels with aggressive swagger. "Sure can, and I don't like it!"

Before Boot had come to Blissful, he had done a spell in jail in San Antonio for bank robbery. *Attempted* bank robbery. Boot had planned to fashion himself into a dangerous character along the lines of Billy the Kid, and had even gone so far as to get a gang together, but on the morning of his first big heist he had been so nervous that he'd left his gun at the hotel. Boot's *compadres* had abandoned him midrobbery, and a consumptive young bank clerk had managed to wrestle him to the ground and hold him till the law arrived.

After serving his time, Boot had managed to secure himself a position overseeing a ranch for the Widow Wallace. Mentioning his days as Boot the Kid never failed to rile him.

When the situation had calmed, Harry turned to Flossie. "So you be a lady, Floss. That's fine. Nobody's got a problem with that. But what about your girls? Why should they have to suffer?"

Flossie howled with laughter. "*Suffer?* Is that what you call bein' deprived of the company of the likes of you?" She snorted in derision. "I'll tell you something truthful, boys. Maybe Lacy's got a point."

"*What!*"

Flossie had to raise her voice to top the shouts of outrage. "You think I'm proud of what I done all these years? Heck, I knew it wasn't right." She stared them all down, one by one. "Is there a single man here who'd want his sister or their mama doing what my girls done? What I done?"

The room fell dead silent. Uncomfortable stares looked anywhere but straight in Flossie's eyes.

The color returned to her cheeks, and some of her old spunk returned. "I didn't think so—and listen to you. Lacy thinks just like you do, and you act all outraged, you pack of hypocrites! But I tell you truthfully, I'm glad my Lacy thinks the way she does. I wouldn't have it any other way. I just gotta make some, well, some adjustments, that's all.''

"Adjustments!" Boot repeated indignantly. "That gal's deprived you of a livelihood. I'd think you'd have a little more respect for the laws of commerce, Flossie!''

Flossie raised her chubby arms to simmer them all down. "I'm sorry. I'm out of the business, gentlemen. Lacy says we're going to open a boardinghouse.''

"A boardinghouse!" Harry Bean piped up. "Who the heck's gonna pay to stay at the Slipper now?''

Flossie shrugged. "You never can tell. Lacy's a good little cook.''

"Oh, sure," Boot said. "Menfolk flocking to the Slipper for the *food!*''

Flossie pushed herself away from the bar and lifted her hands apologetically. "I'm sorry, boys, but now that I'm respectable, that's all I can offer you.''

After Flossie had gone, the men returned morose gazes to their drinks.

"That gal's even turned Flossie against us," George said.

Jacob, who had been working silently, cleared his throat. His Adam's apple bobbed nervously. "B-but didn't you sort of think Flossie had a point?''

Lucas feared he'd have to step in and save his son from an angry mob, and maybe he would have, had the whole room not been distracted at that instant. The doors flapped open and Sheriff Bodine Turner strode into the bar, grinning from ear to ear like he'd just discovered gold nuggets under the jailhouse. "Lord-a-mercy! What a *woooon-der-ful* day!''

A roomful of steely glares met his sunny greeting. As the expressions of the men slapped him full force, the young sheriff took a slight step backward.

"What's so great about it?" Lucas asked.

Bodine's eyes widened in surprise. "Haven't y'all seen the heavenly creature that came in on the stage yesterday? Prettiest thing I've ever set eyes on! And get this—she's Flossie's daughter! I thought Flossie had just been foolin' about having a little girl..."

"Where you been, sheriff?" Boot barked at him in irritation. "That little lady's hit this town like a plague!"

"I heard some of the girls were leaving..."

"*All* of 'em," Boot corrected. "The Slipper's all washed up."

"Oh...I hadn't quite put that all together." Bodine looked a little stricken, and let out a sigh. "I sure will miss hearing that good piano music."

Several men shot each other pointed looks. Unlike Harry, Bodine *did* go to the Slipper for the piano music. More specifically, he went to pay court to the lovely black-haired girl who played the piano. It was no secret that he had fallen in love with Lila Murchison.

"Remember how well Lila played 'Silver Threads Among the Gold'?" Bodine asked mistily. "I'm sure going to miss that."

Lucas passed the man his usual cup of coffee, black and thick with sugar. "She's gone off with Sal." Not that he liked to encourage anyone to run after bad luck, but Bodine was uncommonly fond of Lila.

Bodine stared bleakly into the black liquid. "Well, maybe it's best this way."

Harry shook his head. "If you liked the girl, why didn't you ask her to marry you?"

Bodine set down his cup, scandalized. "I couldn't do that, Harry. You know I'm hoping to go home as soon as I have enough money saved up. Lila..." His face went crimson. "Well, she's not exactly the type of girl you'd want to take home to your ma."

As a silence stretched uncomfortably, and the sheriff looked more and more depressed, Boot broke in with a remonstrance for the storekeeper. "You're a fine one to go around telling people to get married, Harry. You and Myrtle probably haven't spoken a civil word in six years!"

George laughed. "I wish the sheriff would marry the Calhoun girl and take her off to Cicada Creek. Get her out of our hair!''

Bodine chuckled nervously. ''Oh, I don't know about that. She's got some strange notions....''

Lucas sensed more trouble. ''What notions?''

''Well…she came into my office this morning asking me if I would help her get something started. Something she wanted to call the Blissful Decency Committee.''

Howls rose all around, and Lucas heard himself chiming in with the rest of the men. ''*That* is the limit!''

''She might decide to shut this place down next, Lucas,'' Boot warned. ''You know how them suffragette types can't abide liquor.''

Lucas remembered her scathing opinion of his owning a saloon. At the time he'd found her haughtiness a source of humor, since she obviously was in for a rude awakening when she got to her mama's house. He wasn't laughing now.

''And once you empty out Blissful of its women and its liquor, what's left?'' Harry Bean looked like he might collapse into a heap. ''Just my store, and how long's that gonna last when there's no reason anymore for anybody to come here?''

Lucas shook his head. ''Not if we do something to ward off the blow.''

Puzzled faces turned to him.

He laughed. ''Look at us—we're pathetic! There's a score of men like us and only one Lacy Calhoun. Surely we can come up with some plan to fight back.''

At the mention of fighting, hope sparked once more in Boot's eyes and the would-be outlaw snapped back to life. ''Like what?''

Lucas crossed his arms and eyed Bodine. Their baby-faced sheriff wasn't much of a lawman. That was a big part of Blissful's success. Bodine would rather walk over hot coals than deal with any unpleasantness like arresting somebody. But his badge might hold some sway with Lacy Calhoun. ''Maybe somebody might be able to convince our town's newest resident that Blissful might not be the kind of town she wants to live in.''

"But that's the problem," Harper said. "She's trying to turn it into a town she'd want to live in.''

"Then somebody needs to convince her that it's going to be an uphill battle." He leveled a meaningful look on Bodine. "But it's got to be somebody she trusts.''

Bodine's big blue eyes widened. "Oh, no! I don't want to run that little gal out of town. Why, she seemed real nice to me. Real respectable.''

"That's the problem," Harper repeated.

The sheriff really was a bit thick.

Furrows appeared in Bodine's pillowy brow. "Now that there aren't many women in town, should we be chasin' away one of the few we do have?''

"Maybe if Lacy Calhoun left," Lucas pointed out, "the other girls would come back." Shamelessly, he hummed a few bars of "Silver Threads Among the Gold.''

Bodine's ears pricked up, though his expression remained doubtful. "I don't know, Lucas....''

"It's for her own good," Lucas pointed out. "You have to admit, the girl won't be happy here. She'll have to turn the place upside down and remake it from scratch before it'll suit her. And then it won't suit anybody else. And if everybody in town's unhappy, what's going to happen? Strife. Maybe even chaos. You're the sheriff. Isn't that what you're here to prevent?''

That got Bodine's attention. "Shoot, I never considered that!''

Lucas leaned in close, sensing he had taken a major step toward ridding himself of the Lacy pestilence. Bodine, heaven help him, was his first offensive volley. "See if you can't convince her that she'd be better off if she just skedaddled back to the convent.''

"I suppose just talking to her would be all right," Bodine allowed. "She probably *would* be happier going back to the convent if she's such an upstanding high-minded girl.''

Bodine sometimes needed a little mental shove, but once he got that shove he was usually up and running.

When the sheriff left the saloon and headed for the Slipper, Lucas tried not to get his hopes up. Bodine might solve their problem…then again, he might not. But when he returned from the Slipper they'd at least know how firmly entrenched Lacy Calhoun was.

"Sheriff Turner!" Lacy exclaimed enthusiastically. "I didn't expect you to come calling so soon!"

She really was delighted to see someone. Her mother had scurried to her room soon after she'd come back in, claiming she had a headache. Lacy had smelled the distinct odor of alcohol wafting behind her, but had let the matter pass. Flossie's rehabilitation, she'd decided soon after finding a stash of spirits behind the parlor curtains, might take longer than she'd initially calculated.

The sheriff teetered on the threshold, peering nervously into the front hallway. "I'm sorry. I didn't mean to intrude…"

Lacy grabbed his arm. Sheriff Turner was *just* the sort of visitor she needed. As far as she could tell, the sheriff was one of the few respectable citizens in Blissful, besides the storekeeper's family. She wanted the town to see that now only quality people were welcome into her mother's *house*. She tugged him into the parlor, trying to ignore the room's garishness, which she promised herself would be the first thing about the house she changed.

"It's *so* good of you to come by. I wish Mama were here to greet you, too, but she's…" *Drunk,* was the word that came immediately to mind. She gestured vaguely toward the hallway and said, "…unwell."

He removed his hat with a nervous swipe and tapped it against his leg. He looked almost sick…and he couldn't seem to peel his eyes away from the piano in the corner of the room.

Of course Lacy couldn't blame the man for being uncomfortable. She felt a shudder every time she thought of the sordid business that had taken place in this house. And for so many years! Would she ever live down the shame?

"Well, I uh…" He cleared his throat. "Actually…"

"Would you like a piece of pie?"

He stopped stammering out whatever it was he was attempting to say, and his face brightened. He looked relieved to have something to focus his attention on. But wasn't that always the way? Food put people at their ease. She would need to remember little tips like that if she intended to make a success of her boardinghouse.

Which is another area where the sheriff could come in handy. He probably knew everyone, and might be indispensable in helping her find roomers. Flossie had divulged how much money she had saved, and it was a good amount. But it wouldn't last forever. They needed paying boarders, and the sooner they got them, the better.

She dashed to the kitchen and cut into the freshly made pie, still warm from the oven. She'd been up and out at the crack of dawn picking the blackberries. The task had given her something to do after her sleepless night, most of which she'd spent crying her eyes out. The whole dark night she had been consumed with grief. And remembering the nasty things those women had said to her! The names they called her. Why, you'd think that the poor things *wanted* to do what they did for a living!

She trembled at the thought. Of course she had no personal knowledge of the carnal act, but given the alarming intimations she had received at Our Lady of Perpetual Mercy, it had to be a disgusting process endured only for the sake of keeping a man firmly shackled in holy matrimony. That a woman would soil herself that way for a few shoddy pieces of silver was just inconceivable to her.

In the spirit of Christian charity, Lacy had tried to convince a few of the women to stay and help run the boardinghouse— a suggestion that had been met with everything from jeers to Squirrel-Tooth Shirley's spitting on her. No one, not even her mother, seemed to think that they would make much money taking in boarders.

Well, fine. She would show them.

She hurried back out with the pie to find the sheriff standing exactly where she'd left him. Still banging his hat against his knee. Still staring at that piano.

"Please sit down, Sheriff," she said, gesturing to the red velvet sofa. She wondered fleetingly if the sofa could be salvaged—if it would ever lose its bawdy-house taint.

The sheriff did as instructed. She gave him his pie and took his hat, which she set on a gold-painted table that had cupid heads carved on the corners. *Where did Mama get this stuff?*

She perched on the edge of a chair, folded her hands demurely in her lap, and watched the sheriff take a tentative bite of the pie. Immediately, his lips pulled into a smile. Whatever thoughts had been troubling him seemed to vanish.

"Mm-mm!" He swallowed. "That's good pie!"

She shrugged modestly. "Why, thank you. Baking is my only true accomplishment, but it is a useful one. And of course I can sew rather well. And I do enjoy singing and playing the piano."

His face brightened. "*You* play?"

"Yes, though I think my culinary skills will come most in handy when we open our house to boarders. Don't you?"

At the mention of the boardinghouse, he looked as if he'd just been reminded of something distasteful. His face fell, giving him the appearance of a doughy-cheeked little boy. "Oh, well…"

She fought the frown she felt sneaking up on her. "Don't *you* think the boardinghouse is a good idea?"

"Oh, well…" He took another bite of pie and chewed nervously. "This certainly is good."

"I'm so glad you like it." She beamed at him. "I have every confidence that my—I mean *our*—efforts will be rewarded. Mama's and mine. This house seems very…comfortable…and I'm sure there are many in the area who would like a situation where they wouldn't have to worry about cooking and cleaning. The elderly, for instance. Or bachelors.'' She added quickly, ''Bachelors of good character, of course.''

The sheriff's eyes widened. ''You have a point about the cooking and cleaning, Miss Calhoun.''

''Please call me Lacy.''

Two red blotches stained his cheeks. ''I oftentimes sit in my little room above the jail and think about how nice it was when I was home and had my Ma taking care of me, back in Cicada Creek. That's where I come from.''

''I've never heard of it.''

He looked amazed. ''Why, it's a wonderful little town over in East Texas. My family has a farm out there. Nice house, too—almost as big as this one.''

She was struck with a brilliant idea. ''Why, *you* could come live here!''

He looked alarmed. ''Oh, no…'' He shook his head. ''I mean, I'm much obliged, but my duties as sheriff require me to live next to the jail.''

''Of course.'' She tried to hide her disappointment. ''But you see? I'm sure there must be others like you.''

''Sure…'' He caught himself. ''Well, actually…''

Lacy leaned forward. ''Do you mean there's some reason others *wouldn't* want to come live here?''

''No!'' He frowned. ''Well, maybe.''

She finally did slump a little. She couldn't help it. No sleep and the past day's strain were beginning to catch up with her. ''It's the house, isn't it? Its history. People don't want to step foot in here…''

''Oh, no, that's not it,'' the sheriff assured her quickly. ''People *like* the house. Why, the Slipper's been a big part of Blissful since anyone can remember. That's the problem.''

Lacy blinked. ''I don't understand.''

''Well, the thing is…'' He swallowed, then tapped his finger nervously against his plate. ''I guess you could say there's a large bunch in town that want the Slipper back.''

''Surely *you're* not among them!''

His eyes bulged. "Oh, no—I was only telling you why you might meet a little resistance."

She considered this for a moment. "But you see, Sheriff, that's where my idea for a committee for decency comes in. There must be upright people here, and near here, who want this town to be a better place. If we band together, those who actually miss the...what this place used to be...will be silenced."

He stared at his empty plate.

"Doesn't that make sense to you, Sheriff?"

He blinked. "Well, sure. All I was saying was that it might be..."

"An uphill battle?" she finished for him. "Of course! But with courage and determination..."

The sheriff's face was drawn in a frown. He appeared to be wavering.

"You *do* agree with me, don't you?"

He looked into her face and she beamed hopefully at him. Slowly, some wall of resistance seemed to crumble before her eyes. "Heck, Miss Calhoun, if you do everything as well as you bake pies, I'm sure you could be successful at whatever you put your hand to."

Lacy clapped her hands, delighted. "I'm so glad you're in agreement with me, Sheriff. Please let me get you another piece of pie."

She stood, held out her hand for his plate, and watched him relent with a guileless smile. "Oh, what the heck. I'd love another piece."

As he grinned at her, a little spark of hope buoyed Lacy. She had the sneaking suspicion that she'd just won her first ally in the battle of Blissful.

Chapter Three

When the sheriff returned, Lucas wondered if maybe they had their Lacy problem licked. Bodine was grinning from ear to ear.

The Rooster's patrons gathered anxiously around. All had been waiting on pins and needles since Bodine had left, with the exception of Harry, who had gone back to check on his store, and presumably to make sure Myrtle hadn't poisoned Birdie.

"What did you say to the woman?" Harper asked Bodine.

"Did you tell her there was gonna be trouble if she stays here?" Boot pressed.

The sheriff, Lucas noted now, wasn't just grinning. He was in something of a stupor. The men's questions barely seemed to faze him.

Lucas put his hand on his shoulder and gave the man a firm shake. "Bodine! What happened?"

Bodine blinked and turned startled eyes toward Lucas, like a cat awakened from its nap. He swallowed. "Well, I told her that her boardinghouse idea wasn't going to be popular."

"Good!" Boot said.

"And then?" Lucas asked.

Bodine scratched his clean-shaven chin. "Then she sort of…well, she gave me this tasty piece of pie." He grinned again. "Sweet and tart, just like Ma used to make back in Cicada Creek, with *the best* crust."

The men were stunned. "You ate *her* pie?"

"I didn't want to be rude," Bodine said defensively. "And the minute you walk into the house you can smell the aroma from the kitchen. Not like it was at the Slipper before. I guess you could say it sort of caught me off guard."

Lucas had a sinking feeling. "Did you tell her she ought to leave town?"

The sheriff shrugged sheepishly. "Well…not in so many words."

The men groaned.

Bodine, sensing the magnitude of his failure, pleaded for understanding. "I just couldn't help myself. She gave me that pie and…aw, she isn't so bad. Sure, we've lost the Slipper, but how much more harm can one little mite of a woman do?"

Lucas shook his head in disgust. This was precisely why women were so dangerous. The smaller they looked, the more innocent, the better able they were to burrow under a man's skin. Men forgot that these sweet little women had tack-sharp, conniving brains. They did their damage in increments, hoping you wouldn't notice. Then, later, once you were hooked, *that's* when they'd pull the rug out from under you.

"All right," Lucas said, trying to calm the men down. Trying to calm *himself* down. "This was just a first volley—a sort of reconnaissance mission."

"A *what?*" Boot sputtered. "It was a flop, if you want my opinion!"

"Maybe now that Bodine got his foot in the door, one of us should go and give this Lacy Calhoun a firmer warning," Harper said.

Boot looked impatient with this idea. "Why don't we just go break a few windows?"

"Because those are Flossie's windows, you young hothead," Lucas snapped at him. Was it any wonder Boot had spent half his adult life in jail?

"Okay, then let *me* go talk to her," Boot suggested.

"Not you," Harper said quickly. "What we need now is somebody who can state clearly and distinctly all the reasons why that gal should skedaddle out of town. Lucas should go."

Lucas axed that idea. "I've already met Lacy Calhoun, and the woman didn't take a shine to me. If I told her to leave she'd probably stay here out of spite."

Harper sat up straighter. "Well then, if you don't mind my saying so, a more *elderly* man might not be a bad idea. You young saps get all tied up in knots around a pretty young woman. I'm not so susceptible."

Lucas could see the logic in what he said. A woman might be a little intimidated by Harper's eagle-sharp eyes and his somber black clothes. Plus Harper had a financial stake in getting the Slipper back to normal.

"That's a good idea," he declared.

The other men—even, reluctantly, Boot—agreed.

Harper squared his shoulders, mashed his hat on his head, and addressed the men. "I appreciate your faith in me. I will do my best, and God willing, I will return with good news."

Encouraging pats on the back ushered him out the door, and hopeful eyes followed him as he made his way down the dusty street toward the Slipper.

He was gone for two hours—*two hours!*—and when he returned, the crumbs down his shirtfront told the whole sorry tale.

Lucas's hopes plummeted as the old man shuffled guiltily toward the bar.

"That little lady really *does* make a hell of a pie," Harper said.

"What did you say to her?" Lucas asked.

"Yeah, what took you so long?" Boot chimed in. "What were you doin'?"

Harper's sun-browned face took on a reddish hue. "Eatin' dinner."

Lucas rolled his eyes. "For Pete's sake! After Bodine was

done in by that pie, you let the woman stuff a whole dinner down you? Didn't you talk to her at all about leaving?''

''Sure I did,'' Harper said.

''And?''

''She ain't leaving.''

The rest of the men exchanged disgusted looks.

''Harper, you was supposed to give her what-for,'' George scolded. ''You was supposed to *make* her leave.''

All the criticism finally got Harper's back up. ''Last I heard, this was a free country. A body can go where he wants. Lacy's ma owns that house, and she can do what she wants with it. If she wants to start up some fool boardinghouse, well, who are we to tell her different?''

''I didn't hear you lecturing anybody on the rights of man before you went over there,'' Lucas said.

''I hadn't had time to consider both sides back then.'' Harper shrugged and admitted in a much quieter voice, '''Sides, that dinner she gave me set me to thinkin' that it might be nice to have a decent place to eat supper every once in a while.''

''But what about all that hot air about civilization?''

Harper sighed. ''Maybe there's no fightin' it. But as long as we have it, it might as well be able to cook good.''

''Aw, Harper,'' Boot groaned, shaking his head in disappointment.

''For that matter—'' Harper went on ''—the Slipper's not the only place in town that could have girls.'' He looked pointedly at Lucas. ''Why don't you expand your business?''

Lucas brayed at that notion. ''Right now the Rooster's the one place a man can come for a little peace and relaxation. Women change a place. Bring a few girls in here, pretty soon you folks would be having fights over them. There'd be more flirting than card playing. You really think you could concentrate on poker with a girl breathing down your neck?''

Some of the men whose hopes had been raised by Harper's suggestion slumped a little in disappointment now. But everyone had to admit, Lucas had a point. Flossie was the only woman who came into the Rooster, and even her presence changed things.

Harper tilted back his hat. "I guess you'll all just have to become accustomed to goin' farther afield for your pleasures. And I'll have to do something else to earn my bread and butter."

"But what about Blissful?" George asked. "My blacksmith shop barely makes money as it is. We're going to become a ghost town!"

"A ghost town with a pretty fine boardinghouse," Harper added. "That little gal even plays piano pretty nice."

Bodine sucked in his breath enviously. "She played for you?"

Lucas let out a growl. This was too much. Cooking *and* playing piano. If that little viper had managed to bend the iron will of an old codger like Harper, she was obviously even more dangerous than any of them had suspected.

Maybe the old saying was right. If you wanted something done well, you needed to do it yourself.

Lacy wiped a sleeve across her brow and hopped out of the way when the restless wind sent smoke from the laundry fire billowing toward her. Heavens, this was hard work! Harder than she ever would have imagined. She probably should have started this morning. She remembered the starched snowy-white wimples of the nuns at the convent and her own starched white petticoats and aprons and bedsheets, and realized suddenly why Sister Angelica—who had run the laundry—always seemed so crabby. This job would steam the niceness out of a saint.

Lacy was no saint, but in a perverse way she welcomed the difficulty of her task. She intended to scrub clean or boil every square inch of the Satin Slipper, to give the place a ritual cleansing.

A determined hopefulness filled her. Last night she had wept bitter tears, but today she'd been busy making plans and already had received two callers, both of whom were *very*

polite. In fact, Mr. Cooley was quite a gentleman. It was hard
to believe that he had actually been in the employ of a house
of ill repute. She wished that her mother had not sniped at
him so much!

Thinking about Flossie, Lacy tried not to become discour-
aged. Her mother was the most challenging project ahead of
her. Tomorrow she intended to toss her mother's wardrobe
into a vat of whatever somber-colored dye she could procure
at the store. But it would take more than that to transform her
mother. There was a matter of attitude to deal with. Sometimes
it didn't even seem like Flossie wanted to change her ways.
She kept muttering about how the place seemed so empty to
her.

Didn't she understand how hard Lacy was trying to salvage
the Calhoun name from the ash heap of disrepute?

"Isn't it a little warm this afternoon to be doing that?"

Recognizing the resonant, teasing voice, Lacy closed her
eyes in dread. No doubt Lucas had come to gloat because her
mother was...well, wasn't what Lacy had thought she was.
Fine. Let him. *She* hadn't done anything wrong. She was trying to put wrong to rights.

High time somebody did in this town, apparently.

She turned and found the man grinning at her with the same
infuriating, suggestive smile she remembered from the stagecoach. All at once, her self-confidence drained away. When
she remembered telling Lucas with such smug self-assurance
that her mother took in sewing for a living, she wanted to hurl
herself into the pot of boiling laundry water.

He looked her up and down—and took his time about it,
too. She'd forgotten how handsome he was...if a woman were
at all inclined to find that dark, rugged, broad-shouldered look
at all appealing. Lacy decided she was not so inclined. A
woman with an eye on her reputation would do well to keep
her eyes off Lucas Burns.

"I have enough work here to keep me occupied for
months," she replied once she realized that a good first step

in keeping her eyes off of him would be to cease mooning at him. "I don't intend to let a little warm weather stop me."

"Maybe you should. You look a little overheated."

Good thing she had the fire as an excuse for the blush in her cheeks. She didn't want the man to think that his dark gaze and wolfish grin had any effect on her. But the truth was, something in those black eyes of his sent her insides sizzling and popping like the kindling that had started her fire.

She turned away from him and stirred the linens in the boiling kettle. Maybe if she ignored him, he would go away.

"I hear you're quite a little hostess."

Just his husky voice did things to her. He was the devil, all right. "Who told you that?"

"Some of the callers you've had this afternoon. They both took a real shine to you."

"I'm glad." Lucas hadn't come here to compliment her, she was certain of that. No doubt he was here to tell her that she'd done a terrible thing in convincing Flossie to close down the Slipper. The other men, once she'd fed them and got them talking, had nothing but praise for her upright, enterprising spirit. But Burns was another kettle of fish from those men. "I suppose there's a shortage of ladies here for men to visit with."

"There is now," he said flatly.

She lifted her chin. "Yes, but the women left will be more genuinely deserving of the title of lady. Naturally you weren't aware that there were good women in Blissful."

"Sure I was. You drove out a lot of them."

She frowned. "I meant really *good* women."

"So did I."

Lacy sniffed. "You obviously lack a true understanding of what makes a good woman."

"Do I?" Lucas scratched his dark chin in mock contemplation. "Well, let me see... I've always considered Flossie Calhoun to be a fine woman. Am I wrong?"

Lacy glared at him in mute, red-faced anger mixed with shame. That was a low blow—though right on target. How to think of her mother was still a terrible puzzle in her head. All day she'd shifted from hurt to anger to staunch loyalty toward Flossie. Part of her couldn't understand how her mother could have lied to her all those years, could have done what she did; and yet part of her could. Flossie had been trying to shelter her. Lacy admired her for that. But didn't she have other options? Did she have to run a house of ill repute?

She just didn't know what to believe anymore. Maybe that was the most hurtful part of all. Flossie had always told her that she was a widow, that Lacy's father had been a soldier who died during the war. Lacy had always had a clear picture of them together in her mind. But now she wondered how well Flossie had known that soldier. Maybe Flossie hadn't opened the Slipper after she'd been widowed. Maybe they hadn't even been married! Had her father merely been a customer?

These questions burned in her mind, but she couldn't bring herself to speak them to her mother. How could she? It was so shameful, so…

Avoiding Lucas's question, she swung back around and poked at her laundry. "Now that the Slipper is gone, I predict there will be a true flowering of domesticity and civilization here in Blissful."

"Oh, goody!" Lucas's exclamation dripped with sarcasm. He ambled over where she could see him and crossed his arms. "You really think closing the Slipper will be good for this little burg?"

She smiled patiently. "Believe me, Mr. Burns, I don't expect Blissful to change overnight."

"How soon then?" His expression was one of feigned concern. "I might need to know, being a businessman here myself."

"You don't have to worry on that account. The Blissful Temperance League won't be in a position to put you out of business for a while yet."

He nearly choked. "The Blissful *Temperance* League? When did that start up?"

"Tomorrow," Lacy informed him. "I'm holding my first meeting in the town square."

"There is no town square."

"Well, that little patch of buffalo grass next to the stage stop, then. I posted a notice at the general store. Mrs. Bean said she would attend."

"That'll make two of you, then," he grumbled.

She smiled, glad to have ruffled *his* feathers for a change. "From humble acorns grow mighty oaks, Mr. Burns."

His lips twisted into a sour grin. "Please, if you're intending to drive me out of business, feel free to call me Lucas."

She turned, leaving him to stew in his own juices. Unfortunately, she was even more uncomfortable having her back to the man than she was looking into his dark mischievous eyes. "Is there anything you wanted…Lucas?"

The name felt strange coming off her tongue, and it suddenly struck her that Lucas was the first man ever to tell her to call him by his Christian name. Strange that the familiarity would be requested by a man she despised. Or if not despised, then at least had every intention of avoiding.

Trouble was, so far Lucas showed not the least inclination to avoid her.

"Blackberry pie," he announced brashly.

"I beg your pardon?"

"I heard there was blackberry pie to be had here." His voice held the brave quaver of a man stepping up to a challenge. "Unless Harper Cooley ate it all?"

"Oh…" She hesitated, confused. Did he actually plan to stay long enough for her to feed him?

Of course, that would be the neighborly thing for her to do, especially since she had offered hospitality to Sheriff Turner and Harper Cooley. Although technically she didn't suppose she should feel exactly neighborly toward Lucas. "There *is* pie, but unfortunately, as you can see I am very busy at the moment."

"That's okay, I can cut myself a piece."

"I'm afraid—"

"Don't worry, I know my way around the Slipper."

"This is *not* the Slipper anymore!" Although it certainly had been when Lucas Burns memorized the floor plan. Seeing that she wasn't going to get rid of him as easily as she had hoped, she poked her broom handle at him. "If you'll watch the laundry, I'll get your pie."

He grinned as he took the stick. "A piece of cheese would go nice with it, if you have any."

The crust of the man.

Lacy stomped into the kitchen and hacked off a wedge of pie, slapped it on a plate, then marched back out to her unwanted guest.

He frowned as he took the plate. "No cheese—that's too bad."

She rolled her eyes. "I'm sorry to disappoint you."

"Don't lose sleep over it, honey." He carried his pie over to the porch steps, where he sat down as if settling in for a while. Mercy, she hoped that wasn't the case. She wanted Lucas Burns and his dark eyes gone already. The man thoroughly unnerved her.

She turned on her heel and flounced away from him.

"You know, a snippy attitude isn't going to help you much if you intend to take in boarders."

"Snippy!" she exclaimed, realizing too late that her tone sounded…snippy.

"Haven't you heard? People like service with a smile."

"If they're paying, I'll smile plenty."

His eyes brightened. "Ah…already worried about money, are you?"

She lifted her chin. "No."

"Not even a little bit?"

"Mama has a considerable nest egg saved up."

"I don't wonder. She's shrewd, your mother."

"A trait I hope I have inherited."

"Of course, it's a shame you won't be able to *use* any of that money," Lucas said casually.

Her mouth popped open. "I beg your pardon?"

"Well, after all, Lacy...you don't mind if I call you Lacy, do you?" He took a bite of pie.

She didn't care what he called her. She was burning to know why he thought she couldn't use Flossie's money. They needed that money. Was it tied up in some way? Had she been swindled? Or...

Oh, Lord. Was her mother a counterfeiter, too? Considering how her return home had shaped up so far, nothing would surprise her.

"Mmmmm! This *is* delicious pie."

Her head was spinning, though she tried not to show it. She cleared her throat. "Mr. Burns, you said—"

"Lucas," he corrected her.

"You said something about my not using Mama's money."

"Well of course not. I wouldn't insult you by suggesting otherwise."

She opened her mouth, then snapped it closed again, confused. "But you see, Mama offered it to me."

"Naturally, she would. You being her long-absent respectable daughter. But of course everyone knows that you'll give that money straight to charity."

To her everlasting shame, Lacy had never considered doing any such thing. That money was needed to tide them over until they attracted some paying boarders or figured out some other way to earn their bread.

Lucas tilted a startled glance up at her. "I hope you aren't offended by my mentioning money, but since we're both going to be fellow Blissful business owners...until you run me out of town, that is... I thought I could be frank with you."

"Of course," she replied quickly.

"And considering how that money was made...well, I wouldn't think there would be any question of your keeping it. You being a convent educated upright respectable girl trying to shove us all onto the right path."

Her entire body felt as if it were blushing. She certainly hadn't taken the right path into consideration when figuring their next year's budget.

Lucas sighed admiringly. "I expect you'll be sending all that money back to the convent."

"Oh…" *All* of it?

"Or maybe you'll put it to some useful enterprise right here in Blissful," he suggested brightly.

She felt so numb she collapsed onto a stair right next to Lucas. Give up all that money? How were she and Flossie going to get by?

"Yes, ma'am, this certainly is good pie!" Lucas exclaimed contentedly. "You're a very talented little lady."

She smiled limply, barely hearing the man. If she gave away all of Flossie's money, then she and her mother would be poor. Really poor. She had seen plenty of poor people in San Antonio—beggars at the convent gates hungry for the most meager scrap of food. Sunburnt, leathery women with ragged, bent hands. Women who'd never owned shoes, who barely had the wherewithal to dress decently. Women who had to stoop to anything to live.

She looked down at her own well-manicured hands. A shiver went through her in spite of the heat. She'd always pitied those people—from the comfort and safety of Our Lady of Perpetual Mercy. She had never thought of having to be a beggar herself. She had never given the problem of earning her bread a thought at all before this morning. Yet last night she'd told her mother that she'd rather they'd both lived as beggars than have made money Flossie's way. And she'd meant it, but…

But she hadn't thought they'd actually have to.

Of course, Lucas was right. Flossie's money, earned in sin, had to be given to charity. She was sure that's exactly what Sister Mary Katherine would advise.

That Lucas Burns of all people should be the one to point this out to her rankled.

She would have to give the money away, and tonight she would have to tell Flossie that's what she intended to do. She hoped she wouldn't have a maternal mutiny on her hands.

Lucas put down his cleaned plate and gazed at her in concern. "Are you all right, Lacy? You look a little ill."

She stiffened. "I'm perfectly fine."

"Of course! Why, you don't have anything to worry about!" Lucas assured her. "This house will be bursting at the seams with paying boarders any day now."

His tone was way too chipper to be believed. For the first time, Lacy looked at her plan squarely and knew it was doomed. A boardinghouse? In this bedraggled half-dead town? Where would she scrounge up even one person to live in her defunct whorehouse?

"Wait just a minute!" Lucas exclaimed. "I have an idea."

Lacy looked at Lucas gloomily. His ideas were causing her nothing but trouble. She suspected the odious man had come over for the express purpose of distressing her. And how well he had succeeded! What were she and Flossie going to do?

"How much did you intend on charging for rooms?" Lucas asked. "Three dollars a week?"

Lacy had no conception of how much she should charge. But three dollars a week—that was quite a bit of money. Wasn't it? Anyway, more than anyone had ever offered her before.

Suddenly Lucas pulled six silver dollars out of his pocket and plunked them in her hand.

"There," he said, grinning broadly. "For my first week."

Her mouth dropped open. *"You?"*

"Yes, ma'am! Your blackberry pie sold me. My little place behind the bar's not really very homey, and I haven't had a good square meal in I don't know how long. So I guess we'll be moving in this evening."

"We?"

"My son and I. We'll need two rooms, of course. Hope there's something good for supper." Lucas stood and was already beginning to walk away.

She jumped to her feet. "Wait!"

He turned. "Something wrong?"

"Yes! You just can't move in here…with your son." Lucas had a son? Where was this boy's mother?

Of course, given her situation, it would be hard to take the moral high ground on the subject of parentage.

Or on any subject at all.

His dark brows lifted. "Why not? Isn't that what boarders are supposed to do?"

"Well, yes, but…" *But I don't like you,* was all she could think to say. Why would Lucas want to move in? He must have some ulterior motive….

"Of course, if you don't want my six dollars…"

"I never said that!" Remembering those beggars at the convent gates, Lacy held tight to the heavy coins in her hand. Saying what came next, however, was agony. "Of course, you're welcome here." The words felt like sour persimmons in her mouth. "I just didn't expect boarders so soon, that's all."

Lucas laughed at her, reminding her precisely why she didn't want him anywhere near her. "You seem to be caught up short a lot these days, Miss Fresh-from-the-Convent Calhoun."

At his teasing, she quaked with irritation.

He sniffed, his lips twisting into a crooked smile. "And you'll probably be surprised yet again when you realize that your laundry's burning."

Belatedly, an acrid smell reached her nostrils.

Lacy yelped in dismay and ran over to see the huge heap of clothes and linens simmering at the bottom of the nearly dry kettle. She huffed and turned to upbraid Lucas, who after all had distracted her from her chore.

But the slippery saloonkeeper was already gone.

He really *was* a despicable person. And now he was moving in. For six dollars a week, she would virtually be his slave. She would have to cook for Lucas Burns, clean for Lucas Burns. Sleep under the same roof as Lucas Burns!

If she had any pride she would run after him and throw his

six dollars in the dirt at his feet. Right there in the street for all of Blissful to witness.

But, to her consternation, she didn't run after him. Instead, she kept her fist tightly closed around her pieces of silver, and for the first time had an inkling of why a woman would do something she found utterly repugnant for money.

Chapter Four

Upon his return to the Rooster Tail, Lucas received a hero's welcome.

"Did you give her what-for, Lucas?"

"When's she leaving?"

While it was comforting to know that he had the confidence of the other men, Lucas was embarrassed to have to tell them that he, too, had failed to rout the Calhoun menace immediately. But at least he had a plan. He turned to Jacob. "Pack your bags, youngster. We're moving."

Boot's mouth dropped open. "Movin' where?"

"The Slipper."

Jacob let out a whoop of glee while Boot looked like he'd been punched in the gut.

"Wait till I tell Joe and the other boys I'm livin' at the Slipper!" Jacob exclaimed.

Harper eyed Lucas sagely. "You ate the pie, didn't you."

"Sure did," Lucas said.

Boot tossed his hat down on the bar. "If this don't beat all! What can you be thinkin', Lucas? You were our last, best hope."

Lucas laughed. "The trouble with you, Boot, is you don't understand strategy. If you're going to root out a problem, you've got to go to the source. Which is what I intend to do. If Lacy Calhoun wants to open a boardinghouse, let's just show her what a difficult task that's going to be. I figure I can run her out of town much more effectively by living under her own roof than by hiding over here."

A wicked smile pulled at his lips. Oh, there were all sorts of options open to him now! He thought about little Lacy Calhoun, looking so forlorn when he'd suggested that she wouldn't want to spend her mama's money, and had to stifle a cackle of glee. The poor thing didn't stand a chance against him. It was like pitting a sly old fox against a downy chick.

In other words, this was going to be fun.

Harper, a veteran, nodded his approval. "It's called infiltrating the enemy."

A little of Jacob's enthusiasm seemed to fade. "You mean I've got to be mean to Flossie and that other woman, Pa?"

"You behave like you normally do," Lucas told him. "This is no job for a child."

The more Lucas pictured Lacy, with her pouty red lips and silky blond locks, the more eager he was to move into the Slipper. Her wide-eyed innocence was irresistible. Not to mention, it had been a long time since he'd seen anything so pretty. Living next to her, in the same house with her... The way she'd stirred his blood yesterday when he'd held her in his lap hit him again now. The sweet smell of her. The surprisingly warm, fleshy feel of her beneath all that starch.

He swallowed, and when he looked up, Harper was gazing at him with those eagle-sharp eyes. "Sure this is just a tactical move, Lucas?"

Lucas scowled. "'Course."

"Couldn't be settin' your sights on catching a wife now, could you?"

Men erupted in hoots and jeers.

Harper didn't take his eyes off Lucas. "She's a pretty creature. Sometimes the wiliest grasshopper can get stuck in the spider's web." He jabbed his empty pipe at Lucas. "And you're crawling right into it, son."

Lucas smirked. He agreed that Lacy was pretty. He wouldn't be male if he didn't acknowledge that. But unlike most men, he knew the real damage a woman like Lacy could do. He'd been left flat broke, with baby Jacob to care for. A "good" female did that to him. He wasn't likely to take another fall over an irritating little petticoat like Lacy Calhoun. It wasn't that he distrusted all women…but little miss priss Lacy, who thought the way to holiness was making everyone conform to her own rigid standards, had definitely rubbed his fur the wrong way.

"Don't you worry, Harper. I can take care of myself."

Lacy ushered Lucas and his son down the second-floor hallway. "I thought you'd be comfortable with these two rooms," she announced stiffly.

She felt ill at ease walking ahead of Lucas, though she was pleasantly surprised by his son, Jacob, who seemed perfectly nice. Funny how a boy could look so like his father, and yet remind her nothing of him. Jacob's dark eyes were soft and kind, and his voice didn't yet have that deep disarming timbre of his father's. Moreover, his manners were as refined as she supposed was possible in a place like Blissful—in fact, he was one of the best behaved boys she had ever met. He even hurried ahead so that he could open a bedroom door open for her—something that had never occurred to his father to do. Naturally.

She swept into the scrubbed and dusted bedroom, prepared to launch into her speech about how she hoped they would be comfortable here. But when she entered the room, the words died on her lips.

The room was pink. Very pink.

She had known it was pink, of course; only she hadn't realized *how* pink it actually was until now, when she took note of it squarely, in front of male witnesses. The bedspread had been boiled and burned, but its satin still glared out at them in all its bawdy-house loudness. The pink lace curtains drooped over the windows with a marked tawdriness that Lacy had overlooked during her whirlwind of tidying after Lucas had left. She been too concerned with scrubbing floors and dusting and doing anything she could to air out the room. Unfortunately, despite her valiant efforts, the stench of sweet perfume, tobacco and liquor still clung tenaciously in the air.

Or maybe she was just more sensitive to these odors, since they were not scents she'd been exposed to at Our Lady of Perpetual Mercy. Could be that another person might not take the slightest notice.

Behind her, Lucas sucked in a deep breath. "Mmm-mm! That's Squirrel-Tooth Shirley's perfume, all right."

Lacy tensed, and not for the first time wished the man to the devil. Unfortunately, she had taken his six dollars. Lucas Burns was now another cross for her to bear.

He clomped around the room, punching the pillows and peeking out the windows through the pink curtains.

Jacob turned to her with an earnest smile. "This is a nice room. It's very…colorful."

Lacy looked into the young boy's bright eyes and felt hopeful. Such an innocent! Thank heavens she'd arrived in time to save this one. He wouldn't have to come of age in a seedy little sin town.

"I don't like it," Lucas declared.

Lacy whirled in surprise. He was standing next to the washstand, arms folded arrogantly. "You don't like it?"

"It's too big."

"Too *big?*"

Dark brows arched in amusement. "Are you going to keep repeating everything I say?"

She put her hands on her hips and steadied herself against the vexation flashing through her. "This isn't a hotel. I didn't expect you to pick and choose rooms."

"Well maybe you should have," he replied. "People generally expect a little personal service for their money."

Her lips turned down at the phrase *personal service*. She didn't like the sound of that at all.

"Especially when they're paying a king's ransom."

"I'd like to know what king you think could be ransomed for six dollars a week!" she blurted out.

Lucas chuckled softly, and Lacy had to fight back a groan. She would have to train herself to keep a tight rein on her temper in front of this man. Showing her irritation only tickled him. The fiend. "There's another room next door that I was going to show you that—"

He dismissed her offer midsentence with a wave of his hand. "Oh, I know that room. Lila's."

Lacy had to restrain herself from cupping her hands around the boy's ears. How could a man speak so openly of knowledge of these rooms…in front of his son! "Mr. Burns—"

"I thought we'd agreed you'd call me Lucas."

"*Lucas*—" she said with as much distaste as she could inject into those two syllables "—these are the two rooms I prepared for you."

"Well, thank you. This one'll do fine for Jacob. I, on the other hand, would prefer something cozier."

She crossed her arms. "The rooms on this floor are all about the same size."

He grinned. "I know that."

"Then what—?"

"I'd like to see a room on the first floor, if you don't mind."

The first floor was where she and Flossie lived…as he probably knew very well.

Just then, Flossie flurried into the room, and the cloud of lilac scent that traveled with her filled the air. Catching sight of Jacob, she flew to him and gathered him to her bosom for a big hug that made Lacy blush almost as furiously as the boy. Flossie giggled as she looked into his eyes. "I'm so glad you're coming to stay with us! You'll be grand company. Think of all the hands of poker we can play!"

"Mother!" Lacy exclaimed.

Flossie winced and lifted a hand to her ruby lips. "Chuck-a luck, then." She looked over at Lacy's disapproving expression and rolled her eyes helplessly. "Well, we'll think of *something* to do! Do you like your room?"

"I like it fine, Flossie," Jacob explained. "Trouble is, Pa

doesn't like it. Or the room next to it. Says he doesn't want to stay in any room on this floor.''

Seeing Flossie's eyes light up with a possible solution, Lacy scooted over to her and said very pointedly, ''I told him there are no options. None.''

Her mother blinked at her, uncomprehending. ''What are you talking about? Lacy darlin', we've got all kinds of rooms! We've got that nice room downstairs…''

Lacy rolled her eyes. Downstairs was exactly where she *didn't* want Lucas. She and Flossie had agreed that the first floor would be reserved for their own quarters. It would give them a little privacy. ''That's not a possibility, Mama.''

''Well sure it is, hon! There's that beautiful little room right next to yours.''

''Perfect!'' Lucas said.

''It's very cozy,'' Flossie assured him with a wink.

Lucas turned so he could beam that irritating grin at Lacy— the one that made her stomach feel like a flock of butterflies were taking flight inside her. The grin that made her have wildly unladylike thoughts of smacking it right off his face with the force of her hand. ''Cozy!'' he exclaimed. ''That was *just* what I was hoping for.''

''Cozy means small,'' Lacy said flatly.

''That's all right. I'll feel right at home. I'm used to my little place behind the barroom, you know.''

As if he needed to remind her what hole he'd crawled out of. ''I'm sorry. That room is not ready.''

''A competent little woman like you can tend to that in no time,'' he told her. ''And while you're getting it all fixed up, I'll take your mama down to the kitchen and have some lemonade.''

''Oh, I don't know if I should leave Lacy…'' Flossie said worriedly.

Lucas took her arm in his. ''Nonsense. Why, on the stage ride Lacy was crowing about how eager she was to take work off your hands, Floss. She *wants* to help you. Don't you?''

Lacy lifted her chin. ''Of course.''

"Besides, nobody could work around you in that mustard dress, Floss. It's too distracting."

Flossie chuckled happily as she patted his arm. "Oh, Lucas! It'll be so nice to have people around the place again. I can't tell you how dead the house feels now that—" She cut off abruptly, her face flushing guiltily.

In the awkward silence that followed, Lacy had no trouble finishing the sentence. *Now that I'm here.* Tears sprang to her eyes, but she gulped them back.

"Anyhow—" Flossie said quickly to Lucas "—you know me. I love having people around!"

The two sauntered off, leaving Lacy feeling half relieved, half forlorn. She knew Flossie didn't mean to hurt her feelings. Her mother was just gregarious by nature.

Jacob's voice broke into her thoughts. "Would you like some help, ma'am?"

Lacy turned to find those soft dark eyes peering at her sympathetically. His stance was expectant, as if he really wanted to help her. It amazed her again how a boy could look so much like Lucas and yet be so completely different. In this case, the apple had apparently fallen a few miles from the tree. "No, Jacob. And don't call me ma'am. I'll bet I'm not much older than you are."

"I'm twelve." He smiled bashfully. "Well, just eight months short of it, anyways."

"Practically grown," Lacy said. "And I'm nineteen—practically an old woman." Feeling older by the hour, as a matter of fact. "Just call me Lacy."

The boy's complexion grew decidedly beetlike.

"Don't you want to go have some lemonade, too?"

His eyes were saying yes, but he was too polite to jump at the offer. "Are you sure?"

"I can handle changing bed linens by myself."

"All right. Thank you, Lacy."

After he left, Lacy went out into the hall to the linen cabinet to gather the necessary bedsheets and coverlet. From below rose the sound of merriment—Flossie's throaty gusts and Lucas's deep rumbling laughter. This was how she'd always thought of Flossie when she was at Our Lady of Perpetual Mercy. But this, she realized, was the first time she'd heard her mother laugh, really laugh, since she had arrived home. Lacy felt a pang.

Especially since the person making her mother sound so happy was not herself, but Lucas.

"Oh, Lacy?"

Lacy, who was at that very moment crawling into bed, let out a huff. Just when she thought this exhausting day was finally drawing to a much-desired close, Lucas was calling her name yet again—this time through the wall that separated their rooms. She was already dressed for bed and was in no mood to cater to another of his whims.

She didn't even bother going to her door; instead, she braced herself tensely on the edge of the bed. "What?" she hollered back.

"Could you come here a moment?" Lucas asked.

Go into his room? In her nightgown? Was he stark raving mad? "No, I cannot."

"Why can't you?" he asked with annoyance.

It was on the tip of her tongue to retort that she couldn't because she was completely worn out from jumping at his every command. Dinner had been a trial. Lucas had come up with a million different requests. Another glass of buttermilk. More salt. More, more, more. Each time she was forced to hop up from the table and scramble around the kitchen. Then, after dinner, when she served tea, he demanded coffee.

Then, of course, he lit up a cigar in the house, which sent her into fits. They practically came to blows over whether he would be allowed to smoke tobacco in the house. He finally agreed not to, except on the porch or in his own room—the one he kept reminding her he was paying an outrageous sum for. The one that was right next to hers. She could already smell smoke from the noxious weed seeping through their adjoining wall.

But of course, she would rather walk through a bed of rattlesnakes than admit to this man that he was annoying her with his petty little requests. That, any fool could see, what just what he wanted. She might have just left Our Lady of Perpetual Mercy, but that didn't mean she'd just dropped off the tree. She knew a thing or two about human nature, and about how men like Lucas Burns worked.

Knew it from books, at any rate.

Sometimes you just needed to put your foot down. "I can't—" she told him firmly "—because I'm not dressed."

As the answering silence stretched into a long, awkward, suggestive pause, heat radiated through her.

"Not dressed *at all?*" he asked, audibly tickled by the idea.

"I mean I'm not decent!" she retorted. The words echoed back at her and she let out a moan. "That is…"

An infuriating chuckle, muffled only by the thin wall, reached her. "You don't have to explain, Lacy. It's summertime. I have to admit I prefer to sleep in the raw myself."

Lacy's jaw dropped. He was *naked?* She jerked her gaze away from the wall between them in embarrassment.

She certainly couldn't let him go on thinking *she* was naked. "I assure you, I'm wearing nightclothes."

Another of those pauses followed. "Indecent nightclothes?"

"No!"

"But you said you weren't decent."

Frustration and growing anger formed a glob in her throat, making it hard for her to speak. That was just what always happened with Lucas. He goaded her, and then when she refused to take the bait he put words into her mouth so that she felt she had to answer him. But then her answers always came out wrong, or he twisted them so that she sounded foolish.

She managed to keep her voice somewhat controlled. "What was it you wanted, Lucas?"

"There's something I have to show you."

"I'm in bed, Lucas." Not that he cared a fig whether or not he inconvenienced her. "Your problem will have to wait until tomorrow."

A knock sounded at her door. Probably hearing her and Lucas arguing through the wall had roused Flossie. Thank heavens! Maybe she could convince Flossie to tell Lucas he had annoyed her enough for one day.

She frowned. Then again, maybe it wasn't right to be sending Flossie into Lucas's room, either. A groan of frustration built in her throat. Why did the man have to be such a nuisance? What had she done to nettle him so?

"Come in," she said, hoping her mother would have some solution to this problem. Flossie knew how to handle Lucas better than she did.

But when the door opened, it was Lucas himself standing at her threshold, not Flossie. He was still fully dressed in a white shirt, dark trousers and boots. His broad shoulders seemed to fill the entire doorway, and the sight of those coffee-dark eyes sparking at her caused her heart to pound erratically.

She gasped and crossed her hands protectively over her chest. "What are you doing here? Get out!"

In the moments that followed, he gave her a head-to-toe inspection and his expression changed from one of arrogance to amazement. In fact, he looked staggered. "*That's* what you call indecent?"

Her woolen nightgown, one of two identical garments she had made at the convent, wasn't very revealing. It had long sleeves and a high neck—thank heavens! But she still felt agonizingly aware that she had on very few underclothes beneath it. "It's very improper to be talking to you like this."

"Improper!" He laughed. "It's improper to encase yourself in wool in the summertime. You'll smother to death!"

"I would rather not address boarders in my nightclothes, Lucas," she insisted.

Naturally he did not interpret this as his cue to leave. "If you're worried your nightgown will put ideas into a man's head, I can set your mind at ease on that score. That thing you have on would make bulls volunteer to become steers." His brows knit in curiosity. "And what's that color? *Is* it a color?"

"It's gray!" she snapped.

"Reminds me of Elmer the saloon cat's upchuck." He laughed. "The color, I mean."

She closed her eyes, wishing that she could will the man away. Unfortunately, when she opened them again, he was still there. And his gaze was pinned on her chest. She flushed. "What is it you want, Lucas?"

He lifted his gaze to hers suddenly, as if she had reminded him at last of why he was standing there. "The thing is, I'm unhappy with my room."

A scream built inside her, but she swallowed it just in time. She was *not* going to remind Lucas that he had specifically asked for that room. Or that she had gone to a lot of trouble getting it ready for him on no notice. That was just the twisted path he was trying to lead her down. Instead, she lifted her head, as cool as a cucumber, and replied evenly, "As I said, you can take that up with me tomorrow."

Lucas crossed the room toward her.

Did he intend to grab her and take her to his room forcefully? Apparently not, because, to her utter astonishment, when he was within a foot of the bed he turned and then took a flying leap backward. She watched, aghast, as he landed on the bed next to her, flat on his back.

Lacy shot off the bed so fast her rear might have been spring loaded. "What are you doing?"

He groaned and stared disappointedly up at the ceiling. "This one's even worse."

She sputtered in outrage. "What is the matter with you? Have you lost your mind?"

He pushed himself up on his elbows and frowned at her. "Feather beds."

She blinked. "What?"

"I can't abide a feather bed. Not used to 'em. Don't you have anything…firmer?"

Her mouth dropped. "Lucas, do you realize what time it is? I can't go hunting around for corn shucks to stuff in your mattress." She would dearly love to shove a few corn shucks down his throat, however. Anything to cork him up for a little while.

"Actually, I'd prefer cotton wool. Or even straw would do."

She rolled her eyes. "And I'd prefer it if you would get off my bed!"

"How am I supposed to sleep?"

Pushed beyond her limit, she flashed him an exasperated glare. "I expect the same way you slept when you were memorizing the Slipper's layout!"

She would have done anything to withdraw the retort. Especially when she saw the gleeful expression on his face. Mortification pierced her. And she had promised herself she would never mention the Slipper and its shady past ever again. Especially not to someone like Lucas!

He sat up. "Back then, no one was concerned about sleep."

She lifted her chin. "I'm sure I don't care what you were concerned with. If you want, I will look into fixing your problem tomorrow. Right now, I think you should go."

Sighing, he pushed himself out of bed and ambled toward the door. "All right, I guess I can see when I'm licked."

The words surprised her. If he was licked, then why did she feel so wrung out? It was as if someone had milled her nerves through a coffee grinder.

"'Night, Lacy."

"Good night!" she said, with the last shred of civility she could muster.

He was about to shut the door, when he turned. "Oh, and for breakfast tomorrow, don't do anything special. Just a few eggs and some bacon or ham will do for me. And maybe a couple of biscuits. Or flapjacks, if you can make them. I like those better."

"I understand," she said through gritted teeth. She would have agreed to get up at three and make turkey and fixings if it would have gotten the man out of there.

He smiled. "I don't want to be a bother."

"No bother," she said tightly.

When he was finally gone, she collapsed on her bed. Heaven help her—this was just the beginning! She felt like weeping, like giving up.

But she couldn't give up now. Her mission went beyond her mother's needs now, or even the town's. With his taunting, Lucas had changed matters and had made it impossible for her to turn tail and run. Now this was between the two of them. And she didn't intend to let Lucas get the better of her.

Chapter Five

Attendance at the first gathering of the Society for Decency, Temperance and the Beautification of Blissful could generously be described as thin. The meeting was held in the storage room in the back of the mercantile, which the women had decided would be more private, and comfortable, than out in the open sun by the stage stop.

Lacy leaned against a pickle barrel at the front of the room, while Myrtle Bean and her sister-in-law, Birdie, perched on flour sacks as far as possible from Flossie—and, Lacy couldn't help noticing, from each other. The sisters-in-law might be the two most upstanding people in the community, but sour-faced Myrtle and silent, nervous Birdie obviously couldn't stand each other.

She had so many hopes resting on Myrtle and Birdie Bean that she couldn't help being a little disappointed. Myrtle was rather round, but far from being jolly, she seemed like a sour little stump of a woman. Her lips appeared to have spent so long flattened in distaste that they had disappeared altogether, so that her expression was mainly conveyed by the position of the lines on her face and the flash in her deep set gray eyes. The collar of her tight dark blue dress practically touched her chin. Or maybe it was that her chin came down to meet her collar. Lacy couldn't decide.

And Birdie, a wraith, pale almost to the point of being specterlike, did nothing to compensate for her sister-in-law's hostility. She appeared too shy to speak.

The sight of them both showing their backs to Flossie broke her heart. Especially since Flossie seemed to be going that extra yard to be ladylike today. She was wearing her most subdued dress; which, Lacy had to admit, had looked much more subdued at the boardinghouse. The brown dye on the pink had come out a loud shade of orange. Next to the coppery red of Flossie's hair, the color was a little nauseating. And the hat Flossie had picked—her best, she'd bragged to Lacy—was a busy affair with a jauntily curved brim festooned with stuffed birds, nut clusters and ribbons. Flossie swore to Lacy that she was not wearing face paint, yet all the same her lips and cheeks seemed unnaturally red. Maybe all these years of wearing the stuff had permanently tinted her.

Lacy squirmed. She found herself torn between a raw love for her mother, and an equally strong desire to throw a sheet over her.

When Flossie smiled encouragingly at her, Lacy looked away quickly, then felt ashamed of herself. Her mother was doing her best. If anything Myrtle and Birdie Bean's snubs should just make her all the more determined to continue on her quest. Someday, no one would look down on the Calhouns.

She cleared her throat and shot an anxious look at the door. "I suppose this is everyone who could come today."

"If you're waitin' for more females, Lace, this is everyone, period," Flossie declared.

Myrtle Bean stiffened and shot the red-haired woman a quick, disapproving look.

"I thought we could try to come up with some ideas for making Blissful a nicer place," Lacy said, jumping right in. "More appealing to families."

"Impossible!" Myrtle declared.

Lacy was a bit taken aback. She hadn't expected an objection to the first suggestion out of her mouth. "Why impossible?" she asked Myrtle.

The lines around Myrtle's mouth deepened. "With the rough element in this town, you'll *never* attract families. I won't mention a certain establishment—" she barely managed not to flick a glare back at Flossie "—which, I'm glad to say, recently went under."

To Flossie, those were fighting words. She leapt out of her chair with such force that her hat nearly lost a nut cluster. "It *did not* go under! I'll have you know, Myrtle Bean, that the Slipper made more money last week than your store's ever seen in a month."

A flush crept up Lacy's neck. "Mama…"

"We closed on account of Lacy's respectability—" Flossie declared hotly "—and *that's all.*"

She sat back down with an audible thump, sending up a puff of flour.

Myrtle harrumphed. "Be that as it may, this town still has the Rooster seducing good men away from their homes and their domestic duties. Why, I'll bet even my Harry hasn't spent an entire night at home in two months!"

Flossie barked out a laugh. "Wonder why!"

Myrtle glared.

Before a battle could break out between the two women, Lacy jumped in. "Naturally we face certain obstacles…"

"Obstacles! That saloon is a disgrace!"

"I agree completely—"

Myrtle cut her off. "I've been railing about it for years. But nobody would listen to *me.* I was just a voice in the wilderness as far as this town was concerned."

Lacy cleared her throat. "Well, certainly, we should try to—"

"Didn't you hear the gunshots last night?" Myrtle brayed.

Flossie snorted. "Oh, shoot! That was probably just that hothead, Boot, blowing off steam. That's what happens when boys get a little liquored up." Lacy looked imploringly at her mother, so that Flossie added, a little resentfully, "Of course, if it bothers you too much, Myrtle, maybe I can talk to Lucas about it. He's livin' at the Slipper now, you know."

Myrtle jumped out of her seat, nearly causing Birdie to faint. Lacy rushed forward—to Myrtle, not to Birdie. Why, oh, why did her mother have to mention Lucas? Obviously having a booze peddler living with them was not helping the reputation of the Calhouns. At least not with Myrtle. "There's nothing improper about the situation, Mrs. Bean. I've opened a boardinghouse."

"And you've got *Lucas Burns* living there?"

"With Jacob," Lacy added, hoping that would make the arrangement sound more respectable. But Myrtle's expression was still one of shock. Oh, Lord. Now her mother had done it. Now that Myrtle had heard that they had the saloonkeeper living at their house, she probably wouldn't want to have anything to do with the fledgling society.

"He's *paying* you?"

That flat, nasally twang made it sound as if Lacy were prostituting herself, which she hastened to assure Myrtle was not the case. "Six dollars for room and board. And Jacob, I'm sure you know, is *very* nice. It's so much better for the boy to be living in a real home instead of the back of a barroom, don't you think?"

Myrtle's brows shot up. "Lucas Burns is paying you *six dollars* for him and his son?"

Lacy cast about for the correct response. She wasn't certain whether Myrtle was insinuating that she was committing theft or selling herself too cheap. "Yes, ma'am. You see, I have to bring in some cash to keep the house going because Mama and I are giving all her money to charity." There. That should show how serious she was about becoming respectable. Unfortunately, her mother moaned at the reminder of all her lost money; Lacy had to speak fast to cover the sound. "When Lucas Burns offered I felt that I *had* to accept."

Myrtle crossed her short arms over her ample bosom and studied Lacy for a moment, her flinty eyes glinting harshly. Her chest seemed to expand to twice its normal size, which was already considerable. "I see!"

Feeling very small, Lacy burned under the pinpoint intensity of Myrtle's gaze. Maybe Myrtle didn't believe her about the charity.

"How many rooms do you have to let?"

"Just two. Very nice ones," Lacy said, eager to assure her new neighbor she wasn't starting a flophouse. "I'm working on fixing the attic, too, but it's rather hot up there right now…"

Myrtle turned to her sister-in-law. "Birdie, let's pack your bags."

Birdie seemed almost as stunned as Lacy was. In fact, she still looked as if she might faint. When she spoke, her voice was little more than a croak. "Wh-what?"

"Come now, don't play coy!" Myrtle blasted at her sister-in-law. "You know you've always hated living with Harry and me. I'm sure you'd like your own home, wouldn't you?"

As if renting a room in a boardinghouse were the equivalent of having one's own house. Lacy and Birdie exchanged confused glances before Birdie appealed directly to her sister-in-law. "But Myrtle—the *Slipper?*"

"The floozies are all gone, Birdie," Myrtle told her. "No harm in you sleeping where they did. You can't catch looseness like a cold, you know."

Birdie stuttered unhappily. "B-b-but…"

"'Sides, you know you can't stand our cat." Myrtle shot a quick glance at Lacy. "Don't have any animals, do you?"

Lacy shook her head. "That is, just a few chickens in the henhouse, and a cow…"

Birdie flinched. "Cow? Myrtle dear, I don't like animals…."

"Well it wouldn't be in the house, goose!" Myrtle chortled. "Best thing in the world for you, Birdie." She looked up at Lacy. "A dollar a week, you say?"

One dollar? Where did she come up with that figure? "W-why no—it would be—"

Myrtle talked right over her. "Six dollars for a man and boy who'll eat you out of house and home and clomp all over your floors in their dusty boots is one thing, but Birdie's no trouble at all. Why, you won't even know she's there, I'll be bound. *One dollar* would be just right."

"Oh, well…"

"Let's go, Birdie." Myrtle took her sister-in-law by the shoulders and propelled her toward the door.

"Wait!" Lacy called after them. "What about the meeting?"

Apparently Myrtle was too eager to finally be rid of her sister-in-law to discuss decency, temperance, or the beautification of Blissful right now.

After they had gone, Flossie leaned back and laughed. "Can you beat that? Myrtle couldn't wait another second to finally foist Birdie off on somebody else. Guess she thinks she and Harry will finally have that honeymoon, poor deluded woman."

Lacy sagged against a feed sack, feeling dejected. "I had such high hopes!"

Flossie flurried over to console her. "But you got us another boarder, hon. That's good business."

A dollar a week! When Lacy was making plans for the boardinghouse, she hadn't factored in the reality that the town was populated by pinchpennies. But she supposed she should count her blessings. Seven dollars a week wouldn't make them rich, but it was better than nothing. "But what about the society meeting? We hadn't even begun to make plans to make Blissful a better place."

"Oh, that." Flossie waved away that worry with a swipe of a perfumed silk handkerchief. An item that had so far escaped the boiling pot. "Don't worry, Lace. I've got plenty of ideas."

Lacy grunted unenthusiastically.

"Just this morning I was thinking that if you really wanted to draw a crowd to town, we could have a carnival."

She turned to her mother, who was beaming eagerly beneath the brim of that absurd hat. "A what?"

"A carnival. Wouldn't that be fun? I'll never forget the one I attended when I was a little girl in Fort Worth. My daddy took me, and there were all sorts of marvelous things. This one woman there, Alberta the Amazing Bendy Woman, could wind her knees around the back of her neck and write her name on a slate with her toes!''

"Oh, Mama! What good would that do?''

Flossie bit her lip. "I'm not rightly sure…unless you was missing your arms. I bet then that toe-writing trick would come in right handy.''

Lacy took in a slow, even breath. "I meant what good would a *carnival* do? For the town? The point is to make Blissful a better place, not to turn it into a freak show.'' It was too close to being that already, in her opinion. "Besides, a carnival would be just a day-long event, and the people would leave.''

"But it would make money,'' came a voice from the doorway.

Lacy pivoted toward the door, which Lucas was leaning casually against. Looking at him, she felt that same heat start boiling up in her that she felt whenever she was around the man. Which seemed like all the time now. Wasn't it bad enough that she had to live with the scoundrel sleeping in the next room and smell his cigar fumes? That she had to cook his breakfast and dinner? Was he following her everywhere she went now?

She lifted her head. "This society is *not* about making money.''

Of course, at her mention of the society, he couldn't help making a show of gazing around the empty storeroom for evidence of other members of the society.

"Myrtle and Birdie had to leave,'' Lacy explained.

"I might just be an outsider to your little society—'' Lucas said ''—but it still seems to me that if you're going to attract people to this town, you're going to need a scheme that makes money.''

"You're a fine one to tell me my business—'' she fired back ''—when *your* business is what's keeping decent people away from town.''

"My business is all that's bringing people into Blissful right now," Lucas argued. "And if it ever disappears, you can bet this town will blow away like a tumbleweed."

It figured Lucas would position himself as the town's pillar. Its saving grace. The hubris! "It's my intention to show that the town will survive without you and your Rooster Tail."

He bowed mockingly. "In any case, you would still need to scrape some money together to get anything done around here."

It was on the tip of her tongue to retort that she *had* money, but because of his idea about giving it to charity she couldn't use it.

Guilt for such wretched thoughts instantly overwhelmed her. Surely she would have come around to the idea of giving her mother's money to charity on her own…eventually.

"Flossie's idea is a good one," he reiterated.

Flossie beamed eagerly. "Do you really think so, Lucas? I sure did. Why, there were hordes of people at that carnival when I was a girl."

"But that was in Fort Worth," Lacy observed. "Fort Worth is a big place. Where would *we* find hordes of people?"

"Lacy has a point, Floss." Lucas drummed his fingers against the doorjamb. "What you need is a real draw. Bearded ladies. Sword swallowers."

"That's what *I* was thinking!" Flossie said.

Lacy's lips pursed. She knew what Lucas had up his sleeve. He had dreams of bringing a seedy, carny atmosphere to Blissful. Of filling the place up with games of chance and people of questionable repute. Who, she had no doubt, would be just the type of people who would want to while away hours and hours at the Rooster.

"If *you* would like to show your civic pride by swallowing a few swords, Lucas—" she told him "—I surely won't try to stop you."

He guffawed. "I'll bet. You'd probably sharpen those knives yourself, wouldn't you?"

She smiled sweetly. "Anything to help the community."

Needless to say, Flossie was over the moon about the whole carnival idea. It was like trying to sell a horse on oats. "This will be wonderful—just like when I was a girl! We can set up a refreshment stand—" She darted an apologetic glance at Lucas. "Nothing alcoholic. No need to worry about us competing with your business, Lucas."

As if that wasn't the whole point! And what on earth were they even consulting with Lucas for? *He* wasn't a member of their society. And wouldn't ever be, if Lacy had her way.

She was on the verge of telling him so in no uncertain terms when the sheriff wandered in.

"Is this the meetinghouse?"

Flossie greeted him joyfully—as she did everyone. The woman had a knack of hurling herself at people she'd just seen thirty minutes earlier as if they were long-lost friends. "Bodine, you sweetheart! Where you been? You should come have dinner with us sometime."

Bodine took off his hat—something Lucas had *not* done— and smiled a greeting at Lacy. "I'd like that. Word around town is that you're quite a cook, which I can testify to after eatin' that delicious pie."

Lacy felt calmer just looking at Bodine. Now here was a kind, honest man. The type of man Blissful would do well to attract more of. He was respectful and polite, and he certainly didn't leer at her the way Lucas did. He was—if such a thing could exist in Blissful—a gentleman. "I'm glad you came by, Sheriff," she said. "We were just discussing what a bad idea having a carnival in Blissful would be."

"We were discussing the merits of the idea, if I recall," Lucas reminded her.

She glared at him. "Naturally *you* would see only its merits. You would just love to have more victims to lure into your booze shed."

Bodine rubbed his jaw, his brow furrowed. "A carnival, huh? I'm not so sure that's such a good idea."

Lacy crossed her arms and gloated triumphantly at Lucas. *There!* Bodine would stand up for her.

"You'd have to take it a little further than just a carnival," he went on.

Her jaw dropped. *Further?* "B-but surely you're not in favor of such a plan!"

"Why not?"

"Think of the difficulties it would bring here. The lawlessness."

Bodine tilted his head thoughtfully. "Well, now, not necessarily. Not if you did it right."

"That's what *I* said," Flossie put in. "Just have a little fun!" She shot Lacy a nervous, appeasing glance. "Good clean fun, of course…with a few performers."

Bodine worried his lip. "Far as I can tell, the worst part about the carny scheme is that it wouldn't be a constant thing. You'd have it once and then it'd be over. And then what are you left with?"

"How else would we handle it?"

"See, I always thought it would be useful if people had a place to trade goods without goin' from one little town to another, or all the way to San Antonio."

"Why that's a marvelous idea!" Flossie exclaimed. "We could have sort of a trade day. Have some fun things as a draw, but have a purpose to it, too."

"What's anybody going to trade around here?" Lucas asked.

Lacy nodded, and said right after him, "Why would anyone want to travel to Blissful for *that?*"

Suddenly, she and Lucas were staring at each other in astonishment. Good Lord! Lacy's head spun in confusion. *Were they actually agreeing on something?* As they blinked in surprise, it suddenly occurred to her that whether Bodine was right or wrong didn't matter; she *knew* she shouldn't be siding with Lucas.

"Everybody around here's so isolated," Bodine said. "There are all sorts of folks that wait to go to San Antonio once or twice a year to do their shopping and have a little entertainment. But why not give those things to them right here?''

''That's right!'' Flossie seconded.

Even Lacy began to see the possibilities in the plan. Especially now that she noticed how dark Lucas's expression had become. Oh, he had been all for carny geeks and sword swallowers. But the idea of something that might actually succeed in making Blissful a legitimate commercial center appealed to him less.

''We'll have to talk this over with the other members,'' Lacy said, not wanting to be too hasty…and hoping everyone would just forget all about the carnival aspect of the plan in time.

''What other members?'' Bodine asked.

''Myrtle and Birdie and…'' She wished she had some more names.

Flossie laughed. ''You should have seen Myrtle, boys. She was so eager to hie Birdie off to the boardinghouse, she looked like she was going to pop a corset lace.''

''Mother!''

At Lacy's disapproving scowl, Flossie shrugged and laughed uncomfortably. ''Anyway, she was in a big damn hurry. What say we go back and get something cool to drink?''

''Sounds dandy,'' Lucas said, ushering her out the door.

The meeting, apparently, was over, and Lacy felt consumed by disappointment. Nothing had gone as planned. Instead of a nice visit with the ladies of the town, she had been cornered once again by Lucas. Instead of flower plantings and fundraising quilting bees, sword swallowers and contortionists now loomed on the horizon.

Bodine waited for her at the door. ''Are you coming?''

Allowing Bodine to take her arm, she trooped through the store, wondering if she had truly bitten off more than she could chew. Going into the meeting, she had expected to formulate a plan to plant a few flowers around town. But this…a trade day! How could she manage that? And what did it really have to do with resurrecting the Calhoun name in Blissful?

Watching her mother sashay out the door on Lucas's arm, she despaired. How was she ever going to make her mother fit in with respectable people? That is, if she ever found some respectable people who were amenable to socialize with them… Flossie was so loud, so colorful. All the things Lacy had loved about her mother when she'd visited her in San Antonio made her wince now. If she could just change her, tone her down…

She looked up at the bolts of cloth stacked behind the shelf in the mercantile. Maybe she *could* tone her mother down. She just needed to start from scratch. She saw a brown muslin with cornflowers on it, and knew it would be just the thing.

Or at least it might be a good beginning.

The crowd at the Rooster started gathering in the afternoon. Boot was there, and George, and so was Harper. Jacob was at a table in the corner, eating the noon meal Lacy had brought over for him. Apparently she didn't trust Lucas to feed his own son properly during the day. She had knocked at the batwing doors, but had primly refused to step foot into the establishment. However, Lucas had spied her peeking in and sending an unflattering glance around the place.

That glance had caused him—once Lacy was safely out of eyesight—to pick up a broom and attack the floors, which were thick with dust and dried tobacco spit. They *were* pretty disgusting, now that he had his mind fastened on them.

Not that he gave a damn about Lacy's opinion.

Harper leaned back and eyed the food Jacob was attacking like a half-starved coyote. The old man sniffed appreciatively. "Yeast bread. I like that smell."

Boot grunted. "Come over to the widow's then. Seems like all she does is bake. Probably how she keeps so plump."

A wistful smile touched Harper's lips. "The smell of bread reminds me of home. Of good old Tennessee."

Lucas leaned against his broom handle. Harper sure had been acting strangely! In the old days—the pre-Lacy days, which seemed about as distant and golden as the American

Revolution now—Harper had been a windy old crank. Never mentioned his past. He lived in an abandoned shack on the edge of town and didn't seem to care much about what you would call the finer things in life. Something had changed him. "Is that where you come from, Harper? Tennessee?"

He looked uncomfortable. "Long ago, Lucas. Long, long ago."

"I'll bet you wish you was back there now that this town's gone to seed!" Boot said. He turned fitfully to Lucas. "How's your plan comin'? I guess that Calhoun gal must be practically ready to skedaddle back to the convent. Right?"

Lucas resumed his sweeping, if for no other reason than to avoid the hopeful look in Boot's eyes. He hadn't made as much progress as he had anticipated. Oh, sure, Lacy was sick to death of him. He'd pestered her mercilessly since the day he'd moved in. And she'd responded in the most exasperating way imaginable—by taking it on the chin. He had to hand it to her, she had more fortitude than he ever would have imagined.

Now she was becoming adept at staying out of his way. They'd barely had a moment alone together in the past two days. It was frustrating.

More frustrating than he cared to admit to himself, in fact. He hadn't spent the last few nights awake in bed thinking about Lacy's cooking, that's for sure. No, when he closed his eyes at night he was taunted by the vision of Lacy's shapely, compact body swathed in that hideous nightgown. Unfortunately, the mystery of just what was under that nightgown taunted his thoughts more than the voluptuous figure of any saloon girl ever had.

The town really *did* need the Slipper back.

On the other hand, Lacy's cooking seemed to be the only thing on Harper's mind. "Does she make fried chicken?"

Jacob nodded. "Real good, too. It's kind of peppery."

"Ah!" The old man sighed. "Might've guessed that. Any good cook knows a little pepper makes the bird."

Boot drummed his fingers impatiently. "*Is* she about to ske-daddle, Lucas?"

"Sure, Boot, sure," Lucas said. "I just need a little more time...."

"Well, heck! What are you doin' here, then? Let me handle the Rooster some time. Gettin' Lacy out should be your priority now."

Lucas thought about it. Having a night or two free would give him more time to be around Lacy...maybe alone with Lacy...

He swallowed. "All right, Boot. If you think the widow can spare you."

"*Spare* me? Old Henrietta won't even notice I'm gone!"

"You're never there anyway," George pointed out. "Don't know why she keeps you on, myself."

Boot's face went red. "She says she's fond of me."

George practically howled. "No wonder you spend so many long hours here!"

Boot scowled. "She's not *that* bad."

George shook his head. "Too stout for my tastes."

"I'd prefer a stout widow to a skinny young thing like Lacy Calhoun," Boot said. "Wouldn't you, Lucas?"

Lucas, who had been off in a daydream about that very skinny young thing, was startled by the question. "How's that?"

"I don't see how the sheriff could be so wound up about her," Boot went on. "About the only thing good about her is that hair—and who cares about that?"

Lucas thought about that hair. It *was* beautiful—pale and as soft-looking as corn silk. And the way it framed her face, and those blue eyes... And those lips. They were like rosebuds. After fourteen years in a convent, who knew but those lips might never even have been kissed before?

"I like auburn-headed women, myself," George said.

"Since when?" Boot turned on him in irritation. "And for that matter, the Widow Wallace *has* auburn hair!"

"So?"

"So, you were just saying you thought she was ugly!"

"So?"

Boot slammed his hat against the bar. "Either you like some traits in a woman, or you don't."

"You gotta look at a thing from all angles, Boot. And in case you haven't noticed, the Widow Wallace's angles aren't all that appealing."

Boot let out an annoyed grunt and turned back to Lucas. "What do you think, Lucas?"

Lucas blinked. He didn't have a clue what they'd been talking about. Something about hair?

Harper, who apparently hadn't been listening either, sighed and took a long drink of coffee. "Fresh bread, fried chicken, a warm bed," he said to no one in particular. "All the comforts a man alone shouldn't think about."

"*You* sure seem to be thinking about them," Boot told Harper with undisguised disgust.

Harper didn't deny it. In fact, he was smiling. "If you dwell on the comforts, boys, you're doomed. Sweet doom though it may be."

Though no one answered him, Boot and Lucas exchanged knowing glances. It was true; comforts could spell a man's undoing. Because comforts were best provided by the female sex, and once you let females take over your life…

Once you started thinking too much about corn-silk hair and lips as pure as the driven snow you were licked.

Chapter Six

After dinner, Birdie fussed and fidgeted and held back tears until even Lacy looked like she was ready to crumble. The poor woman was not adapting well. Being banished from her old home above the store had obviously hit her hard. When asked if she wanted anything, she would just sniff and say she didn't want to be any bother. Which was more annoying in its own way than if she actually *had* been a bother.

"I think I'll go to my room now," she announced, finally, hopping up from the settee in her quick way. The woman tended to dart silently when she moved, like a minnow.

Lacy was busy sewing, but looked up with a patient smile. "Good night, Birdie."

Birdie hesitated. "Back at home, this is past bedtime." Her lip quivered and she surveyed the room, as if there was something unsavory going on. "But here…"

Flossie looked up from the game that she and Lucas were playing. "Sure you don't want to play, Birdie?"

Birdie jumped. "Me? Play checkers? Oh, no! That is…" She looked longingly at the staircase leading up to the second floor. "Good night!"

"'Night," Lucas said.

One down, two to go. He looked around and noted Jacob, who was close to nodding off in a chair with a book. And then there was Flossie. Getting himself alone with Lacy was no easy task.

Flossie shook her head. "Poor creature. You think she doesn't know how to play checkers? Heck, I'd be willing to teacher her."

"She's homesick," Lucas said.

Flossie drew back. "For old Myrtle? You'd think she'd be thanking her lucky stars to be away from that old biddy. The woman has tormented her for years."

He smiled. "After one night of Birdie's fidgeting and whining, I wonder if it really wasn't the other way around."

Lucas heard a choking noise, and looked up just in time to see Lacy swallowing back a smile.

So…she *did* have a sense of humor, after all. Wonders never ceased.

"I'm glad you could stay in tonight, Lucas," Flossie said. "Though I have to wonder at you lettin' Boot look after the Rooster."

It pained him to be away from his business, but he managed to act as if he welcomed the vacation. In all the years he'd owned the saloon, he had never been absent for long. And if he'd had to be away, he'd simply closed the place down till he got back. But these were extenuating circumstances. He had important business to tend to here.

While he was distracted, Flossie happily hopped over two of his checkers.

Lacy had declared checkers to be far preferable to cards of any type—and certainly preferable to dice—as long as no gambling was involved. At least not with real money. How she reached this decree no one knew, least of all Lucas. Now that Lacy was out of that convent, she seemed bent on re-making the world from scratch. But at the boardinghouse her word was law, so checkers it was. He and Flossie were reduced to using dried black-eyed peas and kidney beans for stakes.

Lacy bent rigidly over her sewing. The way she was going

at whatever it was she was doing, you'd think the future of civilization hinged on her finishing it.

He thoughtlessly slid a checker to another square. Flossie tutted at him. "You better watch what you're doin', Lucas."

He grinned. "I was thinking that after we finished this game, Lacy might play. Doesn't seem fair not to let her have a turn."

"No thank you," Lacy said primly.

"Don't you like checkers?"

"It seems like a very wasteful way to spend one's time." She nodded approvingly over to Jacob, who was plodding sleepily through the battered copy of *The Pilgrim's Progress* Birdie had lent him. "I would much rather read a good book, like Jacob is doing," Lacy said. "If I had the time."

"Reading takes a lot of time, that's for sure," Jacob agreed.

Lucas bit back a smile. "I don't wonder. The way you keep nodding off every few minutes, those pilgrims can't be progressing very far."

Lacy laughed. Lucas caught her eye, and her mirthful gaze scuttled away from his. But the corners of her mouth were still turned upwards.

"I don't think I'll ever make it through this thing," Jacob complained. "It's too dull."

"Of course you will," Lacy said in the overly bright tone of a schoolmarm. "Besides, one doesn't read for excitement. One reads to be enlightened."

Lucas turned to her. "Tell me, Lacy, what *do* you do for excitement?"

Her mouth popped open; she looked as if she had never considered this question before. "Why…nothing at all."

He turned back to hover over the checkers board. "I might have figured that."

When she responded, there was an unmistakable tension in her controlled tone. "What I mean is, I don't need excitement. I'm perfectly content doing my duty. There's so much to be done, I can hardly think of diversions. I've got cooking, cleaning, sewing…"

"Wish your duty could have picked out a more festive pattern for my dress," Flossie muttered in despair as she looked at the material bunched in Lacy's lap.

So the dress was for Flossie. That made sense. No woman in her right mind would pick such a grotesque pattern out for herself. The contrast of the muddy brown and the cornflower blue was truly sickening. Lucas could see what Lacy was up to—she was trying to turn an exotic bird into a sparrow. Trouble was, if Lacy was hoping to draw stares away from her mother, she had picked the wrong fabric. That cloth was so ghastly it was difficult *not* to look at it.

Lacy, on the other hand, was wearing a simple dress of plain blue. Even that modest frock molded to curves that put ideas into a man's head that would have thrown Lacy into fits had she known.

She glanced up as Flossie practically upended her teacup and downed it in one gulp. Flossie hiccuped, and Lacy's eyes narrowed as she looked from the cup to Lucas. Looking guilty Flossie giggled and pushed the cup away quickly. "'Scuse me."

Her daughter's face was now a mask of suspicion. "Mother…"

Flossie jumped up, yawned, and stretched. "Sorry I can't finish the game, Lucas, but I'm exhausted." She crossed over to where Jacob was snoozing again and nudged the boy's leg with the toe of her shoe. "C'mon, youngster. If you're going to sleep, you might as well do it in your bed."

Jacob struggled out of his chair and after saying good-night blearily trudged up the steps to his room on the second floor. Flossie scooted toward her own bedroom on the first floor. Which left Lucas alone in the parlor with Lacy.

A boiling mad Lacy. As soon as the others were gone, she stood up, hands fisted at her sides.

She would have been shocked out of her drawers to know that when she was at her angriest, with color in her cheeks, was when she was at her most desirable.

The glare she aimed at him might have withered a lesser man. Lucas girded himself for another confrontation.

"How dare you!" she huffed the moment the others were out of earshot.

He had some idea of what had her petticoats in a twist, but he wasn't about to volunteer any information. "How dare I what?"

"Sneak liquor into this house, that's what," she answered sharply. "You've been needling me since you moved in here, Lucas Burns, but I didn't think you'd stoop to this. You know my feelings about spirits."

"Needling you?" he asked, all innocence.

She rolled her blue eyes heavenwards. "Don't play innocent with me. No grown man can have as much trouble getting through a meal as you do."

He chuckled. He wondered when she was finally going to take him to task for that. "And no one can be as vigilant about nothing as you are. I don't know where you get the idea that I'm bringing in liquor, but what would be the harm? So Flossie likes to take a little nip now and then…" He might have added that Flossie had probably needed a lot more of those nips since her daughter rolled into town. "You think Myrtle Bean doesn't take a slug of whiskey every so often?"

"That's fine for Myrtle. She's respectable."

"So it's all right for respectable women to drink?" He tossed up his hands. "Where do you come up with these cock-eyed rules to live by?"

"So you deny smuggling in spirits," she said, ignoring his question. "Are you trying to tell me that's *tea* you and Mama have been drinking?"

He shrugged. "You would know. You made it."

A wry laugh erupted from her lips. "I made it, but you polluted it."

"Are you sure you aren't imagining things?" He offered her his own teacup, still half full. He couldn't offer her Flossie's, of course, because it had been drained dry. But he had never seen the point in tea himself. A prissy person's substitute for coffee, was what it was. "Here, take a snort and see for yourself."

He would have expected her to recoil at the prospect of drinking out of a cup used by the likes of him, but apparently her feverish need to prove his corrupting influence overcame any scruples she had concerning hygiene. She brought the cup up to her nose for a whiff, and when she couldn't believe the evidence presented, she took a tentative sip of the liquid.

"See?" Lucas asked her. "Tea."

She replaced the teacup in its saucer with a controlled *clink.* "That doesn't prove anything. For all I know, you could have been swilling straight from a bottle while my back was turned."

An increasingly familiar wave of irritation rose in him. More than just her single-minded devotion to do-goodering was the root of the problem here. Looking at Lacy's beautiful face and trim figure, which he did now at length, much longer than was probably good for him, he couldn't help feeling a stab of regret, as well as natural male desire. "What a waste of womanhood!"

Lacy seemed caught off guard. "I beg your pardon?"

"Has anyone ever told you that you're beautiful, Lacy?"

Despite the compliment, she appeared insulted. Two bright spots of red stained her cheeks. "I suppose you expect me to thank you for that."

"No, I don't. Because while you might be beautiful, and full of vitality and several other traits that are normally desirable in a female, you seem to be bent on being a burr on the backside of humanity."

Her mouth dropped, and a muffled shriek erupted from her.

"You could be a truly appealing woman if you weren't so focussed on telling every person on earth how to live his life," he continued. "Those nuns might have taught you piety, but they sure didn't give you a shred of human understanding, or help mold you into the sort of pleasant woman a man would actually want to be around."

When he stopped talking, he expected Lacy would have

plenty to say, but at the moment she seemed to be having a little difficulty even catching a breath. For one thing, her face was so red he was afraid her brain was overheating. Her mouth opened and closed, but no more sound came out.

He smiled. "Something caught in your throat? Would you like another sip of tea?"

For a moment she looked so overwrought he thought she might actually expire right then and there. Finally she managed to gulp out a sentence. "*This* is precisely why I'm so desperately needed here. Only a reprobate like you would expect a woman to put aside her ideas of right and wrong to make herself more appealing to men!"

He chuckled. "Did you ever think you might *not* be right?"

"When?"

"Just now, for instance. Even when I showed you proof that I wasn't slipping whiskey to your mother, you didn't want to believe me because it didn't line up with your idea that people are either all good or all bad."

"Because I knew you were lying. Believe me, my mother would never swill *tea* like that!"

Lucas laughed. "God knows there's not much else in the way of stimulation around this place."

Lacy dropped her hand and scowled at him. "There! That's just the problem with you. Is that all you can think about? Excitement? Stimulation?"

He stood abruptly, and he saw by the look of tribulation that crossed her expression that she preferred him sitting down. Something about his presence made Lacy Calhoun very nervous...and he didn't think it was just because of what he did for a living. He was willing to bet his last kidney bean that, for all her primness, Lacy felt the same instinctive pull between them that he did. The same shock of male-female awareness, as old as time. Ever since their first encounter in that crowded stagecoach, he'd been living with the memory of the feel of her body against his. It caused a dull ache of desire every time he looked into her eyes, or heard the starchy rustle of her skirts as she passed through a room.

Every time she announced in that honeyed voice of hers that she'd spent the past fourteen years in a convent, a growing awareness scratched at the back of his mind. She was trying to trumpet her goodness; unfortunately, her efforts sent his thoughts scurrying down a much different trail. All those years in the convent...

Fueled by these wayward thoughts, his voice took on a gravelly purr. "Wouldn't you like a little excitement in your life, Lacy? A little stimulation?"

She took a step back. As if pulled by a force beyond himself, he stepped toward her. They continued this cat and mouse dance until her backside collided with the gold cupid table. Lacy braced herself against it and gulped.

"No."

He eyed her skeptically. Given the fact that she wasn't running for the hills, or at the very least calling for mama, he was willing to bet that she was more than a little interested in at least one form of stimulation.

"I—I'm not like you, Lucas," she stammered, her eyes searching his. But from the spark of curiosity in the depths of those blue orbs, she obviously wasn't as unlike him as she wished she was.

"I'll say you're not." He allowed a slow, lazy smile to pull at his lips as he reached over and touched that stubborn, pointy chin. Oh, yes. It was just as he'd suspected from the very beginning. For all her caterwauling about goodness and virtue, seducing Lacy would be as easy as slicing a knife through warm butter.

His gaze strayed downward, to her full breasts and impossibly skinny little waist, pinched in by who knows what means. He bet he could span it with his hands. Which he was just itching to do, he realized as a wave of heat stirred in him. The puzzling thing was how someone so despicably prim and prudish could make him feel all fired up like this.

Nature wasn't always kind, he supposed.

She gulped in a breath and blinked at him. Her expression was frozen in something between fear and curiosity. "You see,

I spent fourteen years at Our Lady of Perpetual…'' Lucas brushed his hand from her chin along her jawline to her earlobe. At his touch, her eyes closed, and she swallowed. ''…Mercy,'' she gushed on a sigh.

''Must have been lonesome,'' he oozed huskily, reaching out to rub her arm with his hand. He could feel her warmth beneath the thin summery fabric.

She gulped again and rolled her shoulder as if to get her arm away from him. As if he would be put off that easily.

Then he looked into those blue eyes. The color of the first blue sky after dawn, when everything seems fresh and clean. They widened. ''Yes,'' she confessed, her voice raw. ''I *was* lonely.''

He stared at her, more uncomfortable with the hitching sensation in his chest than the stirring in his loins. He was so used to her contradicting every little thing. But here she was, speaking honestly with him.

''Do you know how that feels, Lucas? To feel that you've been left alone in the world?''

The frank question penetrated his hide like a dart. *Did he know how loneliness felt?* Mesmerized by those blue eyes, he realized that for years and years it had felt like he didn't know anything else *but* loneliness. If it weren't for Jacob he probably would have snapped long ago.

He felt as if he were going to snap now, but in a completely different way.

Slowly, he nodded as a conflagration of desire and scruples threatened to drive him over the deep end. His throat felt as dry as dust. His body ached. But his wolfish instinct felt paralyzed. He couldn't quite bring himself to lunge.

As their gazes remained locked, she ever so slightly began to tip toward him. ''I have to know,'' she whispered.

In a move that Lucas would relive in his mind about a million times in the days to come, Lacy put her hand on his chest, lifted on her toes, and touched her lips to his. Warm lips that tasted of tea and honey. A trail of fire burned through him, and he clasped her arms, deepening the kiss. And Lacy responded. Oh, not in the practiced way of women he'd known. Or the fervent way of the young love he'd experienced in his youth. But in a tentative, curious way, allowing him to show her stage by stage what a kiss could be.

He did his best. It was a little difficult not to lose himself in the warmth of her. God, it had been so long since he had held a woman like this. This wasn't like going to a woman at the Slipper for some quick gratification. He had forgotten the softness, the tenderness that a pair of warm lips could well up in a man. And she was so small—so delicate in his arms. However rigid and feisty she might be when they argued, she certainly wasn't rigid now....

Fourteen years in a convent. That left a lot of room for catching up. And she was obviously curious....

Lucas wasn't at all put off by the prospect of answering her every question at delectable length. He could have stayed all night, leaning against Flossie's cupid table, tasting the warm buttery sweetness of Lacy's mouth. Could have spent the rest of his life feeling the pressure of her body against him. Could have spent an eternity exploring the feminine curves of her slender frame.

He'd been thinking of Lacy as a girl, but her body was a woman's. Her response to him was a woman's....

A flicker of awareness danced around his consciousness for a moment before he realized what was happening. Something was tapping at him. Lacy was patting him around his torso, and not in a romantic way, either.

In a peculiar way.

He pulled back, frowning. Startled blue eyes met his gaze.

She darted out of his grasp and was halfway across the room before he could stop her. He turned, then felt himself sink against the cupid table. His mind was a jumble of confusion and unquenched lust.

"Oh, heavens!" Her breathing came in rapid gasps, like a rabbit's.

Her words had an effect similar to awakening him from a dream. His heart was still hammering, but his mind was clearing. And he suddenly remembered that none of this was real. This was just a game he was playing with her. Lacy meant nothing to him.

"I'm sorry," Lacy said, still panting.

Sorry? He should have known *this* was coming! No doubt she was now going to deny all responsibility for what had just happened. Wasn't that the way? But she could save her breath. He was only too pleased to point out to Miss Calhoun the fact that she was no better or more saintly than any other human being. "You can spare the prudish denials, Lacy."

"No, Lucas, I have to speak."

He should have known nothing could silence virginal protestations—even the fact that she had so obviously enjoyed the kiss as much as he had. And that she had been the instigator, when you got right down to brass tacks. Lucas was just about to remind her of that fact, when she lifted her hand.

"You have not been drinking," she declared. "I can see that now."

His lecture died on his lips. *"What?"*

"Your breath," she explained. "It didn't have liquor on it…a-and there are no flasks in your jacket pockets."

It took him a moment to sift through this new information. In the back of his mind he recalled her tapping at him in that odd way. Those words of hers—"I have to know"—began to take on a whole new slant. But he could hardly believe it.

"You mean you kissed me to find out if I'd been telling the truth when I slipped liquor into your mother's tea?" His voice cracked like Jacob's.

At least she had the good grace to blush. In fact, she looked like she was on fire. "You *can't* think that I would have kissed you for any other reason!"

He was frozen in shock. She had kissed him like that—for *investigative purposes?* Little Miss Innocent braved the fevered lips of a bad man just to ensure her home remained whiskey-free? He didn't know whether to laugh or direct her to the nearest nuthouse.

As indignation rose in him, just the slightest bit of guilt

tugged at his conscience. Hadn't he had an ulterior motive, too? He had been trying to play "scare the virgin." And then the virgin had turned the tables on him.

But in the end, anger won over guilt. "Lady, that takes the cake! You are, bar none, the most irritating, suspicious female I've come across—and believe me, I've come across some doozies."

She responded with that stubborn lift of her chin.

There. They were back to the normal antagonism again, which Lucas found much more comfortable than jawing with her about loneliness, or looking into her dark blue eyes and panting with lust. Lust which he'd thought was reciprocated. Apparently he'd been wrong about that.

Or had he? Could he really have imagined that she was kissing him back? His mind reeled. Could his instincts about women be so out of kilter?

"I'm sorry—" she said "—if you feel I was devious."

"As if that would be a switch," he gritted out.

"I beg your pardon?"

He strode directly up to her. "In my experience, devious is what females do best."

She crossed her arms. Even though she looked as if she would have liked to sink right through the floor, she stood her ground. "You certainly don't seem to hold women in high esteem, Lucas. The wonder is that you are upset about the Slipper closing at all. At least now there are fewer females in your world to trouble you."

"I could do with one less," he said, stomping past her.

He hurried to his tiny closet of a room. The bed was too small for him, but he'd taken the room because of its proximity to Lacy. Because he'd wanted to crowd her, irritate her, pester her. And now *he* felt crowded, irritated and pestered.

This was working out great.

He tossed his jacket onto the cane-backed chair in the corner and then splashed tepid water from the wash basin in the corner onto his face. What a minx! A prudish little miss innocent.

Fourteen years in the convent, and she still managed to come out of the place with the wiles of a Cleopatra.

He frowned. Interesting that she'd apologized for her ulterior motive for kissing him, but not for the kiss itself. In fact, she didn't seem all that sorry about that. And she hadn't said anything about not enjoying it....

He crossed to the room's little window and looked out at the starry sky, going over the scene in his head. Maybe a few more times than was strictly necessary. Instead of stars he saw the blue of Lacy's eyes.

Thinking about that kiss called for a dose of spirits.

Absently, he reached into his hip pocket and pulled out his flask of whiskey—the one he'd been passing to Flossie during their game. Lacy might be capable of bestowing the sweetest kiss in the world, but she didn't know squat about where a man stowed his liquor.

Once her noodle-weak legs had transported her to the kitchen, Lacy collapsed at the table that she had scrubbed after dinner. What on earth had possessed her to kiss Lucas Burns?

Was she mad? One moment she had been trembling at the fact that he seemed to want to kiss her, and the next... Her face went fiery at the memory of the moment she'd pushed up on her toes to touch her lips against his, just as brazen as you please! As she relived the moment, that meshing of flesh, his hands on her arms, the tickling of his mustache against her lip, her pulse quickened all over again, and she felt that same light-headed warmth.

Oh, she'd tried to regain control. It had taken every ounce of willpower for her to pull away from him and concoct some story about kissing him solely to see if he had been drinking whiskey. She'd thought that would prove that she had only fallen from grace for virtuous reasons.

But what had she really proved? That for all her years in the convent, she had her mother's blood in her. That far from being concerned about Lucas's influence over Flossie, she should worry about his influence over herself.

Her whole body rushed with warmth as she recalled the moment his lips had claimed hers, the shock of liquid heat that surged straight through her. Oh, she admitted it. She had enjoyed every single second of that kiss. She never guessed that a kiss could be any more than two lips touching. It had been a complete shock when he parted her lips with his tongue—and not at all an unpleasant one.

Books, even the racier novels that had been secretly passed around among the girls at Our Lady of Perpetual Mercy, never mentioned that! Nor had any of the girls themselves speculated aloud about the physical actions involved in a passionate kiss.

Now a thousand questions tumbled about her mind. What else didn't she know?

She buried her head in her hands. Oh, heavens. She was barreling down the path to fallen womanhood, and all she could think about was what the next pleasure stop along the road would be. Shameless, that's what she was.

And it was still just her first week out of the convent!

The worst part was the man she had kissed. Fiendish rascal Lucas Burns, overseer of sin city. She could almost have forgiven herself for behaving wantonly with a good man like Bodine Turner. Though perhaps that wasn't possible. That was the sticky part—Bodine, being a good man, probably didn't want a wanton. Which she supposed she now was.

As she gazed absently at the wide puncheon beams of the floor, it suddenly felt as if every ounce of blood drained out of her face. She shivered as a thought occurred to her. A horrifying thought that hadn't come to her before just this moment. What if Lucas told people of her debauchery? News of her shameless behavior would be all over town!

If she reached one hundred years of age, she would never live this down. Never. And if she lived to be a hundred…that left eighty-one years! Eighty-one years of penance, of sackcloth and ashes, of never even thinking about Lucas Burns or kisses. Or even of lips, period.

The time stretched ahead of her like an endless barren landscape.

Heaven help her, after tonight she didn't want to go another eighty years without being kissed. Hopefully not by Lucas Burns. She wouldn't make that mistake again. But she couldn't imagine going another nineteen years, much less eighty-one, without tasting the pleasures of the flesh.

So there it was. Despite all the efforts of the sisters of Our Lady of Perpetual Mercy, she was spoiled.

"Evening, Lacy."

Lacy practically jumped out of her skin. She shot out of her chair and her eyes flew to the open kitchen door. On the other side stood Harper Cooley, carrying a wrapped bundle under his arm.

"Mr. Cooley, you nearly frightened me to death!"

His face went slack in apology. "I'm so sorry. I saw the light on and I hoped…"

"Everyone has gone to sleep," she said.

The man smiled. His tall lean frame, white hair, mustache and beard in the moonlight, combined with his long coat and high hat, made him look rather like a specter of Abe Lincoln. Either that or an undertaker. "Have they? My, my, things *have* changed."

Lacy shifted her weight impatiently to her other foot. Much as she liked Mr. Cooley, the man struck her as rather odd. What on earth was he doing here? She supposed if she wanted to be polite she should invite him in and offer him something to drink, but she was far too flustered of mind to make small talk just now.

He thrust his arms forward, offering his flour-sack-wrapped bundle across the threshold. "For you, Miss Lacy. A house-warming gift."

Her lips parted, and she took the bundle, which was surprisingly weighty in her arms. "What is it?"

He chuckled. "It's usually up to the recipient to find that out, I believe."

Finally, she remembered her manners. "Will you come in?"

He shook his head adamantly. "No, no. It's too late for visitors. I just wanted to drop that by…"

From the way he left his sentence dangling, she sensed there was more he wanted to say to her. "And?"

At her prompt, he smiled gratefully. "I realize that you are primarily concerned with renting rooms, Miss Lacy, but I can't help thinking about the marvelous repast you were kind enough to share with me when you first arrived. Also, the one which you brought to young Jacob this afternoon. You don't know what a home-cooked meal means to a gnarled old fellow like myself. I haven't tasted food like that since…well, for a long time. I suppose a man forgets about the finer things in life when he's been without them for a while."

She smiled. "It was no trouble at all, Mr. Cooley."

His glassy blue eyes brightened. "Then, may I ask, would it be possible to pay you for board?"

She blinked at him. "You mean you would like to come here just for meals?"

"Indeed I would. If it wouldn't put you out."

She frowned. She didn't know how much Harper Cooley would be able to afford. How much spare money could a man living in a solitary little shack on the edge of town possess? After all, she had put him out of a job.

"Come for breakfast in the morning around eight o'clock," she told him. "I'll have a place laid out for you."

His face broke into a beaming smile, so that she was taken aback for a moment by how handsome he was. He must have been quite a man with the ladies in his day. "Tell me, do the others meet for breakfast at the same time?"

She frowned. There weren't *that* many others for him to be concerned about. "Yes, ordinarily. Is that all right with you?"

He smiled a little too brightly to be casual. He seemed very happy indeed. "Fine, fine!" He backed down off the stairs. "I'll see you tomorrow then," he said with a lift of his hat before he slipped back into the darkness.

Lacy turned, bemused by this turn of events. She went inside, almost forgetting the bundle in her hands until it was time to snuff out the lights in the kitchen. The moment Harper was gone, her thoughts had immediately turned back to Lucas. Now she put the bundle down and pulled the object inside out of its flour sack.

Lacy's breath caught. It was a bread box. And yet, to call it that would be to sell the handiwork short. The functional wooden box was painted yellow and decorated with bluebirds. Some of the birds were perched on branches with leaves so lifelike she could make out the veins and the texture of the greenery; others were taking flight into the colorful backdrop. Lacy had never been given anything so pretty. So elegant, really.

For a moment she was able to forget all the problems that had been troubling her mind. Who would have guessed that Blissful, this dry dust-heap of a town, would be harboring something so beautiful?

Chapter Seven

The fact that he had kissed her last night did nothing for Lucas's manners at the breakfast table. If anything, he seemed to think that unwelcome intimacy gave him even more license to boss her around. Lacy was already on pins and needles around the man. She couldn't think about last night without her knees threatening to buckle. Now every time she thought she might be able to take a deep breath and forget about their kiss *and* the man, he was poking his coffee cup toward her.

"Any more of that coffee, Lacy?"

Each time, Lacy gritted her teeth, grabbed the kettle, and refilled his cup.

"I'm surprised you're not about to pop," she couldn't help saying after the third request.

She regretted the remark immediately. His dark eyes danced so brightly, she wanted to toss a napkin over his head. It seemed impossible that the others could miss the sensual, flirtatious glances he kept sending her way. She wished to heaven that she could maintain a quiet dignity around Lucas, but he was bringing out something in her that she'd never even known she had: Sass.

Lucas turned to address the rest of the table. "I need this coffee. Couldn't sleep last night."

Lacy felt the blood drain out of her face. Oh, Lord! He wasn't going to start talking about last night, was he?

He wasn't going to flat-out announce he'd kissed her, was he?

Flossie looked up from her plate in thoughtful concern. She, of course, had no idea what kind of mental anguish Lucas was costing her daughter. "Hope you're not finding your room uncomfortable."

"No, no." His gaze settled on Lacy again; he leaned back and crossed his arms. Oh, he was enjoying watching her squirm! "Funny thing is, I seemed to be haunted by the strangest dream."

This was just the sort of topic Flossie loved to discuss. "What kind of dream?" she asked eagerly.

"Well, let's see…I think I was in a city."

"An eastern city?" Jacob asked, stuffing a biscuit into his mouth. "Like Philadelphia or New York?"

"No…closer to home. I'd say it was a little like San Antone. And for some reason, I was standing on an empty street with a nun."

Flossie laughed. "*You* dreaming of nuns, Lucas?"

He tilted his head, an exaggeratedly thoughtful expression on his face. "The strange thing was, this nun was staring off to the west, like she was looking this way—straight at Blissful. And she was weeping."

Lacy nearly dropped the skillet she was hauling over to the table. Weeping nuns? The fiend—he was torturing her now. She was sure her face was as red as the wood coals beneath the oven.

"That *is* odd!" Flossie said, completely caught up in Lucas's fabricated dream. "Why do you think you would dream about a weeping nun?"

"I don't know…maybe this particular nun was thinking that one of their flock was on the verge of straying…"

Lacy brought the skillet down on an iron trivet with a heavy clang. "Have a biscuit, Birdie."

The already pale woman blanched. She hadn't uttered a peep since whispering good morning as she had scuttled toward her seat at the table. "N-no thank you."

"You need to eat something." Lacy plunked a biscuit onto the woman's place. "You haven't taken a bite."

Poor Birdie looked horrified to suddenly have become the center of attention. It wasn't nice of Lacy to single Birdie out this way, but she would have done anything at that moment to change the subject.

"I think dreams have meanings, tell us what's on our minds," Flossie said. "But why would you have nuns on your mind, Lucas?"

Lacy stifled a groan. She should have known derailing the dream discussion wouldn't be easy.

"I don't know." Lucas grinned up at Lacy. "Would *you* know?"

Jacob's young brow crinkled. "How could Lacy know? It was your dream, Pa."

Flossie slapped the table. "Lacy was around nuns all those years! That's probably what got Lucas to thinking about them."

Jacob's frown deepened. "But why would Pa be dreamin' about Lacy's nuns? And why would the nuns be crying? Unless *that* had something to do with Lacy, too...."

Just when she thought her legs might not hold her upright another minute, Lacy was saved. Harper Cooley knocked on the kitchen door.

"Goodness!" Birdie trembled with alarm. "*More* people?"

Flossie hopped up. "It's Harper!" Lacy had told her about his visit last night. She swung open the door before Lacy could even reach it. "You old coot!" she blasted at Harper. "I should have known you could sweet talk Lacy into giving you breakfast!"

Harper doffed his tall black hat. "Good morning to you, too, Flossie."

"Figures you'd find a way back to the Slipper." She let out a chortle, which died in her throat when realized that she had let the name slip. "I'm sorry, Lace." She turned to their boarders and whispered as if Lacy couldn't hear every word, "We can't call this the Slipper anymore."

Harper nodded his greetings to everyone gathered around the table and then took an empty place. For some reason he seemed a little embarrassed when his gaze fell on Lucas.

"Fancy meeting you here, Harper," Lucas said. "Making yourself comfortable?"

"Yes, thank you," Harper answered stiffly.

"Don't feel doomed?"

"Doomed?" Flossie asked. "What the heck are you talking about, Lucas?" Not waiting for an answer, she turned back to the older man. "Don't you mind Lucas this morning, Harper. He had this bad dream, see, and—"

Lacy clattered a heavy cup and saucer in front of Harper. "I'm sure we've exhausted the topic of Lucas and his tiresome dream." She poured him some coffee, half of which splattered on the table. "Did I show you all the bread box Mr. Cooley made for me?"

She had, but she wagged it back over to the table for another look. The boarders were again duly impressed, and Harper squirmed with modest pride as the women fussed over it.

"Lovely," Birdie said breathlessly.

"It looks like something that would belong in one of them museums!" Flossie chuckled, adding, "but since you're practically a museum piece yourself…"

"You aren't exactly freshly hatched, either," Harper pointed out.

Flossie hooted gaily. "No, I'm a rubbery old hen, for sure. And I never thought I'd live to see the day when I'd have your antique mug staring at me across my own breakfast table, and you not even paid to be here."

He fixed her with those amused gray eyes. "You have a lot to learn about a man's appetites, then."

Lacy cleared her throat warningly before Flossie could come up with a ribald retort.

Lucas was frowning at the bread box. "Since when do you do stuff like that, Harper?"

It figured that Lucas Burns would have no appreciation for a work of beauty.

Harper shrugged. "Guess you don't know everything about me, Lucas."

Lucas slugged down yet more coffee. "You're right. I don't know the first thing about where you came from or what you did. All I know is that you sit around my bar all the time complaining about civilization." He jabbed a finger in the direction of the bread box. "That has all the earmarks of a civilization, if you ask me."

The older man blushed. "I, uh, just thought the ladies would enjoy it."

Lucas laughed. "The ladies, or one certain lady?"

He looked up at Lacy, grinning, and Lacy felt all eyes around the table focus on her again. All except Harper. He kept his gaze on his coffee cup.

"You never were painting birds on things and bringing them over before now," Lucas pointed out. "But then, I guess as everyone keeps saying, things have changed in Blissful."

His devilish gaze locked with hers and sent a shock of memory through her; it was almost as if she could feel his lips touching hers all over again, feel that moment of pure pleasure the likes of which she'd never imagined possible. Even now, for all her regrets, she found herself craving that kiss once more.

Oh, heaven. She wasn't so sure Blissful had changed at all. More likely, it was Blissful that was changing her.

Lucas watched Lacy crossing the yard to the well and couldn't help going over to stand by while she toiled. The purposeful, worker bee way she tackled every little task tickled him. And though he hated to admit it, after last night he found himself drawn to her. Not that this inclination stemmed from any weakness on his part. He figured it was just a natural male impulse. Now that all the girls had left, Lacy was the only good-looking thing in town.

If you didn't count Harper's damn bread box.

He couldn't help shaking his head at that. A man had to be

touched in the head to start fashioning crackbrained things like bread boxes and decorating them with birdies. Poor Harper.

But it wasn't too late to save the sanity of the rest of the men in town. Lucas knew if he could tweak Lacy just a little more, he could send her skedaddling back to that convent. At breakfast her nerves had seemed on the verge of snapping.

He strode over and leaned against a beam holding up the little roof of the well. "Working hard?"

Scowling at him, Lacy let the well bucket drop to the water. She had the withering gaze down pat. If it weren't for the flush in her cheeks and the flicker of heat in the depths of those blue eyes, Lucas would have thought their encounter of last night was just a figment of his imagination.

"Maybe if you were a little nicer to me, I'd give you a hand," he said.

She caught him by surprise by stepping toward him and poking a finger in his chest. "I don't want your help. If you keep carrying on like you did at the breakfast table this morning, I don't want you anywhere near me."

He laughed.

"On second thought—" she hastened to add "—I don't want you anywhere near me in any case."

"Now is that any way to speak to a paying guest?"

"For the paltry sum you're paying me, I shouldn't have to listen to you taunt me."

"I don't remember taunting you."

"What do you call the way you were rambling on at the breakfast table about your made-up dreams?"

He grinned. "How do you know it wasn't a real dream?"

She leveled a disbelieving look at him. "Weeping nuns?"

A chuckle rumbled out of him. "All right—maybe it *was* made up. But I had no idea the effect it would have on you."

"Yes you did. You probably sat up all last night concocting the foolish thing for the express purpose of embarrassing me at breakfast."

"Oh, I sat up, all right," he admitted readily. "But mostly I was thinking about something else."

She looked into his face, and as her cheeks bloomed with pink, he knew she realized what he meant he'd been dreaming about. Her. Their kiss.

"I have to say, I *never* expected such passion from a young lady fresh from all those years in a convent."

The word *passion* seemed to do her in. She hauled up the water bucket with such force he could see the muscles straining beneath her sleeves as she worked the pulley. "That wasn't passion, I assure you."

"Really? What was it?"

"I told you. I was only trying to see if you had whiskey on your breath."

"Oh, that's right. I forgot about that pitiful little excuse of yours. I'll admit you had me fooled at first...."

"It's the truth," she insisted. "Though naturally you wouldn't believe there could be a woman in the world who wouldn't swoon into your arms the moment she found herself alone with you."

"Like *you* did?" As she eyed him in speechless anger, he was consumed with satisfaction. "Lacy, I don't mean to burst your little bubble of virtue, but sniffing a man's breath—which you have to admit is an odd thing for a young lady to want to do—would only take a few moments at most. And yet if you'll recall, that kiss went on for quite a while. You might even say it lingered."

She placed the full bucket on the brick ledge of the well. She was breathing hard, but he couldn't tell if it was from exertion or irritation. Or maybe remembering that kiss fired her up as much as it did him.

She spoke through clenched teeth. "If you had even the slightest shred of decency..."

"That's a club you've excluded me from, remember?"

"I only allowed that you might have a shred. Even if you possessed just the tiniest smidgeon, you would never mention that kiss again. I would think you'd be ashamed of forcing yourself on a woman."

He howled in delight. "I forced myself on you? As I remember it, you were the one who instigated the kiss—er, excuse me, the prolonged exercise in whiskey sniffing.''

''Which I never would have thought to do if you hadn't cornered me like a cat after a mouse!''

''Which *I* never would have done if I hadn't noticed you staring at me as avidly as a kid wanting to unwrap a Christmas present,'' he fired back.

She let out an unladylike snort. ''I'm sure you're mistaken about that.''

''You mean to tell me that in all the time since you stepped on that stage from San Antonio, you never once thought what it would be like if I kissed you?'' Her eyes widened in alarm, and he knew he had guessed her guilty secret. ''It's all right, Lacy. Most healthy people do have thoughts like that.''

''*I* never did, till you!'' she said angrily. Then, as he roared with laughter, she accidentally knocked the bucket back into the well. It landed seconds later with a distant, echoing splash. ''Look what you made me do!''

He was still laughing, but he turned and retrieved the bucket for her. ''*I* made you kiss me, *I* made you drop a bucket? I seem to have quite a power over you.''

She squinted up at him, so tense and flustered that her eyes were almost crossed. Then, after a speechless moment when he feared she was either going to scream or hit him, she surprised him completely. She laughed, too.

And it wasn't just a mere chuckle, or a swallowed guffaw. She put one hand on her tummy and bent over, laughing full out. Perversely, the sight sobered him. Was she going daffy? He watched her fight to bring her mirth under control with a bemused smile.

''I'm sorry—'' she managed to say finally, wiping a tear from her eye ''—I guess I'm just not accustomed to handling your swaggering peacock stance so early in the morning. I started to take you seriously.''

''I was being serious.''

''Believe me, you have no powers. The spell has been broken.''

"Has it?" he said, turning the well's crank.

Her smile fading, she looked him straight in the eye. "It has."

"I wouldn't be so sure. You admit now that you enjoyed that kiss? Because I did."

She blinked up at him, evidently surprised by his admission. But she wasn't any more surprised than he was himself. His own words had caught him off guard, embarrassing him with their raw truth. He stood speechless for a moment, feeling as if the ground beneath his feet was suddenly a bog.

His mind raced, trying to find a way to recover a little of his dignity. After all, why shouldn't he enjoy a kiss? The urge to have a woman in his arms was a primal one, like an itch it felt good to scratch periodically.

With Lacy, though, that description didn't quite seem to fit. Lucas wasn't sure why. He certainly didn't feel at all lovey-dovey about her, so that couldn't explain it. Their relationship was a purely adversarial one. True, he had enjoyed seeing her laugh, and enjoyed the way mirth seemed to dance in those summery blue eyes—until he realized she was laughing at his expense.

She wasn't laughing now. "It doesn't matter to me whether you enjoyed yourself or not." She crossed her arms stubbornly. "It won't happen again."

Her spirited reply helped him remember his mission. This wasn't about kisses, or whether Lacy liked him or not, or how her eyes danced when she laughed. This was just about getting the troublesome gal out of town.

He had seen a melodrama once where a mustachioed villain had overwhelmed the heroine with his oily charm. Lucas attempted his best impersonation of that character now. He leaned in and lowered his voice to a silky purr. "But I'm afraid it will. As long as you and I are living here, Lacy, in this house, I'm sure there will be moments when we find ourselves alone...."

Pursing her lips, she took the bucket from him and transferred the water to the pail near her feet. "Then we'll just proceed like mature adults."

"Exactly."

She rolled her eyes. "Believe me—" she said "—I understand the danger now. I'm sure I can handle you."

He waggled his brows. "Are you?"

For a moment doubt flickered in those blue eyes. Then she tilted her head. "Actually, it's *you* I worry about, Lucas."

He smiled. "Me?"

"You obviously feel vulnerable yourself. Oh, you might try to act tough as cowhide, but last night, when we talked about loneliness, you seemed genuinely moved. I saw it in your eyes. Remember?"

His face went slack. The earth beneath his feet seemed to feel unbalanced again. He had put that part of last night out of his mind. After all, it had just been a trick of the moment that had made him say such a foolish thing.

He drew back. "I hate to disillusion you, Lacy, but a man's apt to say all sorts of things when he's got a woman in his arms."

"Is that so? I wonder..."

Her eyes narrowed on him, and after a moment's hesitation she blurted out, "What happened to Jacob's mother?"

At the surprise question, a sharp pain stabbed in his chest. Nosy woman! No one had asked him about that in years. "She was gone before I ever came to Blissful." He couldn't help adding, "Not that it's any of your business."

The admonishment did not seem to bother her. Or, unfortunately, shut her up. "And you've been here how long?"

"Nine years." To his dismay, the reply had a forlorn, flat sound to it.

"That's a long time."

He looked into her eyes and felt another one of those stabs. *Longer than you could know.* Lacy was just a kid, about the age he'd been when Alice had left him. He shifted uncomfortably, and felt his gaze wandering off toward the sanctuary of the saloon, where he suddenly longed to be. All at once he felt weary and old—far older than his twenty-nine years. And yet here he was standing around playing games with a woman who was little more than a girl.

He pulled his hat forward on his head, shading his eyes. "Long enough," he said finally. And he'd been standing here long enough, too.

Lacy stared at him with an expression too close to pity for his liking. "It's a long time for Jacob to be without a mother," she pointed out.

It's a long time for a man to be without a woman snuggling in his bed.

"We manage," he bit out.

"But he's still so young, and being around the Rooster so much—"

A surprising anger surged through him. "Stop right there. You might be able to tell your ma how to run her life, and the rest of the town, but I don't want your advice."

She closed her mouth. Finally.

He let out a breath—mostly from relief that she wasn't going to tell him how to raise his son. That was one area where he would brook no interference. "I guess as long as there's you and me, Lacy, there are going to be sparks. Of all kinds. You might want to think about that when you consider how long you can keep your boardinghouse scheme going."

She picked up her pail. "Believe me, Lucas, I'll do my best to stay out of your way."

With that, she turned and marched toward the house, her thin shoulders set perfectly straight. As always after a confrontation with Lacy, Lucas had a hard time measuring who had come out the winner.

Snapping beans in the heat of the afternoon was the closest to relaxation Lacy had come to for days. It had been two weeks since she'd opened her boardinghouse, and she was exhausted.

The work never seemed to end. In the morning she was up before dawn to milk the fat cow that grazed in the pasture behind the house. Then, once she started cooking breakfast, the day was devoured by a never-ending cycle of preparing meals and cleaning up after meals. They all seemed to blend into one another. Thank heavens she only had to serve her boarders in the morning and in the evening, but around noon she did have to make something for her mother and herself. And of course she and Flossie couldn't very well eat without offering a little something to Birdie. The woman didn't eat much, anyway. And since Lacy worried that Jacob would get hungry before supper, she always packed a meal for him and carried it over to the Rooster around noontime, too.

It was extra work, but work was what helped keep her mind—somewhat—off Lucas. Woolgathering about that man was becoming a bad habit, but he seemed to have invaded her senses like a disease. When he was around her, she felt quivery, exposed; but when he was gone, she was fretful and perturbed. Her mind lingered, of course, on their kiss.

There had to be something she could do to stop this awful brooding about something that never should have happened. This constant wondering, so fervent it felt almost like hoping sometimes. Hoping that those sparks would happen again.

How could she know a man was bad, and yet still find herself craving his smile, his teasing, his kiss?

Avoiding him didn't help much. During the past few days, she had done an excellent job of staying out of his way. Of course she had to see him at mealtimes, but she sat far away from him, and as soon as the meal was over she busied herself with dishes. She didn't make the mistake of straying into the parlor when he was there alone. Which wasn't often now anyway. Harper Cooley had started lingering after meals, and even Birdie was braving the after-supper get-togethers for a little conversation now and then.

Oftentimes Lacy heard Lucas's voice over the others and she couldn't keep her memory from wandering back to that night when he'd kissed her. Sometimes it came over her so suddenly that she would stop in her tracks and close her eyes to try to ward off the sensation. It never helped for long, however. Lucas's ominous words echoed in her mind. "As long as we live in this house together..."

She knew what he meant. As long as they lived in this house—this town—together, her reputation would be in peril.

She obviously needed to keep herself *very* busy.

Yet lately when she was honest with herself, Lacy had to admit that most of the time she was too exhausted to give two hoots about bringing respectability to the Calhoun name. She hated Blissful. Often she found herself daydreaming of leaving town and running away to a place where no one knew her or her mother. Where no one knew what Flossie had been.

But of course Flossie loved it here. It was her home and Lacy couldn't drag her away. She was still mindful of all that she owed her mother, despite the fact that she sometimes felt resentful. Not so much now as before. Now she blamed herself, too. Why had she been so blind, so naive? If she had just picked up on the clues Flossie had given her, if the nuns had just said something, she could have come home earlier. This would have been straightened out years ago. They wouldn't be in this fix. They—

"Need help?" drawled a male voice from the doorway behind her.

Startled, Lacy slapped a bean into the cookpot and swiveled to tell Lucas to go to blazes—only it wasn't Lucas in the doorway. It was Bodine.

"Sheriff Turner!"

The man smiled at her—and wonder of wonders, that friendly male smile warmed her heart instead of tying her insides into knots the way that wolfish leer of Lucas's did. She had been hoping the sheriff would visit again sooner, but Lacy supposed a sheriff's duties in a town like Blissful kept him very busy.

"Howdy, Lacy. I was at loose ends over at the jailhouse, so I decided to come by to see how you were settling in."

Lacy jumped up and beckoned him through the open door. "Come in and sit down. Would you like a drink?"

"Thank you," he replied politely. "Whatever is handy would be fine."

There wasn't anything but water at hand, but she poured him a glass and he drank it as if it were cold sweet lemonade.

She sat down next to him and smiled apologetically. "I'm sorry about the way I snapped at you, Sheriff. I thought you were Lucas."

He laughed. "Is he still giving you a hard time?"

"Nothing I can't handle," she said with determination.

Bodine peered around the kitchen with approval. "I haven't seen a kitchen this tidy since I was a boy. My ma was a tidy housekeeper, just like you. In fact, you even look a little like she did."

"Did your mother pass away?"

His eyes widened in alarm, and he answered as if his mother dying were an impossibility. "Ma? Gosh, no. She's got the constitution of a mule."

"Oh, well you were speaking of her in the past...."

He leaned back, settling in. "I only meant that you resemble her when she was young, of course. She's older now, and she doesn't keep house much anymore. She leaves that to my sister-in-law." He laughed. "Ma just gives orders now, I guess you could say. She lives with my brother and his wife in Cicada Creek."

"Your home sounds nice. I've never been anywhere but here or San Antonio."

His eyes glistened with nostalgia. "I bet you'd love Cicada Creek. It's green there—most of the year, anyway. And there are big trees. Pine and oak and elm and, oh, every kind you can think of, probably. And you can grow things there, too. That's what my family did. We owned a farm right outside Cicada Creek itself. You've never tasted corn as sweet as an ear grown in Cicada Creek."

She smiled. "It sounds like paradise."

He nodded, but then allowed modestly, "Well, it's not exactly the Garden of Eden, mind you. But I guess it's as close to it as I'll ever come."

"It's a wonder you ever left."

His brows drew together. "Well, I drifted. My brother took over the farm when my father died, and even though there was plenty of work for me there, I sort of felt cramped, like I wanted to see something of the world. But I'm being real careful to save my money now so I can buy my own land someday."

"In Cicada Creek?"

"Or somewhere as good." He frowned. "Though I have to wonder whether there's anywhere as good as home. Ma told me there isn't."

"It's wonderful that you have such ambition, Bodine. I have to admire a man who aspires to make a success of himself."

Unlike a certain other man who seemed only to be interested in making a nuisance of himself.

Bodine's smile reached from ear to ear. "It would be pretty dull to stay a sheriff all my life."

"I would imagine you keep yourself very busy here."

He shrugged. "Not very."

Lacy's jaw dropped. "Really? My goodness, judging from the noise I hear coming from the Rooster most evenings, I'd think you'd been making arrests every night."

"Oh, that. That's just horsing around, usually."

Lacy just managed to keep her disapproval to herself. Or so she thought.

"Not that I hold with folks flaunting the law," Bodine hastened to assure her.

"I didn't think you did," Lacy said quickly.

"No, ma'am. The minute something happens, I'm usually there. Only it isn't always easy to figure out what's happened once the dust settles."

A tremendous noise out on the porch interrupted them. Bodine stared at her, wide-eyed. "What do you think that was?"

Lacy jumped up. "It sounds like the porch fell in!"

The two of them hurried to the front of the house. When Lacy poked her head out the door, Harper Cooley was standing over a pile of lumber that he had apparently just dumped on her porch. "I'm building a swing," he announced.

"A what?"

"A couch swing to hang from your porch," he explained. "Nothing like a swing on a summer evening. Makes a place real homey."

"But—" She looked up and saw Birdie's face dart back behind the parlor curtains. Apparently she'd been startled by the noise, too.

Then again, Birdie was startled by everything.

"But it will be so much work," Lacy said.

The older man winked at her. "Best way to repay you for all those fine meals."

"Never knew you was so handy, Harper," Bodine said.

"Never knew anything about me, you young whippersnapper," Harper retorted as he stared worriedly at his pile of lumber.

"Where did you get all that stuff?" the sheriff asked.

"Never you mind. This is a gift for the womenfolk, so they can sit out here on a fine night and catch the cool evening breeze." Harper looked from Bodine to Lacy and winked. "I'll make it big enough for two, in case you've a mind to star-gaze with a beau."

Beau? Flustered, Lacy attempted to sputter out a response. "Oh, but—"

"I'd say it sounds like a fine idea, Harper!"

Lacy turned to Bodine in surprise. It did? She felt a warmth suffuse her. Did that mean that Bodine was interested in becoming her beau?

This raised an interesting question. How, exactly, did one go about deciding who was a beau and who wasn't? This was a matter that had never been discussed at Our Lady of Perpetual Mercy.

"You need any help with that, Harper?" Bodine asked.

"Heck, no. I've never heard tell you're much of a hand with a hammer and nails, Sheriff." He chuckled. "Or a gun, for that matter."

Bodine took the criticism in stride. "All right. I guess I should get back to the jailhouse then, in case anything happens."

He sounded suspiciously certain that nothing *would* happen.

"Thank you for stopping by," Lacy said quickly. She was sorry he had to go. "I enjoyed hearing about Cicada Creek."

"It was my pleasure." For a moment she thought Bodine might reach for her hand, but he backed away from the impulse.

She leaned against the porch rail, hoping to cover her awkwardness. "Drop by any time."

"I'll take you up on that."

She smiled. "Goodbye, then."

"Bye." He took one last look at her, then turned and ambled back into town.

Lacy's heart raced for an instant. Why, he'd been flirting with her! That was the first time that had happened to her—besides Lucas's taunts, which she didn't count as flirting so much as badgering. It gave her a rush of satisfaction to know that she had drawn the attention of such a good man as Bodine Turner.

"I wouldn't encourage him," Harper warned her.

She turned, realizing that he'd witnessed her mooning after Bodine. "Don't you think he's a nice man?"

Harper barked out a laugh. "Nice—oh, certainly. He'd be a prize catch for any gal. I only meant you shouldn't encourage him to talk about that town of his. Cicada Creek. Once he gets started on it, he never shuts up."

"I think it's sweet that he's so attached to his home, and his mother." A man who thought so fondly of home surely showed a warmth of feeling that seemed unusual in this rough land. "It also proves him to be the polar opposite of Lucas Burns. I'll bet nobody even knows where *he* came from." Or rather, what rock he crawled out from under.

Harper nodded. "No, I don't suppose anybody does. But then a lot of us here are tight-lipped about our pasts."

She bit her lip. "And what about Jacob's mother? I asked him about her and he evaded the question entirely."

"Could be a subject he wants to avoid."

"Obviously." But one could only wonder why. "And that's another thing. I'm sure Lucas has been a good provider for his son, but he certainly isn't seeing to the child's moral welfare very well, allowing him to sit around the Rooster half the day."

"It's summer. School's out. Where's the boy supposed to go?"

"Well..." Lacy didn't have an answer for that. It just seemed plain wrong for that sweet boy to be immersed in the seedy atmosphere of the Rooster at such a tender age. "But of course, the one time I tried to bring up the subject with Lucas, he practically snapped my head off."

"I don't doubt it," Harper said, chuckling again.

She frowned. "What's so funny?"

"I thought we were discussing Bodine, but it appears you've got Lucas on the brain."

"Oh, no—I assure you!"

Harper looked at her with those knowing old eyes of his, and she felt herself begin to blush.

"I'd better get back to my beans," she said, and fled inside.

And she had better train her thoughts *away* from Lucas.

Chapter Eight

At the second meeting of the Society for Decency, Temperance, and the Beautification of Blissful, temperance was the watchword. Now that the Slipper had closed, and Birdie had been disposed of, Myrtle had devoted the past days to brooding over her archenemy, the Rooster Tail Saloon, where her husband still spent a goodly portion of his nights. Thinkingwise, she had put her shoulder to the wheel, and she had devised a plan.

Lacy, who had come to the meeting prepared to talk forthrightly about planting a few flowers to spruce up the town, found her leadership of the meeting usurped. Myrtle arrived armed with heavy chains and padlocks.

"Come along, ladies," Myrtle ordered them. "We have work to do."

Birdie, Lacy and Flossie all stood up and gawked at her in wonder. "Myrtle Bean, have you gone round the bend?" Flossie asked. "What are you going to do with all those chains?"

"I'm going to shut down the Rooster—and you are all going to help me!" She told them her plan—simplicity itself—to chain themselves to the doors of the Rooster. They would form a human barrier to stop men from wasting their lives at that evil watering hole.

"Well?" she prompted them. "Just don't stand there.

Gather your courage and come along. We will have plenty of time to conduct this meeting at the Rooster.''

Flossie was having none of it. She crossed her chubby arms and shook her head firmly. ''Feel free to make a foolish spectacle of yourself if you want, Myrtle, but I think you've cracked.''

Myrtle turned her gaze to Lacy. ''Well?''

Lacy swallowed. Chain herself to the Rooster? She didn't like the place, either, but… ''Isn't that a rather radical course of action?''

Myrtle's face set into a disapproving glower. ''This town needs radical change. I thought that's what you wanted. You agreed that the Rooster is a shame on the town.''

So she did. Lacy felt cowed by the force of those beady little gray eyes boring into her. Her mother's refusal should have strengthened her own resolve, but in fact just the opposite was the case. Without Flossie joining she felt compelled to do as Myrtle said just to show her that the Calhouns were on the side of right in Blissful.

She swallowed. ''Well, all right,'' she said, stepping forward. ''I had planned to talk about flowers….''

''We can talk about that while we're in our human chain formation. Come along, Birdie.''

Birdie, cowering silently behind them, looked like a woman who wanted to disappear. ''But Myrtle, you always warned me against going anywhere near the Rooster.''

''This is different,'' her sister-in-law barked. Then she went over, chains clanking, and took Birdie by the arm. ''Don't be shy. We're all in this together.'' She tossed a frown toward Flossie. ''*Almost* all of us.''

Feeling dazed, Lacy tripped along after them. The sound Myrtle made as she walked sounded like a medieval army in chain mail marching across Blissful. And it did give Lacy a secret pleasure to be on a mission to slay this particular dragon. Lucas had behaved unbearably toward her. Maybe it was time he sampled a measure of the vexation he was so fond of dishing out to her!

When they arrived at the Rooster, it was one in the afternoon. Myrtle sneaked around back and padlocked the back door shut. Then they went around to the front. Birdie, in agony as Myrtle went to work untangling her chains and handing out padlocks, peeked over the doors. She immediately darted back, practically swooning. "Myrtle, there are men in there!"

"'Course there are!"

"But—"

Myrtle clapped a chain around Birdie's arm, wound it around her several times, and then wound the chain itself through the slats on the batwing doors. Then she snapped the padlock through two links, securing Birdie bodily to the saloon. "Don't be a ninny, Birdie."

"Hey!" cried a voice from inside. "What's going on there?"

Myrtle's eyes bugged. "Hurry now, Lacy!" She tossed Lacy a chain, and the two of them went to work winding the chains about themselves.

George Oatley's head poked over the doors. He took in the scene with amazement. "Say, Lucas!" he called back. "Birdie Bean has got herself stuck to your door!"

"*What?*" Lucas's voice made Lacy's hands shake, but she managed to quickly clap the padlock on two links of her chain. Chairs scraped back, and several more faces appeared at the doors. Jacob, too, peered out at her. His face looked delighted. Just last night he had been complaining that nothing interesting ever happened in Blissful.

"Now Lacy Calhoun's chained here, too," George announced, keeping Lucas apprised.

Bootsteps hurried over, but not before Myrtle, enchained across her substantial middle, attached one side of herself to Birdie on one door and Lacy on the other. By the time Lucas looked out his doors, they were immovable. "What the hell…?" He took in the chains and padlocks and let out a string of curses.

Myrtle smirked. "Foul language does not intimidate us, Lucas Burns. We are not going to move until you agree to shut your doors and stop corrupting the men and youth of this community.''

Lucas's lips formed an angry line. ''For Pete's sake, Myrtle. If that was your plan, you might want to take note of the men and child you just managed to lock *in* the saloon.''

Myrtle lifted her chin proudly. ''Don't let him discourage you, ladies. We can still save some others.''

Lacy had to admit to a spike of joy when she saw the aggravation she was causing Lucas for once. The man looked ready to explode. He cursed some more, paced, and then let out a breath. ''Jacob, run and get the sheriff.''

Jacob could be heard running through the saloon, and then hitting the locked back door. ''It's locked from the outside!'' he called.

Myrtle tossed her head back and crowed in triumph.

A thunderous look came over Lucas. ''Then get over here and crawl under 'em!''

Jacob hurriedly did as told, wriggling his small body between Birdie and Myrtle's skirts. Poor Birdie looked like she was dying a thousand deaths, and couldn't hold back a pitiful moan.

Myrtle heard it and announced, ''The meeting will now come to order. Lacy, why don't you tell us your idea for a carnival that the sheriff was telling me about.''

Lacy swallowed. ''Well…''

George was astounded. ''Ya'll are actually going to have your women's meetin' right here?'

''And why not?'' Myrtle asked. ''We're not leaving, so we might as well keep ourselves occupied.''

Lacy tried as best she could to outline what had been said about the carnival-trade day idea. She was embarrassed to have those male eyes staring at her as she spoke, but she soldiered on.

To her surprise, one of the cowboys asked, ''Would there be dancin'? I like to dance.''

''I wouldn't mind selling my old saddle none, either,'' another said. ''Be a good opportunity for that.''

Lacy was surprised by their response. "I suppose we could discuss a dance."

Unfortunately, their meeting was interrupted by the return of Jacob, who had the sheriff and Harry Bean in tow.

Harry's face collapsed into a horrified mask. "Myrtle, what in tarnation are you doin'?"

"I'm trying to help you, Harry. I'm not leaving here till the place closes its doors or you agree never to darken them again."

"But Myrtle…"

Bodine was flummoxed, especially when Lucas commanded him to do something. "Do what? Those are pretty big chains, Lucas."

"Well, order her to unlock the padlocks."

"I've hidden them where you will never get them!" Myrtle taunted.

"Where?"

"They're in my corset."

The looks that went around one man to the other were in complete agreement with Myrtle. No one was volunteering to try to get those keys.

"Now, Myrtle—" Harry whined "—be reasonable. You're making a spectacle of yourself!"

But Myrtle wasn't budging.

A moment later, Lucas appeared again with a spike and a small mallet. To the astonishment of the three women, and the delight of the men trapped on both sides of the Rooster, he methodically unhinged the doors in a matter of minutes. Suddenly, where once Lacy, Myrtle and Birdie had rigidly blocked entrance to this den of sin, they now stood foolishly before the wide-open entrance with the batwing doors hanging off their arms.

"There," Lucas said. "Unchain yourself from the doors and bring them back to me." He glared at Myrtle in warning. "Undamaged."

To say the wind had been taken out of Myrtle's sails was an understatement. As the men around her convulsed with laughter, the woman's mouth worked like a fish. She looked utterly humiliated.

Lucas's gaze met Lacy's and she burned with mortification. So much for giving him a taste of his own medicine. Their experiment in radical tactics had lasted all of fifteen minutes.

The women beat a hasty retreat. By the time they got back to the store, Myrtle was feeling a little more herself again. She unhooked herself from Lacy and Birdie, trying to keep her chin up. "We made a good start. Next time—"

"Next time?" Birdie looked ready to faint.

Lacy had to admit that she, too, was in no hurry to repeat that experience.

"Well, I think I taught Harry a lesson," Myrtle said.

She ended up teaching Birdie one, too—namely, never let herself be volunteered for one of Myrtle's schemes. Somewhere between the saloon and the store, the last padlock key had slipped out of Myrtle's clothes, leaving Birdie attached to the door. Lacy and Myrtle went out searching for the key, but came up with nothing.

"Never mind, Birdie," Myrtle assured the woman, who was now weeping hysterically. "We'll take you over to the blacksmith's. I'm sure he'll be able to cut you loose somehow."

The stunt might have been a miserable failure, but the word of mouth it generated was enough to bring several new members to the third meeting of the Society for Decency, Temperance, and the Beautification of Blissful. Neesa Hart, wife of the doctor in the next town over, had heard about the society through her husband and driven into town for the day. Two farmers' wives from the next county appeared, too. It was just three more people, but Lacy felt vindicated. Her group was now seven members strong, not counting the men who gravitated toward the feed room to eavesdrop.

Even Lucas was lurking about to listen to the latest plans— probably to ensure there were no more designs against his place.

Harper Cooley bumped into Myrtle on his way in. "Oh, sorry, Myrtle—I guess I thought you were a door."

The comment brought gales of laughter—more from the men than from the women. Harry Bean, who had actually closed the store so he could come to the meeting with Myrtle, managed to suppress a smirk, but everyone else laughed openly.

If Lacy thought she was in control of this gathering, she was mistaken. No one wanted to talk about temperance, or decency, or even beautifying Blissful. That fact was very obvious from the beginning of the meeting, when Harper blurted out, "What's this I hear about a carnival?"

Lacy sighed. This idea would not go away. In fact, since the men at the Rooster had heard about it, the town had been abuzz. "What we had in mind—what the sheriff suggested— was more of a trade day."

"With a few performers," Flossie said.

Myrtle, undaunted by her humiliating failure at the last meeting, rose and took charge.

"Those of us in Blissful can donate a portion of the money we make during this day to our women's committee." In fact, Myrtle had even gone so far as to come up with a name— Blissful Day—and a possible date in July. "We should start fairly soon," she declared. "Can't let the summer get away from us."

People generally agreed on this point. Though it was a busy time, summer was also the season when people would have goods to trade. No sense letting opportunity pass them by.

That didn't leave them much time to prepare, though.

"I told Mr. Bean we should put some things on the walkway out front of our store. I plan to hang up decorations, too— spruce the place up."

Harry nodded eagerly. "I've drawn up sketches for how it ought to look. Would you like to see them?"

Apparently, the rest of the town was galloping way ahead of her. Lacy struggled to keep up as they all came up with ideas of plans to lay out booths.

"I'd be glad to volunteer my services," Harper offered. "I will build a pavilion."

"A *what?*" This was from George Oatley, who had come ambling in late. His eyes bugged comically in his fire-burned face.

"A bandstand, George," Harper explained, as if to a child. "All towns in the east are building them now. It's a pavilion that will mark the center of town. Blissful lacks a focal point, a place to gather."

"I thought the Rooster was the focal point," George said.

"Well it won't be once we have a pavilion."

Lucas shook his head. "Harper, I think you've gone loco. What does a town like this want with a pavilion?"

Harper was not to be deterred. "A pavilion would really set Blissful apart, give people a reason to come here and see it."

For a while, the benefits of the pavilion were debated. Cost was a concern, though Harper insisted that it would cost no more than the town wished to spend. This raised a few brows. But at the end of the day, the pavilion prevailed.

"We can have the dance there!" Flossie said, clapping her hands together. "A festival like Blissful Day wouldn't be worth having if you didn't provide a chance for people to step out a little. We can get Jan and Otto to play fiddle." Her enthusiasm for the burgeoning plans made even some of the women who wouldn't sit anywhere near her lean toward her with interest.

Harper wasn't so keen on the choice of musicians, however. "Jan and Otto can't play but five tunes between them, and they're all polkas! They'll wear everybody out."

Harry snorted. "Speak for yourself, you old bag of bones." He gave his wife a surprising squeeze of the hand. While the door-chaining stunt had been a failure in most ways, it seemed to have brought Harry to heel. Maybe he was terrified that Myrtle would think of another way to humiliate him.

So the plans barreled on. One of the farm wives thought there should be a prize drawing, and offered a piglet. Someone else had a cousin who juggled. Flossie volunteered to tell fortunes—an idea that made Lacy quiver with dread. She could just imagine the getup Flossie would put together for that.

As she listened, straining to keep up with the ideas being volleyed about, she seemed to be the only one who was not entirely thrilled at the prospect of having the town overrun with jugglers and musicians and heaven only knows what else.

"I wish we could find a contortionist," Flossie said. "Alberta the Amazing Bendy Woman would be something people 'round here would pay plenty to see!"

It was going to be bedlam. When Lacy happened to look over to Lucas, he was laughing at her. Laughing! Because he knew that she was distressed at the way the plans were now out of her hands. The trade day was snowballing into something impossible for one person to handle. As self-appointed head of the women's society, she was the one person who was ostensibly responsible to coordinate the whole mess. She didn't hear Myrtle volunteering to do *that*.

When the meeting dispersed, he was waiting at the door for her. "Isn't your little society getting out of hand? You all couldn't even think through the stunt at the Rooster very well."

The same thought had crossed her mind, but it would be a cold day in August before she would admit as much to Lucas. Not when she could tell he was just itching to see her fall on her face. "The bigger the better, as far as I'm concerned. If we do raise money at the trade day, there's no end to the good we could do here. Maybe we can even build a church next year. That would be sooner than I expected."

"And just maybe the congregation could get to work on shutting my saloon, is that the idea?"

She lifted her chin and smiled at him. "My, my. You're very intimidated by the thought of a little goodness coming to this town, aren't you?"

The response was what she expected. He straightened. They always seemed to wind up like two cats circling each other. "Not at all. Especially since I know that you're the unlikeliest person to be orchestrating this flowering of goodness of Blissful.''

''With a few performers,'' she reminded him wryly.

He laughed.

''Why do you think I'm an unlikely person to oversee Blissful Day?'' she asked, curious.

''It's the do-gooder sentiment behind the day that has me worried for you. Because after a certain night a few weeks ago I know that you're not nearly as prim as you pretend to be. In fact, I've come to wonder if you occasionally strayed off the convent grounds from time to time.''

Her jaw dropped. ''You are the most insulting, low-minded beast!''

He bowed as if she'd just paid him a compliment. ''Your insults become more superlative as time drags on. I wonder when you'll realize that part of the reason I make you so angry is because you're attracted to me despite the fact that I represent everything you hate.''

She crossed her arms and bit her lip so hard that she almost tasted blood.

''Go ahead,'' he said.

She arched a brow at him. ''Go ahead and what?''

He grinned. ''Hop up and down, stamp your foot, slap my face.''

''I didn't know you were a mind reader.'' She smiled. ''Maybe you should offer up your services on Blissful Day. We could stick you in a booth between Madame Flossie and the prize pig.''

Lucas chortled, then comically jutted out his chin. ''Well...have at it.''

She swallowed her laughter and straightened her shoulders. ''A lady of dignity does not resort to physical violence.''

His neck retracted. ''No, I guess not. Especially when the face she wants to slap is also the face she sees in her dreams at night.''

Despite being a lady of dignity, she howled indignantly. ''I forgot to add vanity to your faults! False vanity, at that. I assure you, I haven't given you a thought for the longest time."

His brows raised in disbelief. "Is that a fact?"

"What's more—" she continued pertly "—I think you should know there is someone in town who might not take kindly to your harassing me in such a lewd way. If you aren't careful, you might find yourself in a fight."

His dark eyes fastened on her with interest. "Found yourself a knight in shining armor, have you?"

"Yes, I have."

As if she had summoned him especially for the purpose of showing up Lucas, Bodine appeared. He looked a little breathless as he removed his hat. "Sorry I'm so late, Lacy. Harper started talking to me out there on the street."

She smiled at Lucas with glorious smugness as she looped her arm through the sheriff's. "That's all right."

Bodine caught the visual exchange between the two of them. "Howdy, Lucas."

"The sheriff is taking me for a drive this afternoon," Lacy explained.

"Sounds snug." The words wrenched from Lucas's lips with such surprising bitterness that Lacy almost leapt in triumph. Was he jealous? What a delicious feeling to get *his* goat for a change.

"We should get going," she said. "I have to get back in time to start supper."

Lucas's lips twisted into a sneer. "Look out, Sheriff. She seems all sweet and innocent, but looks can be deceiving."

Lacy practically yanked Bodine out of there. She was in such a hurry to get away, in fact, that she ignored Bodine's offer to help her up and instead clambered gracelessly into the wagon unassisted.

They drove in silence until they were out of town. Then Bodine turned to her. "Do you and Lucas really dislike each other all that much?"

"Isn't it obvious?"

Bodine bit his lip over the matter for a moment. "Well

sure... But back in Cicada Creek we had a couple of barn cats—an old black tom and a pretty little calico. They always clawed and spat and kicked up a fuss around each other, too, but then every so often we'd find the calico in the hayloft nursing a litter of kittens.''

Lacy thought for a moment that she might jump down from the buggy, then she barked out a laugh. "Believe me, the only thing Lucas Burns will ever leave me nursing is a headache!"

Bodine chuckled along. "Excuse me, Lacy. I don't suppose I should have been comparing you and Lucas to a couple of cats."

"I should say not," Lacy said, forgetting for a moment that just a short time earlier she had made the same comparison herself.

All was quiet inside the Rooster. Too quiet.

As Lucas sat behind the bar, going over the accounts, he noticed an eerie restive silence in the place. But he supposed he should be glad that instead of the usual jawing and complaining and fighting there was some peace around here for once. Jacob, full after his lunch brought by Lacy, was at the table in the corner absorbed in building a house of cards. Harper was at the bar, sketching pictures of pavilions on the slate Jacob had loaned him. Even old fat Elmer, lying in the sun that poured under the doors, his ringed tail barely twitching, seemed even more lethargic than usual.

And then there was Boot, who slumped against the counter, brooding. He thought the whole town was too quiet. "What's the matter with you people?" he exploded all at once.

Everyone looked up. "What are you talking about, Boot?" Lucas asked.

Harper grunted, apparently resenting the distraction from his work. He obviously hadn't a clue what was bothering the man sitting right next to him. In fact, Lucas wondered for a moment whether Harper knew that Boot had been watching him draw for the past half hour.

"What am I talking about?" Boot's voice looped up an octave. "I'm talking about what's going on here!"

Harper blinked at the little man. "There's nothing going on here."

Boot ignited. "That's the problem! Nobody talks anymore. Heck, Harry hasn't been by for an entire week. The man complained about old Myrtle for the better part of a decade, and now he acts like he's attached at the hip to the woman."

"Maybe he's glad to have a little time alone with his wife finally, now that Birdie's off at Lacy's."

"I saw Myrtle over at the store this morning, and she had on a new dress," Jacob piped up. "Yellow. She didn't look half as mean as she usually does."

Boot slapped the bar. "There! See? Everything's changing!"

Harper chuckled. "You make it sound like Harry Bean is the only person you care about, Boot. That sort of hurts my feelings. Lucas and Jacob and I are still here."

"Barely," Boot said flatly. "You haven't said a word since Jacob gave you that slate, Harper. Why the heck are you suddenly so het up about making porch swings and building pavilions?"

"It's a diversion."

"A what?" Boot didn't wait for an explanation, but instead turned an accusatory gaze on Lucas. "Now, I've got all the respect for you in the world, Lucas, but I have to say this plan of yours don't seem to be working."

Lucas tapped his pencil against the ledger. For some reason, Boot's words bothered him. "It's early days yet, Boot."

Boot sputtered. "It's been weeks—and I don't see much progress toward getting rid of our Calhoun menace. All I see is that Lacy Calhoun's got everyone planning trade days and bringing little box lunches over here for Jacob. Not only has she ruined our town, now it appears she's fattening you all up for the kill."

Harper laughed. "I'll admit I feel a little filled out. The food's mighty good over at Lacy's."

"*That's* what I'm talking about!" Boot practically shrieked. "Since when has everyone started calling it *Lacy's?* It's the Slipper, remember? The whole point of Lucas movin' over there was so's we could run the Calhoun menace out of town and get the Slipper back."

Lucas frowned. "The Calhoun menace, as you call her, is more entrenched than we previously guessed."

"I'm worried that with ya'll getting suckered in by her, she's going to be entrenched for all time."

"You have to admit the trade day is a good thing," Harper said. "Bring the town a little excitement. Reason for folks to gather."

Boot grudgingly conceded this point. "Sure, I guess that'll be okay. But that's one day. Meanwhile we're all stuck here for years."

Jacob frowned. "You really feel stuck, Boot?"

Boot whirled. "Huh?"

The boy cleared his throat. "Well, the way you talk, it sounds like you think there aren't any other towns to move to."

Boot whirled on Lucas as if he'd just been wounded. "Listen to that! Your own flesh and blood is practically telling me to leave town, Lucas."

Lucas sighed and motioned for Jacob to pipe down for a while. Jacob was getting smart. Maybe too smart. It was probably time to sit him down for a father-son talk about the dangers of being too rational in this world.

"I can't leave Blissful," Boot said. "Where else could I find a woman like the widow Wallace to employ me? She actually thinks I do a good job."

It was true, Lucas hadn't been as vigilant lately about trying to roust Lacy from their midst as he should have been. The trouble was, she was so slippery. All the times he thought he had the upper hand, she managed to turn the tables on him. He was beginning to feel like the blind bull charging the scarecrow. Just when he thought he was about to come out the victor, he found himself bashed up against a hard, immovable object.

And that object was Lacy.

"Now she's even got the sheriff in cahoots with her," Boot pointed out. "There's another man we haven't seen in a while. Not at the Rooster."

But it seemed to Lucas that he'd seen enough of Bodine in the past week to last him a lifetime. He and Lacy were always together now. You'd think Bodine had hung up his badge in favor of a job as household helper. Afternoons he could always be found sitting at the table, drinking lemonade and helping Lacy peel vegetables or start making bread. This morning the sheriff had come over to the boardinghouse after breakfast to hoe the kitchen garden. Lucas hadn't seen the couple behaving in a fashion that would indicate that Lacy was encouraging Bodine in anything other than housework and taking her on buggy rides...but who could say what went on during those buggy rides?

He swallowed, and his throat suddenly felt very dry. "You're right, Boot. Something needs to be done."

Boot leaned toward him eagerly. "Good, 'cause I've got an idea."

"What have you come up with?"

"Sabotage."

Harper and Lucas goggled at each other in alarm. "Good God, Boot!" Lucas exclaimed. "What do you want to do, blow up the Slipper?"

"Of course not," Boot said. "You think I'm some sort of idiot? The Slipper's what we're trying to save." He shook his head. "I was thinking more in terms of Harper's pavilion."

"*What?*" For a moment, Harper looked like he might bust a gut.

"Well not blow it up, exactly." Boot appealed to Harper. "But maybe if you could manage to make it so it sort of, you know, collapses?"

"Boot!" Lacy seemed to have driven the man to the edge of sanity. Then again, Lucas knew exactly how that felt.

"There are going to be people on the pavilion. You can't have people getting hurt."

"Okay, but couldn't it just collapse right after it's built?"

"From what?" Lucas asked. "The weight of too much air?"

"No one is sabotaging my pavilion," Harper declared hotly.

"But don't you see? If the trade day is a big disaster, everybody'll blame Lacy."

"Why?" Jacob piped up.

"She's organizing the big day, ain't she?"

"I'll sleep under the blasted thing if I have to," Harper vowed.

Boot shot him a disgusted look. "You might just have to, old man, since you pulled down the back wall of your own house to make that damn swing!"

Lucas was taken aback by this news. "You did?"

"It was a sort of spur-of-the-moment impulse." Harper appeared more than slightly abashed. "'Sides, my place is nice and cool now."

"You were showing off," Boot said. "Trying to impress Lacy Calhoun. It's just like I predicted. This town has just been turned upside-down by that woman!"

The news about Harper's house alarmed Lucas more than anything else. While he'd been dilly-dallying, had Harper really fallen under Lacy's spell? The clues certainly all pointed to that. He'd made her the bread box. And then the swing. And now he seemed to be throwing himself heart and soul into building the pavilion.

Lucas shook his head. An old guy like Harper. He'd managed to dodge the bullet of fool-headedness over women for years, and now look at him. Felled by Lacy Calhoun, a girl young enough to be his daughter.

"You're right, Boot——" Lucas said, adding quickly "——not about collapsing Harper's pavilion, of course. But maybe we do need to switch tactics. I had thought the job would be easier than this, but I hadn't figured on the trade day idea taking hold like it has."

"That's why collapsing the grandstand would be such a good idea."

"Over my dead body!" Harper roared.

"We have to be more subtle than that, Boot," Lucas said.

As Boot propped his elbows on the bar, his shoulders sank. "Subtle? That sounds harder."

"It will be. But I think you're on to something."

"Well count me out," Harper said. The older man got up and left.

Lucas drummed his fingers on the bar as Boot watched him anxiously.

Sabotage. Maybe the key wasn't to bring down buildings. He didn't want anyone hurt, and besides, a structure could be rebuilt. "Maybe what we really need to bring down isn't a pavilion, it's a reputation."

Chapter Nine

"Good night, Bodine. I enjoyed our walk."

Lacy could barely see his smile in the scant moonlight. But she knew his expressions well enough by now to imagine how he looked. His face was so sweet, so boyish. He took her hand. "'Night, Lacy. Mind if I come over tomorrow afternoon and listen to some piano music? You promised to play for me sometime."

"That would be wonderful."

"Tomorrow, then."

These goodbyes always seemed to go on forever. Neither she nor Bodine were very adept at bringing a conversation to a close.

"Good night," she repeated.

He let go of her hand. Finally. "'Night."

Before they were compelled to go through one more round of good-nights, Bodine finally turned, took the porch steps two at a time, and hurried back toward his little room above the jailhouse.

She only felt slightly dissatisfied with the evening. It was wonderful to have a beau, which she supposed Bodine was now. Everyone else seemed to assume it. She could tell from the meetings that all the women looked at her with a little more respect now that Bodine had taken an interest in her. Neesa Hart had invited her—and, more astonishingly, invited

Flossie—for tea and cake at her house next week. Even Myrtle Bean was being more cordial. She was making headway.

In those first few weeks, she had seen distrust in the eyes of women she came across. Even Birdie looked askance at her. The looks of those women had told her that they were just waiting for her to take a fall, like her mother. Oh, maybe they weren't hoping for it. She didn't want to believe anyone could be that wicked. But they were expecting it.

Now those looks had stopped. Or maybe they were just better hidden. Either way, Lacy seemed to have earned a small measure of trust amongst the townspeople of Blissful. But she hated to think it was just because of Bodine. She wanted to believe that her work on behalf of the town's welfare was helping to raise her and her mother in the town's esteem, too.

"Nice night."

At the sound of Lucas's voice, Lacy's heart stopped. She whirled, and in the shadowy moonlight caught sight of him lounging in the porch swing. "Lucas! You scared the daylights out of me."

"I was trying to be quiet. I didn't want to bust up the tender scene between you and the sheriff."

A likely story. "You wanted to spy on us, you mean."

Even in the faint light, she could see his smile. Those white teeth glinted like stars. "Sort of disappointing, though. You two don't put on much of a show."

"We weren't aware we had an audience."

The swing creaked as he leaned forward. "That's what I found so interesting. There Bodine was, surely thinking he had all the privacy in the world, and yet all he could muster was a little handshake."

"Not all men have your wolfish impulses."

"What broad experience did you base this conclusion on?"

"I was only stating a generality. You know as well as I do that you're the only man I've ever kissed."

He leaned back again and took a long time answering. As infuriating as the barbed needling that passed for his conversation was, she found that his silence made her even more uncomfortable. Especially since she couldn't exactly see his face, or where he was looking. He was probably ogling her, she thought with a disdainful sniff at the same moment the thought sent a wave of heat shivering through her.

"I've been thinking about that kiss," he drawled.

"I'll bet you have," she said. "I'm sure there are all sorts of salacious thoughts swimming around in your head."

He laughed. "Why? Have they been swimming around in yours, too?"

"You know they haven't!"

"I know no such thing," he argued. "Especially now that I've seen you with the sheriff."

"Bodine and I have a perfectly respectable relationship."

"Yes, I saw that. I was shocked, frankly. Knowing your passionate nature..."

She felt herself rising up on her toes in anger. "I do *not* have a passionate nature. The only person who brings out my passion is you!"

He doubled over with laughter.

Drat! She always seemed to blurt out the wrong thing around Lucas. She stood for a moment, fuming but unfortunately speechless. She was afraid anything she said would be turned against her.

"You flatter me," he said when he'd recovered.

"You know what I meant," she shot back. "All you have to do is open your mouth and I get angry."

"You weren't angry when I kissed you."

"Yes I was." Then she remembered, very clearly, that she wasn't. She had been overwhelmed, transported, and overcome with that warm rush from being in his arms. But she hadn't expressed anger.

She was so relieved that he couldn't see her blush now. Unless he had some sort of night vision, like a rodent—and she wouldn't have been surprised to discover that he did.

"All right, let's say for your pride's sake that you *were* angry. Fine. That doesn't change the fact that I found you a very willing partner in that kiss. Which you instigated."

He would never let her forget *that*. In fact, he seemed not to want to let her forget one single second she had spent in his arms. Heaven knows he managed to insert them into the conversation every time they were alone together. "Only because you were practically standing on my toes anyway," she said, the excuse sounding feeble to her own ears. "Bodine doesn't do that. He doesn't crowd me, or rush me, or irritate me."

"Or kiss you. Or even attract you."

"Bodine Turner is the kindest, sweetest man in this town and I'm flattered that he wants to spend time with me."

"Sure, you're flattered. And no doubt you like parading around the countryside on the arm of a clean-cut respectable man. But you aren't the least bit interested in having the man pull you to his chest and show you a few of the joys of being a woman."

She stomped forward, her mind reeling. It was all she could do to keep her voice down below a roar. "That is the most outrageous thing anyone has ever said to me. I should…" Her hands fisted at her sides. She wasn't sure what she wanted to do.

Lucas had an idea. "Kick me out of the house?"

"I wish I could!"

"Go ahead," he said. "Toss me out on my ear, bag and baggage." That smile of his widened. "Or is there some reason why you want me around?"

"Yes. I need the six dollars."

He laughed. "Money's no excuse when your honor is at stake, is it?"

Did he really want her to toss him out?

Why shouldn't she? Serve him right!

But when she opened her mouth to do the deed, she heard herself saying, "I wouldn't put Jacob out. This seems to be the first real home the boy has ever had."

Lucas chortled. "That's very convenient. Lacy, why don't you just come out and admit that you are chomping at the bit for more of what our kiss gave you a taste for?"

She rolled her eyes. "That's utterly ridiculous."

"Is it?" Lucas took her hand, and to her dismay he pulled her down into his lap with little or no effort at all. She landed with a thump and felt stunned for a moment. But only because he'd caught her off guard. Once she realized he had her in his grasp, she squirmed to get free. She'd forgotten how strong he was. His chest and arms felt like solid muscle. Physically, he was the equivalent of two of her.

Amazing, really. And how was it that a man's skin could feel so different from hers, especially a man who worked indoors all day? He had a different scent, too. A potent mixture of tobacco and leather and man...

Her breath quickened, and she forced herself to stop struggling. She didn't want to give him the satisfaction of a physical altercation. "Turn me loose."

He touched her chin with one hand. Just like last time.

And her heart did a somersault in her chest, just like last time. His eyes glittered at her, and she bit her lip—as if *that* could keep the jumble of contradictory feelings roiling around inside her at bay. "Lucas..."

He didn't answer her. Not with words. Instead, he leaned forward and touched his lips to hers—and oh, heaven, it was even more splendid than she remembered. She'd recalled the feel of his mouth against hers more times than she would ever admit even to herself, but the memory hadn't been as sharp, as intoxicating, as the real thing. The physical sensation drew a moan from deep inside her, and for just a moment she yielded to the delicious temptation.

In fact, she yielded to desires she wasn't even aware she had. Suddenly the urge to loop her arms around the back of his neck and massage the dense muscle around his shoulders was beyond bearing. She simply surrendered, reveling in the way her touch seemed to make him respond and deepen the kiss. He opened her mouth gently with his tongue, sending an answering heat through her.

He tasted her with a hunger that should have frightened her, but didn't. She was too busy exploring at first to take note of the solid pressure of his lap pushing against her skirt. Or his hands, which were exploring her waist, her back. He shifted her in his lap, leaning back to give him access to the top buttons of the front of her dress. So involved was she in investigating the wonderful taste of him, she didn't realize he had undone her dress all the way to her corset until his warm, rough hand skimmed the sensitive skin there. The sensation sent something like a bolt of lightning through her.

She pulled back, sucking in her breath. Her lips formed the word *stop,* but the dark intensity in Lucas's eyes momentarily stole the breath from her body.

Mesmerized, she watched him loosen the fastening of her undergarment and work his hand to her breast. Her breath caught again, and Lucas swallowed her gasp with another kiss. But he didn't remove his hand, which continued to perform a delicious assault on the sensitive breast, circling and rubbing and teasing it until it felt as if every fiber of her was straining against him and straining against the tight fabric confining her.

Time escaped her. They might have been on the swing for just a few moments, or an hour, or a lifetime. All that she could say for sure was that she didn't want whatever he was doing to end.

But Lucas had other ideas. Just when she thought she would have to beg him for something more—though what that something was, she wasn't quite sure—he removed his hand, pulled his lips from hers, and smiled at her.

Though her whole body felt as if it were ablaze, she managed to return the smile with a tentative one of her own. Until she realized that his wasn't an expression of adoration, or even raw lust. Instead, it slowly dawned on her that what she was looking at was a smile of victory. A self-satisfied, I-told-you-so smile.

Her face fell slack, and as she tried to readjust her thoughts, certain physical details began to penetrate her consciousness. The raw warmth of her lips from their kiss. The insistent, impatient throbbing deep inside her. The top of her dress, which was flapping open practically all the way to her skirt.

Lacy grabbed the material of her blouse and clutched it closed.

A warm chuckle rumbled through Lucas. She could feel it, since she was still planted on his lap. She sprang up, and he didn't try to stop her. Why would he? He had already proved his point.

And to underscore it, he stood up and asked with amusement, "Are you still going to tell me that you don't have a passionate nature?"

She didn't know what to say without screaming at him...which she would have dearly loved to do. At that moment she could have let out a banshee wail loud enough to wake the whole house up, rouse the entire town, in fact.

But she couldn't kick up a fuss without drawing attention to what had just happened, and Lucas knew she couldn't. For a few moments, she just stood there panting with anger, feeling as if she were about to explode.

He chortled lightly. "They sure couldn't have taught you *that* in the convent."

When she again saw that wicked smile on Lucas's face, she did explode. Words just wouldn't do. A ladylike slap on the cheek wouldn't suffice, either. She didn't know where the impulse came from, or the skill, but she tightened her hand into a fist, pulled back and rounded on him with such force that the impact of her fist against his cheekbone made a sickening sound—something between a smack and a crunch—and repelled her back against a porch rail. Her knuckles stung, and she flapped her hand in the air at the same moment Lucas brought his hand to his face.

Merciful heaven! She had walloped him beyond her wildest dreams. She knew she should be ashamed of herself—for lots of reasons—and she probably would be, tomorrow. Right now she only felt a satisfaction that verged on hysteria.

"They didn't teach me *that* at the convent, either."

"Do you know 'Silver Threads Among the Gold'?"

Lacy perched on the piano bench, feeling inadequate and

restless. She had warned Bodine that she didn't know how to play many popular tunes, but he didn't seem to believe her.

"No, I don't," she said. "I'm sorry."

He couldn't quite hide his disappointment. "Well, that's all right. It's just one of my favorites, that's all." He smiled at her suddenly. "Maybe if I sang it for you!" He warbled out a few tuneless bars.

After all that, she hated to let him down. "I'm afraid I don't know how to play by ear."

"Oh." Bodine flopped down into a chair and beat his hat against his knee, just like he had in this room on the day she'd met him. Staring off at the piano as if waiting for someone else to materialize there. She wondered who that someone else was. "Well, that's okay. Just play whatever you feel like."

If she were honest, she would have told him that she didn't feel like playing anything. Her hand was still tender from hitting Lucas, so she wasn't exactly expecting her fingers to trip merrily over the keys. But of course she hadn't told Bodine about the scene with Lucas, which would have required an explanation for *why* she had hit him—something she would never tell a single soul. When Bodine had inquired after the bruise along the tops of her knuckles, she had fabricated a tall tale about jamming her hand between the water pail and the well.

So, no, she wasn't honest. And if last night was any indication, she wasn't very virtuous, period. Now Bodine was making her come to the conclusion that she wasn't very talented, either.

By the time she began to play, shakily, she was a nervous wreck. But it was a feeling she was getting used to. Ever since last night she'd felt jittery, on edge. She'd burned the breakfast rolls and lost her temper with her mother later when Flossie had tried to get her to take a rest and let her do the washing up. But Lacy had felt the need to do something, anything, to get her mind off Lucas.

As if that were possible! Maybe it was time to just admit

that Lucas was right. She *did* have a passionate nature. Worse still, she seemed to have a fatal weakness for Lucas himself.

Oh, she'd tried to deny it. She had hoped to heaven being around Bodine would bring out the better part of her character. But it appeared that suppressing her unspeakable lust for Lucas had only made matters worse. It had made her just that more vulnerable when she did find herself alone with him. Just thinking about sitting in his lap last night, the things he had done to her...

Her hands slipped on the keys, turning Mozart into a discordant racket. "Sorry," she said.

Bodine had that faraway look in his eye, though, that made her doubt whether he had heard a note she'd played, good or bad. "That's all right," he mumbled when he finally realized she'd said something.

She resumed playing.

A fine pair they made. Here they were alone, yet Lacy doubted Bodine was thinking of her any more than she was thinking of him. And she didn't even care all that much. It was just like Lucas said last night. She respected Bodine, and thought only good things about him, but she couldn't say she was actually attracted to him.

How could this be? When she looked at the sheriff, her heart didn't thunder against her ribs like it did when she was around Lucas. The touch of his hand at her elbow didn't cause a riot inside her like simply being in the same room as Lucas caused. His conversation, which was never scathing, snide or lewd, oftentimes failed to engage her. He didn't have the same gruff, husky quality to his voice. He didn't make her laugh in spite of herself. His eyes weren't alight with teasing flirtation.

It was disturbing that she could prefer a rascal like Lucas to Bodine. But surely Lucas had some redeemable qualities that would justify her attraction to him.

She stopped playing for a moment and swiveled toward Bodine. "Do you go much to the Rooster?"

"Not so much as I used to," he said, flushing slightly. "I spend more time here now."

He really was *such* a good man, Lacy thought with regret. It was a shame he wasn't...

She gave herself a mental upbraiding. She was about to think it was a shame that Bodine wasn't more like Lucas, which just showed how deeply Lucas had burrowed under her skin. Wishing Bodine to be more like Lucas would be like wishing the springtime to be more like winter. Or the rose to be more like skunkweed. Or...

"Is the Rooster really such a bad place?" she asked.

He laughed. "Heck, no."

Her spirits brightened. "For instance, would *I* be comfortable there?"

Bodine's face went slack. "Why on earth would you want to go to the Rooster?"

She lifted her shoulders. "I don't. I was just curious about what kind of place it is, and when you said it wasn't all that bad..."

His back suddenly went rigid. "Well, no, it's not bad if you're a man, but it's certainly no place for a woman. It's the sort of place where men sit around doing...well, man things. It can get a little rough at times."

She doubted if it got much rougher than what had happened on her porch last night.

"Besides, I'm sorry to say there's some language used in there that would make a sweet thing like yourself blush. You wouldn't like it at all."

"I was just curious."

Bodine chuckled in an indulgent way. "I guess I can understand that. You ladies do seem to have inquiring minds."

At his dismissive tone, the smile froze on her lips. Then she looked up to see Lucas standing in the doorway and her entire body froze.

Lucas had skipped breakfast that morning, so this was the first time she'd locked eyes with him since last night. His dark gaze was like a bolt of lightning to her system. A shiver of desire snaked through her, and her heart was kicking up a ruckus in her chest.

How long had he been watching them?

Seeing her gaze locked on the doorway, Bodine swiveled. "Lucas, you old dog! Come on in and join us."

Before Lacy could pipe in that perhaps Lucas had other plans, he strolled right in and made himself at home on the settee. "Not interrupting, am I?"

"No, no." Bodine frowned at the shiny red bruise on Lucas's cheek. "What happened to your face?"

Lucas's lips twisted into a wry smile and he shot a glance at Lacy. "Guess I took things a little too far last night."

"See there, Lacy? I told you things got rough over at the Rooster!"

Lucas snickered as Lacy writhed in discomfort. "Oh, it can get rough all over in this town."

She wrinkled her nose at him, hoping in vain that this would cause him to cease and desist.

"It's funny—" Bodine said, his brow furrowing at the coincidence "—Lacy and I were just talking about the Rooster."

Lucas's dark eyes honed in on her sharply. "Were you? You haven't been talking about what's going on at Bean's store today?"

"Good heavens, no," Bodine said. "What ever happens there?"

"You can hear some interesting gossip, I understand."

Every fiber of Lacy's being tensed. Gossip? What gossip? Why was he grinning at her like that? Like the cat who had swallowed the cream.

"Oh, I never listen to Myrtle's gossip," Bodine said dismissively, making Lacy want to hug him. He chuckled. "Lacy seemed mighty curious about the Rooster, Lucas. Maybe you ought to give her the guided tour someday."

"That's peculiar. She won't step foot in the place when she brings Jacob his noon meal. She never goes farther than the doors—even when she chains herself to them." Lucas and Bodine exchanged amused glances.

She picked at a nonexistent piece of fluff on her skirt. "I was just curious."

Lucas responded with a knowing grin. "You seem to be curious about all life's pleasures."

Lacy's heartbeat stilled. He wasn't going to start needling her about last night now, was he? Right in front of Bodine?

Of course he would. Quickly, before he could start enumerating those pleasures she was apparently so interested in, she turned back to the piano keys. "What would you like to hear next?"

"Something pretty," Lucas said.

Lacy reeled back toward him. "From you, I would have expected 'Turkey in the Straw.'"

He leaned back and laughed. "Even saloonkeepers like pretty things. But I guess you of all people would know that."

She turned back to the keys quickly and played a few badly recalled bars of Beethoven. Finally Bodine, who looked in danger of nodding off, stood and stretched. "Well, guess I'd better get my nose back to the old grindstone."

She jumped up from the piano. "*Must* you go?" The pleading tone in her voice wasn't there by accident. The last thing she wanted was to be left alone in the house with Lucas. Who knows? Maybe he was considering a repeat of last night! She couldn't let that happen.

Even if a tiny part of her might want to.

Lucas stood and slapped Bodine on the back. "Can't keep the sheriff here listening to music all day, Lacy. The town needs him. Remove his watchful eyes for too long, Blissful might find itself swallowed by a veritable crater of crime."

"Thank you for the music, Lacy," Bodine said with a smile as Lucas tugged him toward the door.

After Bodine had said his goodbyes and was gone, she sucked in her breath and whirled on Lucas. "I'll thank you not to chase my guests away."

Black brows arched. "The sheriff got up on his own volition. Seems he doesn't like piano music as much as he used to."

She planted her hands on her hips. "I'm sure there is a double meaning hidden somewhere in that observation, but

I'm not going to stoop to hunting for it. I'm warning you, Lucas, if you came here thinking for one instant that I'm going to fall—''

Her words were cut off by his curt laugh. "Snuff your wick. There's no reason to get yourself fired up every time we clap eyes on each other."

As if his insufferable behavior weren't the reason why she always seemed to lose her temper around him! "I was perfectly even-tempered until I met you."

"I'm sure you were virtuous nine ways to Sunday, but that's beside the point. I didn't come here to pick a fight, Lacy. I came here to warn you. There's talk in town."

The gossip at the store. She'd almost forgotten about it— but now her heart filled with dread. She swallowed. "Talk about what?"

"You and me."

Anger rallied her. "I should have known you wouldn't be able to hold your tongue!"

He barked out a laugh. "You think I would sit around the Rooster bragging that you slugged me in the face?"

"Well then, who…?"

"We were being watched."

"But…" Who could have seen them? Bodine had left, and everyone else was asleep. At least, she was fairly sure they were sleeping….

The memory of rustling curtains the day Harper had come over to build the porch swing danced at the edge of her memory. "Birdie!"

"Birdie," Lucas agreed.

Naturally Birdie wouldn't have wasted any time running to tell her brother what a den of sin Myrtle had banished her to. Lacy's knees gave way and she sank back onto the piano bench. Oh, heavens! This was all she needed. Here she had been trying to rescue the Calhoun name, but she had instead besmirched it some more.

"Who's been talking?"

"Folks around town. I first heard the news from Harper. He came into the bar fit to be tied. Said we'd sullied his swing."

So the talk wasn't just at the store. It was spreading. Her behavior was being discussed in barrooms, now. "What am I going to do?"

Lucas stared at her long and hard. She wasn't sure what was going through his head. He certainly wasn't expressing remorse for his behavior last night. On the other hand, though his stance was arrogant, the look in his eyes seemed almost sympathetic. "You can always deny what happened."

The prospect of adding lying to her already growing list of sins depressed her. She got up and walked over to where she had left a pitcher of water. Her mouth was bone dry. She took a few deep gulps, trying to calm down.

"I'm sorry I hit you, Lucas," she said. She now felt remorseful about all sorts of things.

He laughed. "I'll bet."

"Not that you didn't deserve it—" she said "—but a lady would have restrained herself. I shouldn't have lost my temper that way. It's just the pressure of everything mounting up on me, I suppose. Weeks ago, I never would have imagined harming a fly."

He pulled off his hat and tossed it to the settee. "Well, Blissful isn't a convent. Not much of the world is, I'm afraid. If you don't want to be faced with real problems, I suggest you go back to Our Lady of whatever-you-call-it, and leave the dirty work of living in the real world to those of us who enjoy it."

She frowned. "That's the problem. I enjoy it, too."

He nodded. "Yes, I recollect that there are some things you enjoy."

There he went again. Always twisting her words to mean something she didn't intend. She shook her head and paced back across the room. Or started to. Lucas caught her arm. The look in his eye caused her heart to leap in her chest.

What was it about those dark eyes that made her common sense unravel like so much cheap cloth?

"Please…" she said, pulling on her arm.

He was about to make a reply when they heard a loud har-rumph in the doorway.

"So Birdie was right!" Myrtle Bean exclaimed. "For shame!" The venerable storekeeper stood, corseted bosom heaving, next to Flossie.

Lacy sprang away from Lucas—too late. Looking into Myrtle's beady little eyes, she saw the damage had been irrevocably done. Flossie also looked astonished, if not quite as disapproving.

"Now, Myrtle, they weren't doing anything," Flossie hastened to assure the woman. "Just standing in the middle of the room, really. No sense kicking up dust over something like that."

Having her mother come to the rescue of her reputation made Lacy feel she had sunk to her lowest ebb.

"*Alone* in the middle of the room," Myrtle pointed out. "Looking all lovey-dovey into each other's eyes. Birdie's warned me about the goings-on around here. She's been telling tales of middle of the night meetings, and saying it's not a fit place for a maiden lady to live. But did I believe her? No!" She shook her head in distaste at Lacy. "But now…well!"

"Oh, for heaven's sake," Flossie grumbled. "That's a lot of hogwash."

Myrtle whirled on her. "Are you calling my sister-in-law a liar?"

"No, I'm sayin' she's a nosy peahen. I don't know what happened out on the porch last night, but I'm sure there's a simple explanation." She gestured to Lacy to explain. "Tell her, sweetheart."

Lacy swallowed.

Flossie goggled at her. "There *is* an explanation, isn't there?"

"Of course!" Lacy said quickly. She looked up at Lucas. "A very logical explanation."

If she was hoping for him to do the gentlemanly thing and rescue her from this embarrassing situation, she obviously had a long wait ahead of her. Lucas merely looked down at her with an amused expression.

"He attacked me!" Lacy said in frustration. She pointed to the bruise on his face. "Look, that's where I hit him. And I've got the bruised knuckles to prove it."

Myrtle came closer to inspect the evidence, as did Flossie, who let out a loud guffaw. "Is that true, Lucas?"

Lacy was pleased to see that he looked embarrassed. "Yes," he admitted. "I...um...*kissed* Lacy, and she kicked up such a fuss that we both ended up wounded."

"There!" Flossie rounded on Myrtle with delicious satisfaction. "Fightin' for her virtue—which is more than I'll bet you ever did when Harry came courtin' you, Myrtle Bean!"

Myrtle puffed up again and shot an arch look at Lucas. "Mr. Bean *never* gave me cause to hit him, I'm sure. Not till we were good and married, anyways."

"That's understandable," Lucas said.

Flossie hooted.

Myrtle glowered at him. "You should be ashamed of yourself—and you with a young son!"

"The youngster wasn't there when I was making love to Lacy, I assure you."

Lacy whirled on him angrily. Did he have to use that term?

"Well you weren't fighting for your virtue the *whole* time," he reminded her. "Just at the end, when I—"

"Stop right there, or I'll take another swing at you, Lucas, I swear I will!"

"Lacy!" Myrtle said, disapprovingly. "More violence is the last thing this town needs, I'm sure you'll agree."

"Not if it's directed at the right people," Lacy said hotly as she glared at Lucas.

Myrtle stepped between them. For a reason that soon became obvious, she was in a forgiving mood. She fixed Lacy with a patronizing stare, then took her hand and patted it. "Now, now. I guess we can overlook this incident. I'm willing to be broad-minded, 'cause I know it would about break

Birdie's heart to have to move back to our house again. She likes it here so."

Her three listeners were staggered. Surely Myrtle wasn't so deluded as to actually believe this! Hardly a night went by when someone's sleep wasn't interrupted by Birdie's wails or worried pacing around the house. In that moment, Lacy felt sorry enough for Birdie to forgive her for being a nosy old snoop, a worrywart, and a daily irritant.

Myrtle dropped Lacy's hand. "Of course, I can't say that I think you're the best person to be leading those meetings of ours, but I suppose everyone deserves a second chance."

While a few days ago Lacy might have been humbly grateful for Myrtle's big-heartedness, now she only just kept a tart retort at bay. "Thank you."

Myrtle brushed past Flossie and steamed her way back to the store. When she was gone, Flossie let out an angry grunt. "Old she-goat!"

Lacy turned back to Lucas. "If you aren't the most villainous rascal I've ever met, Lucas Burns."

He responded with wide-eyed innocence. "What are you huffing at me for?"

"Insinuating that I...that we..."

A long, lazy smile tipped his lips upward. "Well, didn't we?"

Just when Lacy thought she was about to explode, Flossie grabbed her by the shoulders and pulled her back. "Now, now, it's all done now. No sense flying into a tizzy about some silly gossip."

"There wouldn't *be* any gossip if Lucas would just leave me alone!"

Lucas laughed. "If you had stronger willpower, you mean."

"I won't be able to hold my head up in this town, thanks to you," Lacy growled.

"Now it's not as bad as all that," Flossie said. "I'm sure not *everybody* knows. When I was in the store, there were only five or six people there talkin' about it."

Lacy's jaw went slack. Five or six? That was half the town!

And Lucas said the story had already reached the Rooster. "Oh, I'm ruined," she moaned.

Flossie patted her on the back. "Now that's just not the case, darlin'." She chuckled. "But even if it were, in this town you'd hardly be alone."

Lacy let out a wail and buried her head in her mother's ample bosom.

"Don't cry about it," Flossie said. "Nobody around here cares what Myrtle thinks except you. That's your problem."

She turned on Lucas in a fury. "No, *Lucas* is my problem."

His lips twisted into a tight, toothless smile. "I'm sorry. Didn't I warn you there would be problems?"

Yes, he had. And he was right. Maybe they couldn't live in the same house together. Or even in the same town. At this moment she was sorely tempted, maybe really tempted for the first time, to give up and go back to San Antonio.

She felt a jolt inside, then looked into those almost black eyes of his. Was *that* what he wanted? Was this an elaborate scheme to chase her back to the convent?

That thought hurt her more than anything.

Lucas finally turned and snatched his hat off the top of the piano. He jammed it on his head and then started to leave. At the front door, he turned. "Good afternoon, Flossie."

"Bye, Lucas," Flossie said, trilling her fingers at him. When he was gone, she turned back to Lacy. "What's gotten into you?"

Suddenly, Lacy felt exhausted. "Oh, I don't know, Mama. I hope Myrtle *will* forget all this."

Her mother snorted. "As long as we'll agree to keep her sister-in-law for her, that biddy would forgive us anything. I swear, that Myrtle Bean can be so hard, it makes me feel downright sorry for Birdie, even though she is a nuisance."

Truth to tell, Lacy had a hard time sparing many charitable thoughts for Birdie. What cause did that nosy old maid have to spy on her and Lucas? It wasn't any of her business if they...

Lacy moaned.

Remembering her daughter's fragile mental state, Flossie clucked at her sympathetically. "Now, darlin', I don't rightly know what you think of Lucas, but remember this is a small town. It doesn't pay to make enemies, you know."

Lacy wiped her eyes tiredly. "I've tried not to be enemies with anyone. *I've* done everything I can to move here and try to fit right in. But Lucas..." A wave of heat overcame her that could only be interpreted in one way. "Forgive me, Mama, but I hate that man."

"Hate him?" Flossie asked nervously. "Maybe hate's too strong a word. Maybe you just dislike him a little."

"No," Lacy said, standing up. "I hate him."

Hated him, and liked him too much for her own good.

Lacy was bone weary by the time dinner was over. She must have looked beat, because Jacob offered to do the dishes for her.

Was there ever a boy more considerate? Lacy didn't know much about boys—there certainly hadn't been many of *those* around Our Lady of Perpetual Mercy—but she decided then and there that if she did have a child someday, and if it was a boy, she would want him to be just like Jacob.

She refused to let her anger at the father spill over to the son. Lucas might be her mortal enemy—not to mention a big pain in the neck—but Jacob was another matter entirely. He was bright and reasonable, so much so that she almost forgot sometimes that he was still a boy.

He was also a very willing and able helper, methodical and quiet. The chore went quickly. "You're very handy in the kitchen, Jacob," she told him.

"I help a lot back at the Rooster."

"Do you consider the Rooster your home?"

"I guess this is my home now," he said. "But it feels sort of strange. I haven't ever lived in a house with ladies in it before. I never knew my ma."

"I'm sorry."

He didn't comment on that, but he didn't have to. His expression was unbearably sad. "You're lucky, Lacy. You've got the best mama in the world."

Lacy dropped a cup into the water.

"Everybody loves Flossie." He smiled. "When I was younger, I used to wish sometimes she was my mama—you know, when all the other boys at school would talk about their homes."

Her throat felt dry. "I see."

Jacob shook his head gravely. "Pa won't talk about my mama. I guess maybe it makes him too sad. It must have been harder for him, see. I would have been just a baby."

Lacy fought the tightening sensation in her chest, the familiar rush of her pulse. But it was a losing battle. Poor Lucas! How long had he been carrying this pain about his late wife around with him? Perhaps there was more in his animosity toward her than simply, well, animosity.

"I wish I *could* remember her," Jacob said. "I've always wondered if she was pretty. Do you think that's silly, caring about something like that?"

"No."

"Well, *I* reckon it is. 'Cause of course it wouldn't make any difference to me whether she was pretty or not, if we were a family."

"Jacob!"

Jacob and Lacy whirled in surprise at the sound of Lucas's gruff voice. Lacy saw the thunderous look on his face and felt her heart sink. What was he in a swivet about now?

"I need to talk to Lacy," he told Jacob. "Alone."

"Yes sir," Jacob said, folding his drying towel. Lacy took it from him with a silent thank-you, and she felt encouraged by the smile he sent her before he scooted out of the room. Her last confrontation with Lucas hadn't gone so well, because she had gotten overly emotional. But she wasn't going to do that this time.

When Jacob was out of earshot, she squared her shoulders and turned on Lucas. He hulked before her, dark and imposing, but she refused to be bowed. "Before you start lecturing me about putting your son to work, Lucas, I'll have you know that he was kind enough to volunteer.''

"I don't care about that.''

"Then what were you barking at me for?''

"Because I don't like you spying on me.''

Her mouth dropped open. "I wasn't spying.''

A bitter laugh cracked through the air. "I was standing right here. I heard you pumping him for information about his mother.''

She felt like tossing the wet towel in his face. Was there ever a man so provoking? "Then you eavesdropped just long enough to hear wrong, Lucas. He wanted to talk about his mother, and I was willing to listen. Something that you apparently aren't, I might add.''

He recoiled as if she *had* tossed the towel, which gave her an inordinate amount of satisfaction. "I have good reason for not wanting to talk about her.''

The very real pain in his expression made Lacy feel some contrition. However insufferable Lucas was, he had obviously been through a terrible loss. Maybe that even explained a little of his touchiness toward her. "I realize it must be difficult to be a widower—''

"I wouldn't know about that,'' he interrupted.

She stared at him, uncomprehending. "But Jacob said…''

"He doesn't know,'' he answered in a gruff, tight voice. "I've never told him the truth. His mother is still alive.''

Chapter Ten

Damn, he hated talking about Alice.

But as always, watching Lacy's face contort in confusion was almost worth the trouble she cost him. "Still alive?"

"You have this habit of never believing me the first time I say something," he observed. "The way you make me repeat myself all the time, anyone would think you didn't trust my word."

Her gaze narrowed. "Where is she?"

"I don't know."

"You don't know!"

His attempt at a chuckle came out as a dry, nervous rasp. "There you go again."

Her blue eyes searched his face in disbelief. "But you must have some idea...unless you're purposefully keeping Jacob from her."

Naturally she would leap to the assumption that he had stashed her away somewhere. "Believe it or not, Lacy, the former Mrs. Burns has no interest in her son. Never did have, even before he was born."

"That's not possible," Lacy said.

"Oh, it's very possible, I assure you. In fact, if it weren't for the fact that she was waiting for the blessed event of Jacob's birth, I believe Alice would have left me many months earlier. Ours was a youthful, hasty love match, you see. And if there's one thing you can depend on, it's that love doesn't last. Especially when the man barely makes enough money to keep a roof over their heads.''

"But you're very successful," Lacy said.

"You're speaking of now. Back then I was just a farmer, like my parents were before me. And Alice's folks were even worse off than we were. When we first married I was trying to scrape by as a sharecropper, but a drought came and times were hard. And we weren't exactly living high to begin with.''

He was surprised at how vulnerable just talking about Alice made him feel; yet, at the same time, he also felt a sense of release, as if the story was just gushing out of him. He hadn't really discussed the matter with anyone since…well, since forever, really. The few people who had tried to approach him in the months between when Alice had left him and when he had left to start a new life somewhere—anywhere—else, he had met with defensive hostility. They might as well have been poking a bear with a stick. Offers of help, he had spurned. Sympathy wasn't something he'd ever sought. Instead, he'd wanted nothing so much as to crawl off into a cave and hide, like a wounded animal.

Blissful had been his cave.

"I suppose Alice had wanted to get away from home about as much as she wanted to get married. Anyway, love died about halfway through our first dry summer together. We never had a second one.''

Lacy's smooth brow crinkled. "What happened to your…to Alice?"

"After Jacob was born, I knew she was unhappy. I didn't know how unhappy until the day I got a note saying she'd left for Denver with a traveling pill peddler.''

Lacy looked flabbergasted. "And you never heard from her again?"

"Sure I did. When she decided she wanted to marry again, she tracked me down in order to get a divorce.''

"The pill peddler?"

"No, someone else. Richer than the pill peddler, I imagine.

I never saw her again, though. Just dealt with a lawyer, which was fine with me.''

Lacy's mouth formed a round O and she sank down onto a chair by the table. "That's terrible."

The immediate gratification of blabbing out his problems didn't last long, Lucas found. Having Lacy of all people eyeing him with that expression that he hadn't seen in so many years pierced him to the bone. Pity gave him no solace. It just made the past feel raw and exposed. The tenderness in her eyes made him want to crawl out of his skin…or else crawl into her arms and bury his face in that stream of golden hair. He could almost inhale its clean, flowery scent from across the room. Some unseen force seemed to tug him toward her, though he resisted mightily.

As soon as she spoke, however, the tug released, like a taut rope split by shears.

"Why, it's no wonder you're so wrongheaded about things!" she exclaimed.

They were hardly the words of sympathy he'd been expecting. Lucas had to brace himself from stumbling backward. "What?"

Her thin shoulders lifted and her dark lashes swept innocently over those blue eyes. "After all, it's only natural that you'd come away from an experience like that an embittered cynical shell of a man."

"Who says I'm embittered?" A laugh escaped him. A bitter laugh, unfortunately. "If I had been a little older, or a little wiser, I would have realized that Alice was too immature to settle down. Too immature, and too unhappy."

She tilted a doubtful gaze at him. "So you've forgiven her, but intend to be suspicious of the female sex forever after."

"I'm just realistic. I don't get all starry-eyed over women and love, and the idea of home and hearth." God, he hated it when people picked apart his motives. And he didn't like the way having a heart-to-heart talk with Lacy was affecting him. Where Lacy was concerned, he was much more comfortable with argument than discussion. Luckily, in the past month he had become an expert at fostering arguments with her.

"So don't start getting ideas about me," he told her, knowing exactly how she would react to the directive.

Her chin snapped up. "I beg your pardon?"

He chuckled, already feeling much more relaxed. "Oh, I know how you women work. You think you can save us from the torment of bachelorhood."

She gulped and steamed until she was ready to blow. "I have no interest in saving you—from anything! And take my word—that includes flooding rivers and burning buildings!"

He smiled and tilted his head. "So why were you interrogating my son for personal information?"

"For the last time, I *wasn't!* He *volunteered* the information, Lucas. He seemed to want to talk about her—and no wonder! You've told the poor boy so little that he doesn't even know whether she's alive or dead."

"He never cared about it before you came poking around."

"Yes he did. Land's sake, the boy is eleven, not two. You have to know that he's been thinking about these things."

"Are you an expert?"

"On this subject, yes!" She squared her shoulders and blurted, "Do you think I haven't wondered where my father is?"

At the uncomfortable question, he shifted from one leg to the other.

Her face paled. "The sisters always referred to Mama as a widow. When I was a girl, Mama told me my father was a soldier. She said he had died a hero during the war. But now I'm not sure…." She sighed. "So, yes, I am sure Jacob wonders about his mother. It's only natural. Only you're probably too wrapped up in your petty concerns to see his very real ones."

Lucas felt that roaring in his ears that always seemed to come when he'd been around Lacy for too long. How could it be that one woman could irritate him so? But now…. Even when he thought he had girded himself for an encounter, she always seemed to assault him from some new direction, taking him completely unawares.

But this was too much. Criticizing him for not caring enough about Jacob was going too far. "I don't need a nineteen-year-old girl telling me how to deal with my family," he said in a voice as rough as sandpaper. "That's one sphere where I refuse to put up with your meddling."

"I wasn't meddling," she argued hotly.

"Yes you were."

"I only mentioned it because I care about y—" Her words broke off, and she suddenly looked so tense it seemed like her jaw would crack. Her face went scarlet. "I—I care about Jacob."

Lucas couldn't move. He could barely breathe. That wasn't what she had meant to say; her correction didn't fool either of them.

Their gazes were locked. It was agony, but in that moment he felt the need to keep looking at her, to commit every inch of that face to memory. Because God knows he knew he'd be remembering it often enough in the hours ahead.

Cared about him? Lacy? How could that be?

Not long ago she'd been shouting at him like a madwoman about how he was nothing but a problem to her. Could her feelings really have turned on a dime this way?

More perplexingly still, how could he feel this discomfort in his chest, like his heart were hopping up and down and screaming for attention, when every instinct told him that Lacy was the last woman in the world he wanted in his life. She was one hundred pounds of irritation. She was a do-gooder, and as much of a hothead in her own annoying way as he was. Moreover, she was just a kid. Nearly as young as Alice had been.

At that unpleasant comparison, he finally turned and headed out the back door. He had walked clear across the yard before he thought to stop and even question where he was going. He saw the lights across town and fled toward the sanctuary of the Rooster, even as his thoughts were telling him to go back to the boardinghouse and take Lacy in his arms.

Jacob found him later, as he was coming back from the Rooster. Lucas almost didn't see him, it was so dark out. "What are you doing up at this time of morning?" he asked.

When Lucas saw the anxious look on his son's face, and remembered the sharp way he had spoken to him, he felt a deep stab of regret. For so many things. His confrontation with Lacy had stirred up his thoughts. Convictions that before had seemed so firmly set now floated uneasily in his mind.

"I couldn't sleep," Jacob said. "I hope I didn't get Lacy in trouble. I didn't mean to."

Lucas chuckled and put an arm around his son's shoulder. "No, you didn't. But this isn't school, you know. Lacy's an adult—and believe me, she can more than take care of herself."

"You mean like when she hit you?"

Lucas's footsteps froze. "How did you find out about that?"

Jacob shrugged. "I didn't believe that story you were telling at breakfast about falling down the back steps."

Lucas was glad it was dark so his son couldn't see his face go red. Who else hadn't believed him? Or maybe Myrtle had blabbed Lacy's story about fighting for her honor.

"Why don't you like Lacy, Pa?"

"Well…" He swallowed, remembering the look on Lacy's face when she'd nearly said she cared about him. Or when she was listening to him talk about Alice.

Not like her? That wasn't the truth at all. Not now. But how, after all this time, could he change his story? His mouth didn't even seem capable of forming the right words. He wasn't entirely certain what the right words would even be. His feelings were swinging like a pendulum, from hate one moment to its opposite the next.

He cringed when he thought about how he had snapped at her, too, when all she had done was try to help him. She had opened her heart up to him about her own father in order to set him straight. That couldn't have been easy—not if the emotion in her eyes was any indication.

"She's always real nice to me," Jacob said, impatient for his answer. "Maybe I wouldn't like her so much if she'd hit me, but I can't figure why she ever would." He ducked his head. "And anyway, I was sort of hoping that you would like her."

Lucas narrowed his eyes on his son. "Why?"

Jacob shrugged. "Just because. She's real pretty, don't you think?"

Lucas nodded slowly.

"Well, I was thinking that if you liked her, you could…" His words broke off. After a moment's hesitation, he blurted, "After all, Jasper Mayhew's father got married again. Lots of men do."

Lacy had shaken him up so thoroughly tonight that for a moment Lucas's imagination seized on the suggestion. For a startling split second, he thought about a cozy little home with curtains and Lacy in his bed every night. And he was mostly drawn to the bed part, not the curtains. A frustrated heat built up in him at the thought….

And then he recovered some sense. This was *Lacy*. The woman who was whacking him with her fist one night, then telling him she cared about him the next. Or almost telling him. The truth was, even if she did care about him, she didn't look all that happy about it.

And there was Jacob, with that hopeful glint in his young eyes. He wanted a mother, and he didn't even know he already had one.

Lucas let out a long, tired breath. He already had problems aplenty, and now he sensed another one spinning on the horizon, like a whirlwind that would soon be a house-flattening tornado. Maybe Lacy was right about telling the truth—much as it galled him to admit it.

"Jacob, I guess I haven't been fair to you."

Jacob looked astounded. "How?"

Where to begin? Lucas felt as if there was a rock sitting in his chest. He led Jacob over to the front porch of the boardinghouse, and they sat down.

"I want to tell you what happened before you and I came to Blissful," he said.

And then he took another deep breath, and began trying to shore up the damage that a decade of silence could do.

As Lacy finished icing the cake she would be taking to Neesa's the next day, Flossie bustled in. "Oh, how nice! Looks good enough to eat." Then she laughed breezily. "But I guess that's the whole point, isn't it?"

Lacy smiled. She had been alone in the kitchen, but acutely aware of the silence in the house after dinner. Her ear had been especially attuned to the sound of a certain male voice that she had not heard in some time. Where was everyone?

Where, she couldn't help thinking, was Lucas?

Flossie rattled around the kitchen, gathering glasses on a tray for refreshments.

"Let me help you with those, Mama," Lacy said quickly.

Flossie held fast to her tray. "No, darlin', you just go on with what you were doing. I can take care of the other folks."

"But I'm practically finished here."

"No, I insist," Flossie said. "You do too much for me. I should help out with these boarders more."

Lacy tilted her head suspiciously. Usually Flossie would simply let the boarders have the run of the place. At all hours Birdie or Jacob might stumble into the kitchen searching for a glass of milk, or something else they needed. It wasn't her mother's way to wait on them hand and foot. But from the way she was acting now, it seemed that she not only wanted to keep the boarders out of the kitchen, she wanted to keep Lacy *in* it.

"Is something wrong, Mama?"

"No, no! Just trying to do my part." She frowned, distracted. "Where'd that pesky sugar bowl get itself off to?"

Lacy turned, retrieved it from the counter—exactly where

it had been kept since she had returned home—and placed it on Flossie's tray. She was now certain her mother wasn't so much distracted as wanting to appear so. Something was wrong. "Where are the others?"

"I've herded them onto the porch, to keep them out of your way."

Lacy laughed at the idea of the boarders being rustled about like cattle, with Flossie as their unlikely wrangler. "I'll join you all as soon as I have this dish cleaned," she said, nodding toward the icing bowl.

Flossie shook her head frantically. "You just take your time."

Lacy was no longer laughing. What was happening on the porch? "Mama, what is going on? You act as if you don't want me near anyone. Is something the matter?"

"Oh, no! I just..." Obviously uncomfortable with fibbing, Flossie's eyes filled with confusion and then blank panic. Her words died, and her shoulders rounded in defeat. "Oh, honey, forgive me. I was just trying to spare you."

Worry darted in her breast. "Spare me?"

"Lucas is back from the Rooster. He's sitting with Jacob on the porch."

Lacy was hard-pressed not to react to Lucas's name. She turned and shrugged with feigned nonchalance. She felt as hot and fluttery as she had when she had last locked gazes with Lucas. "Is that any reason I should stay cooped up in the kitchen?"

"I was just trying to make it easier for you to avoid him, that's all," Flossie said. "Ever since you two had your dust-up—or whatever it was—I've felt so guilty, Lacy. I can't tell you."

"Guilty? Why?"

Flossie really did look distressed. Of course, her appearance could have had something to do with the sickly green dress she was dutifully wearing, another victim of the dye vat. "Lucas has been a friend of mine since he moved here, but he always seemed a little lonely to me. I was so happy when he came to live at the boardinghouse—I didn't really take your dislike of him into account. I thought you just didn't know him. But if he's been pestering you..."

Lacy blushed deeply. Not because she was remembering the moments she had spent in Lucas's arms, or even the many fights they'd had. Because she remembered now, as she had been recalling all day, his face last night as he had been talking about his wife. Alice. There had been real feeling in his voice. All his bluster and cock-on-the-fencepost posturing had fallen away from him in those minutes, and she had seen for the first time a real human being. A man with real emotions.

To have been abandoned, so young... Was it any wonder he was so defensive all the time?

She blushed because in those moments since her perception of Lucas Burns had changed substantially. Worse, she had nearly blurted out as much.

"I should have seen that you hated him from the start," Flossie said.

"I don't hate him." The words, so hard to admit, came out stiffly.

"Oh, darlin', you're so good you probably don't like to admit to hating anybody."

"I don't hate him."

Flossie fluttered over and gave her a quick hug. "I know you're saying that just for my sake. Or maybe you're afraid if he moved out we wouldn't have money enough to live on."

"Mama, I swear to you—"

Her mother raised her hand to stop her. "I know, I know, it's me that's got us into this pickle. And from now on, if Lucas Burns is livin' here, it's me that'll deal with him. I'll even switch rooms with you if you want."

Lacy stamped her foot in frustration. How could she convince her mother that her views had changed? He was, after all, the same man she had been battling since her arrival in Blissful. The same irritant in boots who had seemed to devil her every waking moment. She herself wasn't sure how permanently her own feelings had changed. Just because she had discovered that he had a heart...

"That won't be necessary," she said.

"Sure?" Flossie asked, concerned.

Lacy nodded. "I am sure I can manage Lucas better in the future."

She just needed to keep a tight lid on all these unfamiliar emotions whirling about inside her.

"What's going to bring people to this thing isn't the selling, it's the dancing."

Bodine and Lacy sat on the edge of the structure going up in the dead center of town. It was positioned in front of Bean's store, about equal distance between the Rooster and the boardinghouse. Harper had been working day and night on his pavilion since the lumber had arrived from San Antonio a few days before. The floor had been put down, though there was still no roof. Everyone was pitching in to get the structure built in time for the first Blissful Day, which was fast approaching. The committee pooled their money to buy the lumber, and Harry and Myrtle were donating paint.

Myrtle had only agreed to give money for the pavilion project when it was promised there would be a plaque put on the pavilion at a later date, with her name prominently displayed beneath the town motto. Not that the town actually had a motto. Myrtle had directed everyone in the women's society to try to think of one. It was the latest bee in her bonnet.

With just a little over a week to go, the pavilion wasn't the only outward sign of change in town, either. George Oatley had whitewashed his lean-to in front of the blacksmith shop, and Harry had gotten himself a new sign. Hardy flowers were being planted in strategic areas with little traffic.

Today Bodine had borrowed George's livery wagon and he and Lacy were going to take signs around to neighboring towns that very afternoon to advertise the event. Not that it needed much advertising. According to the cowboys who came to the Rooster, Blissful Day was the talk of the countryside. And everyone was buzzing about Harper's pavilion. No town around here had anything like it.

"You all need to emphasize the dance more on those signs," Harper told them. "Folks are always drawn to a get-together if there's a little dancing involved."

At the mention of dancing, Lacy's heart skittered in her chest. She had been trying not to focus on this problem. Get up and dance in front of people? She had never done that before!

"Good lord, Lacy," Harper said, looking at her sharply. He put down his hammer. "What's the matter with you? You look redder than the old maid who was listening to the sea captain's parrot."

She lifted her shoulders, trying to exude a calmness she certainly didn't feel. "Nothing."

Bodine looked anxious. "Did we say something to upset you?"

"No…"

Harper laughed. "Something's snapped your garters. Now what is it?"

"Well… It's just all this talk about dancing. We just never did that at Our Lady of Perpetual Mercy. A few girls showed me some steps once…."

Bodine laughed. "Well, is that all?"

Before she knew what was what, he had pulled her into a loose embrace and was showing her an easy two-step. Easy or not, Lacy unceremoniously stomped on Bodine's feet more than once. It was a good thing he was wearing thick boots.

Their lesson quickly drew a crowd. A few men from the Rooster ambled over, including Lucas. Lacy's embarrassment quadrupled.

"Hold her closer!" George heckled Bodine. "Can't dance with a girl when she's practically standing in the next state."

Bodine whirled her awkwardly and she found herself facing Lucas. Thanks to her mother's valiant efforts, she had barely laid eyes on the man for nearly a week, apart from supper. An electric shock passed through her body. He wasn't laughing.

He wasn't even smiling. In that moment, the eyes beneath that dark slashing brow were focussed on her with an intensity that looked like longing.

She swallowed, and suddenly it felt as if her limbs were leaden. She stepped heavily away from Bodine.

"Better show her the polka, Bodine," Harper called gloomily as he measured a board. "God knows Otto and Jan won't play anything else."

Boot Withers was hanging back farther than the others, sucking on an old cheroot. "Anybody can polka."

"Not properly," Harper said.

"Heck, you just jump around. Like this." Holding an imaginary partner, Boot hummed a tuneless ditty and unrhythmically bounded around in the dirt.

His effort drew frowns, especially from George. "You look like a flea, Boot. You don't have to bounce two feet up in the air, you know. You just sort of hop-step-hop—"

Soon, six different men were embracing air and leaping about to nonexistent music. Even Bodine was caught up in the polka debate, and jumped to the ground so that he could join the others.

Harper, leaning against a railing, winked at Lacy. "These boys would evidently rather dance with air than a real woman."

"Not me," Lucas said, leaping onto the raw cedar dance floor. He pulled a stunned Lacy into his arms, holding her close, so that they seemed to be touching all over. Her whole body felt frozen, but the moment Lucas moved, she was right with him, following his steps as if they were somehow instinctive. His dark eyes drilled into her gaze, and though their movements were breakneck, it was the world that seemed to spin breathlessly around them. She wanted to look down at her feet, to make sure she wasn't about to be whisked off the earth entirely. Yet she couldn't drag her gaze away from Lucas.

She couldn't believe she was standing in his arms, in public, for all of Blissful to see. Just days ago she had fretted that she would never live down the gossip about the incident on the porch swing. And now she was whirling in his arms as if she had been born to be in them.

Because, heaven help her, that is exactly how it felt. Even though Lucas topped her height by at least a foot, their bodies seemed to mesh perfectly, seemed to move in perfect harmony. She wasn't stepping on *his* toes. And when he smiled at her, it felt as if that smile leapt to her own lips. The joyful whoop she emitted was surely conjured by Lucas, too—it couldn't have come from her.

When their dance whirled to an end, she felt flushed and exhilarated. Lucas was smiling at her and she was positively beaming.

It took a moment for the peculiar silence around them to sink in. She had to wait for the pounding of her own blood rushing in her ears to subside before she realized that no one was humming anymore. Men weren't dancing with invisible partners. Lacy blinked back at the curious stares aimed at her and Lucas from everyone around them, and a flush crept through her body. One moment the atmosphere had been buoyant and merry, and the next it was suffused with tension. This was the hardest the men had looked at her since she had chained herself to the Rooster.

Boot Withers spat, causing several others to shuffle uncomfortably.

Bodine stepped up and took her arm protectively. "Ready, Lacy?"

Her throat felt so tight she could barely form words. Especially when she saw Lucas's sharp eyes hone in on Bodine's hand on her arm. He *was* jealous.

Confusion flurried in her mind. How could that be? He disliked her so. He just wanted to get rid of her.

Bodine handed her up to the seat of the wagon and then climbed on with her. He clucked at the horse and as they pulled through town, Lacy had to try mightily not to twist around to look back at Lucas.

"I'm sorry that happened," Bodine said to her. "Lucas can be so unpredictable."

She swallowed. "He's part lunatic, I think."

Bodine chuckled. "You look flushed. Are you all right?"

"I guess I'm not used to dancing."

He nodded. "Dancing can make a body a little dizzy, I guess."

Lacy closed her eyes and visualized Lucas's dark eyes. As she did so, she could practically feel his strong arms supporting her. A temporary madness swept over her. She had to stifle the impulse to jump off the wagon and sprint all the way back to town—back to Lucas. She couldn't blame *that* on dancing.

"Can I get you some tea, Birdie?"

Birdie jumped at the unexpected question. "No thank you," she replied in a breathy voice. "I was just going upstairs. I wanted to go to bed earlier, but there's such a racket up in the attic…"

Lacy frowned. "In the attic?"

Birdie couldn't look her in the eye. "I believe there's a dice game transpiring up there."

So that's where everyone had disappeared to! Lacy crossed her arms and glared up at the ceiling as if she could see right through the plaster.

"I don't like to complain," Birdie said in the trembly, reedy voice she always used to complain. "Heaven knows I told my dear brother that I didn't want to be any trouble. I realize that others might not hold the same opinion of games of chance—and other things—that I do. But when I see a nice man like Harper Cooley going to the dogs…well, I have a hard time holding my tongue!"

"What's happened to Harper?"

Birdie pivoted around anxiously before leaning in toward Lacy in confidence. "I saw him go up there. With your mama and that *Lucas Burns.*"

The distaste Birdie used to say Lucas's name was so pronounced, Lacy had difficulty keeping a straight face. But then mere weeks before she had also spat the man's name like a curse. What had changed? Not Lucas. She was fairly certain he was what he had always been. He didn't appear to be a man who would change himself to suit a woman.

Which meant that *she* had changed. She harbored feelings for him that couldn't be accounted for in rational terms. When Lacy looked into his eyes, she felt a longing she didn't understand. Something swelled in her chest when she thought of him, which didn't happen when she thought of, say, Bodine. Lucas was on her mind incessantly. Though frankly her thoughts about the man never progressed far beyond those few tawdry moments on the porch swing, or their wild dance in the pavilion—moments she'd turned over and over until they were threadbare.

She couldn't say what it was about Lucas that caused this feverish, achy feeling inside her. She just knew that she'd never been more restless in her life.

"I always thought Harper Cooley was such a nice man—" Birdie droned on sadly "—despite the fact that he worked here."

"He *is* nice!" Lacy replied so snappishly that Birdie actually jerked back in her chair and nearly stabbed herself with her embroidery needle. Did Birdie think there was actually some taint that rubbed off on someone just from being around a saloonkeeper and an ex-madam?

Well, actually, *she'd* thought that at one time, too.

She shifted in her seat, flustered. "I'm sorry, Birdie."

Birdie bolted up stiffly, gathering her embroidery to her chest. "I think I'll retire now. I'm sure I have some cotton wool to block out the noise."

Lacy had to bite her tongue to keep herself from giving her detailed directions on where to stuff that cotton wool.

But then, when Birdie had flitted away, she sagged into her chair and felt a dull sting of loneliness. The problem was, she was at loose ends. She sighed and snuffed out the lamps. Jacob had gone to bed. Birdie had gone off to sulk and plug up her ears. Everyone else was throwing dice—not an activity she would ever partake of. And she noticed that she hadn't been asked to, either. They had even sneaked up to the attic, like naughty children hiding from a schoolmarm.

Lacy supposed there was nothing left for her to do but go to bed, too.

She paused as she passed the staircase. She tilted her head, but could hear none of the racket Birdie had been complaining about. She went up a few steps and listened again, but she still didn't detect any noise. In fact, she was all the way to the small attic stairs before she even heard the animated voice of Flossie carrying through the wall. Forgetting that she had intended to retire to her room for the night, Lacy climbed the narrow staircase. It felt as if an invisible cable were attached to her, tugging her toward the attic.

Toward Lucas.

In the long, narrow room, lit by a single candle on a crate, Flossie and Harper sat at an old low table playing chuck-a-luck. Flossie's face was full of color, and Harper was laughing while Lucas looked on.

The three glanced up as one when Lacy appeared. Flossie greeted her with her usual enthusiasm and seemed so absorbed in the game that she didn't bother to hide what she was doing, or apologize for it. And Lacy, for once, didn't want her to. A week ago, she might have given her mother a lecture on games of chance, but now she didn't have the heart. Flossie looked like she was having fun.

"You want to play a round?" Flossie asked.

"No thank you," Lacy said, perching on the edge of a shaky ottoman.

"Snake eyes!" Harper said, chuckling gleefully.

Lacy tried to keep her eyes focussed on the game, but she felt a tug of awareness drawing her gaze toward Lucas. Sure enough, when she glanced over his dark eyes were aimed straight at her, just as they had been through dinner. Ever since their dance, the air between them had seemed electric.

"You've made good progress up here," he said.

She and Flossie had been trying to clear out old things and

make it another bedroom. They had mopped and tidied, but the creaky old bed with the yellowed mattress cover in the corner and the mishmash of old furniture pieces stacked about looked less than welcoming. There was other clutter, too—wobbly chairs and a dusty wardrobe full of cast-off clothes. A resting place for empty jars and bottles stood in one corner, and nearby was a steamer trunk full of odds and ends she couldn't convince Flossie to part with. "We've got a ways to go yet."

A smile tugged at his lips and her gaze was drawn to his mouth. Her skin felt feverish, her throat dry. *What was happening to her?*

"Are you all right?" her mother asked worriedly. "You look a little woozy, hon."

Lacy spoke, though her words cracked in her throat. "I suppose it's the heat." It was true; she felt hot all over.

For a few moments, the only sound in the room was that of Harper and Flossie shaking the dice in their hands and flinging them across the tabletop. Then, once Harper had won, Flossie tossed up her hands. "You old coot! I've a hunch those dice are loaded."

Harper grinned at her as he stowed his lucky ivories in his pocket. "You just don't have the touch, my dear."

Something about the way Harper said "my dear" to her mother made Lacy snap out of her daze and turn her attention to the older pair. Something was different tonight. It took her a moment to figure out what it was.

Oh, yes. They weren't sniping at each other with quite their usual vigor.

"Maybe we should take advantage of the moonlight tonight," Harper suggested.

"What for?" Flossie asked.

"Perambulation."

Flossie blinked at him. "Huh?"

"A moonlit walk, Floss," Lucas translated for her.

Flossie bit her lip and fixed an affectionately suspicious

gaze on Harper. "And what do you intend to do out there in the moonlight?"

"Talk your ear off, I reckon," Lucas said. "That's what he does most of the time."

Laughing, Flossie relented. "I guess a walk would do me good." She stood and dusted off her skirt. "Anyways, it's bound to be cooler out there than it is in here."

That was the truth. The room had a torrid stillness that Lacy felt the sudden urge to escape. She rose and started to follow them out, but Lucas stopped her with a light touch to her arm.

Her gaze jumped nervously to his eyes. No matter how light his hold was on her, the touch felt searing. "We should go, too," she said.

He smiled down at her—and not that ferocious grin she was so accustomed to. This smile had a hint of sincerity in it. Of warmth.

"You have my arm," she told him.

"I know."

Her stomach gave an uncomfortable flutter. "I think I might catch up with Mama."

"That's one of the reasons I have your arm." When she looked at him questioningly, he explained, "To give the old folks a head start."

"To get me alone is probably more like it," she blurted out.

"*That* was the other reason. Though to my credit, I mostly wanted to give the others a little solitude."

Understanding dawned, and her mouth parted in wonder. "You mean Mama…and Mr. Cooley…"

Lucas chuckled. "No one's more surprised than me. First I thought the man was just lured over here by the food, and then I thought it was *you.*"

That news startled her. "Me?"

"Well, you are younger than Flossie—and prettier, if you don't mind my saying so."

Her heart slammed against her ribs. That sounded almost like a real compliment—and he wasn't following it up with a lecture about all the things that were wrong with her, either. Such a rush went through her that she felt light-headed. This was what it must be like to be tipsy, she thought.

"I should go," she said, pulling herself free. To her surprise, and slight disappointment, he released her.

"To be their chaperone? I think Flossie can take care of herself. Besides, I'm sure Harper has nothing but honorable intentions."

"Oh." She tried to steady her breath. "Then I suppose there's nothing wrong with that if they…"

Her words petered out. She looked up at Lucas and willed herself to stop thinking about the porch swing, dancing, or how his lips felt against hers. Her mother might be safe with Harper; she, however, was in a more precarious position. One look into Lucas's eyes was enough for her to know that *his* intentions weren't honorable.

Worse, she didn't want them to be. Oh, she tried to grab hold of her senses. In her head, voices screamed for her to flee down the stairs just as fast as her legs could carry her. She tried to call up the stern faces of Sister Mary Katherine and Myrtle Bean and Neesa Hart, but they merely flashed before her eyes and then melted to a blur. Her heart was beating frantically, yet she remained unable to move a muscle.

"Harper and Flossie seem to be taking it slow," he said, his gaze burning into hers.

They were standing so close. Lacy felt as awkward as a novice on the stage—all jangling nerves and trembling. She didn't know what to do with her hands or her feet. "It's good that Mama can show such—" she swallowed with effort "—restraint."

"Mmm," he replied, between a grunt and a growl.

"It's so much better to…" A glint in his gaze sent a shiver through her. "…to take things…"

He stepped forward, so close that they were just a whisper apart. "Slow."

He brushed against her lightly.

"Yes." The heat of him, that male scent, overwhelmed her

senses and sent a shiver through her spine. She put her hands against his chest, and that simple contact was enough to make her feel as if she just might melt against him. She saw his head dipping toward hers and gasped, more in anticipation than in surprise or fear. "Oh, Lucas!" She looped her arms around his neck.

"Oh, hell!" he growled back, with such urgency she knew that he was as lost as she was. The way he expelled his breath was like the last shred of his inner resistance snapping. Like a dam bursting after gallantly resisting a torrential onslaught.

His mouth came down hard on hers—not that she was complaining. They feasted on each other's lips like two starving people. She pulled herself as close to him as humanly possible, reveling in the solidity of his body, the strength of him. Her movements were greedy and a little impatient. She immediately wanted him to do what he had done before, on the porch swing.

Without her saying a word, he sensed it. It was as if her thoughts had passed to his hands, and with no logical method, he tugged at buttons and unfastened hooks and yanked at laces. Urgency prevailed. By the time his hand touched one breast, Lacy was already breathless. She let out a moan and buried her face in the crook of his neck as he worked a kind of alchemy. The scent of him—a combination of whiskey and tobacco and sweat—was like an opiate, making her feel energized and torpid at once. She nuzzled the skin there and then flicked her tongue to sample the salty taste of him. He groaned, then sank down to his knees.

Lacy, still on her feet, was momentarily mystified. What was he doing? She gaped down at the crown of his head in confusion as he clawed more at her stays until her breasts were completely freed from the confines of the corset. *Oh heavens, was he going to…?*

As his mouth devoured one tight aching bud, her back arched. She moaned in a voice that she had never heard before, barely recognized as her own. She would have collapsed if his hands hadn't been firmly holding the backs of her thighs through her bunched skirts. She had never imagined that a man would do this—never imagined anything could be so pleasurable. Her hands massaged his hair, which managed to be both coarse and soft. It was just another contradiction that drew her inexorably to him.

Everything about him, about what he was doing, seemed strange, foreign, and delectable. One hand reached beneath her skirts and skimmed up her leg, causing an earthquake inside her. But when the same hand pushed between her legs and touched the most sensitive flesh there, Lacy thought she might faint from the sensation that washed over her.

"Lucas," she whispered, half terrified.

"Shh…"

The protest died in her throat. As his ministrations grew more intense, so did the pleasure. Moment by moment, she relinquished a little more control, until she was thrashing against him, lost in the onslaught of pure sensation. After a few blinding moments of searing heat, she drooped against him, damp with sweat and utterly exhausted. She couldn't believe she was still just standing there, leaning against him, when seconds before it had felt as if she were being carried away to another world entirely.

Lucas rose slowly, holding her tight, and kissed her again. "So sweet…" he murmured.

He picked up her bone-limp body and crossed to the bed in a few economical steps. Heaven knows, her legs couldn't have held her another moment. Her insides were liquefied, molten. She gratefully allowed herself to be placed on the old thin mattress of the bed.

Lucas looked down at her with such heated desire in his eyes that she felt as if her whole body might catch flame. She seemed to bloom with heat as he lowered himself on top of her. She was still half dressed and so was he, but she could feel the tautness of Lucas's body through their clothes. Every muscle seemed tensed, as if a great power were harnessed within him. And that harness was about to snap.

He kissed her hungrily, and she felt flustered, hot, confused.

She'd assumed that it was all over. But as he pressed his body full against hers, there was no mistaking how he desired her.

She gasped, feeling his hardness. He let out a groan, reached down, and shucked his pants in a few quick moves. Before he came down on top of her again, he pushed up her skirt, massaging her again as he had before; the same madness built inside her again, only this time there was even more urgency in his movements. Fear and curiosity and need built inside her in equal measure, but when Lucas positioned himself on top of her, one look into that dark, burning gaze of his seared all doubt from her mind. Heaven help her, she wanted him so badly.

He entered her with one quick thrust; pain and heat flashed through her, bringing forth a cry that he swallowed with a kiss. She buried her head against his shoulder and clung to him as the pain subsided and was replaced by an undeniable need. She moved her hips, tentatively, and he responded with another thrust, and then another, until they were moving in some instinctive, primal rhythm. She gave in completely to the whirlwind of fire she was being sucked into, until the heat was so intense she felt almost senseless and cried out Lucas's name. He answered her cry, then took her to heights she never dreamed mere mortals could reach.

Chapter Eleven

He should have been kicking himself for what he'd done. He should have been running for the hills. Instead, Lucas didn't seem able to rouse himself from the bed, or from Lacy.

A million emotions rushed through him, none of them expected. Tenderness. Possessiveness. Shock.

But how shocked could he be? He had dreamed of Lacy Calhoun. He would have to be the world's most outrageous liar to pretend that the thought of bedding her hadn't crossed his mind about a thousand times since the infernal girl had stepped off the stage.

Had he actually thought he would? That was another question.

Only now it wasn't a question at all. It was a done deal. And he couldn't pretend that the deed had been done with any ulterior motive, with any devious design. It had just been pure impulsive desire. He'd wanted Lacy. Ever since their dance at the pavilion, it had seemed that their fate had been sealed. Lacy was a fever in his blood, and her appearance in the attic after dinner had seemed like an answered prayer. He hadn't been able to take his eyes off her.

But what had landed the fatal blow on his waning restraint had been the realization that she wanted him. *Really* wanted him. Her eyes had told him so. He had detected in those blue orbs an emotion he hadn't seen for a long, long time.

Maybe it had been a trick of the candlelight up here. The flickering glow cast deep shadows around the odd-shaped room. The roof that made the walls around them formed a sharp V up to the ceiling, giving it a tent-like feel. He looked down at Lacy, so beautiful lying next to him. Her skin looked as fine and delicate as porcelain. And her face, unguarded, was a different landscape entirely from the defensive, combative mask he usually saw there. She looked so peaceful and relaxed. Her hair swept over her cheek like a shimmering waterfall.

He was filled with awe at her beauty. And he was also filled with something else, a feeling he didn't recognize at first. Elation.

For so long he had muddled along, doing his business, raising his son. Maybe he had forgotten about what it felt like to simply be happy. But now, deep inside, he was almost giddy. Making love to Lacy had gone against every shred of reason. He might have heeded any number of alarms going off inside his head. But he hadn't, and now he felt...jubilant. If he weren't concerned about waking Lacy, he would have raised a shout, punched the air, or pulled her into his arms and swung her in a circle so that her feet never touched the ground.

He wished then that they were somewhere far away from Blissful, from prying eyes, from their own prejudices. Yet the very real world of the small town around them would intrude, probably sooner than later. There would have to be a reckoning.

He was gently brushing his hand through her corn-silk hair when her eyes swept open. At first sight of him, her lips tilted in a sensual little smile of memory. And then, as her senses slowly awakened, taking in the heavy air that smelled of sweat and sex, a transformation occurred. The brow that had been so childishly smooth and untroubled in sleep, pinched. The dreamy eyes cleared and widened. The mouth that had been crooked sexily dropped open.

She bolted up. "Lucas!" Her gaze honed in on his bare

chest—his bare everything—and she turned a painful-looking shade of crimson.

He grinned.

She criss-crossed her arms over her bared chest.

"It's a little late for that gesture," he pointed out.

Her cheeks flamed. "What time is it?"

"Don't worry. You just fell asleep for a few minutes. It happens sometimes after—" At the look of mortification in her eyes, he took pity on her and didn't say the word love-making aloud. That just might do her in. "Well, when you're tired."

She clasped her dress with one hand and lifted her other up to her cheek. There was no doubt that she was fully awake now. Awake and remembering every single moment that had occurred between them on this bed. "Oh, my!"

He chuckled. "That's just what I was thinking."

Tears sprang to her eyes, but to his surprise she didn't turn on him in a fury. Instead, her eyes pled for understanding. "Don't make fun of me. What am I going to do?"

He lifted his hand to her chin and tilted it upwards. "For one thing, you're not going to hang your head."

She came as close to hopping up and down as a person could while sitting down. "But I *should* hang my head! What I did—and with *you* of all people…"

A low hum started in her chest and grew in volume until a keening wail finally heaved out of her.

His lips twisted into a frown and he dropped his hand. The reckoning was coming more swiftly even than he had feared. He tried not to take offense; he knew what she was, and that she believed him to be an irredeemable rascal, no matter what else she might feel. He had anticipated the state she would be in when she awoke to cold reality and realized that she was a sensual woman and a fallible human being. But he still couldn't help the disappointment that stabbed at him.

"Let me guess," he said. "You're horrified by what you've done."

"Oh mercy, yes!"

"I'm everything you despise. You're worried what people will say."

"Yes!"

"In fact, you *know* what they will say." He looped his voice up into a matronly trill. "'How could a nice girl take up with a bad man like Lucas Burns?' Myrtle Bean will prattle on to anyone who will listen to her." His eyes widened in mock surprise. "Who knows but they might not even let you in those decency meetings anymore. Myrtle might just bar the door when she sees you coming."

At the prospect, Lacy half laughed, half writhed as if in agony.

He was tormenting her, he knew, but he couldn't help himself. "All you can hope is that no one finds out...but then again, here we are right above Birdie's bedroom."

Lacy gasped.

"And this mattress squeaks, if you'll recall."

As if to demonstrate that unfortunate fact, she fell against the squeaky mattress with a moan. "I'm just ruined in this town!"

"Yes, but how do you think I feel?" he asked.

The question levitated her. She lifted up and searched his face in disbelief. *"You?"*

"Certainly," he said. "You're so concerned about your own reputation. I've got one, too. Have you spared a thought for what *my* friends are going to say?"

She stared at him long and hard before deciding he was joking. She laughed faintly.

Unfortunately, he wasn't joking. Not entirely. If news of this got out at the Rooster, he wasn't sure what he would have to say for himself. He had failed them. He had promised that he would get rid of the Calhoun menace, but he had only managed to fall prey to her as no one else in town had. How had that happened?

He looked over at her, sitting disheveled across the bed, lips still red from their kisses, and he didn't have to waste another thought on that question. How on earth could he have helped wanting her?

Would he want to do without her, even at the risk of all the badgering he was going to receive from the men at the Rooster? No sir. He could no more resist Lacy now than Adam could resist Eve after she had handed him that big juicy apple.

At the thought of pleasures ahead, defensiveness rose in him. Why should he have to justify his actions to anyone? Stranger things had happened than a man developing a yen for a beautiful woman. So he had gone from wanting to rid himself of Lacy to wanting to bed her. If the men at the saloon couldn't understand that...

He sighed. The men at the saloon would never understand that. "Maybe we shouldn't tell anyone about this just yet."

"*Just yet?* Must we ever?"

He scratched his chin. "Well...not if you don't want to."

"I don't!"

Again, he tried not to be offended. He knew where she was coming from. And he didn't particularly relish the idea of word about them spreading, either. Still, a man wanted to think that the woman he had just shared the most intimate experience in life with would feel proud to walk with him down the street, arm-in-arm.

On the other hand, maybe it would be better if they just eased the town into accepting their liaison. If it just seemed to happen without anyone noticing...

"All right," he said. "If you're so worried about your reputation, we can just keep this under our hats."

She sank back down with relief. "No reason why anyone *should* know. It was just one slip, after all."

He smiled. "Just one?"

She looked over at him. "Of course." Then, as she took in his expression, she swallowed. "Wasn't it?"

"That depends."

"On what?"

"On how you feel about this." He leaned over and touched his lips to hers, once again sampling the honeyed sweetnes of that mouth. She tasted like nectar, and her arms moved up to drape around him like it was the most natural thing in the world.

He looked down into her eyes. Clearly this wasn't over. Not by a long shot. "I want you. Right now I'm having a hard time imagining a day, even an hour, when I *won't* want you."

Temptation danced in her eyes, mixed with trepidation. He kissed her again, coaxing a response from her.

Then, to his eternal relief, she sent him a wicked little smile. "I can keep a secret if you can," she whispered.

"Lacy, honey, I've made up my mind."

As her mother barreled into the kitchen, Lacy flinched. And not just because she had been woolgathering about Lucas and would have been startled by any sound. All morning it seemed that she had been merely going through the motions of life while her mind was firmly fixed on what had happened twelve hours before, up in the attic. She should have been wild with regret; instead, it seemed as if she were lit from within. She might have been floating, she felt so weightless, so buoyant, so alive.

And yet at the same time, her mind was absorbed in this impossible, intriguing tangle. *Lucas?* Could he really have been the man who was so wonderfully tender? Who had made her say—and oh, heavens, *do*—all manner of things she had never dreamed of?

Flossie came to an eye-crossing stop right in front of her. "I want you to teach me to be good," she announced.

It was what Flossie was wearing that truly made her flinch. She had finally put on the brown dress Lacy had taken such pains to sew for her. It fit oddly, yet no one could say it was immodest. In fact, its high collar threatened to choke her. And the pattern of little blue flowers against the brown was not only sedate, but also slightly nauseating.

Lacy was too busy being appalled at being the creator of that wretched garment to respond to Flossie's statement, so

Flossie pulled out a chair and flopped down next to her. "I want to learn to be respectable and ladylike, like you."

"Like me," Lacy repeated dully.

You're one day too late.

Every time she recalled the sensuous feelings that had slammed through her at Lucas's touch, at the feel of his body against hers, in hers, she feared she might fall into a swoon. Yet, far from being ashamed by her brazen behavior, what was now uppermost in her mind was when she might be able to be alone again with Lucas. Which, to her way of thinking, put her in the back of the line of people who should be instructing others how to be good.

But of course she couldn't tell her mother what had gone on up in that attic. All those years she had worked—in her own way—to send Lacy to the convent...and look what happened! The minute Lacy got out she'd gone and fallen into the arms of the very man she swore she hated.

Flossie noticed her discomfort, but completely misinterpreted it. "I guess I can understand why you're surprised. Tell you the unvarnished truth, I wasn't wild about the idea of being ladylike when you first got here."

She tried to focus on her mother's words, but her thoughts strayed like mischievous children, and her mind harkened back to that first day she'd come to Blissful. She had been so naive, so sure of herself and her own goodness. And then her virtue had crumpled after a little over one month.

She didn't know what to say. She felt humbled. Before she had stepped foot off that stagecoach, everything had seemed so clear in her mind. There were good people, and there were bad people, and she placed herself firmly in the first category. But it turned out that she wasn't nearly so good as she thought she was, and the bad people were who she cared about most.

"I want the ladies at those meetings to stop looking at me funny," Flossie said.

Remembering the meeting that morning, the one that seemed to go on forever because she couldn't concentrate for thinking about Lucas, Lacy chuckled mirthlessly. "I thought they were looking at me."

Her mother's blue eyes widened. "You? Why would they look at you?"

Lacy had an easy answer for that. *Because I've changed.* To her own eyes when she looked in the mirror, the transformation was so obvious, so radical. Her cheeks were glowing, her eyes were glittering, and her whole body seemed to be strung to a different key. She had scarlet woman written all over her.

Yet the whole town—even her own mother—persisted in treating her the same as they always had. Perversely, their attitude made Lacy, who had awoken that morning expecting to be exposed, all the more edgy. Were they all blind?

"Of course, you *were* standing at the front of the room." Flossie frowned. "For a little while, at least. The way Myrtle bumped you aside so she could take over really got my goat."

"Myrtle is better at conducting meetings than I am."

"Nonsense. She's just more pushy, is all. And I for one wanted to smack her!" Flossie ducked her head and eyed Lacy sheepishly. "I guess that's not a very ladylike impulse, is it?"

Since she had belted Lucas in the face, and since the urge to smack Myrtle seemed to come over her every time she met that esteemed lady, Lacy could hardly throw stones.

"Can you do it?" Flossie asked.

Lacy frowned, surprised. "Hit Myrtle?"

Flossie cackled delightedly. "No, teach me to be ladylike! I tell you, I'm all afire to learn now."

Trying to concentrate on the matter at hand, Lacy gave her mother a closer look. Besides the plug-ugly brown dress, Flossie was wearing no jewelry but a demure cameo at her throat, and she had pulled her hair back a little more tidily this morning. There wasn't a trace of face paint on her, and the air was dull in its lack of perfume. Nevertheless, there was color in Flossie's cheeks, and her eyes were sparkling brilliantly. Even subdued, she could outshine anyone.

"What's brought on this sudden change of heart, Mama?"

She couldn't believe this shift in attitude had been entirely sparked by a sudden urge to please Myrtle Bean.

Flossie actually blushed. "Well...I didn't want to say anything, knowing how worried you are about appearances and such...but I got a beau." She vibrated with laughter. "Isn't that silly? Look at me, I'm acting like a schoolgirl."

Lacy smiled, remembering that walk she'd taken with Harper the night before. "Nothing silly about it at all. I might have known George Oatley would catch your eye someday."

Flossie's face fell, and then, after studying Lacy for a moment, she howled with glee. "As if I could fall for that red-faced fellow!" she hollered, clapping Lacy's arm so hard she nearly pushed her off the chair. "I swear, Lacy, I never knew you to tell such a joke." Suddenly, she sobered. "It *was* a joke, wasn't it?"

"Yes."

Flossie looked relieved. "I guess you know it's that old fool Harper Cooley who's caught my eye. Only he ain't such an old fool as I thought. The thing is though, it turns out he's real respectable. Or was. Can you believe that?"

"At this point, I'd believe anything."

"You know he told me that he was a real architect type back in Tennessee? He went to school and everything! Worked in Knoxville for years but then his fiancée died of consumption a week before they were to be married. The poor man nearly died of heartbreak, and lost all sense of purpose. So he came west, working all sorts of jobs till he got to my place. Funny a man could drift like that for years and then land right here on my doorstep, don't you think?"

Lacy thought about Lucas, saying he'd come to Blissful after Alice had left him. Harper wasn't the only man who had settled in this little town to hide from trouble. "No."

"Harper said it wasn't till you came to town and we opened the boardinghouse that he saw me as a real woman, not just a character." She laughed. "I guess before he just thought I was some old floozy. And I didn't think much better of him! Isn't that odd?"

Lacy nodded.

"Though I always did think there was a certain dignity in the way he dressed," Flossie said thoughtfully. "And I was right. Harper's from good people. That's why I gotta get respectable."

"But I think Harper likes you as you are now."

Flossie gaped at her as if she'd lost her last lick of sense. "*As I am?* A man like Harper?"

"But Mama, until just recently, Harper worked for you. You always referred to him as an old coot. Whatever he might have been decades ago, now he's living in a shack on the edge of town. A shack missing one wall, even."

Flossie laughed gaily. "That old idiot! I still can't believe he did that, can you?"

Lacy was beginning to rethink entirely her notions of what was believable and what wasn't. This was a brave new world to her, a world that was more complicated than she had ever imagined back at Our Lady of Perpetual Mercy. A caring mother could keep a bordello. A barkeep could make a good father. A virtuous woman could fall in the beat of her heart. Compared with these things, a man tearing his own house apart to make a porch swing didn't sound so odd now.

Flossie blinked at her. "Well, can you make me respectable?"

Lacy swallowed. Just a month ago she had wanted nothing more than to make her mother respectable. She had such big plans. It had taken her just over a month to realize that she didn't know the first thing about anything. Now she felt like a gosling being asked to give flight lessons.

Her mother stood at attention, waiting for instruction. "What should I do?"

"Well..."

Don't go near that attic, was all she could think of.

A rap sounded at the door, and Bodine poked his head in. "Am I interrupting?"

Flossie whirled and hurried over to him. "You're just in time. Lacy's giving me a lesson in being ladylike."

As Lacy stammered a denial, Bodine chuckled. "No better teacher, I'll reckon."

"She was just tellin' me…" Flossie frowned and turned back. "What was you tellin' me, Lace?"

Lacy swallowed. "I…um…"

"Don't you go breathing a word of this to Harper," Flossie said to Bodine. "I don't want him to think that I'm going ladylike on account of him. That old buzzard's head is big enough as it is."

"Harper sparkin' you, Flossie?"

The question reduced Flossie to peals of girlish laughter. "Hee-haw, Bodine. As if we were a couple of kids!" She looked over at Lacy and sobered. "Mind you, there's nothing untoward goin' on. So far we've only held hands." She blushed. "And maybe a peck or two."

At least someone in the family was showing a little restraint.

"Now what was you sayin' to me, Lacy?"

Lacy's mind was a blank.

Bodine cleared his throat. "My ma always says that you can tell a real lady by her hands," he volunteered helpfully.

Flossie latched onto that tidbit like a locust bug on a cornstalk. Her eyes flew to her own hands, which were red and plump. She clucked unhappily. "Are ladies allowed a few liver spots?"

"Ma never gave particulars. She said you could just tell." Bodine cast his gaze over to Lacy. "Let's see your hands, Lacy."

Flossie was all for this idea, though Lacy immediately put them behind her back. If you could tell a lady by her hands, she was suddenly seized with the terror that upon examination hers would be as brown and shriveled as old walnut shells.

But her mother pulled them out, and revealed them to be as they always were. Tidy, if redder than when she lived at Our Lady of Perpetual Mercy. That, she was nearly certain, was a vestige of doing dishes and washing, not of her night of sin.

Flossie clucked her tongue. "Such pretty little things. Did you ever see such delicate little hands, Bodine?"

Bodine looked deeply into Lacy's eyes and flashed her a big smile. "No, ma'am. I guess Ma was right about bein' able to tell a lady."

Lacy flushed and pulled her hands back instinctively. She had never felt so uncomfortable; she wanted to fly from the house. "Would you like to go for a walk, Bodine?" Maybe she would be able to catch sight of Lucas if they walked through town. "I need something at the store."

"Nothing would please me better," Bodine said. When they were outside, he confessed, "I have to admit, I was hoping I could coax you out for a walk."

She squinted up at him in the glare of the noon sun. "Really, why?"

He blinked down at her. His expression was decidedly uncomfortable. If not disappointed. "I just felt like walking, I guess."

Lacy thought back to last night, to her mother's going out walking with Harper. Walking held more meaning than she had previously supposed. She felt suddenly that she was betraying Lucas. Yet she and Lucas agreed that they would keep their relationship a secret for now. And how better to shield herself than on Bodine's arm?

Instinctively, she slipped her hand on his elbow, a gesture that brought more of a reaction than she had expected. "W-what I mean to say is—" he said "—is that I sure enjoy just being around you sometimes, Lacy. I guess you're the best woman I've been around since I left my ma."

Lacy tilted a glance up at him, feeling another wave of guilt hit her. "You shouldn't compare me to your mother, Bodine."

A cloud descended over his face. "Pardon me, Lacy, I didn't mean to be unfair to you."

She would have laughed, had he not looked quite so serious. She felt a pang of pity then for Bodine, who seemed to have difficulties just as thorny as her own. Given his estimation of his dear mama, it would be a wonder if he didn't die a bach-

elor. Because it was perfectly obvious that no one could hold
a candle to the paragon of womanly virtue that was Mrs.
Turner of Cicada Creek.

That night, Lacy lay in bed, worrying. What was she going
to do? There was no way that she could pretend she didn't
care for Lucas for very long. Dinner had been an agony. True
to their pact, Lucas hadn't let on that anything had changed
between them. He barked for more coffee, more rolls and a
second helping of chicken. But this time when she sloshed
coffee in his cup, she felt a thrill run through her at being so
close to him. She handled his rolls lovingly. And she only
hacked off the parts of the chicken she knew he especially
liked. No wings.

To her mind, their affection was practically transparent. She
already felt close to bursting with the news. How many days
could she keep it a secret?

She tossed and turned forever until she heard a creak of the
door opening. She surged up to sitting and was startled to see
a streak heading toward her through the inky darkness. Her
lips parted in a shout of surprise, but Lucas stopped her
screech with a hand over her mouth.

"Don't scream—you'll wake up Birdie."

Her scream transformed into a delighted laugh.

He crawled into bed next to her and burrowed under the
covers before he would release his hand. And when he did
take his palm away, it was only so he could lower his lips to
hers and kiss her as if they had been parted for months. And
now that she thought about it, it did seem so long since last
night. The day had been an agony of wondering where Lucas
was, and what was to become of her, and whether he cared
for her as much as she cared for him. But all her troubles
vanished the moment they touched. Anxiety fell away, replaced by this wonderful new activity, and this happiness she
felt so strongly that it threatened to overwhelm her.

They kissed until she was very ready to make love again,
but to her surprise, Lucas pulled her into his arms and nuzzled

her affectionately. "I missed you. I swear I couldn't stop thinking about kissing you the whole damn day."

The words were almost sweeter than kisses. *Missed her?* This was Lucas talking? She sank against his chest with a contented sigh. She could definitely become accustomed to this. "Me, too! This seemed like the longest day of my life. Well, since a month ago."

He frowned. "A month ago?"

"The day the fancy women left town was a pretty long one, too."

"That was a long day for everyone." She took a playful swat at him, which he easily ducked. "Besides, you're a sweet little liar. I saw you with Bodine at lunch, strolling around town as happy as you please."

Her mouth popped open. Surely he couldn't think she felt the same way about Bodine that she felt about him!

"I'm just teasing, Lacy."

She sagged against him again in relief. "You're still infuriating, you know."

"No more than you are," he said, bending down to kiss her nose. "Infuriating and, unfortunately, irresistible."

A frown pulled at her brow. "Why unfortunately?"

He shook his head. "Because I didn't expect this. I never meant to get tied down again."

She might have told him that he wasn't exactly tied down now—that was something that was frightening her a little. She wasn't a fool. She had read just enough novels to know that when love came before marriage—and without it—disaster followed. Usually for the woman.

But of course this wasn't a novel. Lucas was very real. What she felt for him was far more potent than anything she'd read about in fiction.

"You're a pessimist, Lucas."

"You're right. But I've got a little more experience than you do to back up my outlook." He gazed so adoringly into her eyes that she felt as if she might melt then and there. Who would have guessed how tender those coal-dark eyes of his could be? Certainly she never had, all those weeks he'd been so awful to her. "But it doesn't matter now. I don't want to compare you to anyone else, Lacy. I know you're not Alice. God knows I should be older and wiser, but somehow I feel just as giddy and inexperienced as a pup."

He certainly didn't seem inexperienced to her—especially when his hand made quick work of the buttons on her nightgown and his hand reached inside to caress one already aching breast. She caught her breath and bit down on her lip at the sharp pleasure of his touch. She had been thinking of this all day, yet memory didn't even come close to doing the reality justice.

Feeling bolder than she had last night, she leaned against him and kissed him on the mouth. He seemed pleased by her initiative, and rewarded her with another dizzying kiss.

The next day was a busy one at the boardinghouse. Lacy was trying to spruce up the place in anticipation of Blissful Day, and she had set aside the morning for washing the front windows of the house on all floors. She had thought the task would be a nice break from the usual routine of cooking and chores, but it turned out that washing windows was onerous work. When she'd started, she hadn't anticipated the amount of water she would be drawing from the well, or how often she would be scurrying up and down on a chair, or how hard it would be to make the dust coated windows look clean and not streaky. Luckily, she had more than twice her usual energy…. Thanks to Lucas she had gotten much less sleep than usual, yet her body hummed with vitality.

It was well after noon before she remembered Jacob's lunch. She scrambled down from her chair on the front porch and ran to the kitchen to throw a quick meal together. There was bread and cold ham and fruit, which wasn't exactly a feast, but would have to do for today. She vowed that tomorrow she would make up for her shoddy meal planning. Meanwhile, she did have a special treat she had prepared this morning before she'd started all the madness with the windows: a chocolate layer cake to take to the Rooster. She could present it as a gift to all the men there—her way of including Lucas in the noon feeding. She felt an irresistible urge to nourish him, but if he still wanted to keep their relationship a secret it would look mighty peculiar for her to be taking him food.

She stuffed Jacob's haphazardly prepared meal into an old tin she used for this purpose and grabbed the plate holding the chocolate layer cake with her other hand. Then she headed over to the Rooster.

It was a clear day, and hot enough to make everything in sight seem just a little droopy. But in spite of the fact that she was indeed achy from her work that morning, not to mention from her nocturnal activities, and that she was working up a sweat just by crossing town, Lacy felt anything but droopy. There was a kick in her step as she got closer and closer to Lucas's place of business. She was even beginning to soften in her attitude toward the Rooster. After all, there wasn't much fun to be had in this area. If men wanted a place to gather, who was she to say it was wrong? Just because there was liquor there, and fights broke out, and men probably gambled away more money than they ought to have...

Well, that wasn't *all* Lucas's fault. He wasn't forcing men into the Rooster.

She neared the Rooster's door and heard George Oatley's voice. "You've got to quit riding Lucas so hard, Boot. The man knows what he's doing."

"I'm beginning to wonder if he does!" Boot sputtered back. "Heck, you saw him dancing with her the other day. Dancing with her real close. I'm beginning to think that he's got a soft spot for that Calhoun woman."

Lacy stopped in her tracks. *Oh heavens, it* did *show!*

Her ears burned. She knew she shouldn't be standing at the door listening, but hearing herself discussed was just too tempting. The heels of her shoes felt glued to the hard-trodden earth.

George chuckled. "I've noticed him showing a certain partiality toward her myself. But what does that prove? He's a man, and she's about as pretty a creature as this town's seen.''

Lacy smiled. George Oatley really wasn't that bad, she decided then and there. Just because he was always a little sharp smelling from sweat... She gave herself a mental reminder to make a special point of being nicer to him in the future.

''Proves he's forgotten his promise,'' Boot said. ''Didn't he say that he would get rid of her for us?''

Lacy's smile faded.

''Well, sure, but maybe this is just part of his plan.''

''How?''

''Well...remember what you told me he said about sabotaging her reputation? Guess he thought that if he couldn't annoy her back to the convent then maybe he could send her running for other reasons. I'm willing to bet this is all just part of what you might call his grand scheme.''

Her blood turned to ice.

''I hope it works!'' Boot huffed. ''I'll bet if we got the Slipper back to normal before Blissful Day, we'd have a lot more people comin' to town.''

George laughed. ''You make it sound like it's civic pride that makes you want the Slipper back, when you know it's just because you miss the women!''

''Well who don't?''

''If you ask me, Harper don't. *He's* the one you should be worried about, what with him disappearing.''

Harper had disappeared?

Lacy wished she could say she was as interested in eavesdropping for news of her mother's beau as she was to find out what people were saying about herself. But the truth was, her head was spinning so she could hardly hear their voices anymore except as a vague murmur. She was suddenly clammy from perspiring profusely, and so choked for breath that she feared she would faint.

Lucas's grand plan? Ruining her reputation?

She could hardly believe it.

But at the same time, she couldn't *not* believe it, much as she would have liked to. The horrible scheme made too much sense. While she had thought Lucas had undergone a miraculous change of heart, he had actually just hit on a miraculous way to get rid of her. He was counting on her to run back to San Antonio in shame.

She'd even suspected as much! But then, right after that, he had told her about Alice, and looked at her with soulful eyes, and made her think that he actually had a heart. Oh, what a performance he'd given! All that fake joy and jibbering on about how he'd never expected to be tied down again. How could she have been such an idiot, such a gullible fool?

How long did he intend to keep her dangling along this way?

Suddenly, she remembered the ease with which he had seduced her. All it had taken was a dance, a few husky words, and an available attic. The things they had done, the words they had spoken in passion, raced through her mind and the hard earth turned spongy beneath her feet. Her skin felt like it was on fire as she remembered the time they had spent together—every tender (she had thought!), loving, passionate moment.

Despite the fact that she had been on her guard against him practically ever since coming to Blissful, she had still been duped. The man had cannily used the animosity she felt toward him and turned it on its flip side. He had used her innocence against her. He had laid a sensual trap, and she had foolishly leapt directly into it.

She closed her eyes as mortification hit her in one solid, overwhelming wave. Oh, why couldn't the earth just swallow her up now?

"Lacy?"

That voice! Her knees wobbled. Lucas was the last man on earth she wanted to see right now, but apparently she was not going to be given a single moment to order her jumbled thoughts. She should have known there would be no escaping him. Especially not when she was right next to his primary lair.

"What are you doing here?" he asked. "Are you all right?"

His voice oozed concern. He was still playing the game, not realizing that the jig was up.

She forced herself to open her eyes, slowly, and stare straight into those dark eyes. Those eyes that had flashed at her so often in anger, and then in passion, now simply squinted at her with worry. And, seemingly, concern.

What a loathsome, scheming toad.

"You look ill. Is it the heat? Can't you talk?"

Oh, how she wanted to talk! There were a million things she would have dearly loved to spit out at him, but her mouth felt dry, and her jawbone was so stiff it might have been rusted at the hinges.

"Lacy?"

At the sound of him saying her name, she began to quake. Tears sprang to her eyes, but she would be hanged if she would let Lucas Burns see her cry over him.

"Here, let me help you," he said, reaching to take her arm.

She flew backward. "Don't touch me!"

His face contorted in confusion. "If you're feeling poorly, at least let me take some of that stuff off your hands."

Lacy glanced down. She had forgotten all about the food she was carrying. But of course it didn't even seem that Jacob was in the saloon. And as for the cake...

She remembered something Lucas had said to her weeks ago. "You take the cake," she said aloud.

Lucas's face screwed up. "Huh?"

"You said that to me," she bit out angrily, knowing she was probably raving but well past caring. "Well now it's my turn. *You* take the cake!"

To punctuate her words, she hefted her scrumptious chocolate layer cake and heaved it straight at Lucas's deliciously shocked face.

Chapter Twelve

Moments after the sugary cannon hit its target, Lucas was still standing in place, sputtering out sponge cake, completely baffled. One minute he'd been strolling along, preoccupied with the peculiar news about Harper he'd heard at the store, and then… Come to find out, he'd been strolling right into a hurricane. His face was sticky with icing. Chocolate goo dripped off his face and plopped to the ground in clumps.

As if he needed any confirmation of how foolish he looked, Boot and George appeared, peering over the saloon doors. Once they got a look at him, they both doubled over laughing.

"What happened to you, Lucas?" George asked. "Couldn't get enough of Lacy's baking?"

The two men dissolved into whoops.

Lucas glowered at them. "I need to speak to Miss Calhoun in private, if you don't mind."

"Oh, we don't mind!" Boot said gleefully, trying to contain himself.

The two men retreated, cackling.

Lucas rounded on Lacy, who was still standing defiantly where she had been when she lobbed the cake at him. He grabbed her arm and pulled her out of earshot of the saloon.

Lacy bristled at his touch. "You let go of me, you duplicitous creature! You sidewinder!"

His face screwed up in puzzlement—he could tell because

the icing cracked on his skin. He felt like throttling her. Last time he had seen her they had been snuggling under the covers, dewy and spent from lovemaking. And now this.

What the hell had happened?

"Have you gone out of your mind?"

She stamped her foot and yanked herself away from him. "Yes, I have!" she bellowed, in a voice so low it sounded like it came from somewhere deep, deep inside of her. "I must have been crazy to believe that you cared one iota for me!"

She was hopping mad now, and he put his hands on her shoulders to calm her down. But the gesture had the exact opposite effect. "You liar!" she shouted. "You underhanded Casanova! You—"

"Lacy, would you calm down and tell me what's happened to get your petticoats afire?"

She balled her hands into fists, a gesture that made him take a cautious step back. He was familiar by now with the lady's temper. And her swing. "You know very well what's got me riled up. You've been playing me for a fool!"

"*What?*"

"Don't try denying it."

"But I do deny it."

Hurt and contempt warred in her eyes. "Naturally! You don't have an honest bone in your body. Even when your despicable scheme has been revealed in all its malicious glory, you don't want to admit you've been found out."

"Would you stop speaking in riddles?"

She tossed her head proudly. "It's no riddle any longer, Lucas. I know all about your master plan."

Irritation and confusion were struggling in his mind. "Well maybe you can tell me about it, because I have no idea what you're talking about."

"Your plan for getting rid of me. Apparently it's common knowledge that you moved into the house just to try to annoy me out of town. And then when that didn't work, you decided you would seduce me!" As she spoke the words—which described what seemed to him now a wild and sinister exaggeration of his original intent—his face paled.

And yet she could obviously tell by his reaction that her accusation had at least a kernel of truth to it. "How did you intend to humiliate me, Lucas? At what point were you going to tell the world that I was your...your whore!"

The word was nearly her undoing. And his. She started shaking so violently that he took a step toward her, to pull her into his arms. She stiffened and hopped back. "Don't come near me. I don't even want to look at you anymore. I don't want you at the house. Pack up your things and move out today, or I'll pile your every last belonging in the street and make a bonfire."

"That's it?" he said angrily. "You don't want to hear my side?"

"Your side is as plain as day. The pity is I was stupid enough to be blind to what was going on for so long. But I guess you counted on my inexperience to make me an easy mark."

He shook his head. "I don't know where you've been hearing these things—" He stopped, remembering Boot and George falling over laughing at the sight of him having been assaulted with cake by Lacy. Lacy was Boot's nemesis. "Unless you've been listening at doors."

Her cheeks, already red with anger, brightened further. "Only because I couldn't help it. I'm obviously a common topic at your place of business!"

"You should know better than to listen to gossip like that. And you should especially consider who was doing all the running off at the mouth."

"I have considered the fact that he was your friend. So close that you let him look after the saloon while you were seeing to running me out of town." She stared at him and then shook her head in revulsion. "I mean it, Lucas. I never want to have anything more to do with you."

"That's a tall order in a town the size of Blissful."

That pointy chin of hers jutted up proudly. "I suppose that's what you were counting on all along. That I wouldn't want to live in the same town as you, when all was said and done. You thought I'd crawl back to San Antonio, back to the sisters. But don't think you're running me out, Lucas. I'm not going to give you that satisfaction.''

"Oh, for Pete's sake," he said, though he really felt like cursing a blue streak at her. Didn't she have any idea what these past few days had meant to him? Did she really think that he was the kind of man who would sneak into a lady's bedroom and make love to her like there was no tomorrow, all just because of some harebrained plot to get rid of her?

Didn't she care for him enough to trust him one tiny bit?

Obviously not. The set of her jaw and the cold fire in her eyes told him that she was in no mood to listen to his side of things. Trying to talk reason to her would be like trying to reason with a tree stump.

He crossed his arms. "Don't worry, I'll pick up my things this afternoon. I'll send Jacob for them."

At the mention of Jacob, she seemed taken aback. A cloud crossed her expression. "Jacob can stay."

"Jacob's home is with me. We managed very well before you blew into town," he reminded her.

She didn't contradict him. At least she wasn't going to start throwing being a slipshod father at him again. That might have been the last straw.

"Goodbye, Lucas."

By the Lillie Langtry dramatics in her tone, you'd think she really did believe she would never see him again. He shook his head. "You know, I was actually beginning to believe you had a little womanly understanding in you."

She laughed bitterly. "When it comes to you, Lucas, I've got all the womanly understanding now I care to have. You've taught me a lesson I'll never forget!"

To punctuate that declaration, she spun on her heel and stomped back toward the boardinghouse, leaving him as bewildered as he'd ever felt in his life. And that included when Alice left him.

Alice. He *would* have to think about her right now! Of

course, when his wife had left him, the event was preceded by a slow burn. But this—this really struck him out of the blue.

He remembered that he was standing in the street with cake on his face and darted back inside the Rooster. When the doors flapped shut behind him, he was faced with his two sniggering customers. Seeing the seething anger on his cake-encrusted face was no deterrent to their ribbing.

"Hilarious!" he snarled at them as he crossed to the back of the bar. He took a dishcloth from the washing tub and started trying to undo the damage. When he glanced at himself in the mirror over the bar, it was all that he could do not to jump back. It wasn't the cake icing that troubled him—it was the pained look in his eyes. Anyone looking at him right now would think that he actually gave a damn about Lacy Calhoun kicking him out of her house, out of her bed.

He bit out a curse and tossed the towel back in the water harder than he'd intended, slopping liquid on the floor. More mopping up he would have to do. Not to mention, how was he going to explain to Jacob that he had gotten them kicked out of their new home? Jacob actually liked living at the Slipper.

Well, he had to admit that *he* had enjoyed it, too. Harper had been right. He had sashayed right into the spider's web and been trapped good and well. Home-cooked meals, a soft bed, a woman's smile…these weren't things that were hard to get used to. Nights spent in Lacy's arms wouldn't have been hard to get used to, either. Pity he'd only had two of them.

And the reason he'd only had that few was still staring at him.

"Sorry, Lucas," Boot said in a decidedly unrepentant voice. "We didn't know the weasely woman was standing right there, listening to us."

"Imagine a lady eavesdropping like that!" George exclaimed.

Never mind the fact that the duo had obviously been eavesdropping on him and Lacy. If Lucas had any doubt of that fact, Boot's next words laid that doubt to rest. "She must have been listening for a long time if she heard me talkin' about the master plan.''

George looked at him curiously. "So…*did* you intend to humiliate her, Lucas?''

"'Course he did!'' Boot exclaimed. "What do you take Lucas for, some pavilion building lunatic like Harper turned out to be? I always knew the man was crazy. And now look—he's bugged out.''

George bowed his head. The day before, apparently, Harper had borrowed the livery wagon. Said he was running an errand. He didn't say where he was going, or for how long. And now a day had passed, and Myrtle Bean said she'd seen him sneaking a bundle into the back of the wagon. A bundle would fit just about everything Harper owned.

Some suggested that he wasn't coming back. Lucas wasn't so sure. Two nights ago he had seemed uncommonly attached to Flossie. But the man was a drifter, and he did seem prone to whims.

George obviously still held out hope for getting his wagon back. "Can't believe you'd speak against Harper, Boot, as many hours as we've sat around this here bar, talkin' to the man.''

"I'll bet he finally just went plum loco. He was always warning us against civilization, and then he got suckered into it himself.'' He frowned. "Though maybe leavin' wasn't so loco after all. Maybe he got out just in time to save himself.''

"Save himself from what?'' George asked.

"From womenfolk getting their claws into him. Look at the way Flossie's been acting about him. Fluttering about him like a girl with her first beau!''

"Sounds to me like you're jealous,'' George said.

"Jealous?'' Boot squealed.

"I'll bet you wouldn't mind having women twittering around you,'' George said.

Boot spat. "I guess if I wanted a little female companionship I could turn on the charm as well as anybody. I just don't have a weakness for the domestic, is all.''

George laughed. "You just don't have a face for attracting a wife, is more like it."

"And I suppose *you* consider yourself a dandy!" Boot laughed. "You with your red face."

"Yeah, but I got manners."

"Like I ain't got 'em!" Boot exclaimed.

Lucas let out a long breath. The cake in his face had been all but forgotten in favor of Boot and George's usual squabbling. Only now as he listened to them argue over nothing, the same as he had been listening to them argue for the past several years, the future seemed very bleak.

Jacob brought a new pan of water in from the back. Then he leaned over the bar, looking dully out at the men assembled in their usual clumps. A few, like George and Boot, held forth at the bar, while others played cards or hunched over dominoes at the tables. It was the typical crowd, but Lucas noticed his son's brow pucker as he watched them all through narrowed eyes. Like he was seeing them all for the first time.

Lucas sometimes did that, too. Especially when he felt restless. And now, this first night after being kicked out of the boardinghouse, it felt as if he were taking a good look at Jacob for the first time in a long time. He seemed different. Older. Lucas didn't think he had grown, actually—though at this age he seemed to be growing faster than a sycamore. The real change was in his expression.

Lucas felt a pang; his son's spirits looked like they'd just hit bedrock. Which pretty much described his own feelings today. But Jacob...he didn't like to see him so low. Next time he went to San Antone, he swore to himself that he was going to bring back a whole armload full of books. Enough to start one of those lending libraries, if he had to.

Which sounded just like one of those do-gooder schemes of Lacy's. Maybe that crazy woman really *had* gotten under his skin.

Jacob eyeballed him anxiously. "Pa, are you all right?"

"Huh?"

"You looked sort of sick. Are you feeling poorly?"

"No," he said, straightening. "I feel fine, and so will you, tomorrow. In the morning you'll realize that you don't miss that place one bit. We're better off on our own. Always have been, haven't we? Just because there was good food over there, and some different company, that doesn't mean we wouldn't have gotten sick of the place eventually. If we'd spent as long there as we have right here, we probably would have started taking it all for granted. Or even begun to tire of it. Anyone can wear on your nerves, kid—Boot, Birdie…Lacy…anybody. You'll see."

Jacob's worry looked like it was on the upswing. "I never mentioned missing the boardinghouse."

Lucas frowned. No, he hadn't. Damn. "Well, I just guessed that's what was on your mind. It would be, naturally."

Jacob tilted his head. "Do *you* miss the boardinghouse?"

Lucas cleared his throat. "No. 'Course not."

"'Cause if you do, what are we doin' back here?"

He hadn't had the heart to tell Jacob that they had been evicted, much less why. "We're here because this is where we belong. It was just foolishness that made me move us over there to begin with—it was wrongheaded of me. Let that be a lesson. Nobody's infallible, Jacob."

Jacob blinked up at him. "Infallible? You mean, you make mistakes, too?"

Hearing the question put to him in his son's cracking adolescent voice, Lucas felt remorse overwhelm him. Mistakes? Who was he kidding? He couldn't even begin to count the blunders he'd made. To Lacy, to Jacob—yes, even to Alice, if he cared to go back that far.

But right now, the wrongs he'd done to Lacy preyed on him most of all. He just assumed she would know that he'd had a change of heart. Didn't his actions show it? But apparently her faith in him wasn't enough to withstand a little barroom gossip. And why should it be? He'd never been square with her before.

And now he wasn't sure when he'd ever get the chance to win her over again.

"Yes—" he croaked humbly "—I make mistakes." Gigantic, foolish ones.

"Well, shoot. I knew that." Jacob stretched and yawned. "I guess I'll hit the hay after all, if there's nothing more here for me to do."

"Sure, go ahead."

Boot glanced up at him. "Good to have you back, Lucas."

Lucas laughed. "Wasn't aware I'd been anywhere but here."

"You know what he means," George said, shaking his head. "You spent too long at the Slipper. That place is a bad influence now."

Boot tutted in disgust. "Just look what it did to Harper!"

He still wasn't back.

George, smarting over his wagon and never missing an opportunity to needle Boot, scoffed. "You're just bitter, Boot."

"Bitter? Why?"

"'Cause Harper's probably gone to San Antone." George snickered. "Maybe when he comes back we'll find out if they're still talkin' about Boot the Kid."

Boot grabbed George by the shirtfront, and Lucas knew then and there that it was going to be a bad night.

He just didn't know how bad.

Misery abounded at the boardinghouse. To Lacy, it seemed like the evening would never end.

She had sworn she wasn't going to shed a tear over Lucas Burns. There was no profit in it. She had known all along what he was. Allowing herself to fall in love with such a creature showed bad judgement; letting herself languish away for him now that she had been reminded of what a low character he really was would only be degrading herself further.

But it was difficult to fight back tears when Flossie was such a mess. Her mother had been weeping on and off all day, ever since word came from Myrtle that George said Harper had borrowed—perhaps stolen—his wagon the day before and roared out of town. And Myrtle said she had seen him carrying a large bundle.

The bundle was the detail that had thrown her mother over the edge. Flossie was positive that Harper had skedaddled.

Tensely, Lacy bit the tail end of the thread off the potholder she'd just finished and threw the square onto the pile of the ones she'd already completed for the craft booth on Blissful Day. Then she immediately picked up several squares of material to start the next one. At the rate she was going, the world would have more potholders than there were pots to hold onto.

But her fingers seemed to have a will of their own—to stay busy. Her emotions might be under tight control, but she had become a sewing dervish with trembling fingers that moved at the speed of lightning. Who knew what would happen if she stopped making potholders?

She might crumble. Like Flossie.

Her mother swooned on the settee. "*Gone!* Without a word."

Lacy jumped up and poured her mother another glass from the lemonade pitcher. "He'll be back, Mama. He wouldn't have left forever without saying goodbye."

"You don't know these drifter types!" Flossie wailed.

"Harper wasn't like that," Lacy said.

Her mother honked into a handkerchief and then swiped at her red-rimmed eyes. "It happens all the time! You don't know the stories I know, Lace. Men leaving without a word, women left behind to shift for themselves." The drama of it proved too powerful for her, and she sank again.

"You don't have to worry about that."

"Oh, no," Flossie said with a ragged sigh. "I'll get by, I know…all alone…"

The boardinghouse did feel more lonely than before, especially since Birdie had gone to bed early tonight. The tension in the air had proved too much for her nerves.

It was wearing on Lacy's, too.

Flossie shot up suddenly. "You think it was the fortune telling booth, honey?"

Lacy frowned. All day, it had been difficult to keep up with her mother's frantic thoughts. Especially when her own thoughts weren't exactly sanguine. "What?"

"Well, I know you haven't said so in so many words, Lacy, but I could tell you thought that my fortune-telling idea wasn't exactly respectable."

Lacy's cheeks felt hot. "But after all, it's for charity, Mama."

Flossie sighed. "That's what Harper said, too—but maybe he was just bein' polite. Maybe he really did think it was sorta low class. Could be he wasn't telling me the truth."

Lacy mumbled consolingly, but her heart felt so sore that she broke off. She would never have thought Harper Cooley was a liar, but what did she know? Lucas had managed to deceive her, too. "Does any man ever tell the truth?" she blurted out.

The question rattled Flossie out of her gloomy frame of mind. "Why, of course they do! What cause do you have to ask such a thing?"

Lacy fumed silently, and shrugged.

Flossie ran over and gave her a hug. "Now I don't want my bitter experience to rub off on you, Lace. You're so young and sweet—you got your whole life ahead of you. Things might seem slow to you now, but just wait. You'll find a man."

Squirming inside, Lacy bent her head over her needlework.

But Flossie went back to the settee, and the look on her face told Lacy that she was again preoccupied with Harper. "I reckon that bundle had his extra shirt and his Ralph Waldo Emerson, and now he's going back to the drifter life. Or maybe he's going back to Tennessee, and real respectability."

"Or maybe he's coming right back here to stay," Harper bellowed from the doorway. He was standing clean-shaven in a new suit, and holding a large rectangular box.

The two women gaped at him in shock, as startled as if they were confronting a ghost.

Gasping, Flossie leapt up from the settee and crossed the room in one bound. Then she simultaneously yelled at the man and smothered him in a hug. "You old leathery coot, where have you been! And what happened to your whiskers?"

He chuckled indulgently as he rubbed his jaw. "Lopped them off in San Antone."

"But you left without saying a word—poor George thought you'd stolen his wagon."

Harper chuckled. "I just paid him double what that rickety old buckboard is worth. And as for you—I figured you'd be glad to see the back of me."

Flossie's eyes practically glistened as she looked at him. Without his beard and in his new suit, he seemed more dignified than ever. "Holy smokes! Look at your new duds!"

He leaned the box against the wall, tucked his thumbs in his lapels and turned like a swell to model for her. "The man in the store said the president wears one just like it."

Flossie hooted. "But there ain't been a president who wears a hat like yours in many a year, Harp."

He doffed his old stovepipe hat. "Consider it a sign of loyalty to my hat brand. And consider this—" he presented Flossie with the box "—a token of my esteem, Floss."

Flossie was like a kid on Christmas morning. She clasped the box to her breast and practically skipped back over to the settee. When the top of the box was lifted, an awestruck sigh escaped her parted lips. She reached in and pulled out a dress of the most dazzling shade of royal blue that Lacy had ever seen. The garment was made of silk that shone deep and rich, and had a low-cut neckline beaded with tiny pearls. Three rows of pearls lined each cuff.

"Why, it's beautiful!"

Harper came forward. "It's one of a kind. Because you're one of a kind."

Flossie burst into tears and hugged him, and for a moment Lacy feared she would follow suit. She sniffed happily as the couple embraced, and forgot her own troubles for a moment.

Flossie finally pulled back, unable to keep herself from taking another look at the eye-catching dress. It was exactly the kind of thing Lacy wouldn't have wanted her mother to wear. "You old fool! I'm sure you spent too much money."

"I'm not a man without means, Floss. I might have been a drifter, but I was never a spendthrift, so don't worry your mind on that score."

"It looks like it will fit me to a T!" she said, impressed. "How on earth did you guess my measurements?"

Harper grinned. "I'm afraid I have to confess to a bit of theft. I stole a dress from your clothesline."

Flossie's hands lifted to her cheeks. "My brown dress with the little blue flowers! I wondered where that went!"

"It went to San Antonio—and then it went to charity." He took her hands. "Please promise never to wear anything that hideous again, Flossie. You shouldn't hide yourself in drab browns. You used to dress with so much liveliness!"

Flossie laughed happily. "I thought you'd prefer me looking ladylike."

"I prefer you Flossie-like."

Flossie released a sigh of relief and took Harper's arm. Deciding she had been a fly on the wall long enough, Lacy got out of her chair and began to creep silently toward the door. She might have made her exit complete unheeded by the old lovers, except that halfway to the door, a sharp pop cracked through the air. Following on its heels were three more.

"What was that?" Lacy asked, whirling back toward them.

Flossie chuckled. "Sounded like some shenanigans coming from the Rooster."

Shenanigans! Those were gunshots. Lacy rushed to the window and stuck her head out.

"Probably just one of the boys lettin' off steam," Harper said with a shrug.

Lacy sank down on the sill. Her heart was thumping so she could barely catch her breath.

"Honey, what's the matter with you?" Flossie asked. "You've heard noises like that before."

But I've never imagined one of those bullets hitting Lucas before.

Birdie skittered down the stairs in her nightgown and slippers. Her eyes were saucer-wide. "Did you hear that?"

"Probably Boot Withers—he always totes his gun now, when he doesn't have a bank to rob," Flossie said.

"I don't know how you can joke about violence that way," Birdie scolded her. "It's a shame on the town."

Harper chortled. "I'm not so sure about that. I think it just shows our town has the usual number of idiots running around drunk in it."

"Speaking of the Rooster, maybe we should all take a snort," Flossie said. "I could use one, after the day I've had."

She went over to the window seat, dug beneath a stack of blankets, and produced a bottle. Back in her vigilant days, Lacy had never thought to look there.

"You better have some, too, hon," Flossie told her. "For medicinal purposes. You're almost as twitchy as Birdie here. You look like you got a bellyful of bedsprings."

"Spirits won't help what ails me, Mama."

Flossie frowned as she took a jigger out of the china cabinet. "*Is* something ailin' you?"

Lacy wondered if it would be helpful just to get the whole sad tale out in the open. Maybe if she testified to her wrongdoing, her foolishness, it would relieve her of the misery sitting in her chest.

The decision whether to make a confession was taken out of her hands. Hectic bootsteps clumped up the porch stairs. Jacob burst into the parlor, huffing excitedly. He was wearing a peculiar outfit of a nightshirt tucked into wrinkled pants, and his cheeks were red from the dash across town.

Lacy was across the room in a heartbeat, holding Jacob's arms in a clawing grip. "What's happened? Is it Lucas?"

Jacob nodded and shook his head frantically, trying to get the breath to speak.

The blood drained out of her. Lacy looked at him, horror overtaking her. Oh, Lucas! The man was gone—and her last vision of him would be with his face covered with cake! Remorse threatened to overwhelm her.

"Tell us everything," she demanded. She was shaking like a leaf.

Jacob gulped for air. "It was a gunfight—a deadly one, it

looks like. Pa sent me ahead to ask Flossie if we could borrow a bed.''

He sent ahead to make arrangements for his own deathbed? Lacy bit back a sob at the pathos of that. But it was like him, wasn't it? He was so strong...

''He and some of the others should be here any moment now,'' Jacob said.

Harper had already disappeared—probably to go help.

Flossie glanced out the window and then started bustling around the room. She snatched up the brandy bottle again. ''Guess we really do need it for medicinal purposes. I'll set up your pa's old room, Jacob. It's right near me and Lacy.''

Lacy knew she should be moving, but she was still in shock. ''How is he, really?'' she asked, unable to look Jacob in the eye. *He* was so brave, so relatively composed, when for all he knew he was about to become an orphan.

''He's unconscious now.''

''Unconscious!'' Then she wouldn't be able to tell him good-bye! Or that she forgave him, even if he *had* acted abominably toward her. Forgiveness was so important, and suddenly she felt full to the brim with it.

''He was shot in the head. Could be he's lost a lot of blood. Boot's gone to fetch Dr. Hart.''

The sounds of voices could be heard outside, and Lacy jumped up and tried to compose herself. She had to pull herself together. She hurried to throw the door open wide and was nearly flattened by a man walking backward through the door.

Lacy hopped out of the way; then, as she looked down at the patient, she nearly fainted. It wasn't Lucas. It was George Oatley! Shuffling along the hallway with the men, she looked up at the man who had nearly plowed over her moments before and discovered *that* was Lucas. Lacy nearly fainted.

''Where's Flossie?'' Lucas demanded.

Lacy gulped and pointed. ''There...your room.''

The men bypassed her and she sank against the wall, struggling to absorb the basic facts. George. It was George who was injured. Not Lucas.

A hysterical laugh burbled out of her.

Flossie dashed out into the hall. "Oh, there you are! Could you boil some water? Lucas says he's sent for the doc, but heaven only knows when he'll get here." She rifled through the linen closet for a sheet and came out with one of their best. "We gotta do what we can to stop the bleeding."

Lacy nodded and fairly flew out to the well. Now that she knew it wasn't Lucas hurt, she was beginning to function normally, if under heightened urgency. When she had pulled the water, she ran back inside and started a fire in the stove.

After she had gotten the kettle on, Lucas came in. He looked less frenzied than before, though plenty worried. It would have been hard to believe that their encounter with the cake had just been this afternoon, except for his wariness as he approached her.

"How is George?" she asked him.

He shrugged. "I'm not sure. He's still unconscious. Looks bad to me."

She frowned. "I'm sorry."

"He's a good man."

She nodded, then after a moment of silence, foolishly blurted out, "When Jacob first came in, I thought it was you who was hurt."

"Thought your dreams had come true?" Lucas asked, the humor in his tone falling flat.

"No!" No matter what she had said to him that afternoon, she couldn't believe he would believe she wanted him dead. "Of course not."

"You were probably all set to weep bitter tears at my funeral," he said.

His dark presence, leaning so insouciantly against the door, made her uncomfortable in that same old way. When his eyes met hers her chest clutched just as it had when she had feared he had been shot. That feeling seemed to have wiped away all the seething animosity and hurt she had been sitting on all day.

She looked away. "No, Lucas."

"Well, you can pack away your hankies and your dancing

shoes. As you can see, I'm hale and hearty, all in one disreputable piece.''

Her lips twisted. He sounded almost bitter—as if *she* were the one who had wronged him. Wasn't that typical? She straightened her shoulders and shot an irritated glance his way. "So I see."

"I'm sorry circumstances have forced me to sully your pristine kitchen with my presence," he said. "I was going to see if you needed any help, and maybe offer you the opportunity to lecture me on the evils of barrooms."

That last thought had never entered her mind. She had been so caught up in the idea of Lucas's escape from death that she hadn't gotten around to blaming him for the accident. "You don't sound as if you need a lecture. You've apparently come to that conclusion all on your own."

A pained look registered on his face, and she immediately felt remorse. "I'm sorry, Lucas—"

He cut her off. "Don't be. I'm the one who's sorry." He shot her a piercing look. "For a lot of things."

Heat shimmered through her—but that was insanity. Nothing had changed; he had deceived her. She was just reacting to the physical closeness of him, to the same dark eyes that had bewitched her before. She turned and stared at the kettle, using all her effort not to react to his beckoning gaze.

"Lacy...?" His voice had that purr to it again.

She gritted her teeth. "Hadn't you better go see how George is?"

After a moment, Lucas pushed away from the door. "All right. I'll do that."

It was probably the first time he'd ever done anything she'd asked him to.

But when he was gone, Lacy felt an almost irresistible impulse to call him back to her.

Chapter Thirteen

The anxious town held its breath as George hovered between life and death. At the boardinghouse, Flossie, Lacy and even Birdie took turns keeping a vigil at his side. A bullet had grazed George's skull, and he had a fierce, swollen lump on his temple from falling after he'd been shot. His face, what parts of it weren't swathed in bandages, was pale from loss of blood. Yet Dr. Hart's initial prognosis—that before dawn the blacksmith would be toiling for his maker in the great forge beyond—proved false. The physician's subsequent predictions that George would be gone by noon, by supper, and by the next morning, were also wrong. George did not regain consciousness, but neither did he appear in any hurry to give up the ghost.

He had always been on the contrary side, men at the Rooster agreed.

At the boardinghouse, the women were simply glad that their nursing efforts so far had not been in vain.

But at the store, the mood was much different. Harper Cooley noted it when he went in to buy some nails from Harry. After making his purchase, he hightailed it over to the Rooster. Lucas was glad to see his old friend this morning. A sane face was welcome after the insanity of the past two days.

"The doctor's saying George might not live till evening," Lucas said gravely.

Harper dismissed this forecast of doom. "I doubt the doctor has any more idea what's going to happen than I do. The matter's just between George and God now, and you know as well as I do that George is a fellow who likes to argue. This thing might not be settled for a while."

Lucas pushed a cup of coffee toward Harper. "I'd rather have it unsettled than lose George."

Harper nodded his agreement, then eyed him through a squint. "Trouble's brewing, Lucas."

"What kind of trouble?"

"Over at Harry's they aren't taking kindly to the incident that put George in his present fix. Myrtle was sayin' something ought to be done."

"About what?"

"About the Rooster in general, and whoever shot George in particular. There's not much doubt who did shoot him, over there."

Lucas frowned. "It was an accident."

Harper's iron-gray brows soared. "According to those folks, and the folks at the boardinghouse, there were four shots fired. Mean to tell me Boot accidentally pulled the trigger four times? Even I wouldn't have expected him to be that inept!"

Lucas sighed. He could trust Harper, and it would be good to get this off his chest. "George and Boot had been arguing all night. When they pulled out the guns, I told them to simmer down and go home. They left, all right, but instead of heading home I guess they decided to use each other for target practice. But I don't think Boot meant any malice. After he saw what he'd done to George, he was so upset he nearly shot his own toe off. I told him to go fetch the doc, keep his mouth shut about what happened, and then ride back to the Widow Wallace's and stay put there for once."

"I don't know if that's going to help. The way they were talking at Harry's, they smell Boot's blood. It's always stuck in Myrtle's craw to be living side-by-side with an outlaw."

Lucas sighed in frustration. "That idiot! I told him if he

kept being such a hothead, something like this would happen.''

"I guess we all knew," Harper said, pulling at his mustache. "But we none of us did anything about it, did we?"

"What were we supposed to do?"

"Tell him to stop spending his life at a bar and go home.'"

Lucas couldn't help bristling at the implied accusation. His own culpability had been preying on his mind. "What, have you decided the town should close down the Rooster now, too?"

"Heaven's sake, Lucas. Don't *you* be such a hothead. I was just suggesting that we all bear a little responsibility here. 'Course, Boot is ultimately the one who will have to face the music if George doesn't come to and corroborate his story of it just being a case of barroom shenanigans that got out of hand.''

Lucas felt a pang. The music Boot would have to face would be solemn. After his bank-robbing career, the law would not look kindly on murder, accident or no accident.

Harper downed the last of his coffee. "I'm finishing the pavilion today. But first I'm going to pay a call on George and his ladies." The laugh he managed was rueful at best. "Bet the fellow's never had so much female attention."

After Harper left the bar, Lucas decided he would visit the store on the pretext of buying some candy for the Florence Nightingales at the boardinghouse. He wanted to do something for the women who were taking such good care of George anyway.

Who was he kidding? He wanted to do something for Lacy. Their last meeting hadn't gone as he had hoped. When he had seen her the night of the accident, he had intended to try to make peace. He'd meant to apologize. But then she'd said something snippy and he'd responded curtly...and things went downhill from there. For some reason he just wasn't able to tell her what was really in his heart. Maybe that was a good thing, though, if she didn't want to hear it. No sense in a man' spilling his guts if the lady was in no mood to listen. No need to make a damn fool of himself.

Again.

He knew immediately upon entering the store that Harper had not been exaggerating about the subject or the tone of the conversation. The moment the door swung open, Myrtle and Neesa fell silent, and Harry looked at him guiltily. He could feel their eyes follow him as he strolled over to the counter where the candy jars stood in a line and inspected the peppermints and licorice whips and lemon drops. His eyes fell on the jar of licorice, simply because he could never understand why people would stick anything so black and peculiar-tasting in their mouths. He couldn't abide the stuff, himself. He pegged Lacy for the lemon drop sort. Sweet and sour.

Usually when a person walked into Bean's store, Harry or Myrtle would be right on top of them within seconds. They weren't pushy, exactly; it really wasn't in Harry to try to sell his neighbor an item he didn't want. He wasn't peddling anything; he was just helpful. And Myrtle, thin-lipped though she was, could always put aside prejudices for the sake of commerce. But today commerce seemed to have ground to a halt.

Lucas drummed his fingers on the countertop and decided the best route might be to pretend they were being helpful all the same. "Guess I'll get a bag of lemon drops," he said, as if someone had actually asked him what they could do for him today.

Harry, breaking free of the invisible cord that seemed to bind him to Myrtle these days, finally rushed over. He pulled out a small sack and began filling it, smiling nervously at Lucas all the while.

Bodine entered the store, greeted everyone, and strolled up next to Lucas. "Hi there!" He eyed the bag Harry was filling and then glanced playfully over at Lucas. "Got a sweet tooth today?"

Lucas grunted self-consciously.

Bodine elbowed him. "I thought I might pick up a little of Lacy's favorite candy. Seein' how she's working so hard and all. Ma always says you can tell a good woman by the way she tends the sick. Could you fix me up with a bag of licorice, Harry?''

Harry obliged, and meanwhile the women closed in behind him. Slowly, the tense atmosphere began to ruffle even Bodine, and he realized that he and Lucas were surrounded. He turned and smiled anxiously at Myrtle. "Hey there, ladies," he said with a polite nod to Neesa, too. "How are you today?"

"We're fine," Myrtle replied crisply.

Neesa chimed in, "Unlike poor Mr. Oatley!"

At the reminder of George, Bodine looked stricken. "Yeah, poor old George. I don't guess there's been any news for the better?"

"No news," Neesa said. Then she added with a bluntness that bespoke a gruesome relish, "Except that my husband says he will mostly likely not live to see the sun set."

Bodine's expression grew more pained still. And no wonder. At the thought of George dying, Lucas felt a sharp kick in his stomach. It would be a sore thing to lose such a friend.

"And if he does die, something will have to be done," Myrtle said.

Bodine looked confused. "Well, naturally. We'll have to send for a preacher, I reckon."

"We'll have to send for a judge," Myrtle corrected him, not without exasperation. "As sheriff, you should be less worried about his burial and more concerned about the trial for his murder."

"Murder!" Bodine recoiled physically at the word, as if it were something he would rather not get mixed up with.

Myrtle and Neesa puffed up as one. "That's what it would be if the man dies."

Lucas turned to Bodine to reassure him. "It was an accident."

Myrtle pounced on Lucas now as if he were a mouse who had just scurried out of a hidey hole. "*You* would know, I suppose, since the deadly incident happened in your establishment."

Bodine frowned. "No one is dead."

"Yet," Neesa said.

"He's as good as dead now," Myrtle said. "Doc says he's in what you call a coma. And I say if a man can get the noose for murdering, surely there should be an equally stiff penalty for coma-tizing."

"I think George will pull through," Lucas said with more optimism than he actually felt. "He's always had plenty of spunk."

"Maybe when it comes to avoiding work!" Myrtle agreed resentfully. "I took him a drawer pull to repair once and it was six days before he got it fixed." Her tone indicated that he was being equally shiftless in taking so long to die. "But it's no wonder a man develops such slipshod work habits when he's being continually tempted to idle his life away over a glass of liquor."

Lucas stiffened. He was wondering when she would get around to this subject.

Bodine tilted his head. "George had has—a taste for alcohol, but he mostly was drawn to the Rooster for the company, I imagine."

"I believe *that* like I believed men were drawn to the Slipper for the piano music!" Myrtle bellowed.

Candy bags crinkled in Harry's nervous hands.

"Lila *did* play a might fine piano," Bodine said, a little wistfully.

But Myrtle was obviously in no mood to debate the point. "The point is, Sheriff, drunkenness and general lawlessness in this town have gotten out of hand. Your friend Miss Calhoun—no matter what I may think of her personally—has gone to a lot of trouble to organize an event to try to draw people to this town. Hardworking, decent people with families, we hope. But no decent people will want to come to Blissful, for any reason, if it's known that killers here walk free."

"I don't know what Henrietta Wallace can be thinking!" Neesa exclaimed in disgust.

Bodine stepped back, flabbergasted. "The widow Wallace *killed* someone?"

Myrtle took a deep breath and turned her eyes heavenward as if searching for patience. "We're not talking about Henrietta Wallace, we're talking about her ranch help, Boot Withers!"

"Everyone knows what kind of man he is," Neesa said. "Spent nearly two years in a San Antonio jail! A young man like that who goes bad so early is clearly irredeemable."

"No chance of anyone being redeemed in Blissful as long as it remains so lawless and wild!" Myrtle said.

Bodine finally took offense. "Well now, I'm not so sure about that. Just because we've got the Rooster..."

"And a murder," Myrtle reminded him.

"It's just an almost murder," Bodine pointed out. "I tell you frankly, Mrs. Bean, I've never heard of a law against coma-tizing someone."

Myrtle lifted her several chins. "Maybe it's just never come up before. But now it has, and you should do something about it. You're the sheriff."

Bodine had never looked so unhappy about that fact. But then, this was perhaps the first time he had ever been faced with a thorny problem. "You heard Lucas here say that it was just an accident."

Myrtle snorted. "The incident will be a blight on this town, and on your record as sheriff. But if you have no intention of even investigating, maybe the citizens of this community should take the law into our own hands."

Lucas and Bodine exchanged anxious looks. For all its being a hurrah kind of place, Blissful had been basically peaceful. Fights, but no killings. But frontier justice wasn't unheard of in these parts.

"Something needs to be done," Myrtle said. "If the matter isn't settled soon, Blissful Day could be a loss. And look how much trouble everyone's already gone to!"

"My husband was making rounds yesterday, and he said

over in the next county, mothers are saying they wouldn't let their boys step foot in this town," Neesa told her.

Lucas, who had been trying to stay calm, felt his blood reach the boiling point. Two men's lives hung in the balance now, and all these two women could think about was whether people would buy their potholders at Blissful Day. And there was Harry, Boot's old friend, standing by and not saying a word! What had happened to this town? Whatever happened to loyalty?

Maybe it was like Boot said a while back. Men had stopped sticking together.

"The way the doctor talks, you might as well send for the judge," Neesa declared.

"Before you send for the judge, you need to arrest the man!"

Lucas couldn't take any more. "If you want to arrest any-one, Bodine, arrest me."

Bodine pivoted toward Lucas, eyes bulging. "You?"

"*I* shot George," Lucas stated flatly. "So you'll save your-self the trouble of an investigation if you just toss me in jail."

"Lucas, you got to be kidding!" Harry exclaimed, in spite of the glare it cost him from his wife. Having Lucas in jail would probably suit Myrtle fine. He wouldn't be able to run the Rooster.

Damn, Lucas thought. He'd have to close for a while. And he would have to explain to Jacob somehow, and find a place for him. It irked Lucas to play into Myrtle's hand this way, but he couldn't allow the town to go after Boot. Guilty he surely was—guilty of being a hothead and having hotheaded cantankerous friends. Guilty of drinking too much, Lucas ad-mitted. But anyone who thought he would actually mean to hurt George didn't know Boot or George.

He faced Bodine and put out his hands in a gesture of sur-render.

Bodine gaped at him. "You shot George? Why?"

"He said something disparaging about..." Lucas couldn't

think of anything that would rile him up enough to fire a gun at someone. "Well, about a certain lady."

Something flashed in Bodine's eyes. A flicker of belief, maybe. "About Lacy?" he asked in a low voice.

Lucas nodded. Bodine would readily believe gunplay would break out over his precious Lacy.

"But you never seemed to care if people insulted her before."

Lucas shifted. Damn. He hadn't counted on Bodine actually thinking. "This wasn't something a man could ignore."

Feeling the ladies' hovering presence, Bodine's face reddened, and he cleared his throat before Lucas could have the opportunity to describe the alleged insult in colorful language that might be all right at the Rooster but certainly wasn't fit for the candy counter at Harry Bean's store.

"I guess you'd better come on down to the jail, then," Bodine said hazily, as if he couldn't quite believe the words he was speaking.

"Wait!" Harry exclaimed.

Lucas turned expectantly, hoping Harry might finally come to his or Boot's defense before his wife. Instead, the man held out the two bags. "Don't ya'll want your candy?"

"Doctor Hart says the poor soul won't live to see another sunset," Birdie said breathlessly. Tears welled in her eyes. "And he was so nice to me when he cut that saloon door off my arm!"

"He was?" Flossie asked in surprise.

Birdie flushed. "He smiled at me."

Flossie mopped a warm cloth over the strip of George's forehead that wasn't covered by a bandage. She was decked out in her new blue dress—the most flamboyant nurse a man could ask for. "The doc doesn't know what he's talking about."

This wholehearted disrespect for a man in a position of authority made Birdie quake as if the very earth were rumbling beneath them. But for Lacy, her mother's staunch belief in

George's ability to buck the doctor's doom-and-gloom predictions were what kept her going. For nearly two days their lives had been consumed with taking turns nursing a patient who showed no response to their ministrations, except perhaps by not getting worse. His pulse remained faint, his temperature cool, his skin pale. He looked like what he was—a man on the brink. But as stubbornly as George refused to sink into the hereafter, Flossie refused to believe that there was any reason why he should.

"A bump on the head and a little gunshot wound," she said dismissively. "I've seen men live through worse. Much worse. Haven't you, Harper?"

Harper, who was sitting quietly on the other side of the bed, his eyes fixed more securely on the nurse than the patient, nodded. "In the war."

The front door had been left wide open, so no one was surprised when Bodine appeared. His eyes were dazed. "I brought you some licorice," he said without preamble.

As if sleepwalking, he handed the small bag in his hand to Birdie, who was so surprised she nearly dropped it.

"What's wrong?" Lacy asked him.

"Plenty! I've just locked up Lucas in the jail!"

Lacy gaped at him wordlessly. It felt as though her legs might fold like an accordion beneath her weight.

Flossie tossed her cloth into the washbasin and hopped out of her chair. "Lucas? In jail? What for?"

"For murdering George."

"Murder!" Harper hopped up, too. "But George isn't dead yet."

"Isn't likely to be, either," Flossie said determinedly. "Have you gone bug crazy, Bodine?"

Bodine looked like he might crumble from stress. "I don't know. I was at the store and Myrtle Bean and Neesa Hart and even Harry were after me to arrest someone—said the town looked bad with people just shootin' each other and getting away with it. Said that someone should go to jail for comatizing George. I told Myrtle plain and simple that there's no such thing as a law against coma-tizing. Leastwise, I've never heard of one. And then Lucas up and confesses to shooting George!''

"But he couldn't have!" Lacy said.

"But he says he did."

Flossie and Harper exchanged doubtful looks. "It ain't likely," Flossie said.

"But what could I do?" Bodine asked. "There was everybody tellin' me I should send for the circuit judge. And there was Lucas, confessing." He looked at them all, one by one, pleading his case. "I couldn't very well make Lucas *un*confess."

"Well I can!" Lacy said.

Before she could think twice, she raced out of the house toward the jail.

Lucas was just easing his bones onto his cot and settling in to life as a jailbird, when the jailhouse door flew open and Lacy appeared, red-faced, gulping in frantic breaths. "Have you taken leave of your senses?" she shouted at him.

As hellos went, it left a little to be desired. Still, he was so amazed to see her at all he sat up with a breath of surprised pleasure. "Thank you for opening that door. It gets a little hot in here without a breeze."

She marched up to the iron bars and gripped them hysterically, almost as if *she* were the one locked up. "I don't know what is going on inside that fat head of yours, Lucas Burns, but you've *got* to tell Bodine the truth about what happened to George."

"Maybe I did tell him the truth."

"You didn't shoot George."

He raised a brow, reached into the small bag resting on the old blanket on the bed, and popped a lemon drop into his mouth. "How do you know I didn't?"

She rolled her eyes. "No one believes you did it."

"Myrtle does."

"She *would!*"

"Harry believes it. So does Neesa Hart."

"Nobody at the boardinghouse believes it."

"That's good. I might need a few people to attest to my character before long." He chuckled. "Don't worry. I won't be summoning *you* into court."

"Don't joke, Lucas. Not when your neck could wind up in a noose."

"After our last conversation, I would have guessed that you would want a front row ticket to my necktie party." He shot her a level look, then held out the little sack. "Lemon drop?"

Her nose wrinkled.

"It's a good thing we'll never have to worry about court-ing," he said with amusement. "We could never agree on sweets. To my mind, there's nothing nastier tasting than lic-orice."

She opened her mouth to argue the point, then seemed to lose her train of thought to exasperation. "Lucas, I did not come here to argue with you about candy!"

"I figured that," he said, sucking thoughtfully on his lemon drop. "Thing is, I'll be switched if I know what you are doing here, Lacy, especially when the sheriff's not about. A jail is no place for ladies. You shouldn't be here."

"You shouldn't, either."

Though he was surprised by the conviction she spoke the words with, he refused to let himself take any comfort in her declaration. Lacy had proved herself unpredictable. Tomorrow she might just as easily wish he were in jail as out of it.

He put a hand over his heart. "I'm touched by your faith in me."

"I don't have a lick of faith in you," she corrected. "I just don't think you'd shoot a man."

"And you're always right, naturally," he said, remembering how irritatingly cocksure she could be. "You have everyone's character pegged, right down to every little reaction to every last contingency. It must be amazing to be you."

She was speechless for a moment, and he could tell she was biting back a retort. "I don't know why you're fighting with me over this. If you had the least bit of consideration for others, you would tell Bodine that you didn't shoot George. Bodine feels just awful for locking you up in here.''

A little light of understanding dawned. ''I see—so it's Bodine you're worried about.''

She looked flustered. ''Well…yes. Of course. And what about Jacob? What must he think when he discovers that his father is in jail.''

''That's why I sent Bodine over to Flossie's. I was hoping that Jacob could take advantage of your hospitality for a few days.''

''We never wanted him to leave,'' Lacy assured him honestly.

''Good. That's a weight off my mind.''

She frowned, as if taking weight off his mind wasn't at all what she intended when she stormed over here. ''Then you intend to just stay here?''

''Yes, I do.''

''Until when?''

''Well, I'm hoping George will pull through.''

''But what if he doesn't live?'' she asked, her voice rising. ''They could really try you, Lucas. Myrtle already wants Bodine to send for the circuit judge.''

''Things move slow in these parts,'' he said calmly. More calmly than he felt, actually. ''This way, at least you all can go ahead and have your big Blissful day, and you won't have to worry about the bad influence of the Rooster.''

She looked flabbergasted. ''Who cares about that?''

He laughed. ''Don't tell me you've lost your taste for battle when you're finally winning the war.''

She lifted her chin, and something about the defiant gesture, the spark in her eye, took him right back to the moments when he had held her in his arms. Even when he had been making love to Lacy, he realized, he had never felt as if he had actually been in control. For all her jawing about being ladylike and innocent, there was at her core a tough, independent spirit. She wasn't Flossie Calhoun's daughter for nothing. You could strip her bare, but her spirit was one thing you couldn't strip away from her. Maybe that was why she could always turn the tables on him. He had set out thinking that he could beat her back by teasing and intimidation, but she had come right back at him each time and matched him with her own brand of strength. Seduced him with it, in fact.

He looked at her blue eyes and felt himself being seduced all over again. All she had to do was point her chin up and bat those eyes at him, and he felt his loins quicken in response. God he wanted her. How was he ever going to get her back?

Lucas didn't like the turn his thoughts were taking, especially when there were iron rails separating them and there was absolutely nowhere for his lust to go. Lacy apparently didn't like the direction his mind was moving in, either, because as she stared into his eyes and read his transparent thoughts, two blotches of red rose high in her cheeks. Her mouth opened and closed for a moment without making a sound, as if it were taking her a moment to work up the spit to speak audibly.

When at last she did find it, her voice was small. "You *didn't* shoot him, did you, Lucas?"

Lucas laughed so hard he nearly choked on his lemon drop. "I was wondering whether you could actually be so sure of yourself—especially since you know my bad character so intimately."

Mentioning intimacy to Lacy was like waving a red flag in front of a bull. "I don't know why I'm bothering to beg you to save your own skin," she said heatedly. "You've already got more people worried about you than you deserve!"

"You don't have to worry," he said. "I absolve you."

She huffed and turned toward the door. "Even when you're helpless, you're impossible."

"And even when you're mad as hell, you're adorable."

The unexpected compliment only ruffled her more, and in a moment, she was gone as quickly as she had appeared. But he was pleased to see that she had left the door open.

* * *

"Lacy!"

At the sound of Myrtle's yoo-hooing at her from across the road, Lacy stopped in her tracks and for the first time muttered a genuine curse to herself. Damnation! She was hot, and confused, and when she turned, Myrtle was hurtling toward her across the dusty street, her ample bosom heaving as one tightly corseted unit.

What did *she* want? Hadn't she caused enough trouble for one day?

She didn't have long to wonder, because in no time at all, Myrtle was bearing down on her. "My dear girl, *what* were you doing at the jail?"

Lacy's mind raced for some explanation, but came up blank. She had just been telling herself she had to have been crazy to go in there; rationalizing this foolishness to Myrtle Bean was beyond her. "I don't know...." She stammered for a moment. "I heard that Lucas was in the jail, and naturally I was worried...about Jacob."

The minute the name came to her lips, she breathed a sigh of relief. Thank goodness—she could use the boy as her excuse. "But then Lucas told me that Bodine had gone to the boardinghouse for the express purpose of asking Flossie to look after Jacob, so—"

Myrtle's little bitty eyes bugged in horror. "You mean Sheriff Turner wasn't even at the jail with you?"

"No, he—"

"And you two were *all alone?*" Myrtle gulped like a beached fish. "For all that time?"

Lacy frowned. How long could she have been in there? Long enough for at least one busybody to take notice, apparently. "He *is* behind bars, Mrs. Bean."

"Thank heavens for that!" Myrtle exclaimed. Then she swelled up proudly, as if she were personally responsible for taking a vicious criminal off their streets. "Of course I always knew that Lucas Burns was a disreputable type, and that barroom of his has been a scar on our town for years and years. But I never thought he would *kill* a man!"

"He didn't." Lacy swallowed.

"From what I've heard, he may as well have. George can't last much longer, the doctor says." Myrtle fanned herself with her palm. "To think—it might just as easily have been my Harry!"

Lacy smiled tightly. "Yes, from the stories I've heard about Harry, it *might* have been."

Myrtle drew back. "Well! I'd say that insinuation was rather uncalled for, Lacy."

"I'm sorry," she said quickly. The last thing she needed was to have Myrtle on the warpath against *her*. "My only excuse is that I'm tired. Between working on things for Blissful Day, and seeing to George…"

Myrtle put a hand on her arm, but the forgiveness in her words didn't quite reach her eyes. "Of course! You should go home and rest. Lord knows none of us should be out in this hot sun if we can help it."

Then why are you? Lacy just managed to hold her tongue this time.

"So do you know if Sheriff Turner is still at the boarding-house?" Myrtle asked.

"I expect so."

"If you see him, maybe you can use your influence," Myrtle said. "The sheriff likes you so."

The words brought another wave of heat to Lacy's cheeks. After she had thrown herself away on Lucas, she didn't deserve a good man like Bodine. Especially after she had run off like a madwoman to see Lucas the minute she'd heard he was in jail. And what had she received for her troubles, her concern? Sneering and stonewalling!

She tapped her toe angrily as fresh anger welled up in her. "What would you like me to say to the sheriff, Mrs. Bean?"

Myrtle leaned in and said in a confidential voice, "We need to get a circuit judge here as soon as possible to try this case."

"But George isn't dead."

"Pshaw! Everybody knows he's as good as dead."

Lacy glowered. It was beginning to seem that half the town seemed awfully eager for poor George to kick the bucket.

"Anyway—" Myrtle went on "—once people hear that the town is doing something about the problem of violence and drunkenness, it's bound to make them more likely to come to Blissful Day."

"Doesn't rushing a man to trial just so we can have a good turnout strike you as a little unseemly?"

"Nonsense! You said yourself you wanted law and order in this town."

"Yes, but—"

"And you can't deny you've hated Lucas Burns from the get-go."

Hated him…and loved him…and then hated him again. Now she wasn't certain how she felt. She only knew she couldn't quite work up the gusto she'd once had for her enmity. Even though he had teased her, tricked her, seduced her.

"He *is* in jail, Myrtle. He can't hurt anyone from where he is."

Myrtle was not appeased. "The best way to get rid of a rotten egg is to bury it. Same's true with criminals."

Lacy blinked at her. Good heavens! The quality of Myrtle Bean's mercy was more than a little strained. It was strangled within an inch of its life. It was hard to believe Myrtle's opinion meant so much to her before. Looking into the woman's eyes now, Lacy saw only goodness run amok, and a woman who had completely forgotten that understanding, forgiveness, and tolerance were also virtues.

"Besides—" Myrtle said, heedless of Lacy's thoughts "—prisoners can always escape."

"The bars in that jail seemed secure to me."

Myrtle's lips turned down. "Oh, certainly. The bars are secure. But what if he had an accomplice?"

Yes! Why hadn't she thought of that?

For a fleeting moment, the thought of taking Bodine's keys, sneaking into the jail at night, and shooing Lucas out the door took hold of her mind. But only oh-so-briefly. And she immediately felt ashamed of herself. This was what Lucas had done to her. He had corrupted her, just like Myrtle claimed he had corrupted Harry.

And at that moment, she made a resolution. Come what may, she would get Lucas Burns out of her blood. Out of her heart. She was going to claw her way back to sanity while she still had a reputation to speak of.

"I'm sure that won't happen," Lacy said with confidence. "And if it makes you feel better, I'll speak to Bodine about the matter of the judge." And she would. She would tell Bodine that she didn't think a judge should be sent for.

Myrtle nodded, satisfied. "Wonderful. Don't forget the quilting bee tomorrow. Have you thought of a motto?"

Lacy stared blankly at the woman. "A what?"

"Motto, motto!" Myrtle trumpeted. "We were trying to think of a town motto at the last meeting, remember? For the plaque!"

Lacy hated to admit that she remembered practically nothing of the last meeting. That had been the day after she had first made love with Lucas, when her head was still in the clouds. "I guess I forgot."

"Well get to work on it then. We need something with zing!"

Myrtle turned and marched back toward the store.

Lacy's heart felt heavy as she watched her go. Quilting bees and hanging judges. She certainly had a lot to keep on her mind these days.

Chapter Fourteen

"You're bearing up so well," Lacy told Jacob. "Everyone's so proud of you."

Jacob, sitting on the top step of the porch, stretched his stiltlike legs. She thought she could detect a blush in his cheeks. The truth was, Jacob had seemed pleased to return to the boardinghouse, even though he surely must be worried to death inside.

"I'm all right," he said. "Though I think Pa might be afraid."

The chains supporting the porch swing were given a near-fatal yank as Lacy bolted to attention. "What would he be afraid of? A trial?"

Jacob dismissed that notion out of hand. "He told me not to bother myself about that. He says that won't come about, probably. He told me..." His mouth slapped shut for a moment. He finished more quickly, "Well, he told me not to worry."

She leaned forward. "What? What did he say?"

Jacob shook his head and announced soberly, "I'm sorry, Miss Lacy. Pa told me several things in the strictest confidence." The proud tilt of his head announced how he felt about shouldering such a responsibility.

That fact only made her that much more rabid to know what Lucas had said. But of course she couldn't force a boy to break a promise—especially not a promise to his own father. She leaned back in the swing, brimming with frustration. She picked up her sewing again and blindly stitched at a handkerchief for her booth. If idle hands were the devil's workshop, no one could accuse her of doing commerce with Old Scratch. Which just showed how wrong proverbs could be. She had made so many potholders and pencil cases and doilies and handkerchiefs that she probably could crank them out in her sleep. Her hands might be busy, but her mind was idling, and most of the time it was idling on one subject: Lucas. Sitting in that jail cell.

"Is there some problem you haven't told us about?" she asked. "If there's anything we can do...."

Jacob shook his head. "When I said he might be afraid, I meant he could be worried that I might leave. To go find my ma."

That statement struck her like a thunderclap. Lucas had told her that Jacob didn't know about Alice. She cleared her throat, feeling she needed to tread carefully. "Do you know where she is?"

His lips screwed up. "Not exactly. Pa said somewhere around Colorado."

She couldn't help asking, "When did he tell you this?"

"Just a few nights ago. He sat me down on the porch and told me all about how it was when he was married, and how my ma left when I was still in diapers."

"Oh." That must have been right after she had taken him to task for keeping Jacob's mother a secret from the boy. That fact astounded her. Lucas had actually taken her advice?

"I guess I knew all along she was probably alive," Jacob said. "I know a few boys who lost their mothers." He ducked his head and stammered, "I—I mean, whose mothers had died. But those boys all know where their mothers are buried. Their families put flowers on the grave on special days, and have pictures out on the mantel. But I never saw any pictures, and Pa never mentioned a grave to me. He never mentioned her

at all. Do you think maybe he was scared I might run away
to her?''

A lump formed in her throat. She remembered that she had
noticed a bit of loneliness in Lucas's eyes from the very first,
despite the fact that he ran a busy place. And then there was
his defensiveness about Jacob. She wouldn't be a bit surprised
if Jacob was right.

"Or maybe he felt embarrassed. But heck, other people
leave their families, I've heard. Norman Dougall over in Tate
went to California one day, and he only left his family a short
note and a dollar and twenty cents.''

"Oh, my.''

Jacob wrapped his shoelace absently around his finger. "I
reckon a dollar and twenty cents was all he felt he could spare
from his journey, but I guess Squirrel-Tooth Shirley needed
more than that to raise three daughters, 'cause she sent them
away.''

Squirrel-Tooth Shirley? Why, that was the name of the
woman who had spat on her! Lacy could well understand why
a man might want to abandon *her.*

Her lips twisted into a thoughtful frown. Of course, back
when the woman was simply Mrs. Norman Dougall—probably
before she had assumed the habit of expectorating on her enemies—she might not have been so terrible. Lacy had to admit
that events in life had a way of making people do things they
might not consider possible. Look at herself! Lying with a man
not her husband...and *she* didn't even have the excuse of being down to her last dollar and twenty cents. No, she had acted
out of sheer animal desire.

And the consequence? Daily she feared she would discover
evidence that she was with child. She had gone so far as to
sneak a look at the nursing book her mother kept in the corner
cupboard in the kitchen. She had read with dawning mortification what the results of her rash acts could be: the cessation
of menses, the onset of sickness and the tell-tale swelling as
the baby grew inside her.

How would she explain *that* to Myrtle Bean? Just thinking

of the shame of it made her break out in a cold sweat. Moreover, she would have additional explaining to do to the child, when the child became old enough to ask questions. She didn't allow herself to believe that if she ended up in such a quandary Lucas would do the gentlemanly thing and marry her, even if he hadn't been hanged by then. The man obviously didn't love her, and he had every reason to be shy of matrimony. Perhaps she would be forced to make up a mythic parent and a tale of woe, like that soldier on a battlefield in Tennessee. Only for her it would be a gold rush that proved irresistible, say, or a fatal bolt of lightning.

Oh, lord, what was she going to do?

"But I don't think I ever will go find my mother. I think we've done pretty well with just the two of us."

Lacy thought of Flossie and of all the things she'd always had. Good clean clothes, a safe roof over her head, an education. A lump caught in her throat. Flossie's whole life had been about providing for her. She could hardly wrap her mind around the sacrifices she had probably made, especially in the early days.

"Oh, Jacob. I hope you told him that."

"Oh, sure, I said something like that. Since we were talking man-to-man and everything. I also told him it would be okay with me if he got married again."

Lacy's throat felt as if she had swallowed dust. "I'm not sure—"

"I'd like him to find a good wife, though. Someone like you."

"Oh!" Lacy didn't know what to say to *that*. Except that, as usual, Jacob seemed to be way ahead of his father.

"I was hoping we would move back here after Pa gets out of jail, but I don't think that's going to happen," Jacob said. "He said it was a mistake to move over here in the first place."

Her breath caught. "He did? When?"

"Right after we moved out. He told me he wasn't…" Jacob

squinted "...infallible, I think it was. He was acting really odd that night."

As Jacob spoke, Lacy felt as if she were catching the words and cupping them in her hands so she could study them later. And so she did. Long after Jacob had run off, Lacy sat on the porch, thinking. Lucas had been sorry about moving into the boardinghouse....

Sorry he'd tricked her?

But if he regretted how he had treated her, why hadn't he told her so?

She expelled a long sigh. Hadn't she vowed to get Lucas out of her blood? And yet an innocent comment from Jacob had set her to brooding. Most likely Lucas had just meant that he was sorry he ever laid eyes on her.

If she kept on going this way, one day *she* would snap and run off to California, just like the man who'd left Squirrel-Tooth.

Later, after checking on George as he always did, Bodine lingered. Lacy brought him some tea in the parlor. Jacob was in the yard in back of the house, taking advantage of the last of the sunlight. Birdie, who was growing ever more devoted to nursing George, was watching the patient. And soon after Flossie had greeted Bodine and invited him to slip off his coat and stay for a while, she had announced her intention to find Harper and take a walk.

"George sure is bucking Doc Hart's predictions," Bodine said.

Lacy somberly scooped out sugar. "Yes, but he's not getting any better. How long can a man remain this way?"

"Maybe George figured he needed a rest."

She tried to smile as she handed him the cup and saucer. But in addition to wishing George would get better, she worried what his continued unconscious state would mean for Lucas.

Bodine sipped the hot brew appreciatively. "You certainly make a fine cup of tea, Lacy."

"Thank you." She cleared her throat. "What if, for instance, George never recovers? Then Lucas would be charged with his murder, wouldn't he?"

He looked miserable. "Maybe so. I sent a letter to Judge Wygant to see if he has a legal opinion on the matter. He's supposed to be coming here soon. I just don't know…"

For the past few days, Bodine had looked like a man who had taken on a burden only to make the terrible discovery that it was more than he could bear. His normally jovial face was wracked with worry lines, and his shoulders seemed stooped beneath the weight of carrying half the town's need for justice and his own friends' life-and-death problems. "To be honest, Lacy, I'm thinking that my days in Blissful might be numbered."

Lacy looked at him, concerned. "You're leaving?"

"Hope so."

"But you can't leave *now!*"

He looked disturbed that she might think he was running out of Blissful in its time of trouble. "No, not while things are so up in the air," he agreed. "But I always did say that I intended to go back to Cicada Creek, soon as I had a little money saved. And—"

His words broke off abruptly.

Lacy leaned in. "And what?"

"Well, I don't want to be forward, Lacy, but I don't see a reason for beating around the bush. I guess there's no woman in Blissful I admire as much as you."

The statement startled her. "Really?"

He nodded, then looked puzzled. "Who else would I admire? You're practically the only woman here."

She didn't have an answer for that. "Oh, well…thank you." She lowered her eyes. "I'm not sure I deserve admiration." In fact she was sure she didn't.

Impulsively, Bodine lurched forward and clasped her hands. "Oh, but you do—that is, I think so. Why, you've got all the qualities my ma said I should look for in a woman. You're sweet-natured and handy around the house, and I swear nobody keeps a better weeded garden than you. And of course you've got virtue to spare. Ma thinks that's important.''

She cleared her throat. He was right about the weed-free garden, at any rate. ''Thank you.''

He ducked his head. ''I guess I don't have to tell you how pretty I think you are. Ma never set much store by that—pretty is as pretty does, she always says. And for all my brother's wife being the belle of the county at one time, Ma certainly doesn't think much of *her*. But of course, Ma's not a man.''

''I guessed not,'' Lacy agreed.

''But enough about Ma,'' Bodine said. ''You've got all the qualities *I've* been looking for in a woman since I left Cicada Creek, Lacy. I guess you could say I've soured on sheriffing, and now that I want to go back home, I sure would hate to go back empty-handed. That is to say…''

His words died out and she looked into his shining, hopeful eyes, and she suddenly felt her heart pound erratically, as if it were trying to lift and sink at the same time. Just this afternoon she had been worried about what she was going to do. She had prayed for an answer to all her problems…and here he was.

''Bodine, are you asking me to marry you?''

He nearly collapsed in a heap in her lap. ''Yes, yes, I am. I didn't mean to. That is, I didn't come over here this evening with that in mind. If I had, I would have brought something for you, a trinket or a box of chocolates or some kind of little gift. But I just came to check on George, and then I got to talking about my plans and my ma, and…'' He looked up at her again imploringly. ''Will you?''

Lacy drew up and tried to look deep inside herself. Maybe she didn't love Bodine, exactly. From what little she had experienced of it, love was a dangerous emotion that robbed a woman of clear thinking. One thing was certain: Bodine would not use her and cast her away. If he said that she was the woman that he wanted to take back to Ma in Cicada Creek, she didn't have to worry that he had some ulterior motive or scheme in mind.

She just had to worry about Ma.

But of course Bodine was operating under the delusion that she was some sort of domestic saint, when in fact she might at this moment be carrying another man's child. How could she even think of marrying him under those circumstances?

Then again, how could she not? After all, she didn't *know* whether she was in the family way. And if she gave Bodine his pledge, and he gave her his, what would be the harm? From that day forward, she would dedicate her life to making him a happy man.

She hesitated, wracked by indecision. Yet when she looked down into Bodine's blue eyes, they were still clear and hopeful. He seemed to see nothing of the doubt flooding through her.

"What do you say, Lacy? Can I convince you to become Mrs. Bodine Turner?"

"Full house," Flossie said, laying down her cards on Lucas's bunk.

Lucas tipped back in the chair he had pulled out of the sheriff's half of the room. "Did you come over here just to depress me, Floss?" He tossed his losing cards down next to her winning hand and laughed.

Flossie took a tug on a cigar. "If I meant to do that, I wouldn't have to play cards."

He frowned. When Flossie had come sashaying in tonight with the sheriff's keys, a bottle of rye, and a deck of cards, her arrival had come like a breath of sunshine. Now, from the worried look in her eye, he wondered if something was up. Maybe she had just been trying to put him a frame of mind to receive bad news. "Is something wrong with Jacob?"

Flossie laughed. "Oh, no. Jacob is as happy as a pig in a poke. Don't worry about that. He's still what he's always been—better than you deserve."

"I'm relieved to hear it."

"No, the news I have is bad in a different way. Bodine was over at the house when I left."

"I didn't figure you conjured his keys out of thin air."

Flossie tilted her head. "When I left them, Lacy was going to make tea for the two of them to have in the parlor."

He chuckled, though he had a disturbing inkling of where this discussion was headed. "Am I supposed to be bent out of shape about a tea party?"

"It depends on where the intimate little tea party leads," Flossie said.

Lucas felt a sharp strangling feeling take hold of his chest, and drew in a breath. He let it out slowly, trying to get hold of himself. "The sheriff's been buzzing around Lacy since she got here."

"But lately, there's been something different in the air, and in Bodine's face. He's been a different man these last few days, Lucas. He used to act like a young man with all the time in the world to make up his mind what he wanted to do. But now that Myrtle is pestering him about his job, and he's got you locked up here, I don't think he likes Blissful half as much as he used to. And I can't blame him. This situation has him in a hell of a fix."

"So he wants to run home to Ma."

"I expect so." Flossie chortled. "Can't say's I blame him. That ma of his sounds like she would walk through a bed of copperheads to protect her boy. That's probably why he left Cicada Creek to begin with—and why it would feel so good to run back now."

"And you think he wants to run back with a wife in tow...."

"I expect he realizes that's the only way he'll ever have any independence from Ma Turner if he does go back there."

Lucas thought about it. The image of Lacy marrying Bodine Turner nettled him. But why, exactly? Lacy hadn't come back to the jail since their first brief encounter right after he was locked up. And she had made it clear, many times, that she thought he wasn't good enough for her.

But Bodine was. Oh, yes. Bodine the Virtuous would be a perfect match. Unless, of course, Bodine found out she wasn't quite as sin-free as she pretended to be. But that information would never come from his own lips.

Unless, of course, he got *very* desperate.

"What's all this got to do with me?"

Flossie rolled her eyes impatiently. "I might be a little slow on the uptake, but I've been puttin' some things together. When she heard you were locked up, Lacy didn't come running over here to make sure the bars were good and tight. I bet ten dollars you'd be heartbroken if the sheriff married my daughter."

He squinted at her. "What's your real stake in this, Floss? I imagine Bodine would make you a fine son-in-law."

"Maybe so. But Lacy's been acting strange lately. Bothered." She eyed Lucas pointedly.

"How do you know she's not bothered by Bodine?"

"Because Bodine isn't the type to get any woman bothered. He doesn't have a rough edge on him—and if you don't mind my saying so, Lacy looks like she's been up against some rough edges lately. I'm willing to bet she wants you."

Hope rose in him, then popped just as quickly. He let out a sigh. "Even if it were true, I'm hardly in a position here to bust up a courtship, Floss. I'm practically a condemned man, remember? Is that the sort of suitor you want for your daughter?"

Flossie pursed her lips. "Lucas, when are you going to end this foolishness and stop covering up for Boot?"

He blinked at her innocently. "Covering up what?"

"What, my fanny!" She exhaled a puff of smoke at him. "You know and I know that you didn't shoot George. I doubt you've pointed a gun at another man in your entire life. That fight with George had all the earmarks of something a hotheaded idiot like Boot Withers would pull."

"You weren't there," he reminded her.

"I didn't have to be. You didn't shoot him, Lucas. I know it in my heart. You're a good man, and you're covering for him because you're afraid with his history the townsfolk would want a little frontier justice."

"Wouldn't they?"

"They still do, only it's you they're focussed on now." She shook her head. "I don't know what you did to keep Boot out of town these last few days, but it's probably the first time in his life he's ever done anything anyone told him to do. He's probably driving Henrietta Wallace up a tree. What would you do if Boot skipped out?"

He frowned. "Everything will be fine so long as George is alive."

"I wouldn't count on that too strongly."

"Is George worse?"

"He's no better," she said. "And I wouldn't count on people around here to wait for the law to arrive to dispense justice."

"No one's bothered me yet."

Flossie gathered up her cards. "I can see you're going to be stubborn about this."

"What do you want me to do, Floss? Break jail?"

She looked meaningfully at the unlocked cell door. "Why not?"

"For one thing, I don't think Bodine would like it."

"Nothing he would like better. He's been worried sick about your being in here."

"If I leave, he'll have to be worried sick about my escaping. Also, he'll have to tell every sheriff in the surrounding area to keep an eye out for me. I'll be a hunted man."

Her brows arched. "But those sheriffs won't be hunting in the right place."

"Where would the right place be?"

"Right under Bodine's nose."

Lucas studied her. She wasn't kidding. She wanted him to walk out of there with her tonight, and he had a sneaking suspicion of where she intended him to go. The one thing he wasn't sure about was whether she was more concerned about his welfare, or the fact that she feared her daughter was about to marry a man she didn't love.

Come to think of it, Lucas wasn't sure which of those things bothered him most, either.

"I don't want you to get involved in this, Flossie. It's enough of a mess already."

"I *am* involved," she reminded him. "The victim is unconscious in one of my bedrooms. The sheriff is having tea in my parlor. Why not have the so-called killer in my attic?"

Bodine stayed to help Lacy wash up the tea things. As they stood side by side, her washing and him drying, Lacy had a flash of vision of the way the rest of her life was going to proceed. The years ahead would be purposeful, solid, comforting. She would have a real companion and helpmeet. And if her life was a little predictable...

Predictable was good, wasn't it?

"I'll bet I know what you're thinkin'," Bodine said, stacking a saucer on an already cleaned one.

"You do?" She hoped not.

"You're already thinking about your wedding dress," he guessed, about as wrong as he could be. He looked into her eyes and laughed. "I'm right, aren't I?"

She smiled. "Well..."

"I'll bet you make the prettiest bride Cicada Creek's ever seen."

The comment threw her for a loop. "But won't we be married here?"

His face fell. "In Blissful?"

"Well, yes. It's my home."

"Oh." For the first time since she had given him her answer, he seemed a little displeased. "I guess that's right. I just expected that we'd get married in Cicada Creek, with my family there."

She shrugged. "I don't suppose it really matters. But maybe it would be better if I met your mother after we're legally man and wife. That way she won't be able to talk you out of going through with the ceremony."

Bodine roared with laughter. "As if my mother would do that! Ma's going to love you, Lacy."

Lacy wasn't so sure. And she noticed that Bodine wasn't suggesting bringing his mother here for the wedding, either. Was that because he was ashamed for his mother to find out about Flossie?

As if beckoned by her thoughts, Flossie came in, a little breathless. "Hello!" she greeted them. "How's George?"

"About the same," they said at the same time.

They were even already speaking in unison. That had to be a good sign.

Bodine cleared his throat. "We've got a little news for you, Flossie."

Flossie tilted her head, smiling. "Oh?"

"I guess I should have asked your permission first," Bodine said, a little of his good cheer disappearing as he recalled this lapse in form.

Flossie dismissed his qualms. "Oh, never mind that. I wouldn't have it in my heart to turn away anybody Lacy decided to marry."

Bodine and Lacy exchanged glances, then laughed. "How did you know?" Lacy asked her.

Flossie came over and gave her a little hug. "Gut feeling, that's all. Guess you could say there was something in the air."

"But I didn't even know myself that I was going to ask her," Bodine said. "It just came out."

Flossie clasped her hands together. "An impulsive proposal! I wouldn't have thought of that coming from you, Bodine. Shouldn't you have written your ma first?"

"Ma's going to love Lacy. Anyone could tell that who knows the two of them. Lacy's just Ma's type."

"Well, *that's* a compliment to make a girl blush!"

Coming from Bodine, it was. But Lacy couldn't help noticing that this was the second time in the course of a few minutes that he had announced that his mother would love her—almost as if he were trying to convince himself of that fact.

"Congratulations to you both," Flossie said, enfolding Bodine into a hug next. "Best of luck. Though I've a notion you won't need it."

She winked at Lacy.

Lacy swallowed. To her it seemed they would need more luck than she had the nerve to pray for. Still, she tried to smile back at her mother and Bodine and act more confident than she felt.

After Bodine had thanked Flossie, and turned down her offer of a toast, he announced it was time he went home. "Where did I put my jacket?"

Flossie lifted her hand. "You two stay right here," she commanded. "I'll get it."

She turned and left the room in a flurry, leaving Lacy and Bodine standing awkwardly side by side. Bodine was practically glowing. When Flossie came back, she handed him the coat with a big smile. "It was lucky you came over tonight, Bodine."

"Sure was!" Blushing furiously, he stooped slightly and brushed his lips fleetingly against Lacy's cheek. "'Night!"

"Good night," Lacy said, marveling at how her husband-to-be seemed giddier than she was by their first kiss.

When Bodine had rushed out the door, she felt strange facing her mother again. Flossie was still beaming at her. "Well, well! This is a big night for you, honey. Your first engagement."

Lacy laughed at the unexpected remark. "My only engagement, I hope."

Flossie waved her hands dismissively. "Nonsense. I know young people—you're always getting engaged and unengaged. It doesn't mean anything."

Lacy frowned. "But I intend to marry Bodine, Mama."

"Of course you do," Flossie replied with a trilling laugh.

Lacy traipsed after her, griped by how easily her mother

could shrug off as inconclusive such a life-changing decision "But Mama, I *really do* intend to marry Bodine."

"That's what you said."

"And you like Bodine. When we gave you the news, you hugged him. You couldn't have seemed more pleased."

"Well, an engagement is always good news," Flossie said "Besides, I have some news of my own that I was just bursting to tell you."

Lacy felt jolted. Of course she knew what the news was Her mother and Harper were getting married! She felt frozen for a moment, unsure of how a daughter should react to her parent's betrothal. But then her heart was flooded with such happiness for her mother that she flew over to her and hugged her joyously. "Oh, Mama, that's wonderful."

"What is?" Flossie asked, drawing back.

Lacy's smile evaporated. "Weren't you going to tell me that you and Harper are engaged?"

Flossie hooted. "Now how could I tell you that when didn't even go anywhere near Harper today? The man's so busy with that pavilion you'd think the future of mankind were riding on it."

"But I thought you were out walking with him."

"That's just what I told that so-called fiancé of yours so could sneak off with the keys to the jail."

"*So-called?* Mama, I—" Lacy stopped, and gulped anxiously. "The…jail?"

Flossie grinned. "That's the surprise! I brought Lucas back with me."

"Back?" It felt as though a little man were inside her chest hammering crazily to get out. "Back *here?*"

Her mother nodded. "If you want to see him, he's i the—" But Lacy didn't even hear the rest. She didn't have to. She knew where in the house Lucas would be, and she was already on her way.

Chapter Fifteen

Lucas was just settling in when he heard footsteps clattering up the stairs. Lacy flew into the dark room.

"Lucas!"

He was about to tell her to be quiet when she ran right into an old chair. Woman and furniture collapsed to the ground making more racket than he would have thought possible, given that the chair wasn't very big, and neither was Lacy. He stooped down and pulled her back up to standing, and for the first time since he'd gotten the cake in his face she didn't try to swat him away or go stiff as a board. Even when she was back on her own two feet she clung to his forearms.

"Lucas!" she repeated, as if she just couldn't believe he was standing before her.

He was having a hard time adjusting, too. Even though he hadn't spent that long enjoying the hospitality of Blissful's jail, he still had to admit he preferred freedom.

"Why are you standing here in the dark? I can't even see your face." She turned and bumbled around the room a few moments more until she found the candle.

"I believe that's the point," he said. "And if you could hold your voice down to a whisper—"

"What?" She lit a match.

"Don't—"

As the illumination struck her face, Lucas swallowed his

words. He doubted he had ever seen her prettier than she was at this moment. The soft glow did magical things to her lively eyes, and made her blond hair seem almost like a halo around her face. Looking at her, he was hit with a powerful longing almost as forceful as a physical blow. Maybe it was just the candle glow, or the fact that this was the room where they had made love the first time. Maybe he was just remembering the way the flickering candle had played off her naked skin that night....

She blinked. "What were you saying?"

Steady, boy. "I was saying, don't light that candle, but I suppose it's all right just for a moment." It would give him something to dream about. "But I would appreciate it if you wouldn't keep shouting my name. No sense in me leaving jail if you're going to get me thrown right back in."

Her blue eyes widened, and her lips parted. "Lucas!" She scurried over until she was practically standing on the toes of his boots. "Don't tell me you broke jail!"

He considered. "Technically I didn't break anything. Flossie had the key."

Her hands flew to her cheeks. "Oh, no!"

"What did you think, that I had received a pardon?"

"I wasn't thinking at all. I just heard that you were here and…"

He lifted his hands to pat her thin shoulders. "And you came right up to see me. I'm touched."

The disbelief in her face transformed to a scowl. "You're touched in the head!" she said in a desperate whisper. "What will happen when Bodine discovers you're gone?"

"I saw him ambling toward the jailhouse just now from out the window. He should be sounding the alarm any minute now."

She looked almost frantic. "Everyone will think you're guilty!"

"They probably think that anyway."

"But now they'll know it. Oh, Lucas, why didn't you just stay where you were?"

"Flossie convinced me it was a good idea to get out of there."

"She *would!*" Lacy stormed. "But they'll come looking for you here."

"No they won't. The way Flossie and I figure it, they'll assume this is the last place I'd go, since the man I shot is lying unconscious downstairs, and my son is staying here, too. And especially since the sweetheart of the town sheriff lives here."

A shadow crossed Lacy's face. "Oh, no!"

"What's the matter?"

She shook her head. "Lucas, you'll have to go."

"Go where?"

"I don't know—back to the jail. You can't stay here. Birdie's just downstairs."

"Flossie told me she was looking after George tonight."

"She is now, but her room is just below here. If she hears you moving around later, she's bound to tell."

"Then I'll tippy-toe so she won't hear me." When her expression became more frenzied, he touched his knuckle to her chin and lifted her face so that he could look her directly in the eye. "It's not Birdie you're worried about, is it? It's Bodine."

Her breath caught. "Yes. You see, Bodine and I..."

He felt his own expression go slack. "You what?"

"Well, I was just telling Mama that Bodine asked me to marry him tonight."

For a moment it felt as if all the air had been sucked out of the room. "And what was your answer?"

Her gaze tore from his and shot off to a dark corner. "I said yes."

His hands dropped. "You can't be serious."

"Why not? Bodine is a good man—"

He rolled his eyes. "Yes, yes. A good respectable man. In other words, the opposite of me."

"Yes!"

"But have you broken the news to this pillar of virtue that you aren't such a pillar yourself?"

For a moment she looked like she might lash out at him, but then those thin shoulders sagged. "No, I haven't," she admitted.

"Don't you think you ought to?" He managed only a listless chuckle. "I imagine confession would be right up your alley."

"What purpose would that serve?" From the quickness of her answer, and the heat in her voice, he could tell that she had formed this argument already. "Really, it would just be causing undue trouble. I'll make Bodine a good wife, I know I will." She ducked her head. "Especially once we're away from here and settled in Cicada Creek."

"That'll be cozy—you, Bodine and his mama."

She tossed her head. "It won't be like that. Bodine wants to buy a place of our own."

"Let me guess... Somewhere close enough where dear old mother can visit several times a week." He chuckled. "You'll *love* to have someone tell you how to run your house, Lacy."

"I'm sure Mrs. Turner is a very kind, very good woman and that we'll get along famously," Lacy said with a clenched jaw. "And anyway, I'm not marrying Mrs. Turner, I'm marrying Bodine because I respect him and care for him and—"

"And because he asked you," Lucas finished.

A glower settled over her features, and she crossed her arms. "I couldn't very well marry him if he didn't ask me," she snapped. "For that matter, I would think you'd be happy he did. You should be doing handsprings—you're finally getting what you want. I'll be leaving Blissful."

She had him there. A few weeks ago he *would* have been doing handsprings. But that was before...well, before he'd gone and lost his head. The world had changed so much in so short a time that Lacy's leaving town now seemed only like the sourest kind of victory. No victory at all, in fact.

He grunted. "So you shut down the Slipper and practically elevated Myrtle to the status of morality mayor. In fact, you've almost made it so the only fun left in this town is teasing you, and now you're leaving. I ask you— Is that fair?''

She laughed in spite of herself, but soon was serious again. Her gaze cut anxiously toward the window, then to the door. "Oh, Lucas. Any minute now there's going to be a manhunt."

He waved away that fear. "Bodine and whoever he rounds up to look for me will think I hoofed it off to San Antonio or Laredo."

"And so you should!"

He laughed. "I'm gratified that you would care so much about my escape."

"Of course I care," she said, blushing. She added quickly, "About Jacob, especially. What are we going to tell him?"

"Flossie's going to tell him I'm right here."

"You're telling him *the truth?*" she asked, aghast. "Lucas, the more people who know where you are, the more danger you're in."

"I trust Jacob. And he deserves to know the truth."

Frustration was evident in her eyes. "I don't understand why you want to be here, anyway. If you stay here, you'll be caught, and when they catch you, you'll look guiltier for having run."

"Well, maybe they'll be more lenient on me since I didn't run very far." The argument wearied him. Lacy was engaged to the sheriff. His jailbreak had come too late to stop that from happening. Now he just had to make sure matters weren't carried any further. He crossed over to the bed and fell on it with a squeaky thump. "And as for why I'm here, I decided that if I was going to be confined in Blissful, I'd prefer this bed to the one at the jailhouse."

"How can you talk so flippantly?"

"There's nothing flippant about it. This bed has better memories." He grinned. "Care to join me?"

At his raised-brow leer, she stepped backward. "All right, stay here and get caught. See if I care."

"I think you *do* care."

''Only that you're putting all of us in this house in a quandary.''

He eyed her closely. ''I suppose it is a bit of a fix for you. And yet I notice you're not running off to tell Bodine…like a good wife would.''

A loud knock sounded on the front door. Even though the sound was muffled for being two floors down, it was impossible to miss the urgency in it.

''Speak of the devil.'' A smile tugged at his lips. ''That'll be your intended, come to tell everyone that the prisoner has escaped. Aren't you going to go to him?''

Lacy stood rooted to the floor.

''Surely you don't believe there should be any secrets between a man and wife.''

Red suffused her face just before she blew out the candle with a huff. Her footsteps marched toward the door. ''I'm not his wife yet!'' she snapped in parting.

Would she ever be Bodine's wife?

Lucas feared that was a question that would plague him for the rest of the long night…among others. He needed to figure out how to come between a headstrong woman and her wrongheaded engagement. But seeing that he was stuck in an attic, he felt at a distinct disadvantage.

Birdie was more fidgety than ever at breakfast—and it wasn't long after she sat down at the table that she felt compelled to announce why. ''I heard noises last night.''

Forks dropped. Cups clattered into saucers. Jacob's eyes cut nervously toward Lacy, and Lacy stared guiltily down at her hands.

She could feel Harper's gaze on her, and she knew that Flossie had told him where Lucas was. And Flossie had of course told Jacob. Which meant that everyone at the breakfast table knew there was an outlaw in the attic, except for Birdie.

After Bodine had announced the jailbreak last night, every able-bodied man in Blissful had searched the whole town. The whole town, that is, save the boardinghouse. Lucas had been infuriatingly right again. No one figured he would have the gall to hide out in the same house where George lay in a coma.

Flossie was the first to pull herself together. "You're *always* hearing things, Birdie."

Birdie, who usually would be put off by such a dressing-down, shook her head adamantly. "It sounded like something in the attic."

"That was me," Lacy blurted out. "I was in the attic, looking for—for—for—" Her mind was a blank.

"Lace!" Flossie said, and Lacy looked up at her, thinking her name had been called. For her cluelessness, Lacy received a sharp kick in the shin from her progenitor. "I sent you up to look for *lace* for your wedding dress."

"That's right!" bleated Lacy. Glad to have a change of subject, she asked, "Did I tell you that the sheriff and I are engaged, Birdie?"

Birdie's lips turned down. "Yes, you did."

"Oh." So much for hoping to divert Birdie's attention with her big news.

"You've announced that engagement of yours twice already since I sat down," Harper pointed out. "But I suppose if it makes you feel better, or helps convince you that you really are going to be hitched, you can keep on announcing it."

"Now, Harper, a girl naturally bubbles over at a time like this," Flossie said. "If she gets a little repetitive, it's just natural."

Birdie's head tilted. "I wouldn't know about that, of course," she said primly. "I've never been engaged. All I know is, I heard something last night. And it didn't sound like Lacy."

"Probably the wind," Flossie said.

Lacy and Jacob chimed in that this was probably the case.

Birdie's eyes narrowed. "Noooo…I don't think there *was* a wind last night. I had my window open, and the air was perfectly still in my room."

Birdie, the human weather vane. Lacy suppressed a frustrated sigh. What were they going to do? The woman was already suspicious, and Lucas had only been up there one night. All it would take was one wrong move...

"What with all this talk about Lucas Burns being a fugitive, and hearing that noise, I didn't get a wink of sleep!" Birdie exclaimed.

Nervous glances were exchanged all around. Then Jacob, as if someone had poked him, piped up, "It was Elmer!"

Lacy swung around to face him. "Elmer?"

He nodded. "Elmer's the Rooster's cat."

Birdie let out a strangled cry. "A c-cat?" Judging from her terrified expression anyone would think she feared felines more than felons.

"He's just a sweet old tom cat, and no trouble," Jacob said. "I couldn't very well leave him back at the saloon, could I? Not with the place all closed up like it is." His voice was laced with such genuine worry, she decided the boy had a future as a thespian. Lacy could have hugged him. She would go over this morning, fetch that cat, and give it the best meal it ever had.

"But I don't like animals in the house," Birdie said, turning to Flossie. "You said there wouldn't be any animals. You promised Myrtle."

Flossie considered. "Well now, I *did* say that. But that was before the saloon closed. Jacob's right, we can't just abandon the poor creature."

"But what if he bites someone?"

"He's not a dog, Birdie," Harper said. "I imagine if you leave Elmer alone, Elmer will be glad to do you the same favor."

Birdie did not seem at all satisfied by that kind of compromise. "But if he's going to be keeping people up at night... I would hate to think of him disturbing poor Mr. Oatley."

A wave of irritation slapped Lacy. When did Birdie get so brave? She'd spoken more this morning than in the last four weeks combined. Lacy was nostalgic for the time when she wouldn't have offered a peep at the breakfast table, much less argued with anyone.

"Best thing for George if the cat did wake him up," Harper said.

"I'm speaking of his peace of mind. And besides, a cat in the house..." Birdie shivered. "Don't you think you should keep him out of the attic?"

"Elmer will take care of any mice that decide to take up housekeeping up there," Flossie said. "Which would you rather have, Birdie, rodents or a cat?"

The word *rodent* nearly unhinged poor Birdie. "Mice? I didn't know—"

"'Course we have mice. All houses have a few little critters, after all," Flossie said. "Elmer will be worth his weight in gold."

Birdie fell silent, and there was palpable relief around the table. Knowing how Birdie hated animals, the Elmer story would ensure she didn't go up to the attic. Also, it gave them some explanation if Lucas made noise again.

Birdie pushed her scrambled eggs around her plate and took a nibble at a biscuit. As she chewed, her eyes were narrowed. Then, while the others were gulping down food in relief that the subject of what was in the attic was settled, she declared, "It didn't *sound* like a cat."

Lacy bit back a groan.

"I heard a *loud* noise," Birdie said with growing self-confidence. "Louder than a cat could make."

"Elmer's a big cat," Jacob explained.

Just when Lacy thought they were done for, someone knocked at the front door. She and her mother looked at each other nervously.

"Could it be the doctor?" Lacy asked.

Birdie shook her head. "It's not time. He said he'd come this afternoon."

"Bodine always comes in the back door at this hour," Lacy said.

Harper threw down his napkin, chuckling. "I know one way to solve this mystery," he said. "I'll go see who is at the door."

Birdie looked on the verge of expiring from nerves. "What with the news about Lucas Burns, everything seems unsettling."

"I doubt it's Lucas knocking at the front door, Birdie," Flossie said. "Fugitives from justice don't knock, as a rule."

"Lucas never knocked anyway," Lacy mumbled under her breath.

She and Jacob were chuckling secretively at her joke when Harper reappeared in the doorway. In that moment, all thoughts of fugitives and cats and attics vanished. Next to Harper was a woman—a woman whose face brought a gasp from Flossie.

Lacy could barely identify the dark haired woman as one of the women who had fled Blissful on the morning after she arrived, but her difficulty wasn't simply because she didn't know the woman very well. The woman was battered almost past anyone's recognizing her.

One side of her face was scraped as if she'd been slapped with a tree branch. That was bad enough. But the other side was truly horrifying. The eye was swollen shut, her lip showed a scabbed-over cut, and her cheek was shiny and blue tinged with yellow. Staring at the bruise, Lacy felt sickness rise in her throat.

Once she had recovered from the initial shock, Flossie leapt from her chair and ran over to the young woman. "Lila! Honey, what *happened?*"

Lila, who said not a word, flung herself into Flossie's arms and dissolved into sobs.

It was some time before the poor woman was composed enough to get her story out. She was too embarrassed to speak before Harper, Jacob and Birdie. When the others had left the breakfast table, Flossie sat Lila down in front of a plate of eggs and smoked ham and coaxed the tale out of her.

"It was a rougher bunch at Sal's than here at the Slipper," Lila began tentatively. Given the woman's damaged face, neither Lacy or Flossie questioned that statement's veracity. "There was one man in particular, Mr. Sewell, who was awfully mean. You wouldn't have had him here, Flossie—but Sal was different. He beat up another girl named Nell, too. After what happened to Nell, I told Sal I wanted to leave. To come back here.''

That was the first time Lila actually acknowledged Lacy. She smiled at her with a rueful wince. ''I remembered you asking us that morning we all left whether any of us would like to stay. I'm sorry I didn't take you up on that offer, but all the other girls were leaving, and I didn't see how I could stay and still make a living. And then there was another thing...'' For a moment, her face was twisted into a puzzled frown, as if she were remembering something more hurtful than a beating. ''I figured it was time I left Blissful anyway.''

She swallowed and then took a deep breath, returning to the original thread of her narrative. ''When I told Sal I wanted to come back here, she said I owed her money on account of I wasn't as busy as the other girls. So I stayed, thinking I could pay off my debt to her. But I couldn't get ahead. Things weren't too busy there, and Sal claimed she had expenses startin' up the house.'' She shuddered. ''And then two nights ago she told me to entertain Mr. Sewell, and when I wouldn't do the thing he wanted me to...''

Flossie's eyes filled with tears, and she put her hand over Lila's and squeezed it. ''Oh, honey! I'm so sorry.''

''It's not your fault.''

''But it is. It was me who first took you in after you left your home.''

Lila ducked her head. ''My father wasn't much better than the man who did this to my face.''

Those words stunned Lacy more than anything she'd heard so far. What kind of life had this woman had? It was almost beyond her imagination. And what had she done to deserve all the troubles that had been heaped on her?

''I could have done something for you,'' Flossie said, agitated. ''I could have given you money and told you to go set yourself up in a respectable job. But I looked at things different then. I just didn't think...'' She whipped out a handkerchief with her free hand and dabbed her eye. "Well, you know I never wished this on you, Lila."

"I know." Lila nodded at her reassuringly. "Would it be all right if I stayed here for a while, Floss? Just till I'm on my feet again?"

"You can stay forever if you want," Flossie said. "You know how I feel. I've missed you something awful!"

At that heartfelt exclamation, Lacy felt moisture well in her own eyes. Why, Flossie was acting as if she looked on this woman almost as…a daughter. And Lila had come to her in a moment of distress, just as a daughter would have. For some reason, she hadn't looked upon the exodus of the fancy women as her mother losing friends. And yet her mother clearly cared deeply about Lila.

And Lacy could see why. In spite of her wretched appearance, Lila was clearly a sweet soul. She had a genteel bearing and good manners, for all the roughness she had experienced in her short life. In fact, something about her dull, steady gaze made Lacy feel faintly foolish and half formed.

Flossie and Lila's conversation was interrupted by the sheriff's abrupt arrival in the kitchen. Lacy was glad to see him. She was an unwanted third party in this reunion, and Bodine's taking her for a walk would be an excuse for her to get out of the house.

One look at Bodine, however, and Lacy knew she wasn't going anywhere. As he gazed at Lila, he was practically green.

Lila's bruised lips parted. "Hello, Bodine."

He looked into her eyes and his expression darkened, as if a thundercloud had rolled across his face. "Who did this? I'll kill him!"

And though Lila soon convinced him that killing wouldn't be necessary, Bodine's expression when he'd made the offer stuck with Lacy. It was the first time she had ever seen him angry. In fact, it was the first time she had seen her fiancé overcome with any kind of emotion that didn't involve his mother.

* * *

The next evening, Lacy and Bodine sat on the settee. Flossie was perched on a chair by the window, trying to finish her fortune-teller's costume in the waning light. Her needle whipped at the gauzy material in quick, uneven stitches. Every once in a while she muttered a curse when the wild needle poked her finger. It was practically the only talk in the room; with Flossie distracted by needlework, the house had lost its main source of chatter. Jacob was horsing around outside with a friend whose family was camped outside of town for Blissful Day, which was the following day. Birdie was holed up in the sickroom reading aloud from *The Pilgrim's Progress*—a book, Jacob had informed them earlier, that wouldn't wake anyone from a coma.

Lila was seated at the piano, playing old melodies that pleased Bodine no end. Listening, he had a smile on his face— a smile that seemed to turn into a troubled grimace every time his gaze met Lacy's.

On one of these occasions, Lacy returned the tense smile and strained to initiate some conversation. "I think it's sweet how devoted Birdie is to looking after George, don't you?"

Bodine stared at her for a few moments, as if the words were taking longer than normal to absorb. He was in such a daze he seemed not to register the names Birdie or George. For a moment Lacy wondered if the man even knew where he was.

"Bodine?"

He jumped. "Sure, sure!" He frowned. "What was the question?"

"I said, Birdie certainly seems devoted to nursing George, doesn't she?"

"Does she?" Bodine asked. "I hadn't noticed."

Hadn't noticed? In the past few days Birdie had discovered her calling in life. She was with George practically every waking moment. Lacy had even heard her talking to the man— *talking*—to him! Apparently Birdie didn't mind conversing with the opposite sex as long as that person couldn't form a reply to scare her with. But Birdie was growing bolder since she had taken over the care of George.

But ever since Lila had arrived in town, Bodine had seemed focussed exclusively on her, so how could he have noticed Birdie? Lacy didn't know what to make of the change in the man. He kept staring at Lila with a sort of calflike expression.

He never stared at *her* that way. There was only one man who had ever looked at her that way—unfortunately, he was a duplicitous schemer.

Not to mention a fugitive from justice.

Lacy crossed her arms, flopped against the backrest, and sighed. Bodine didn't notice that, either. All of a sudden, he started singing along with the piano in a warbly baritone.

"Silver Threads Among the Gold!"

As though mesmerized, he stood, strolled over to the piano, and leaned one elbow against it. The way his eyes sparkled when he looked down at Lila, it was as if he was enraptured.

Lacy could only sit through one treacly verse. "I think I'll stretch my legs," she said.

Bodine didn't hear her.

Flossie pricked her finger and barked out another curse without looking up.

Lacy headed for the front door, but at the last moment turned and ran up the stairs. She doubted anyone saw, much less cared, where she went.

"Just the woman I wanted to see!" Lucas exclaimed cheerily when she barged in on him.

"At least *someone* wants to see me," she said, relieved.

Amazingly, the man was not the least bit edgy from his days of confinement in the attic, and before that, the jail. He had been in better humor this past day than she had seen him in for some time. Which just showed what an ornery creature he was.

"I have a surprise for you," he said.

A surprise? She couldn't help leaning forward eagerly. "What is it?"

"Close your eyes."

She stared at him skeptically—with her eyes wide open.

He feigned hurt. "Don't you trust me?"

"Yes, I trust you to stick a bug in my hand, or crack an egg in my hair."

He guffawed. "That's schoolyard stuff even Jacob's grown out of. Now be brave and close your eyes."

She suspected she was being more gullible than brave, but she managed to squeeze her eyes closed.

"Now hold out your hands."

Reluctantly, she did so, and in the next moment, he placed something on her outstretched palms. It didn't feel like a bug. It was too heavy, and the bottom was cold. Like glass. She opened her eyes.

At first she couldn't quite understand what she was staring at. She was fairly certain it was a whiskey bottle. But it was decorated so prettily she almost didn't recognize it as such. The glass flask had been pasted over with bits of material to give it a crazy quilt pattern. The neck was festooned with bits of ribbon and a cluster of grapes from one of Flossie's old hats. Out of the top grew flowers—a mismatched bouquet of cloth daisies and gardenias, and real dried heather and paper rolled to look like roses. And out of the center peeked the face of a little bird, a wren perhaps, fashioned out of cloth with a leather beak, real feathered wings and tiny buttons for eyes.

A delighted laugh bubbled out of her.

"Do you like it?"

"Oh, Lucas—it's ridiculous."

He seemed to take that as the highest compliment. The odd thing was, he was so eager for her reaction, and appeared so pleased that she liked it. "It is, isn't it? You wouldn't believe how much sweat I've expended over such a stupid damn thing."

She pivoted around, spying objects he might have used. An old sewing basket of scraps. A feather pillow. Flossie's old hat boxes. And of course, the bottle itself—there were plenty of those lying around. He had made liberal use of all the junk in the attic, and from it constructed a tiny masterpiece.

"It's very clever," she said with real appreciation. "I wish you had more time—we could have sold these at our craft booth tomorrow."

"Sell?" he asked, appalled. "I wanted to make you something unique. It was the only sort of bouquet I could put together for you here in my hiding place."

It was then that she understood that Lucas wasn't just showing the bouquet to her, he was giving it to her. As a present. For a moment she was so flustered she didn't know what to say.

"Why on earth would you go to such trouble?" she asked, astonished.

"A man wants to give a woman flowers." He stepped closer. "I don't have to translate what that means for you, do I?"

A blush rose in her cheeks. Bodine hadn't given her any flowers since he'd picked a bunch of Indian paintbrushes for her on one of their rides, weeks ago. And now here was Lucas of all people toiling away at this silly thing, when she was engaged to another man. True, if she were tempted to smell the bouquet, it would probably bear the perfume of old whiskey, but she nevertheless found herself clutching at the gift as if Lucas had just handed her a basket of the most fragrant red roses.

And the way he was looking at her! She went warm all over as his gaze settled on her face, her lips. Given that Lucas had seen her stripped naked, and had made love to her and whispered the most intimate things imaginable to her, she should have been immune to what a simple little gaze could do to her.

But she wasn't. And when he stepped forward, rubbing his thumb along her jaw, she shivered so she half expected him to laugh at how easily he could arouse desire in her. But he wasn't laughing. His lips weren't set in their usual sneer; his eyes weren't twinkling at some secret joke. Instead, when she looked into those dark depths she saw...

What she'd seen when Bodine was looking at Lila.

Tenderly, his lips came down on hers, and she was wrapped in his warmth. She leaned into his broad, rock-solid chest as if she were coming home. She had missed this, wanted it without consciously realizing it. Despite the tension she could feel in his shoulders, his kiss was achingly sweet.

How long had it been since she had kissed him? A week, perhaps? And yet it felt like much longer. She clung to him, pressed needfully against him, and filled with happiness when his tongue parted her lips. She felt that frantic yearning build in her, that burning need that Lucas seemed to trigger so easily. Throwing caution to the wind, she pressed her hips against him suggestively.

Lucas pulled his lips from hers. He smiled, and gently pressed his forehead against hers, nuzzling her. He was being cautious with her, she thought in confusion, trying to absorb this new turn of events. He wasn't ripping at her clothes, or wheeling her toward the bed, or growling suggestively in her ear. He was behaving as if…

She frowned, and stepped back. A slight throbbing began in her temples. Piecing together what was happening was difficult. It almost seemed…no, it *absolutely* seemed…that Lucas Burns was behaving like a man in love.

She gasped, and clutched her whiskey bottle to her breast. "You are a monster!"

His head tilted slowly. "Am I?"

"You know you are! For weeks you've tormented me, plagued me. You tricked me and seduced me into your bed. But this your most suspicious change of tactic yet!"

"What is?" he asked.

"Being *nice!*" she sputtered. "Just when everything was going so perfectly, you have to try to trip me up by doling out little presents and sweet kisses and…"

His gaze darkened in doubt. "Are you sure everything was going so perfectly?"

"Of course!"

"You mean you're happy sitting down there with Bodine and Lila?"

Her mouth dropped open. "What do you know about that?"

"Flossie told me the sheriff's barely left the house since Lila got back."

"So?" She hated the hysterical tension in her voice. "He's got a kind heart."

"Certainly does," Lucas agreed, and his voice was peculiarly without malice. "Especially when it comes to that woman."

Her curiosity reached a fever pitch. Lucas knew what no one else was telling her. She was certain he would be able to confirm everything she suspected about Bodine and Lila—that they had been lovers. That they were still in love.

She opened her mouth to ask him, then snapped it shut again.

The fact was, she was so certain, and Lucas's expression was so transparent and hauntingly sympathetic, that she didn't even have to ask. Her little dream of escaping life's messier emotions by marrying Bodine was evaporating like a dewdrop on an August morning.

And the most frightening thing was, she was relieved.

Chapter Sixteen

Lacy had dreaded Blissful Day from the beginning. She feared the event that was supposed to raise money for Blissful and give it a reason for being would bring more pandemonium than profit.

And when the big day arrived, the town was close to Bedlam. Despite Myrtle's fears, news of the escaped near-killer had not kept people away. Far from it. Judging by the dust, crowds and congestion of horses and wagons lined up on the main road, every community within a fifty-mile radius had emptied itself out and descended upon Blissful. The few flowers the women's committee had planted about the town were soon trampled, and by afternoon the bunting around the freshly painted pavilion and the welcome sign across the store bore a fine film of red dust kicked up by scores of horse and mule hooves.

The craft booths and refreshment tables had done good business for the town, but the outsiders who had come in to sell wares, swap horses, or just enjoy a day watching more activity than folks around here usually saw in a whole year, seemed satisfied, too. Finally, around the time the blazing sun of afternoon was giving way to the still of early evening, there was a lull in commerce. Loitering adolescent boys swung their legs off the backs of wagons as they showed off their purchases and swapped stories with friends they hadn't seen since school let out. Lacy had spied Jacob with a group of his friends. Women gravitated toward whatever shade could be found to talk and drink lemonade. And the smaller children, worn out from a day of excitement and games and gorging on cake and watermelon, lay on picnic blankets and under wagons, dozing.

In short, the day was a huge success. For everyone, Lacy thought as she looked toward the empty Rooster, except Lucas. Judging from the steady stream of men she had seen disappearing behind one of the larger wagons, only to come stumbling out the other side later, laughing as only drunks or fools could in this heat, she bet the Rooster would have done a booming business this day.

But Lucas was still up in his attic.

She'd been thinking about him all day. Daydreaming, she would lose track of conversations and give people the wrong change. Every time she looked toward the boardinghouse, all she could really visualize was the occupant of its topmost room. When she imagined how his eyes looked when he had spoken to her last night, she felt as though there was an earthquake trembling inside her.

Her mind kept going back to that little bouquet he had given her. A lover's gift. Did Lucas love her? *Could* he? She had been so quick to decide that he was a shallow, selfish, devilish sort of creature. And he certainly had hurt her…though Jacob had intimated that he regretted that. Did his gift mean that he had turned over a new leaf and was truly ready to make amends? She knew he was capable of love. Look how caringly he had raised Jacob from a baby; how he loved him.

He had never said, however, that he loved her.

She buried her head in her hands and felt a lone trickle of sweat between her shoulder blades. That was probably the last drop of moisture she had left in her. Birdie had promised to relieve her for a spell at the boardinghouse booth, but apparently she had become so caught up in taking care of George that she hadn't been able to spare the time. So Lacy was left to man the table the entire afternoon—and now was as dried out and leathery as a strip of jerky. That Birdie! She was on the verge of making a fool of herself over George.

Almost as big a fool as Lacy felt herself becoming on account of Lucas. She groaned at that unpleasant thought. Maybe she was being duped again, plain and simple. Lucas had decorated a whiskey bottle, and now she was rushing to make all sorts of excuses for his past behavior. She wanted to believe that he was good because she loved—

Her mind hit a snag before the thought could be completed. Oh, lord! She definitely needed to get out of the heat. Love Lucas Burns?

"Hello there."

The sound of Bodine's voice startled her. She looked up just in time to see him sinking down onto a chair next to her. Like most everyone else, he appeared withered from the heat. His ever-present smile was gone as he mopped a handkerchief across his brow. But it wasn't the heat that put the trouble in his eyes. Something was worrying him.

"What's wrong, Bodine?"

"I just spoke to Flossie."

Right now Flossie was Madame Flossie, who was doing her fortune telling business in a tent a stone's throw from Lacy's craft booth. "What did Mama say to you?"

"She told my fortune." He sighed. "It wasn't good."

Lacy bleated out a laugh, which died the moment she saw the torment in Bodine's eyes. "I'm sure you have to take anything she says with a grain of salt...."

"She predicted Ma wouldn't like the bride I took home to Cicada Creek," he announced, as if this were news that could not be doubted.

Lacy's brows beetled. "She said *that?*"

His expression was pure misery.

"But that's outrageous!" Her engagement was on shaky enough ground without her own mother undermining it, too. "Bodine, you know that's not true."

"Then why would she have said it?"

She leaned close to the sheriff and placed her hand on his.

"Bodine, Mama's just playacting. She's no more a fortune-teller than…" *Than you're Wyatt Earp,* she almost said. She bit her lip. "I just wouldn't put too much faith in what she says. It's all just to make money for the town, you know."

"Oh, sure," Bodine said. "I know." Yet his brow was still lined with worry. "You think she meant that *you* wouldn't be my bride?"

Lacy sighed. "I imagine she barely registered who she was talking to. There have been more people in and out of her tent today than have sneaked behind Jud Tanner's whiskey wagon."

"Because I can't figure how Ma wouldn't approve of you," he said, lost in thought. She doubted he had heard a word she'd said. "'Less she finds out about your mother, and I'm going to try to avoid that."

The comment, spoken in such an offhand way, caused Lacy's spine to stiffen. "I beg your pardon?"

He blinked at her. "We can't tell Ma about Flossie."

"But what if Mama wants to come visit us in Cicada Creek?"

From the look in his eye, Bodine was apparently filled with horror at the thought. "Why would she do that?"

"Because I'm her daughter!"

He scratched his chin. "Well, I don't suppose people in Cicada Creek have to know what she was."

Were the people in Cicada Creek all fools? "Even *I* knew what she was, Bodine—and I'd been in a convent for fourteen years. Besides, I don't want to live on pins and needles, waiting for your mother to overhear some gossip."

"If you could manage to tone your mama down a little…."

At that inopportune moment, Flossie meandered out of her tent and stretched lazily in the sunshine. She was wearing her gypsy costume, which consisted of a low-cut peasant blouse and several scarves tied at her waist and fluttering loose to disguise the fact she was wearing nothing but a petticoat beneath them. Another scarf was wrapped around her head, but plenty of bold red curls escaped the covering. And her face!

After over a month of lecturing her mother against wearing makeup, Lacy saw that Flossie had seized this opportunity to hit the face paint with abandon. Her lips were scarlet, her cheeks glowed red, and her eyes were lined with black and colored blue below the brow.

All this time Lacy had been trying to keep her mother from looking like a floozy, but on this, the day when the most people would see her, Flossie looked just like what she was. Brazen. Independent. Scarlet.

And Lacy finally had to admit that she liked her better that way. Harper was right. Color suited Flossie best. The face paint highlighted her smile, her bright eyes. Standing out in the sunlight, tossing off wisecracks to passers-by, Flossie was in her element again. She seemed happy.

"I like Mama just the way she is," Lacy said. "I thought you did, too. You always acted that way."

"Well, sure. Here, she's fine."

"She's fine anywhere, Bodine," Lacy said with a sudden voracity she had not expected. "I won't have anyone looking down on her."

"It wasn't that…."

"Yes, it was." Lacy wondered for a moment if she was making more out of this disagreement than it was worth. After all, who knew whether or not Flossie would ever even want to go to Cicada Creek? More and more, Lacy was doubting she'd ever see the place herself. Maybe after watching her fiancé mooning after another woman for a few days, Lacy was just spoiling for a fight. Or maybe Lucas's gift was encouraging her to argue with Bodine. Or maybe she was just irritable from sitting in the sun all day selling potholders. Whatever the reason, she couldn't stop herself from saying testily, "You think your mother would look down on my mother, so you suggested that we just pretend Flossie is something other than what she is."

Bodine, to her surprise, grew a little fierce, too. "Well, heck, Lacy, you have to admit that what she is isn't very good. You were ashamed of her yourself when you first arrived—

that's why you raised such a ruckus about making Blissful a better place, remember? You said you wanted to save the Calhoun name.''

The reminder stung. She wasn't sure how she would react, now, to the news of what her mother had been doing all those years. She just knew she wasn't comfortable with the way she had acted then. ''I feel differently now.''

He tapped his hat nervously against his leg. ''Just because you've had a change of heart, you can't expect the whole world to. Or my ma. Who *would* want a madam's daughter for a daughter-in-law?''

Anger choked her throat. ''For heaven's sake, keep your voice down,'' she hissed. ''And I'll thank you to remember that she is a *former* madam.''

His tapping became more forceful. ''Why, for that matter, who knows what Flossie did before she became a madam? She might have been a loose woman herself.'' His eyes widened.

''Yes,'' Lacy said, wondering if Bodine truly hadn't considered this possibility before. It had plagued her own mind so often that she found his naiveté almost unbelievable. ''That's probably true.''

''Well, then.'' He jumped up and emitted a surprised cry. ''It wouldn't be so different than me taking a prostitute into my ma's house!''

She crossed her arms over her chest, which was rising and falling with the angry gulps of breath she was taking. ''That's one way of looking at it.''

Bodine slammed his hat on his head and swung around to stare at the boardinghouse. ''I always said to myself that I could never do that—that I couldn't insult Ma that way.''

''You seem to have devoted a lot of time to the problem of marrying a prostitute and taking her home to your mother, Bodine.''

She doubted this was a preoccupation that troubled most men.

But now she really understood. Bodine had been silently

suffering through his own dilemma these past weeks—and for who knows how long before that. His discomfort those first days at the boardinghouse made sense now. He had been mourning Lila's leaving. And Lacy had happened along at just the right moment to gum up the works. If not for her, perhaps he would have ridden after Lila weeks ago. Maybe Lila would have been spared her present misery.

He pushed back his hat brim, looking as uncomfortable as she'd ever seen him. "I, um…" His face turned crimson as he faltered and then failed to think of any reply to her observation. "I'd better be going."

He was right. There was really no more to be said now. "All right. I'm finished here, too."

He hesitated. "Do you want me to help you carry your things back to the house?"

She shook her head. "No thank you. I can manage."

"Okie-doke," he said quickly. "I'll see you at the dance tonight, then."

He tipped his hat and then he was gone.

Though Lacy looked at the little table she'd set up to sell her goods and knew that she needed to carry it back inside, she found it hard to move. Flossie, discovering her standing alone, strolled over. "Looked like you and the sheriff were exchanging war words."

Though she hadn't meant to, Lacy heard herself blurting out petulantly, "Mama, how could you tell him his mother wouldn't like me?"

Flossie fanned herself with a Spanish-style fan. "I didn't remember saying anything about you."

"But he said you told him his mother wouldn't like his choice of bride."

"Oh, I see," her mother said. "So you're still planning on marrying Bodine, are you?"

Lacy tossed her hands up in the air. "Mama!"

"Well, that's good, sweetheart. You won't get an argument from me."

A strangled cry erupted from Lacy's throat. "I'm not looking for an argument—I'm just looking for a little acceptance. And some certainty." But of course now she was all but certain that she wouldn't marry Bodine. And that wasn't Flossie's fault. She sank down again and moaned in despair. "Will anything in my life ever work out right?"

Flossie rushed over to reassure her. "What are you talking about, honey? Of course things work out. Look at all you've done so far. Blissful Day's been a big success. Why, I took in twenty-three dollars just telling fortunes, and I plan to do more tonight. And I'm sure other people made just as much. And if all of us in the society donate most of the money to the town—why, that's a lot of improvement that can be done!"

Lacy shrugged.

Flossie gestured grandly to all the mess around them. "None of this would have happened if you hadn't come back to Blissful, honey. And what about me? You've made life better. Oh, sure I miss the Slipper sometimes, but look what your coming here's done for me. It's all your doing that I've got Harper because Harper said he never would have snapped out of his old drifter life if the Slipper hadn't closed down so sudden."

She grunted.

"I should have brought you back to me years ago, Lacy, and gone respectable. I've got ideas now that I never would have had before you came to town."

Dread shivered through Lacy. "Ideas? What ideas?"

Flossie pulled over the other old chair from the attic and took Lacy's hands eagerly. "I didn't want to say anything just yet, what with all this commotion going on around town." Her brow crinkled. "And of course everything is so up in the air with Lucas, and the George situation."

Lacy's heart felt heavy at the reminder.

"But see, I've got this plan about what to do with all that money I'd saved," Flossie explained eagerly. "You know, the money you said I should give to charity?"

"We were going to send that to Our Lady of Perpetual Mercy," Lacy said.

Flossie waved a hand through the air. "I still plan to send the nuns a goodly chunk, after all they done for you. But seeing Lila again has given me this other idea, and I think it's a good one. Why send all our money to San Antonio when there are things we could be doing right here in Blissful? If it's all right with you, Lace, I'd like to turn the boardinghouse into a sort of refuge for women like Lila."

Lacy's breath caught.

"You heard Lila," Flossie continued. "She wanted to get away from Sal weeks ago, but she thought she couldn't. Some of these women keep the girls practically enslaved, you know. But if the girls knew that there was a place they could escape to…"

"A sanctuary," Lacy said. "But how would we keep the place going?"

"We'll probably be scraping by a lot—" Flossie replied "—but we could have fundraisers like this one, couldn't we? And Harper said he would help out."

"Harper?"

"He's got some money set by, he says. And we've got those five acres behind the house. We could make the garden bigger and maybe build a larger barn so we could have more animals…"

Build a barn? "Mama, that's quite a project."

"Harper showed me some plans this morning. He says he could do it himself." At the look Lacy aimed at her, Flossie blushed. "Do you mind that I told Harper first?"

"Of course not."

Her mother eyed her nervously. "But do you think it's a bad idea? I even thought of a name for it. Dove's Rest."

"I like that," Lacy said.

"You do?" Flossie's eyes widened. "Harper said it sounds like a cemetery for birds."

Lacy laughed. "I like the name. I like the whole idea. I'm proud of you for thinking of it."

It certainly never would have occurred to her. No, Dove's Rest would have to originate with someone as big-hearted as her mother. What had Sister Mary Katherine told her? A good heart can always find good works to do.

Lucas had it right from the very first—Flossie had always been a good woman, in spite of everything. Lacy just hadn't been able to see it plain.

Flossie's eyes filled with tears. "I guess I wanted to make you proud of me, Lace—just a little."

"I am!" Lacy felt her own eyes brim. "I love you, Mama."

Overcome, Flossie pulled her to her bosom and for a moment Lacy was enveloped in a comfortingly perfumy embrace. And though she was just months short of being twenty, and had known a man's love, and was pledged to be married, just burying herself in her mother's arms felt so good, so soothing that she couldn't pull away. For a few moments she did not want to give up that cocoon of total acceptance and love.

But finally Flossie sat back and dabbed at her eyes with a handkerchief she pulled out from the blousy sleeve of her shirt. "Enough crying, now. I want you to go and get some rest so you'll look pretty and fresh for the dance tonight."

"Pretty and fresh might be wishing for too much. Right now I feel like an old rag."

Flossie gave her a pat. "You just need a nap."

"I need to take all these things inside," she said, gesturing toward the table.

"Don't you worry about that. Harper and I will do that when he gets back from making sure no one spills watermelon juice on his pavilion."

Lacy was too tired to look a gift horse in the mouth. "Thank you, Mama."

She got up and made her way back to the boardinghouse. Even when she was still a ways off, she could hear piano on the air, coming through the opened windows. Lila was playing "Silver Threads Among the Gold"—a tinny old tune Lacy was thoroughly tired of after a few short days in the woman's company. But Lila did play beautifully, so it was difficult to complain.

As Lacy stepped inside the front door, she was nearly run over by Birdie, who was carrying a tray. Birdie stopped so fast, some of the broth in the bowl on the tray slopped over the brim. "You're back already?"

Lacy grunted. Apparently Florence Nightingale here had forgotten all about taking turns outside. "How's George?"

Birdie's face creased into that mask of worry and fondness familiar to everyone in the boardinghouse now. "About the same—though his fingers squeezed mine when I touched them." Birdie blushed furiously. "Do you think that was unseemly?"

If Birdie's face hadn't been so painfully anxious, Lacy would have laughed. "I'm sure it was only done in the spirit of good nursing."

Birdie went a shade redder. "Of course!" She skittered down the hallway to go pour more nourishing fluid down her charge.

The music stopped. Curious, Lacy poked her head in the parlor. Lila, with her still bruised face, was peering at her over the piano. She always seemed nervous when someone new entered a room. Was she afraid the man who had beaten her up might come after her? Was she awaiting someone else?

"Please don't stop on my account," Lacy told her, going in. "You play so well. I never practice enough."

"I get plenty of practice, playing where I work. Worked," she corrected. She looked down at her hand and sighed wistfully. "I wish I could go hear the music tonight. The dance sounds like fun."

Like everyone else, Lacy had just assumed that Lila wasn't going to the dance. With her face looking like it did, why would she want to? Lila hadn't left the house once in two days.

Maybe that was the reason she had a pent-up look about her now. Lacy studied the woman and realized that she couldn't have been a day older than herself. Her eyes were more world-weary, and her clothes more eye-catching. But beneath the surface, Lacy recognized the same youthful impatience that had often thrummed through her own bones when she thought of tonight. Lila's leg was twitching slightly, as if in time to music that could only be heard in her own head. She wanted to go to the dance…and not just to listen, either.

She wanted to dance.

And why shouldn't she? She was young, and if it weren't for the beating she had taken, she would have been the prettiest woman in town. Normally men would be fighting over her. And Lacy could think of one man in particular who would give a lot for the privilege of taking Lila for a turn around the pavilion.

Lacy heaved a small sigh of her own, and suddenly felt as if she were the steady point in this messy triangle. She crossed the room to where Lila was sitting. "You'd like to go to the dance tonight, wouldn't you?"

Lila shook her head quickly—quickly enough to indicate that she had given this question laborious thought and decided that this was the way she should answer it. "I couldn't go. I'm a fright to look at. And nobody would want me there in any case."

Lacy crossed her arms and smiled. "I know one person who would."

Lila lifted her green eyes to Lacy's. There were equal measures of hope and hopelessness in her gaze.

"Besides—" Lacy went on "—I didn't ask you if you *could* go, I asked you if you wanted to go."

Lila still wasn't ready to admit that. She raised her hand to her bruised cheek. "But my face."

Lacy wasn't the best person to assess whether all the damage to Lila's face could be remedied through artificial means, but she was willing to experiment. "We can do something about that."

"We?" Lila's voice was a squeak.

Lacy took her hand and tugged her upstairs.

Nearly two hours later, she stepped back and felt as satisfied as Cinderella's fairy godmother must have once upon a time. Lila was transformed. She was wearing Lacy's favorite white dress, trimmed with a spray of delicate Cherokee roses at the high collar. She had a pink ribbon in her hair to match the sash at her impossibly tiny waist. Her hair they had laboriously curled and braided. The soft curls fringing her forehead and spilling down her cheeks distracted from what bruises a keen eye might have otherwise been able to spot. But for the most part, face powder and rouge camouflaged that damage.

Lila blinked in amazement at her demure reflection in the full-length mirror in Flossie's room. "I can't believe it!" A tear spilled down her cheek.

Lacy lunged for the dresser and found a clean handkerchief in Flossie's top drawer. She yanked one out and handed it to Lila. "For heaven's sake, don't cry. You'll streak."

Lila laughed and dabbed at her cheek. "I'm sorry. I don't want to ruin your handiwork. I just never thought I'd look like my old self again. But you made me look better."

Lacy swelled with pride. "I had good raw materials to work with." She gave the dress another wistful once-over. "Heaven knows my white never looked so stylish on me."

Lila blinked at her in alarm. "But what are you going to wear? And what about the time?" She gestured toward the window, and the sun that was starting to lower in the sky. "The dance will start any minute now, and you've spent so much time helping me dress that you're nowhere near ready yourself."

"I'll tidy up and be right down," Lacy told her. "We can go to the dance together."

Lila looked relieved at the suggestion. "Oh, thank you. I wasn't sure I could brave going amongst all those people all alone."

Lacy patted her hand. "You won't be alone."

Lila left, and Lacy turned to shut Flossie's handkerchief drawer. It was then that something caught her eye—a silver frame hidden beneath another handkerchief. Curious, she lifted the frame out of the drawer and studied the eerily familiar faces in sepia staring back at her. One was Flossie, twenty years earlier, all in white and holding a bouquet. The other was a man in a Confederate soldier's uniform, standing with a hand protectively at her shoulder.

Lacy's heart drummed.

The man was her father, without a doubt. She might have been his double, if she had been born a boy. He had her same pointy chin and compact frame. He looked very neat in his uniform, and sported a thick mustache that no doubt was supposed to make him appear older than he was. Because he was young—so young that Lacy ached for him. He didn't have long to live, and he looked so solemn.

But maybe he was just solemn in contrast to his bride. Lacy's gaze strayed over to her mother's likeness. Despite the dignified pose she had struck, a merry smile crooked at her mouth. Her shapely but plump frame was encased in a dress busy with frills and pleats and ribbons. No frumpy war bride calico for Flossie. She had gussied up for the occasion, from her hat trimmed with what appeared to be gardenias right down to the bows on her slippers.

She must have seen this picture before, Lacy realized, when she was a little girl. Flossie must have showed it to her. This was just the way she had always imagined her father—but she probably hadn't been imagining at all. She had simply forgotten she'd seen the picture.

Now she felt shame for doubting her mother. Flossie hadn't lied about the soldier who was her father, and probably not about the fact that he had died so bravely in Tennessee. Lacy hastily covered the photograph with the handkerchief, feeling small for her suspicions.

What else had she been wrong about? Could it be that Lucas hadn't been as devious as she had assumed after overhearing George and Boot? After all, she had refused to hear Lucas's side. She'd been so certain he had done her wrong.

Why had she been so bent on thinking the worst of everyone?

In her own room, she splashed cool water on her face, changed into a light blue muslin dress, and ran a comb through her hair. She could already hear the music coming from Harper's pavilion. This was her first dance, yet try as she might, she could not work up any enthusiasm. What was the matter with her? Her heart should have been skipping. She should have been worried about whether she would be a wallflower, or whether the decorations they put out would be pretty, or who would be there. She should have been more worried about the fact that she couldn't dance very well. She'd only had that one dance with Lucas.

Recalling the spinning, breathless moments she'd spent in his arms that afternoon not so long ago made her freeze in her tracks. For a few minutes she indulged in remembering how he had looked that afternoon—tall, devilishly handsome and even a little sheepish at his lack of self-control. Maybe that was when she first realized that something had changed between them. Really changed.

And it hadn't changed back, apparently.

She released a groan and stamped toward the door. Her footsteps hurried down the staircase, but her spirit straggled. Part of her wanted to dart up to the attic to check on Lucas. She hadn't seen him since last night, when she had taken him to task for being nice to her.

She met Birdie again at the bottom of the stairs. The dutiful nurse was carrying a pitcher of water now. Lacy began to wonder if George was in peril of drowning.

"Aren't you going to the dance?" she asked Birdie.

Birdie's eyes flew wide at the question. "Me? Goodness, no!" She let out an anxious twitter of a laugh. "I'm not much of a dancer, I'm afraid. And besides, someone must look after Mr. Oatley tonight."

"That's very good of you."

Birdie's face would have put a tomato to shame. "Well, I...that is...I wouldn't want you to get the wrong impression..."

She turned to scuttle away and nearly ran smack into Lila. Birdie gasped at the change in the young woman.

Lila smiled self-consciously. "Lacy was kind enough to lend me one of her dresses for the dance."

Birdie's eyes, already wide with surprise, nearly popped. "*You're* going to the dance?"

Lacy felt her face go stony with anger. Was this a harbinger of what was to come? What had been delightful for herself was apparently seen as completely inappropriate for a woman of Lila's reputation. When she detected the hurt in Lila's eyes, she wanted to shake Birdie by her twiglike shoulders. "Of course she's going," she said, a determination forming in her mind. "Doesn't she look pretty, Birdie?"

Birdie, when faced with such a direct question, was bullied into letting go of her snub. "W-well, yes. She does."

"I think she'll be the belle of the party, don't you?"

Birdie gulped. "Y-yes, I imagine so, though I wouldn't know about those things." She began backing away. "I must get back to George."

When she was gone, Lila looked as if her heart had sunk to the heels of her dancing boots. "I shouldn't go. It will just cause a stir, and with Myrtle and Neesa there looking on, no man's gonna want to dance with me anyhow."

Lacy pulled her out the front door. "Everyone will want to dance with you. And Myrtle might stare, but she won't dare say anything. Trust me."

The evening was still and warm, though the worst of the heat had lifted. The music seemed to lighten the air, too. As they threaded their way toward the pavilion, they received scores of smiles. And if a few of those people looked twice at the sight of one of Flossie's old girls gussied up for the dance, Lacy was propelling them along so quickly and purposefully that neither she nor Lila had time to notice.

They did notice the beauty before them. Torches had been brought out to light the area around the pavilion, which was itself lit by what looked to be a hundred candles. With its gleaming white paint and festive bunting, the structure glowed brilliantly against the twilight. She understood now why Harper was so feverish to build his bandstand. It was a masterpiece.

"Lila!" Flossie raced over, exclaiming at the change in her friend. "Honey, you've been transformed!"

"You look lovely," Harper agreed.

Lila blushed, and was stammering out a paean to Lacy's skill, but Lacy cut her off impatiently. "Mama, have you seen—" All at once, she caught sight of Bodine. "Never mind! Come on, Lila."

She tugged Lila straight over to where Bodine was standing. The pavilion was too small for many couples to dance, so an alternate dance floor had been designated on a patch of grass nearby. Bodine was standing to the side, watching the couples twirl to the insistent polka music. Lacy sped straight up to him and presented Lila.

For a moment the sheriff was too astounded to say a single word. Which suited Lacy fine.

"Bodine, would you mind looking after Lila tonight? I have a slight headache. I think I need to go home and lie down."

Lila protested. "But Lacy, you never mentioned—"

"I'd be happy to!" Bodine exclaimed, cutting her off. Once Lacy had handed Lila over, placing her hand on Bodine's arm, it was clear he wasn't going to let her go. Belatedly remembering his manners, he glanced at Lacy. "Would you like me to walk you back to the house? If you're not feeling well..."

She shook her head. "No, no. You two should dance while the music lasts."

Bodine was only too glad to oblige, and as he swung Lila onto the grass patch, it seemed for a moment that the crowd parted a little. Lacy spotted Myrtle's red-faced reaction, as well as an indignant glare from Neesa and a few of their acquaintances. But there was such a crowd at the dance, many from so far away, that the stir Lila feared creating was buffered, and then probably was forgotten by all but those gossipy few.

Lacy stepped back, thinking she would talk to her mother

for a moment about this small triumph, but Flossie and Harper were on his bandstand, laughing and dancing. And though the festive atmosphere would have been irresistible at any other time, tonight she didn't feel like celebrating. Or, rather, the only person she wanted to celebrate with wasn't here.

She turned on her heel, went back to the boardinghouse, and marched straight up to the attic. She didn't bother to knock, but barged right in on Lucas, who was standing a few steps back from the window.

"I thought that was you," he said after she had closed the door. It was darker in the attic than it was outside, and her eyes took a moment to adjust before she could see his handsome face.

"You should be enjoying the dance," he said. "What happened? Did some cowboy step on your toes? Or did you just leave something behind here?"

"The latter."

"What was it? Your gloves? A fresh hankie? A moonstruck fiancé?"

She rolled her eyes. "Good heavens, you're infuriating! I came up here to make peace, and all you can do is be snide."

He stepped toward her with interest. "I'm sorry, I had no idea you had chosen this big night to bury the hatchet. Has the music affected your brain?"

She laughed in spite of herself. "I suppose it has. I was standing by the beautiful new pavilion, and I realized the only person I cared to dance with was right here."

He reached forward and held her hands in his. "What about Bodine?"

"He is otherwise engaged."

"Lila?"

Lacy sighed. "I suppose I should be jealous, but I can't be. She *is* nice."

"That's not why you aren't jealous," Lucas said, pulling her closer. "You're not jealous because you never loved Bodine. Because you're in love with me."

She stared up into those dark eyes and felt a certainty she

hadn't felt perhaps since getting on the stagecoach to Blissful all those weeks ago. Her heart expanded until it seemed to be pushing against her corset lacings. "Heaven help me. I am!"

He laughed. "Well, don't sound so horrified. You've just finally come to your senses."

She shook her head. "I've lost them, I think."

The smile faded from his lips. "I never meant to hurt you, Lacy. When you first came here, we were at war, and I thought anything was fair. I behaved in ways I'm not proud of. But even then, you twisted my intentions around, so that when I was trying to gain the upper hand, I was actually losing it. But believe me, when we made love, I had no ulterior motive. Those were the best hours of my life."

His words poured over her like a warm shower, lightening her heart. "And I called you a sidewinder," she said, shaking her head. "Among other things!"

"But you've changed your mind about that?"

She nodded. "Right now you're the most desirable man in all of Texas. Maybe the whole world."

"Even though I'm a rascal?"

"And a fugitive," she reminded him.

"And a whiskey peddler?"

She smiled. "Don't push me too hard, Lucas. I'm still adjusting."

A deep chuckle rumbled in his chest and he gathered her close to him, treating her to a quick twirl around the room. She felt so happy, her feet might have been floating. They fairly skipped across the floor in time to Jan and Oly's jaunty tune. When they came too close to the window, Lucas pulled her away from it, and she turned full against him.

His lips descended on hers feverishly and roughly, but she didn't care. She was eager to kiss him again, to feel the hard warmth of his mouth against hers. He smelled of sweat since his incarceration up in the hot attic, but she didn't mind that, either. Their tongues touched and she let out a sigh of surrender. It felt so good to be here, in his arms again, and so sure of herself.

Lucas pulled away from her mouth and touched his lips to her chin, her jaw. They kissed as if they couldn't get enough of each other. And that was how Lacy felt. Voracious, greedy. He rained kisses down her throat that made her back arch at the thrill of it. His hands caressed her back and made quick work of her dress buttons. Hungrily he freed her from the restrictions of her corset, fell to his knees, and fiercely teased one of her breasts until the bud was tight and aching. He took it between his teeth, and she gasped, holding onto his shoulders to keep herself from melting bonelessly to the floor.

The music still played in the background, but it became fainter and fainter as Lucas continued his loving ministrations. This odd-shaped little room lit only by the reddish setting sun became their own private world. It didn't matter that the biggest crowd in Blissful's history was gathered just outside; in here they were the only man and woman on earth.

They had shared so little time together, but even her little experience had raised her expectations, so that when Lucas's hands skimmed the backs of her thighs she thrilled with anticipation. She knew what she wanted. She wanted Lucas, and the kind of fulfillment she knew she would only find with him. He was right; she loved him. Loved him and wanted him as she never dreamed it was possible to want a man. It didn't matter what he did or who her mother was—the only consideration was how she felt in her heart. The realization filled her with a feeling that was joyful and slightly terrifying all at once. The future seemed to be unfurling before her, with layer upon layer of trouble and complications, yet all she could do now was cling to the present. Cling to Lucas.

While he held her like this, she couldn't believe that anything would ever come between them again. It didn't seem possible that this private world could be shattered.

But it could. And it was.

A gasp rent the air, causing them both to freeze. Lucas looked up into Lacy's eyes, but she couldn't catch his gaze for long. The gasp had not been the result of passion. It hadn't even come from her. Instead, the sound of shock had come from the doorway, where Birdie stood, her narrow pinched face slack with astonishment. Behind Birdie stood Myrtle, fanning herself furiously. And behind Myrtle stood Flossie, her hand covering her mouth. Lacy guessed she was probably covering a smile—like the one that was stretched across Harper's face.

But no one's expression matched the openmouthed confounded look on the face of Bodine, who brought up the rear.

Lacy was too mortified to move, much less say anything. Yet she found herself wanting anything but this agonizing silence, and the unbearable intensity of all those eyes focussed on her.

When someone did break the silence, it was the person she would have least expected to pipe up at a moment like this.

"I *knew* it wasn't a cat," Birdie declared smugly.

Chapter Seventeen

If Lacy lived to be a hundred, she doubted she would ever fully understand how she went from an innocent young woman of unimpeachable character to brazen fugitive's moll in just a matter of weeks.

It wasn't that she was ashamed of what she had done so much as she was awed by the knowledge that everyone—*everyone*—knew about what had happened in that attic. Not only had she and Lucas been caught with him on his knees and her with her dress half off, at precisely when the most possible people were gathered in Blissful to hear about the scandalous goings-on at the boardinghouse, but they'd also had the additional bad luck to have Myrtle Bean as a prominent member of their audience.

And once Myrtle knew something, the world and its wife knew it.

A crowd had gathered when Bodine had emerged from the boardinghouse with Lucas walking in front of them. They proceeded solemnly to the jail, though several of Lucas's friends had come up to greet him. They all wanted to know what Lucas had been up to during his fugitive days. Of course if they just would have waited a minute and given Myrtle a chance, they wouldn't have had to ask.

Lacy had stayed back at the boardinghouse—and she hadn't left her room since. All night she had sweated and turned, her heart racing. How could she face people? What was she going to do?

She couldn't stop recriminating herself. She should have followed her instincts and left weeks ago, off to a little town that had never heard of the Satin Slipper, or Flossie Calhoun. It would have been so easy then. Before she had been so crazy as to fall in love with the last man in the world she should ever have cared for.

Now that he was back in jail, worry about Lucas gnawed at her. She took the blame for that, too. By going up to the attic last night instead of staying at the dance, she had sealed his doom.

But those moments alone with him—who knows if they would be their last—were precious to her. The way he had looked at her, touched her, and the warmth of his words still seemed to caress her. The memories held her upright, and gave her a reason to keep going. She *would* figure out a way to free Lucas, which probably wasn't going to be a cakewalk while Myrtle was up in arms.

Of course, even if she did manage to get Lucas out of jail, what would happen after that was anybody's guess. She had told Lucas she loved him, and meant it, but he had not made any sort of pledge to her.

She tried to console herself. So she had made a spectacle of herself, and would probably spend the rest of her life living down her shame... So she had gone and fallen in love with a man whose days might be numbered to a very few, and deceived the town's sheriff in the bargain... So she had behaved like a hypocrite and now probably had earned the scorn of the entire town...

Let he who is without sin cast the first stone.

But that platitude really wasn't all that comforting as long as Myrtle Bean was just across town, no doubt hunting for a good rock to bean her with. And Neesa! Lacy shuddered to think of having to face all the women on the committee.

Jacob knocked on her door. For someone who had just been contemplating a life of solitude, Lacy was excessively glad to have a visitor. She hadn't spoken to a soul since she had turned down Flossie's offer of breakfast this morning.

"Come in!" she said to Jacob, tugging him into her room. "How have you been?"

He looked a little perplexed. "You mean since yesterday?"

Had it been just less than twelve hours since all the hubbub of Blissful Day? It seemed like years ago. Such was the gulf between her former relatively blameless life and the long grueling road that lay ahead, the one on which she would have to claw her way back to respectability.

"Did you have fun yesterday?" she asked, trying momentarily to put aside thoughts of the long grueling road. "I saw you with your friend Joe."

He shrugged, suddenly taking on that reticent air youngsters had when adults pried too closely in their affairs. "I guess so. We managed to stay out of trouble."

Unlike some people.

"Good!" she said brightly.

"I was just over at the jail," he said.

Her chipper facade melted. "You saw your father? How is he?"

"He's fine. He beat me at checkers."

Lucas was playing checkers! The thought gave her a rush of happiness...mixed with annoyance. Lucas was playing checkers? That sounded awfully...calm.

Apparently worry wasn't gnawing at him.

"Oh!" Jacob said, remembering. "I have a message for you."

Her heart tripped. "From Lucas?"

"No, from the sheriff. He came back here with me. Says he wants to talk to you."

The announcement filled her with dread. But she supposed she couldn't hide from Bodine forever. Much as she might like to.

What was she going to say to the man? What *could* she say? All through the night, she had practiced a hundred different excuses and explanations, but at the thought of actually using one of them, her memory mutinied. Any excuse she might come up with would be self-serving and flimsy to his ears.

After Jacob had gone upstairs to his room, she ventured out, attempting to hold her head high. That became difficult, however, when she walked into the parlor and saw Bodine standing there, red-faced but stony. He glanced at her briefly, then turned away.

Bodine Turner was a wounded man. Lacy might have saved herself worrying over those hundred excuses. He didn't appear inclined to hear even one of them.

After a few moments pregnant with tension, he cleared his throat. "I debated whether or not I should've come over here, Lacy. After..." He crimsoned a shade deeper "...after last night I was pretty sore. Still am, if you want to know the truth."

"Bodine, I—"

He held out his palm, making her fall silent. "I should tell you that I came here to ask you to release me from our engagement."

The statement caught her up short. A laugh lodged in her throat. *Of course* he was calling off the engagement! Didn't he think she knew that?

"There's no way now I could take you home to Cicada Creek," he told her.

She shook her head, biting back a subversive chuckle. "No," she said soberly. "I don't imagine Ma would understand."

"No, she wouldn't." He turned, and his blue eyes seemed to darken as he gazed at her. "*I* don't understand. You always seemed so nice. Oh, sure, I heard whispers around town— something about you and Lucas and the porch swing—but I didn't pay them any mind. I trusted your word when you said you didn't even like Lucas."

Her mouth opened to reply, but he interrupted her. "I never dreamed when I asked you to marry me that you were just using me to cover Lucas's escape."

"What?"

He lifted his chin. "You agreed to marry me the same night he broke jail. That couldn't have been a coincidence."

"Yes, it was," she argued. She had come into the room fully expecting to take complete responsibility for not being faithful to their engagement. She already had her hair shirt on anyway. But to hear him mangle her motives, and make them sound worse than they were, got her back up. She couldn't not defend herself, especially when Bodine's anger had to be more wounded pride than real disappointment in her. Just yesterday he had been pining after Lila—not exactly a man clinging lovingly to their engagement!

She didn't want this encounter to dissolve into a finger-pointing squabble, however. "I intended to marry you, Bodine, and truly hoped to make you a good wife."

His eyes registered doubt, but he shrugged magnanimously. "Well, I guess we should just bury the past."

"Yes, I suppose so." She doubted there was anything she could do that would make him believe her.

"Well, that's all," he said, smashing his hat back on his head. "I just figured you ought to know that I didn't intend to marry you, and that I'm going home anyhow."

She looked up, surprised. "Back to Cicada Creek? Alone?"

The man looked like a monument to wounded pride. "I've been a bachelor this long. I guess I can shift for myself."

At that moment, she stopped thinking about herself for the first time since the events of the night before. Maybe truly for the first time in all her twenty years. She saw that her actions had had consequences, and she rushed forward to try to shore up some of the damage. She clasped his hands, and though he tried to withdraw them she held fast.

"Oh, Bodine, don't be a fathead!"

His eyes widened in offense.

She ducked her head. "That is to say, don't let your heart turn bitter, Bodine. I know it looks as if I weren't completely on the square with you, but Lila loves you. Don't doubt her because of me."

His eyes registered hope, but his body remained stiff. "Well, I guess we'll just have to see about that. I don't intend to leave till the trial's over, at least."

Her heart went still. "Trial?"

"The circuit judge replied to my letter. He's coming to town tomorrow. I reckon that's when we'll know what's gonna happen with Lucas."

Judge Davis Wygant was sixty-two and suffering from chronic lumbago. He had come to Blissful in order to settle a case involving a disputed property line, and he didn't particularly relish the extra duty of dealing with a murder case. Or a near murder case. It all seemed irregular to him, and nothing nettled him more than irregularity.

The civil case was dispensed with quickly. The other matter, however, looked more troublesome. Clearly, he should have retired last year.

There had never been anything like a murder trial in Blissful before, so no one was sure quite what to do. There was no place to have a hearing. The little jailhouse, with its one cell and tiny office for the sheriff, was too small to accommodate the crowd that had gathered when the judge arrived. Some were holdovers from Blissful Day, who had decided to stay to see how it all turned out.

How it all would turn out was a matter of intense interest to Lucas, too. He had been counting on time being on his side. But now his time was up, and the outcome he had thought would save him had not come to pass. George was still in a coma. No one had heard from Boot since the night he went riding off for Dr. Hart. Lucas hoped he was still at Henrietta Wallace's farm—but if he was, it would be the longest spell he had ever spent at the place. Maybe he had decided to cut and run.

Since there was not enough room in the jail, the judge announced he would conduct a hearing to sort the matter out at the pavilion. A crowd gathered there around noon. To Lucas's surprise, Lacy showed up at the jail slightly before he and

Bodine and the judge were to begin the short processional over to the pavilion.

"I sent Jacob to his friend Joe's till tomorrow," she told him in a rush.

"I'm surprised he went," Lucas said. He tilted his head at her. "He really must be uncommonly fond of you."

"I didn't want him to be here for this."

Lucas shook his head. "I doubt they're going to hang me today, Lacy."

The judge whirled his head toward them. "Hang you?" he barked. "No, no! No time for that today!"

That comment didn't seem to bring Lacy much relief.

It was not the first time she had been here in the past twenty-four hours. To Bodine's irritation, she had come twice yesterday, bearing meals.

After the way they had been parted, Lucas's seeing her with a wall of metal bars between them was something akin to torture. He longed to take her in his arms again, bury his head against her alabaster skin, smell the sweet soapy scent of her. More than once he found himself on the verge of making all sorts of promises and plans that would be downright foolish for a man in his position to make. There was precious little he *could* say, what with Bodine hovering about. The sheriff wasn't about to let his prisoner escape a second time.

Lucas couldn't give her solid assurances of their future, so he tried to keep her bucked up by appearing his old self. By teasing her, and making light of his situation. He liked the way she had boldly walked down the road through town, carrying the meal tray, knowing full well that all eyes would be watching her after the attic incident. That showed spunk. But he didn't like the worry in her eyes.

By the time she came to walk him to the town hearing, that worry had escalated to a frantic dementia. As Bodine let him out of the jail cell, she rushed past the sheriff and took Lucas by the arms. "You've got to tell them the truth, Lucas."

He smiled and kissed the top of her head. Which he thought showed admirable restraint.

"I think Mama and Harper know something—I saw them talking early this morning. But now they've disappeared."

"Maybe they eloped."

She sent him a scowl that caused a little field of dimples to appear on her chin. "You shouldn't joke at a time like this."

"All right," he agreed as Bodine reached over to snap handcuffs on him. "But you'll have to forgive me if I don't spend much of this morning pondering the whereabouts of two aging lovebirds."

"Time to go, Lucas," the sheriff said.

Outside, the tension in the air was palpable. The drone of murmured conversation coming from the pavilion died when Lucas and the sheriff stepped onto the street. Judge Wygant led the way, carrying a chair in one hand and a Bible in the other. He was as thin as a switch, with a gray beard and dark eyes shaded by bushy gray eyebrows.

"Never held court out of doors before," he grumbled.

Bodine looked truly apologetic. "Sorry, Judge. Want me to carry your chair for you?"

The judge drew up as if he'd been stung. "No thank you." He huffed along a few more paces as before adding, "It sure is hot."

It didn't seem to bode well that the judge was already cranky this early in the proceedings. Nor was Lucas heartened to see Myrtle Bean and the four other ladies of the women's committee standing on the top step bearing a sign that read, IT'S TIME BLISSFUL WAS PEACEFUL.

Catching sight of their thin-lipped welcome wagon, the judge stopped, studied the sign, and shook his head. "I should have retired last year."

Myrtle stood her ground as the judge approached. "Judge," she announced, "we the ladies of the Society for the Beautification of Blissful, save one of our founding members—" she glowered pointedly at Lacy "—we believe that this matter should be treated with utmost seriousness, and that action should be taken immediately. Otherwise, you might as well drive a stake through the heart of all the progress we've made here in Blissful.'' She puffed up and pronounced importantly, "We might be a tiny town, but we have a big future.''

Her cohorts clapped enthusiastically.

The judge was not so impressed. "Gadzooks, woman! At least let me sit down before you start lecturing me.''

Several in the crowd whooped with laughter as the judge pushed past her and then carefully positioned his chair in the shade the pavilion's roof afforded him. Lucas took the opportunity to cast a glance at Lacy. She was looking up at him, and when her anxious blue eyes met his gaze, he felt an astonishing wave of tenderness for her. After all that had happened, she was standing on the top step, opposite Myrtle. Standing up for him in front of everyone. She looked every bit as frantic as she had at the jailhouse. Her whole body was strung as tight as barbed wire. He tried to give her a reassuring smile.

Once the judge was settled to his liking, he turned to the sheriff. "Now then. I understand this town is in something of an uproar. You've got a man in a coma, and a man here you say shot him.''

"Yessir,'' Bodine agreed. "That's about the long and short of it.''

"So the man isn't dead.''

"He's as good as dead,'' Myrtle interjected.

Wygant flicked her an annoyed gaze, then pivoted back to Lucas. "You've been in custody for how long?''

"About five days, on and off.''

"More off than on,'' Bodine countered with a little sting in his tone.

The gray shrubby eyebrows of the judge rose. "That's right—broke jail.'' He looked Lucas up and down. "That doesn't speak well for you.'' He grunted. "Or for the sheriff.''

Once the laughter had died down, the judge took a deep breath to say something more. But he was cut off by Lacy, who hopped up the last step and raced over to him. "Lucas didn't do it. He's covering for someone—and if he's covering for someone you've got to let him go!''

Of all the dumb things! What did she think she was doing?

If he weren't wearing these cuffs, Lucas would have put his hand over her mouth to shut her up.

The judge gave her a displeased sizing up. "Who are you? His attorney?"

"No, I'm Lacy Calhoun, his…friend." She blushed, and obviously tried to ignore the sniggers behind her. "But I know he's covering for someone. He didn't do it. Don't I have the responsibility to step forward if I know you have the wrong man?"

"Yes—" the judge admitted "—if you've got proof."

That stopped her cold. Lacy looked helplessly up at Lucas, then back at the crowd, which was waiting to see if she could come up with something.

And did she ever. Taking a deep breath, she turned back to the judge and announced, "*I* shot George Oatley."

Shocked murmurs rippled through the crowd, and the judge looked like he might faint. "*You* did?"

"She's lying," Lucas broke in.

She glared at him. "No, I'm not."

"She was at the boardinghouse," Lucas told the judge. "She was there when we brought George's body in."

She whirled on him, hands planted on her hips. "So? I shot him and then ran back to the boardinghouse."

Lucas pleaded with her, "Lacy, please—I know what you're trying to do, but it won't work. No one's going to believe you."

A loud harrumph came from Myrtle. "Don't be so sure!"

For once, Lacy saw Myrtle's hostility as being in her favor. She turned back to the judge in triumph. "You see? Those women will vouch for my low, devious character. *I* did it. So you can just tell the sheriff to take those cuffs off Lucas and put them on me."

The judge's openmouthed gape was punctuated by a gunshot that startled everyone. The judge jumped out of his chair and peered out over the crowd. Everyone turned, in fact, to see an old wagon barreling down the dusty road toward town. Next to it was a rider on a black horse. As the figures grew closer, Lucas recognized Flossie sitting in the back of the wagon. Flossie's red hair was hard to miss. Boot was driving, and there was an unfamiliar woman sitting next to him. The rider of the black horse was Harper.

They sped into town, driving right up to where everyone was gathered. Harper hopped off his horse and helped Flossie down, and then, slowly, Boot climbed off the wagon and did the same for the other woman. All at once, everyone realized they were looking at the reclusive Widow Wallace.

Henrietta Wallace was a dark-skinned woman, plump, with meaty arms and puffy cheeks. Her eyes were wide set and brown. Under no circumstances could she claim to be a beauty, except perhaps for her thick auburn hair. But there was something in her quiet bearing, in the perfectly starched and pleated calico dress she wore, that bespoke a great personal pride, in spite of her being something of a hermit. As the crowd parted for her and Boot to ascend the pavilion steps, she smiled cordially to the people she passed.

Boot looked just the same—and yet somehow different, too. He was wearing his same work clothes, with the addition of a small black tie. But the clothes were clean, and he was freshly shaved. His jittery manner was somewhat calmed, too, so that he'd lost a little of that half-cocked swagger he usually had.

He walked straight up to the judge and announced, "I'm here to turn myself in for shootin' George Oatley."

Judge Wygant sighed. "Many more confessions like this and that jail cell's gonna be mighty crowded."

Boot shook his head. "But I'm the one who really did it." He took his gun out of his holster and placed it at the judge's feet. "That's the gun I shot him with. We was drunk, and I didn't mean him any harm. Shoot, he was practically my best friend. But I can see now that I gotta pay for what I done." He nodded over at Lucas. "Lucas is just covering for me because he knows I'll probably hang for my crime on account of I'm a notorious outlaw."

The judge's eyes widened. "Who are you?"

"Boot Withers," he said. "Boot the Kid."

"Never heard of you," the judge said dismissively. Then he crooked a thumb toward Lacy. "And why is *she* covering for you?"

Boot turned to Lacy, and his eyes registered shock. "Shoot, I don't know! But I do know she's sort of crazy, so that might be the reason."

The Widow Wallace nudged him. "Anyhow," Boot continued, "I'm here to do my penance, whatever it might be. But as a last request, I'd like you to marry me and Henrietta here."

A collective gasp went through the crowd, followed by a few hoots. "That's fast work, Boot!"

"Yeah, it just took him two years!"

"Maybe if you'd tended to your work more, she would've married you before now!"

Boot scowled at them. "Ever since I confessed to Henrietta what I done, she's been very understanding. She says that I just never had a good family to watch over me, and maybe that's true. But she's agreed to be my wife now, and to help me turn over a new leaf—if I don't wind up hanged."

"Well!" The judge stood up. "This is irregular. Most of the time I don't care for that. But marrying you seems less irregular than ordering you tried for a near-murder, so that's okay by me. I can marry you now, though of course we'll need to get the correct paperwork done later."

Boot took Henrietta's hand and smiled at her.

And so, with astonishment, a large crowd was on hand to watch the Widow Wallace transformed into Henrietta Wallace Withers. After the ceremony, the sheriff took the handcuffs that had been on Lucas's hands and clapped them onto Boot.

"Wait!"

At the thin but loud scream, everyone turned to see Birdie speeding toward them, waving her arms as if trying to stop a train. Her wiry dark hair fell out of its bun so that she looked like a lunatic woman by the time she reached them all. She was so winded from the unaccustomed exertion she could barely speak. After several heaving breaths she managed just two words. But they were doozies.

"He's awake!"

Dazed after his long sleep, George Oatley stared out from his bed as if he were beholding a world transformed. And perhaps he was.

A large crowd hovered around him. First there was the judge, who introduced himself and explained the quandary George's coma had put them all in. Then there was Boot, standing with the Widow Wallace—now Mrs. Withers, as Boot proudly announced. George blinked several times on hearing that. Lucas and Lacy stood arm in arm, staring down at him. The sheriff, Flossie and Harper flanked the other side of his bed, while in one corner, almost unnoticed by the others, stood Lila.

But obviously the oddest thing for him to wrap his mind around, and understandably so, was the presence of Birdie Bean, perched right next to his pillow, clasping his hand and gazing down at him with loving eyes. He was still peering up at her with confusion, and a little fear, as the judge questioned him.

"So you'll attest that your shooting was what you would call accidental?"

"Well, as best as I remember it," George said. "Heck, I think I shot at Boot first." He looked over at his old friend. "Isn't that so?"

Boot laughed. "I guess—though I'm a little hazy about it myself." He looked apologetically to all those gathered around. "But I've turned over a new leaf, George. I'm done with drinkin' and arguin'. From this day forward, I'm an upright married man. No foolin'."

George looked dumbfounded, and a little saddened. "You were right, Harper. Goodness sure hit this town like a sock in the jaw."

Harper laughed. "Well, maybe it needed a little shaking up."

Several people proceeded to catch George up on what he had missed. Blissful Day. The closing of the Rooster. Lila coming back. George was astounded. "That's more than what's happened in this town in the past ten years combined."

Lacy felt herself being tugged away into the hall, toward her room. When she and Lucas were alone, out of earshot of the others, he took her into his arms and treated her to a long, passionate kiss, to which she gladly surrendered. She was so filled with relief and joy that she didn't care that the others were just a room away. After the stress of the past days, she was so happy she could barely keep her hands off of him.

They were interrupted by approaching footsteps. Lucas pulled her into the open door of her room. Lila scooted down the hall, and then was followed by the sheriff. Bodine couldn't have seen Lucas and Lacy hovering in the doorway, or he surely wouldn't have caught up to Lila, twirled her into his arms, and kissed her hungrily right then and there. Lacy looked into Lucas's eyes, startled. She gestured that they should step away from the door, but he put his hand over her mouth so they wouldn't risk interrupting them. They remained silent.

Bodine, however, had plenty to say when he came up for air. He pulled Lila to him and exclaimed in a rush, "I should've done this a year ago!"

"Oh, Bodine, why didn't you?"

"I wanted to, but I was so wrongheaded. So full of notions that don't make a lick of difference to me now. I love you, Lila—I'm not gonna be happy till you're my wife. I'll live here or we can go back to Cicada Creek. It doesn't matter so long as we're together."

Lila's answer was another kiss. Bodine lifted her into his arms and carried her away—where, Lacy didn't know. But she was happy—for both Bodine and Lila. She leaned into Lucas's broad chest with a wistful sigh.

Lucas took her by the shoulders, turned her around, and said huskily, "Bodine's got the right idea."

Her stomach performed a delicious flip. "Don't tell me you want to move to Cicada Creek now, too."

Laughter rumbled out of him. "No. I was thinking about the other thing."

She tilted her head. "*What* other thing?"

He let out a huff of irritation, but his dark gaze was so loving she could tell he didn't really mean it. "I'm asking you to marry me. Do you want me to get down on bended knee, or should I just carry you off caveman style like the sheriff did his lady love?"

"A simple proposal will do," Lacy said primly.

His lips screwed up into an affectionate lopsided smile that made her heart feel too big for her chest. "Will you marry me, Lacy?"

The words were ones she never expected to hear from him. And even though he had given her fair warning that he was going to say them—she'd even *asked* him to say them—she was a little overwhelmed. She sank against the door frame.

His brow puckered. "You're not going to say no, are you?"

"Everything's been so strange lately, and happened so fast. Are you sure you want to marry me, Lucas?"

"Of course I'm sure!"

She lifted her shoulders. "Maybe you just feel obligated."

He drew back. "Why should I feel obligated?"

He had to ask? She reminded him, a little indignantly. "You ruined my reputation!"

"That's right, I did." He scratched his chin and stared down at her, considering. "But you had something to do with that, too, if you'll recall."

"Me?" she squeaked.

"Don't play Miss Innocent," he said, skimming a finger down her throat and across her shoulders. She shivered, and felt her body quicken in anticipation. "Because I know better." His voice was a suggestive, husky whisper. "Besides, it wouldn't do for the wife of a saloonkeeper to have *too* sterling a reputation."

"Lucas…" The name, so hated once, seemed to dissolve

in her mouth like butter. "Think of all the problems there would be. We would argue."

"Mmm," he agreed, bending down to nibble at her ear.

She inhaled sharply. "Constantly."

"And make up," he purred.

She was practically panting.

"Please say you'll marry me, Lacy Calhoun," he said, pulling her closer, so that she could feel the coiled hardness of his body against her own. "If I really ruined your reputation, the least you can do is allow me to make an honest woman out of you. Especially when I'm so fool in love with you."

With an exhale that was half laugh, half wail of desire, she relented. "All right! Yes, I'll marry you."

He grinned. "I sort of knew you would."

Before she could give him a well-deserved swat, he covered her mouth for another searing kiss. Her body ached with desire, but she was also bursting with happiness. When he broke away, she said excitedly, "Should we let everyone know? Let's go tell Jacob!"

That dark gaze she'd come to adore bore into her, making her quiver with desire. Her whole being responded, and she pressed against him suggestively. "On second thought," she said, in a husky voice that would have made Sister Mary Katherine weep, "let's do a little more damage to my reputation first."

He smiled, took her hand, and gently closed the bedroom door behind them.

ITCHIN' FOR SOME ROLLICKING ROMANCES SET ON THE AMERICAN FRONTIER? THEN TAKE A GANDER AT THESE TANTALIZING TALES FROM HARLEQUIN HISTORICALS

On sale September 2003

WINTER WOMAN by Jenna Kernan
(Colorado, 1835)

After braving the winter alone in the Rockies, a defiant woman is entrusted to the care of a gruff trapper!

THE MATCHMAKER by Lisa Plumley
(Arizona territory, 1882)

Will a confirmed bachelor be bitten by the love bug when he woos a young woman in order to flush out the mysterious Morrow Creek matchmaker?

On sale October 2003

WYOMING WILDCAT by Elizabeth Lane
(Wyoming, 1866)

A blizzard ignites hot-blooded passions between a white medicine woman and an amnesiac man, but an ominous secret looms on the horizon....

THE OTHER GROOM by Lisa Bingham
(Boston and New York, 1870)

When a penniless woman masquerades as the daughter of a powerful marquis, her intended groom risks it all to protect her from harm!

Visit us at www.eHarlequin.com

HARLEQUIN HISTORICALS®

LOOKIN' FOR RIVETING TALES ABOUT RUGGED MEN AND THE FEISTY LADIES WHO TRY TO TAME THEM?

From Harlequin Historicals

July 2003

TEXAS GOLD by Carolyn Davidson

A fiercely independent farmer's past catches up with her when the husband she left behind turns up on her doorstep!

OF MEN AND ANGELS by Victoria Bylin

Can a hard-edged outlaw find redemption—and true love—in the arms of an angelic young woman?

On sale August 2003

BLACKSTONE'S BRIDE by Bronwyn Williams

Will a beleaguered gold miner's widow and a wounded half-breed ignite a searing passion when they form a united front?

HIGH PLAINS WIFE by Jillian Hart

A taciturn rancher proposes a marriage of convenience to a secretly smitten spinster who has designs on his heart!

Visit us at www.eHarlequin.com

HARLEQUIN HISTORICALS®